BEWILDERED

Micah reached up and touched Jody's cheek with the tips
of his fingers. His touch was so light she might have missed
it if her heart hadn't responded with so much excitement.
"Jody," he said. "why do you confuse me so?"

"I'm as confused as you are. I've never met anyone like
you."

Micah looked as if he wanted to kiss her, but he stepped
back, his eyes filled with intense longing. "I'll not
compromise you. You can trust me."

Jody was so sure she wanted to. She found she was hoping
he would put all that trustworthiness aside and kiss her.

ELIZABETH CRANE

Time Remembered

LOVE SPELL BOOKS NEW YORK CITY

LOVE SPELL®

October 1997

Published by

Dorchester Publishing Co., Inc.
276 Fifth Avenue
New York, NY 10001

ISBN 0-505-52223-3

The name "Love Spell" and its logo are trademarks of Dorchester Publishing Co., Inc.

Printed in the United States of America.

For winter's rains and ruins are over,
And all the season of snows and sins;
The days dividing lover and lover,
The light that loses, the night that wins;
And time remembered is grief forgotten,
And frosts are slain and flowers begotten,
And in green underwood and cover
Blossom by blossom the spring begins.

From *Atalanta in Calydon* (1865)
by Algernon Charles Swinburne, 1837-1909

Chapter One

When Jody Farnell first saw Whitefriars, she was struck with the beauty of its design and its deplorable condition. Obviously left vacant for some time, the house had fallen prey to vandals who had scrawled unrepeatable words and suggestions on walls and floors alike. The real estate agent clutched her purse and stepped gingerly around some ragged blankets on the floor. "It could be cleaned, I suppose," she said, then quickly corrected herself. "That is, I *know* it could. I could give you the name of a man who will haul off this old furniture and trash."

Jody nodded. The owner apparently had taken everything he had considered worth salvaging. She was examining the carving on the mantel in the front parlor. "When did you say it was built?"

The agent checked her notebook. "In 1798. It stayed in the same family until 1980, when the last of them died, leaving no heirs."

"It's been empty since then?"

"It was rented some years ago, but only for a short while. It's so large, the price must have been prohibitive. Now it can be had for a song." She looked around uncertainly. "I have to admit, it needs a lot of work."

"That's an understatement." As Jody looked around, she tried to keep her features expressionless to hide her growing enthusiasm for the property. It was exactly what she had been looking for. "Will the owners come down on the price?"

"Probably." The agent touched a hanging shred of wallpaper. "If it sells at all, it will keep it from being demolished. That would be a shame. At one time it must have been the prettiest house in Joaquin. Of course, there are some finer ones toward Shreveport," she added. "Here in Louisiana we have always had beautiful plantations."

Jody kicked at the corner of a dilapidated sofa. "I'd like to make an offer on it." She could see the agent's relief.

In due course a deal was struck, and three weeks later the final papers were signed. Jody now owned Whitefriars, moldy walls, crumbling plaster, and all.

Anxious to get started, she hurried out to her new home. As she inspected it again, she grinned with satisfaction. She already knew that under the surface debris, the house was sound, and on closer examination, she concluded that the improvements that had been made over the years would be easier to remove than she had first thought. The vandalism didn't faze her; she had seen worse.

Rescuing old houses was Jody's avocation. She had bought her first one while she was in college, primarily because it proved cheaper for her to buy an older house than rent somewhere else, but also with the idea of improving the property while living there and selling it after graduation. By the time she had received her diploma in architecture, she had finished restoring the house, and she made a tidy profit on its subsequent sale. In the four years since, she had bought and sold three houses, each project proving to be more lucrative than the one before. Whitefriars was a more ambitious undertaking than the others, but it also held greater promise.

Jody had come to Joaquin, Louisiana, not only to look for a plantation home to restore, but also because she felt she needed a change of scenery and some distance from the several men she had been dating off and on, none of whom held her interest beyond the end of a given date and all of whom were pressuring her for a more intense relationship. She had liked the town at first sight, it being the sleepy sort of place that stayed pretty much the same from decade to decade, and had taken a room at the town's only motel while she surveyed potential restoration properties. The people she met were friendly, if somewhat more conservative than those with whom she had been involved in Baton Rouge, but change was what her situation dictated, and change it would be.

The same day she made the offer on White-friars, she impulsively rented office space and contracted for a sign out front of the office announcing her services as an architect. She knew the demand for an architect in this small town was going to be slim, but she had a comfortable sum in her savings account and would not need much income for living expenses since she planned to live at Whitefriars during most of the restoration. Of course, she had had no guarantee that her offer on Whitefriars would be accepted, but instinct had told her that her chances were good, and she had been prepared to offer more if her initial bid had been rejected.

Jody glanced at her wristwatch and looked down the stairs into the expansive foyer. She had invited her new friend, Angie Wilson, to come see the place, and had expected her to be there before now. Angie operated a flower shop in the building adjacent to the one she had rented, and during the past several weeks they had discovered they had a good deal in common. Angie's only irritating habit was that she was seldom on time for anything, and today was proving to be no exception. As Jody headed down the upstairs hall for another look at the bedrooms, she heard someone call out from below.

"Jody, are you in here?"

"Up here, Angie," she answered as she hurried back to the landing at the top of the stairs. "Come on in."

Angie entered hesitantly, looking about in obvious trepidation. "Are the floorboards safe? Are you sure this was a good idea?"

Jody laughed. "It looks worse than it is. Of course it's sound; otherwise I wouldn't have bought it. Come on up. I'll give you a tour."

Angie gingerly made her way up the stairs, careful not to let the dusty walls touch her white slacks.

and pale pink blouse. "I had no idea it would be such a mess."

"That's why I got it so cheap." Jody led the way to the master bedroom. "Look at this view!"

It was huge, like all the rooms in the house, and had French doors leading out onto an upstairs porch. Beyond its large windows on the south wall, the Petite Coeur River flowed gently past the plantation, its path through the expansive fields surrounding Whitefriars marked by swaying river willows. Cows belonging to neighboring farms dotted the verdant meadows, and in the near distance a mockingbird was calling.

"Isn't it beautiful?" Jody crossed her arms and hugged herself. "This is my best house yet. And look at the mantel. Under the paint, it's marble! Can you imagine anyone painting over a marble mantel?"

Angie looked around the room. "Didn't you say you were going to live here while you're working on it? I mean, I hate to be the voice of doom, but this place has a long way to go."

"I'm having the electricity checked this afternoon. If the wiring is sound, I'll move in as soon as I can get this room clean enough to live in."

"Won't you be afraid out here? You don't have any neighbors. What if the vandals come back?"

"I'm putting new locks on the doors and glass in the windows. Once it becomes obvious that someone is living here, I won't have any trouble." Jody looked back out the window. "I grew up in the country. I won't be lonely. Besides, you'll come visit me, won't you?"

"Yes, but I just hope you know what you're doing."

"I do. You won't recognize this place when I get through with it."

Once the trash and dilapidated furniture were hauled away, the house looked better. Jody spent days cleaning the floors and walls in the rooms she intended to live in, then moved her belongings into the house. Angie helped her get settled, but she continued to give Jody the impression that she thought Jody had lost her mind. But Jody was too busy and too excited to care.

She began the restoration process by researching the house's history in hopes of finding a picture of it in its earlier days, spending so much time in the Joaquin library that it seemed like a second home. After days of digging, the pieces of the puzzle began falling into place. The house had been built by one Josiah Deveroux at a time when the Petite Coeur must have been larger; he had kept his own boats on the river and used the waterway to move his crops of cane and cotton from Whitefriars to the Mississippi and, eventually, on to New Orleans. Jody surmised that the plantation must have been enormous at that time, perhaps a thousand acres or more, for it to have supported the production of both cotton and cane. Diligently, she continued her quest for more information.

The plantation had apparently survived the Civil War without a scratch and had been kept intact until early in the 1900s, when a portion of it was sold to pay overdue taxes. In the years hence, the huge holding continued to be pared down periodically, until nothing but the ten acres and the house she now owned were left.

In the microfilm records of old area news-papers, Jody found many pictures of twentieth-century Whitefriars—the owners often had rented it out for weddings and garden parties—but even in those pictures taken as early as the turn of the century the improvements were already in place.

Having done all she could on her own, Jody went to the librarian and asked for help finding pictures of Whitefriars prior to 1900.

"Might be something in our plantation section in the back room," the woman said. She took Jody through a door marked "Employees Only," and led her into the stacks and down a long aisle devoted to Civil War Louisiana. "We pride our-selves on being a good resource library for that time period, but we limit access because many of these books are quite old and fragile. I'm sure you'll handle them with care, but that isn't true of all our patrons." As the woman scanned the book spines, she added, "There won't be many photos, you understand. Cameras were quite new then." She pulled a thick book from a shelf and handed it to Jody. "Try this one. It's a history of this par-ish. There's a good section on Joaquin, with quite a few sketches and reproductions of paintings of the period. Now, remember, these books mustn't leave this room."

"I understand. Thank you." Jody took the book to a table nearby and sat down to read it.

The book, compiled by residents of the parish, contained family stories, as well as information about the original owners of the plantations and houses of the area. It was exactly what Jody had hoped to find.

One story in particular caught her interest. Whitefriars had been owned by Micah Deveroux immediately before the Civil War. His father had died at a relatively early age of unnamed causes, leaving young Micah orphaned at the age of eighteen and in charge of his own plantation. Jody had to admire him. Micah not only made the plantation flourish, but he'd apparently freed his slaves soon after his father's death. For him to have been able to pay wages for the labor necessary to work the plantation, which had been done previously for free by slaves, said a great deal for his management abilities, as well as for the family's fortune. Jody knew most people would not have been able to handle such a difficult task at the same age.

A few pages farther into the book she found a painting of Whitefriars as it had looked in 1860. The ancestor who had written of the house described it as being bright with sunlight and filled with flowers inside and out. Jody liked that. Whitefriars must have been a happy home for one of the family to have remembered it being so cheerful.

On the next page she found a picture of Micah Deveroux. The tintype, then still a relatively new invention, showed a handsome man in the prime of his life. He had dark hair and his eyes seemed to be light. Blue, she assumed. Instead of the typically somber expression found in most old photos, he wore a faint smile, as if he found life exciting, and his eyes were bright with intelligence. As she read the text surrounding the picture, she found her eyes returning again and again to the photo. For some reason she couldn't fathom, his face was compelling, almost hypnotic to her.

"Great," she muttered to herself. "I find a fascinating man, and he's been dead for nearly a hundred years."

The librarian, who had positioned herself nearby apparently standing guard over the ancient tomes, must have overheard Jody's utterance, for she looked in her direction. From the expression of mirth on the woman's face, Jody could tell she was amused by Jody's unintentional comment. Jody didn't think the subject was humorous at all. She had never found anyone she liked well enough to date exclusively, let alone marry. In her hometown of Grand Coteau, she had had several boyfriends, and in college in Baton Rouge there had been others. But since then, she had dated only sporadically, preferring more often than not to spend her time after hours working on whatever restoration project she had under way. Although the spare social life she led was her own choice, at times she wondered if at 26 she was losing out on life. Her family certainly thought so and told her as much in every letter.

She glanced back at Micah Deveroux's photo. What had he been like? Was he as personable as his picture implied?

As she read on, she discovered the book contained quite a bit of information on Micah; he was evidently a favored ancestor as well as a colorful one. There were paragraphs describing how he had freed his slaves and strong hints that he had been part of the Underground Railroad to help other slaves escape to freedom. He had been known as an innovative builder and had drawn plans for houses for friends and even for a few of the stores in Joaquin. He had been the first to try several new methods of farming cotton and for cooking cane into syrup and sugar, but there was virtually nothing about his private life.

He had evidently married, since the person who had written the account was also named Deveroux and Micah had had no brothers. Or was this writer the offspring of a cousin? Jody looked back at the picture. He was too handsome not to have been popular with the ladies. Why was there no mention of a wife?

She finished her research, photocopied the pages that described Whitefriars' interior, and, on impulse, copied Micah's picture as well. Before going home, she stopped by the courthouse to look for additional information on Micah, but her search yielded only a few documents about his freeing the slaves and the purchasing of some additional land. No marriage certificate was on file, but neither was a record of his birth or death.

For the next few days, Jody was quite busy at Whitefriars, discovering the original colors of the rooms. She spent hours painstakingly peeling off layers of wallpaper. Once the original paper was exposed, she carefully recorded the patterns and colors in her notebook. To get a history of the paint used over the years, she covered a ball with sandpaper, then twisted it in a circular motion on the painted door frames, mantels, and banisters. The circular sanding not only revealed the colors of paint used, but the order in which the paint had been applied. She took particular note of the original finish applied to the wood, which in some cases had been a clear varnish that an untrained eye might have missed.

The colors used over the years had been splendid, for the most part. In a layer between the dark, somber tones of Whitefriars' earliest days and the stark and uninspired whites and off-whites of more modern times, Jody discovered the walls had been hues of robin's egg blue, sunny yellow, and primrose pink. The latter color at least hinted at a woman's touch, but Jody reminded herself that a number of generations besides Micah's had lived in the house and that this method of tracing colors was not intended to pinpoint the year a particular color was used. It was possible that the clear, cheerful colors had been ordered painted by his mother or perhaps a daughter, assuming he had produced a family. Somehow, Jody was sure, however, that Micah had lived in the house when the walls were at their prettiest.

The library was the greatest challenge. Many of the shelves were filled with moldering books and stacks of receipts and other papers from the 1930s. She had put off going into that room until last, because it promised to be more time-consuming than all the others. She knew better than to throw away the books and papers stored there without inspecting them carefully; they might contain valuable information about the house or its history.

On the Saturday she had decided to devote to cleaning off the shelves, Jody dressed in jeans and a pullover top and surveyed the disorder. Generally, the books were an aging variety of schoolbooks on algebra, geometry, and the like, along with a few volumes from recent times on farming, secretarial skills, and household hints. None was of any particular interest to her or of any collector value, as far as she knew, but nonetheless, she made neat stacks according to when the book was published and whether she intended to return them to the shelves or to donate them to the library. She had always loved books and couldn't bear the thought of throwing them away.

In a cardboard box, in a dark corner of a top shelf, she found more papers. She started to put them with the 1930s receipts, but a date caught her eye: 1872.

Jody sat down on the floor with the box in her lap and slowly removed the brittle papers, being careful not to break them. They were mostly farming notations in a masculine but beautiful script. The ink had long since turned brown and the pages had the musty smell of old paper, but they were a treasure to her. They were dated from the time when Micah Deveroux had lived at Whitefriars, and she was positive they had been written by his hand.

At the bottom of the box was a thin book. When she took it out and read the word *Diary* on the cover, her heart beat faster. It was too much to hope for, but when she opened it, Micah's feathery script covered the page. She carefully closed it and put the volume on the stairs so she would find it easily when she went up to bed. She told herself she was interested only because it might contain information she needed to restore the house, but she didn't believe it. Nevertheless, she turned her thoughts back to her work.

Her investigation of the house showed that, as she had guessed, it had been much smaller originally and that the back wing had been added just prior to the Civil War, when it had seemed that cotton would be king forever. The library was in that wing, and when she sanded through the layers of paint and varnish, she found cypress wood. Her excitement grew.

Whitefriars was yielding more pleasant surprises than Jody had expected, and her thoughts turned to the idea of keeping the house and using it as her permanent headquarters. It could be run as a bed-and-breakfast to support itself and was close enough to Shreveport and Caddo Lake to bring in tourists. Lately she had given thought to putting down roots somewhere. Perhaps this would be the best place.

Her mother had called Jody the night before to tell her that another of her younger cousins was getting married, and put renewed pressure on her by hinting strongly that everyone in the family was wondering why Jody wasn't settling down. Jody had explained, once again, that she had yet to meet anyone she wanted to marry, but as usual her mother hadn't listened. Jody's older brother had completed his family, and her younger sister was expecting her second child in a few months. Her mother had said she was worried Jody would be alone forever. Jody intentionally omitted mentioning that she, herself, was beginning to wonder about that, too.

She worked herself to near exhaustion trying to keep her mind off being lonely, but the diversion that had worked for her in the past failed her this time. The truth was that Jody was tired of being alone. She had enjoyed her independence and the moves from house to house in the past, but it was getting tiring. Whitefriars, she thought, might be different. She might want to stay there and reap the benefits of her hard work.

At last she had the library freed of years of accumulated dust and dirt, and the books and papers were organized. The house was beginning to feel as if it belonged to her. Ordinarily she didn't get this feeling until some of the wall coverings were restored. This was a good sign, she decided.

Through for the day, she went upstairs and ran water for a hot bath. Ordinarily she preferred taking showers, but her muscles ached from reaching, lifting, and scrubbing, and she knew a hot soak in the tub would ease her discomfort. After pouring bath oil into the water, Jody stepped into the claw-footed tub, which fortunately had been recently re-porcelained, and sank in up to her chin. With her eyes closed, she breathed in the perfumed steam and felt her tired muscles relax. The house, too, was settling for the night, as evidenced by the pops and creaks that occasionally broke the silence of her bath. The noises were peaceful, not at all alarming, as if the house were breathing out a long, deep sigh as it bunched its muscles, preparing to protect and shelter her, as it had protected generations of Deverouxs.

Although she had accomplished the first step in relaxing, getting her body slowed down, her mind continued to whir. If she were to stay here, she would need to do something with the house to make money, because the income she could expect from her work as an architect in this rural area, even after she became well established, might not be enough to support her. The mortgage and taxes and utilities on a home this size were considerable. The thought of using Whitefriars as a bed-and-breakfast inn occurred to her again, but she had no idea how much she could hope to make with such a venture. The financial risks might be great, but she had never shied away from taking such chances before. Besides, if things didn't work out the way she hoped, she could always sell the house and move on.

With her decision made, Jody took a slow, deep breath and willed her mind to relax. Idly, she looked up at the ceiling. This room had been originally used for some other purpose, of course, but what that might have been was long ago lost. Many other things had changed as well over the years. Modern invention had had a profound effect on people's lives. As Jody thought about that, it occurred to her that with every change had come more convenience, though not without a price. Life moved faster and was far more complex these days than she imagined it had been when Whitefriars was built. Back then, there had been no such thing as a woman living alone on a plantation and having to make ends meet all by herself. For a moment she wished she had been a part of that slower life-style.

Jody washed with languid movements. The bath was relaxing. The perfumed oil pampered and soothed her. Slowly she slid lower until her dark brown hair floated on the water and fanned out about her head. Then she reached for the shampoo and began to scrub her scalp.

Later, towel dried and feeling much happier, Jody went into her bedroom and sat on the bed. Her thick, terry-cloth robe was belted about her middle and her hair, cut in a straight pageboy style, was gleaming. She preferred her hair short for it was easier to maintain and required no rolling or even a blow-dry. It suited her routine perfectly, even if her mother and aunts said it would have been prettier with a curl in it.

As she picked up the diary she had found in the library, she noticed how incredibly old and musty it was. She turned the slim book over slowly, wondering what it would be like to have the psychic gift of psychometry and be able to know about its author from touch alone, then set aside the romantic thought. She opened the book and began to read.

The first page began without preamble, as if Micah had kept other diaries before and was accustomed to their use. "Today was fair," he had written, "a good 'lay-by' day. The children in the quarters were laughing and singing because they won't have to chop cotton anymore until next year. Saw Sally."

Jody wondered who Sally was. A girlfriend? A cousin? She read the next day's entry.

"Camilla was here. Her children want me to help them build a playhouse down by the river. I was able to talk them into playing in the meadow instead. It's too easy for a child to drown. I'll have my men build them a place under the old crabapple tree."

Jody smiled. This reference must be to his sister and his nieces and nephews. She was glad to see he took an interest in their play as well as in their safety. Not many bachelors would be so kind to children. She read on.

"Sally has left for Charleston. She says she will miss me. Emma was by earlier to ask me to dinner. Tomorrow I'm to ride with Katie."

With a smile, Jody touched the page. She could imagine his handsome face with its enigmatic half-smile and him bending over the book as he wrote the words. As owner of this plantation, he must have been considered the most eligible bachelor in the parish. The next few pages had to do with what machinery he had had repaired, which fields he would let lie fallow the following spring, and which of his mares he would have bred. Buried among the farm notes were the terse words, "Katie has decided to marry Elwin Nestor from New Orleans. She should have been more patient."

What had he meant by that? Would he have proposed to her if she had not been in such a hurry to get to the altar? Or did he not propose because Katie was too impatient a person? She wished she could unravel all the mysteries of the diary.

The next page changed her mind about Micah's cavalier attitude toward women. "I begin to wonder," he wrote, "if there is anyone for me in all the world. I know many women of all descriptions, but none of them touches my heart in such a way to make me love her above all other women. I must marry in order to have heirs to take Whitefriars and my name after me, but I had hoped their mother would be a woman unlike any other."

Jody felt tears well in her eyes. For all his popularity, she could feel Micah's loneliness reach out to her down through the years. She could understand that kind of loneliness.

"I find myself recalling a dream I have had on numerous occasions. In the dream I find a woman who has appeared seemingly from nowhere and who is as unlike anyone I've known as a unicorn is to a plow horse. At the end of the dream, she always whispers 'Remember me,' and vanishes. I know I shouldn't put stock in dreams, but it haunts me. Claudia says I'm being foolish, but Camilla says it means something when a person dreams the same dream more than once. Claudia is probably right this time, I'm sorry to say."

Jody closed the book and put it on her bedside table. How sad, she thought, that Micah with his dashing good looks and fortune would be as lonely as she was. It didn't seem fair. Had he ever found his unique woman or had he finally settled for one of the women he had known since birth? She hoped he hadn't settled.

Micah's dilemma wasn't unlike her own. Jody removed her robe and lay down before turning off the bedside lamp. She knew several men who would make good husbands. One of them had even proposed, and she knew a phone call would bring him to Joaquin in record time. But she felt no love for any of them. As hard as she had tried to convince herself that settling down with one of them would have been prudent, she hadn't even come close.

The darkness lay soft in the room. Beyond the windows moonlight shimmered in silvers and blues. A breeze lifted the curtains, then waned, letting them flow back into place. Jody had always liked the calm of night. It had always seemed magical to her, a time for miracles, a respite from the reality of daylight. She remembered how as a child she had always made a wish on the first star she saw and how she had gazed at the moon and wondered what marvels might be up there. She had always been a dreamer and had never entirely lost her conviction that wishes could come true. Micah Deveroux seemed to share at least some of her philosophy. A realist would not hold out for a "unique" woman when he had several parishes of suitable, though ordinary, ones to choose from.

She rolled to her side and closed her eyes. It didn't matter. Micah Deveroux was sleeping in the churchyard along with the rest of his family and hadn't dreamed his dreams or made a wish on any star for nearly a century. She would gain nothing by lying awake and thinking about him.

No matter how logically she put it, however, Jody couldn't get Micah out of her mind. He must have slept in this same room. Almost certainly he had been born here as well, and had probably died here. The idea wasn't alarming. Death held no specters for Jody. She liked the idea of the continuity of lives begun and ended and begun again in the house. She sat up and looked around the room. Where had the furniture been then? She owned very little furniture of her own, and in the dim moonlight the room looked bare.

As she thought about the closet that had been added beside the bathroom, she wondered if the room she was in had originally been longer or if the space for the bath and closet had been taken from the adjoining room. Until she took the carpet up, it would be difficult to tell. The floorboards would show where the original walls had been. Had his bed been more or less where hers was now or had he put it on one of the other walls? The room was so large, it might have been arranged any number of ways.

Feeling restless, Jody got up and went to the window and gazed down at the river. The Petite Coeur flowed past Whitefriars, lazy and silvery in the moonlight, and watching its passage soothed her soul. A breeze touched her face and lifted her hair as it had the curtains earlier. Jody breathed in the fresh air and sighed. Where was her unique man, the man she could love beyond all others?

"I hope you found your woman, Micah," she whispered. "If you did, maybe there's hope for me, too."

The night wind touched her cheek and Jody went back to bed.

Chapter Two

"At first I thought a bed-and-breakfast inn would be the way to go," Jody excitedly explained to her friend. "Then I had this really great idea." She leaned forward eagerly. "Picture this, Angie. What if I start a historical village like the one at Williamsburg, Virginia?"

"A village?"

"I could start small. If I restore Whitefriars to its original state, complete with furniture, I might qualify for a state or federal low-interest loan or get a grant from a foundation interested in the preservation of historic homes. I can hire crafts people in the area to come here and demonstrate quilting or horseshoeing and so forth."

"I don't mean to be pessimistic, but why would people in Joaquin want to come out here and see someone quilting? Most of them do things like that themselves."

"I'm thinking bigger than Joaquin. I'm talking tourist trade. We're near Shreveport, but far enough into the country to lend an air of mystique."

"But Whitefriars is only one building. You said *village*."

"I own ten acres. I can buy other vintage buildings in the area and have them moved here. I'd have to go slow at first, of course, but in time, this could be a big tourist draw. Maybe never as elaborate as Williamsburg, but who knows? I don't think there's anything like that in the South."

"I never heard of anything." Angie sipped her iced tea and looked thoughtfully about the room. "You might have something there."

"I've been concerned how I can afford to live here. Not many people in town need or want an architect, but I like living here. What do you think? Will people be for it or against it?"

"Who can tell? People around here aren't much for changes, but in a way, this is going back to the way it used to be. They may be all for it."

"I'm going to give it a try." Jody smiled at the room, and in her mind she saw it the way it would be. "I have to at least try. And I've decided to restore it to the Civil War period. Tourists link that more with the South, and most aren't all that aware of our French heritage. Besides, the Civil War has been better documented and will be easier to research."

"When will you get started?"

"Right away. I'm going to start looking into financing for the project this afternoon." Jody sighed happily. "If things go in my favor, I may be able to keep Whitefriars after all."

*   *   *

The financing Jody applied for was approved more quickly than she had dared to hope, and she also received a rather generous cash donation, with no strings attached, from a group of local businessmen who were willing to support anything that would bring tourists and their money to Joaquin. She had been working only a few weeks, but already she had finished painting some of the downstairs rooms and had sent samples of the various wallpapers to a company in New York that specialized in the replication of antique wallpaper. Whitefriars bloomed in its new colors, and Jody thought it really did seem as if it were filled with sunshine.

As the summer progressed, she began the search for furniture of a type that would have been used in the house during the Civil War period. Word about her venture had spread throughout the town, and as a result, she received several windfalls. One of them was a telephone call asking her to come to one of the older houses in town.

The door was answered by an elderly woman who leaned on a cane as she led Jody into the house. Jody looked about with interest. She had seldom seen so many antiques in a private home.

"I have everything my grandparents owned," Miss Neston said. "All that and then some." Pride was evident in her voice even though it cracked with age. "See that chest over yonder? My great-grandfather brought it here from France when he came to Louisiana as a boy. It's my oldest piece."

"It's beautiful." Jody followed the woman into

the back parlor. "I've never seen such a wonderful collection."

Miss Neston laughed. "I never thought of it as a collection. Just furniture." The woman gradually lowered herself into a chair. "I heard tell of what you're planning to do with Whitefriars. Sounds like a good idea to me. Just a shame one of our own young folks didn't think of it first."

"I intend to hire all local people for the crafts, or at least as many of them as I can."

"I wish I could work there myself. Can't though. Got too old." Miss Neston laughed as if this were a joke.

Jody smiled. "I need all the advice I can get."

"You need more than that. You need furniture." Miss Neston gestured at the room. "You're sitting in it."

"I don't understand."

"The furniture in this room, most of it, came from Whitefriars."

Jody's eyes widened as she looked about at the marble-topped tables and velvet-tufted chairs. "It did?"

"When Benjamin Deveroux died I had my nephew buy as much of the furniture as he could. He kicked up a fuss, but he did it. Said I didn't need any more old furniture."

"I can't believe it. This really belonged to Whitefriars?" Silently, Jody tried to determine whether the pieces were old enough to date back to the Civil War.

"Sure did. I can even tell you where they sat. My family has always been friends with the Deverouxs. That chair you're in was in the back parlor, over by the window that faces east. The others like it were also in that room. So was the fern stand over there and the knickknack shelf. The marble tables were in the front parlor and the secretary was in the office. It was against the inside wall near the door."

Jody recalled the diary entry that had made the Neston name familiar to her. A man named Elwin Neston had married the impatient young Katie, who was also being courted by Micah Deveroux.

"I'm getting to the point where I can't live alone anymore. I'll be eighty-five in October. I have to do something with my belongings because I'm to move in with my youngest niece next month. My nephew thinks he's going to have the burden of selling them, but I don't want that. I don't need the money and neither does my niece, so I've decided to give them to you."

"To me?"

"To Whitefriars, really. I hate the idea of them being sold into separate places. They belong together." She fixed Jody with rheumy blue eyes. "I want a promise, though. If you don't make a go of Whitefriars, I want them donated to a museum where they can be enjoyed by everybody."

"I agree. We can draw up a contract stipulating that."

Miss Neston nodded. "Done. As soon as I leave for my niece's house, I'll have them delivered."

"Thank you." Jody was almost at a loss for words. "I can't tell you how much this means to me. But won't you miss them? Can't you take your favorite things with you?"

"I'm taking my great-grandfather's trunk and things of sentimental value and my bedroom suite, but I can't fill my niece's house with old furniture." She paused, as if she were thinking for a minute. "There's a Bible, too. Over there on the top shelf of the secretary. You might as well take it with you now so it doesn't get misplaced."

"The Deveroux family Bible?" Jody felt her pulse quicken.

"That's right."

She went to the secretary and opened the glass door. The musty smell of old books assailed Jody's nostrils, but to her that scent meant nostalgia and some sort of connection to a bygone era. One of the books was a Bible, which was quite large, and as she took it from the shelf, she found it was even heavier than she had expected. She held it to her bosom as if it were a baby. "I can't tell you how much this means to me. I'm overwhelmed."

Miss Neston waved at her. "Nonsense. I'm just being logical. A person who wants to do what you're doing will take care of my things. That's all." She looked as if she might be close to tears.

Jody took her hand to reassure her and said, "I'll take the best of care of them, I promise. And I'll have a legal contract drawn up to guarantee that if anything happens to me, the furniture is to be sent to a museum and kept together and on display."

"Thank you."

Jody suddenly realized that as grateful as she was for receiving the furniture, Miss Neston was equally relieved that she had found a good home for her treasured things.

Once Jody was seated in her car, she put the Bible on her lap and reverently caressed its old leather cover. Carefully she opened it to the leaf where family births, deaths, and marriages had been recorded.

The entries had been done in several different hands and different inks, a few of which were faded almost to oblivion. Josiah Deveroux married Elizabeth Cartier in March 1795 and died in 1816. In 1816, Lucien married a woman whose first name was Dorothée, but whose last name was no longer readable. Two years later they had the first of several children, a boy named Antoine. Antoine married first Celina, who died in childbirth along with the baby, then Julie, who was the mother of Micah.

Jody touched Micah's name, apparently written in the bold script of his proud father. On November 3, 1842, Micah was a tiny newborn at Whitefriars. It seemed so far in the past when she looked at the dates. Yet she had researched so much about Micah's life that at times he seemed to be almost her contemporary.

She read down the list of babies born to Antoine and Julie to where Micah's marriage should have been noted. His name was there all right, but the name beside it was smudged and illegible. Try as she could, she couldn't make out the letters. A search of the list showed no record of the wife's name at the birth of their babies or any mention of her death. For that matter, Micah's death was also unrecorded. But then, so was that of his grandmother. The list was kept for the family, and she thought perhaps the bereaved children either couldn't bring themselves to write the date or had thought they would never need a reminder.

She closed the Bible and started the car. With the Bible beside her, she felt as if her enterprise was indeed going to come to pass.

When she reached Whitefriars, Jody put the Bible away in a safe place in her bedroom and went outside. The day was sunny but not so hot as to be uncomfortable in the shade. Whitefriars was situated so that a breeze always seemed to touch it. Jody walked across the yard and tried to imagine her village as it would be in the future.

Behind a row of ancient oleanders out back of the main house was a double row of wooden cabins. Jody had been in and out of them often during these few weeks, but now she looked at them in a different light, envisioning crafts people working in them. Originally the cabins had been built as slave quarters, and the oleanders apparently had been planted to block the view of them from the house. Most of the cabins were in poor shape, having been unoccupied quite a long time and obviously uncared for, and several were in truly deplorable condition.

Jody made mental notes as to whether each cabin could be saved or whether it was too far gone to be worth the effort. Most were salvageable, and she thought the materials from the ones that were tumbling down could be used for authentic repairs on the others. Most of the cabins had but a single room, though some had a shedlike structure built onto the back to serve as extra sleeping space. It saddened Jody to think of entire families living in the tiny places, and of being owned by someone else. The idea of slavery had always been repugnant to her.

One cabin that sat slightly apart from the others was in better condition. Unlike most of them, it had a plank floor and a small window in the south wall, though the window was boarded up. As she had seen the interior of this particular one only once before with a peek through the door and was not sure what to expect inside, she stepped in carefully and waited for her eyes to adjust to the darkness.

Like all the others, it had only enough room for a bed and perhaps a chair and table. Jody took a closer look at the tiny fireplace, the only possible source of heat, and wondered how the occupants had managed the winters. Louisiana as a whole had relatively mild winters, but here in the northern part, the temperature usually dipped below freezing several times each year.

The remnants of what had been a wooden chair were piled in one corner, and suspended from the low rafters were what was left of long-dead plants, possibly herbs that had been used for cooking or medicinal purposes. Then her attention was drawn to some odd graffiti on the walls.

These scrawls were different from those she had found in the main house, apparently having been made many years before, because they were almost hidden by years of grime and wear. As she examined the marks more closely, Jody discovered that they were not graffiti at all, but rather crude drawings of animals and leaves of plants that were unfamiliar to her, and some sort of unrecognizable symbols. The closer she looked at the walls of the cabin, the more of the odd and disquieting drawings she found. After looking at them for several minutes, trying to understand what she was seeing, she ventured a touch and discovered that they had been burned into the wood. Whoever had put them there had not meant for them ever to be eradicated.

Even the untrained eye could see these drawings were not meant merely for decoration. The animals were snarling with fangs and appeared quite fierce despite the simplicity of the drawings. Even the peculiar symbols were embellished with sharp points and jagged edges. Jody was reminded strongly of voodoo trappings she had seen once in New Orleans.

Suddenly the cabin seemed too close and still. She stepped out into the sunlight and rubbed her arms. It took a while for the sun to warm her. For a moment she stared at the cabin. She had never felt anything quite like that before in her life.

She decided that the cabins, and this one in particular, would have to wait a while. Her efforts would have to be spent first on the main house. She hurried back to the more familiar surroundings.

Fired by renewed enthusiasm, Jody went to the library and began the shelves. The paint gave way with relative ease, and she was gratified to see grains of cypress start to emerge.

At suppertime she stopped work long enough to eat a quick sandwich and watch the news on TV, then went back to work. She liked this room and could already see how she would decorate it. A large desk would be here; oak, of course. And lamps with green shades. She thought maybe pale blue curtains since the walls would be the natural wood and more somber in tone than the other rooms.

As she moved from the inside wall to the one that held the fireplace, she noticed something.

This wall was broken by a short hallway into the drawing room. She had always assumed that the hallway traversed the space taken up by the two fireplaces, which had been placed back to back. But now she realized that the fireplaces could not account for all the extra space between the two rooms.

Jody's curiosity was aroused. Could it be because the library was in the new wing and whoever had added it had not understood the principles of architecture? She immediately dismissed this possibility. The wing was beautifully done in every other respect, and it blended perfectly with the older rooms.

She went into the drawing room and studied the wall from that angle. There was no closet or anyplace where a cupboard might have been boarded up. She had removed most of the wallpaper down to the bare boards, and they were uniformly old. No wall had been added after the house had been built.

Going back to the library, she looked more closely at the shelves. The wood there was a perfect match to the wood on the wall she had just cleaned.

Standing in the doorway, Jody measured the enclosed distance. Nearly five feet were unaccounted for. Surely no builder would sacrifice five feet of a room to a mistake in planning. She tapped on the wall, but the wood was so thick she couldn't tell if there was a hollow space inside or not.

Jody had never encountered a mystery like this. Visions of secret rooms leapt to her mind. This could be a secret room such as was used to hide runaway slaves in the underground railroad!

Her excitement was building fast. She recalled the strong hints in the parish history that Micah Deveroux had been part of the underground railroad. If this were such a room, Whitefriars would have a unique attraction all its own. But where was the door?

She went outside and searched for anything that could have been used for an entrance into the house. She even took a flashlight and crawled under the house to look for a trap door; all she found, however, were spiderwebs. Soon it became so dark she had to give up the search outside.

Going back to the mysterious wall, she felt over every square inch, looking for a clue as to how to get inside. No panels yielded to her touch and she could find no hidden spring latch. At last she sat down on the floor to rest. It was possible she could be mistaken. The drawing room had once been the back wall of the house, and it was not inconceivable that the new wing had been added in the easiest if not the best way.

The fireplace was inset between the walls of shelves and the mantel, and unlike the others in the house, was of wood. She had stripped away enough of the older finishes to know it was made of walnut, not cypress, but she hadn't thought much about that. It could have been bought before the shelves were put in place, or it could have been chosen because of its carvings and in spite of its not matching the rest of the room. Someone, possibly the vandals, had built too large a fire in it, and the outside was blackened with a thick soot. She had put off cleaning it until later. Again she felt all along the shelves, even jiggling them to see if that would trigger a hidden door to open. As before, her search was useless.

There was one other way, but she had reserved the idea as a last resort. She could cut into the wall from the drawing room side. Since the drawing room would be covered with wallpaper as soon as the new paper arrived, no one would ever know a hole had been cut. But she hated the idea of damaging the house in any way. Once she could see inside, however, she would be able to tell at a glance if a secret room was hidden there or if the extra space was only a mistake on the part of the builder.

She went back to work on the walls and busied her mind, trying to determine some other way to find out what was in the space. By the time she was too tired to continue working, she had come up with no alternative ideas and had decided to cut into the wall before putting up the drawing room paper.

After her bath she sat on her bed and took out Micah's diary again. She opened it to the page where she had left off and resumed reading.

"Claudia was here today. She is encouraging me to court Emma Parlange. It would be reasonable for me to do so, since her family's land adjoins mine and it would almost double Whitefriars' acreage when she inherits it. As she has no brothers or sisters, it is sure to belong to her on the death of her parents.

"Emma isn't a bad choice. She's pretty enough and seems biddable by nature, and if she isn't particularly intelligent, what does that matter? Her family is as Creole as mine and her lineage as long. I'll give it consideration."

Jody shook her head in exasperation. How unintelligent had she been for him to have noted it? Had he never heard of genetics? Then she realized he might not have known about genes and that if he had, the genetic influence on intelligence might not have been known yet. She decided that didn't absolve him. Who would want to marry someone who couldn't carry on an intelligent conversation? Or maybe, she thought, that was not as important in the marriages of his day.

"We've come a long way," she said to herself. Maybe this Emma had more to recommend her than her conversation. Her land and wealth, for instance. Now that Jody had the family Bible, she knew the Claudia he referred to was the older of his two sisters, but why did she care if he married or not? Had it been that important for the son and heir to marry and produce an heir in his turn? It would seem so.

The next few pages were filled with Micah's plans for repairs to the horse barn and with his disgust at Reconstruction politics.

Jody put down the diary. That had not occurred to her. This diary was written only six years after the end of the Civil War. From all she had read in history books and novels, the South was still a ravaged mess, in constant turmoil over carpetbaggers and the like. From Micah's diary she could see he had relatively few thoughts about the war and seemed to be none the worse for the local politics. For that matter, why had Whitefriars not been burned by Yankee troops?

Jody supposed it must have been spared due to its location. While it wasn't far from modern interstate highways, it could have been far off the beaten path during the war. Joaquin hadn't been the site of any battle she had ever heard of, and Whitefriars was not along the path an army would have taken getting between Shreveport and New Orleans. Nor was the Petite Coeur a large enough waterway to be important to the invading army. Whitefriars had evidently been saved by a stroke of fate.

Had Micah served in the army? He had been only eighteen when the war began, but younger boys than he had enlisted. She tried to imagine the man in the tintype photograph in a gray uniform with cannonballs flying around him, but she couldn't. He didn't look like a soldier. Killing didn't fit with his gentle smile. Perhaps Whitefriars' inhabitants, like the house, had gone through the war untouched. Given her viewpoint on slavery and the fact that the house might have a secret room for smuggling runaway slaves north, she liked the idea. Surely if Micah were part of the underground railroad he would not have fought to continue the practice of slavery.

She reopened the diary to another day's entry. "Katie Neston was by to see Camilla. Camilla says she is already bored with Elwin. I thought she would be. Katie always was impetuous. It's not a good trait in a wife—at least not one of the Neston wives. Elwin could bore a saint half to death."

Jody had to smile as she thought of the old Miss Neston she had just met. She seemed to have inherited some of Katie's spunk, if not her impatience. Her nephew, who had deplored her buying more old furniture, sounded typical of the

Nestons Micah had known.

The page read, "Went to Camilla and Reid's party. Saw Zelia Ternant. Valcour was there, but she never sat with him. Now that he can't dance she seems to think he can't see or hear either. She was flirting with me and several others all evening. It's a pity the cannon didn't take Zelia and leave Valcour with his leg."

So the war had touched his friends, at least. Perhaps Jody had been too quick to decide Micah had not been a part of it. Or maybe he had fought for the North, and Whitefriars was spared for that reason.

For the next few weeks Micah had only listed the foals born and the status of the various fields of crops. Then the words seemed to leap up at her. "I proposed to Emma tonight and she accepted. I expected her to show maidenly resistance. She says she loves me. Maybe she does. The marriage will be next year. She favors the month of April."

The terse sentences told her more than their content. Micah was engaged to be married, but he was not happy about it.

"Claudia held another party in Emma's honor. Camilla says she thinks Claudia is overdoing it and I agree. You'd think this was the match of the century to hear Claudia talk. I know she's glad to have her particular friend in the family, but Claudia tends to go overboard at times. Camilla says it makes her own efforts look sparse, but as I told her, any more parties would be too many. Camilla no longer says she dislikes Emma, out of respect for me, but I know her feelings haven't changed."

Jody noticed there was still no mention of Micah's emotions toward his betrothed. That changed on the next page.

"Emma and I had a disagreement yesterday and made it up today. I convinced her that I still love her. She cried copious tears and I had to apologize twice before she would hear me, but it's done. I hope she lets the matter die. I only did what any gentleman would do for a stranger in need."

Jody frowned. What did that mean? Had Emma quarrelled with Micah for doing someone a service? "Copious tears" seemed like an odd reaction to a fiancé's charity. She closed the book. Reading it tonight made her feel as if she were invading Micah's privacy. She silently chided herself for thinking such nonsense. How could she be invasive of a man who was dead and buried for half a century?

All the same, she felt a strange uneasiness, and the last notations remained lodged in her mind.

Chapter Three

A month later the library wall still had not yielded its secret, nor had Jody had the heart to cut into the drawing room wall to see what might lie inside. Jody had long since finished reading Micah's diary, but she was no closer to learning if he had married Emma.

Diary entries had detailed several parties where he had seen Emma, and there were a few references to a mysterious "she," but the other woman was never named and his comments seemed guarded. The diary had ended abruptly the night before he was to marry Emma. Jody was intrigued, but she could find no other clue as to why or if Micah had married Emma as planned. Because of her interest in this, the secret room—if indeed there was one—had taken a back seat.

Jody had written to several craft organizations in Joaquin inviting the members to consider possible employment at her proposed village. She received acceptance letters from several almost immediately.

"I read your note at the last meeting of the Busy Needles Quilting Society," one read, "and everyone there expressed enthusiasm. One of our members suggested that a small store might be set aside to sell the crafts. Are you agreeable to the suggestion?"

Jody smiled with relief. She had been afraid no one else would share her excitement for the undertaking. A craft store would be ideal. Quickly she ran through possible places to put it. Not in the house. Whitefriars was too important to devote a room in it to a profit-making scheme, even if the money would be necessary to make the village self-supporting.

The barns were too large. In the winter people would be too cold out there to want to shop. Besides, she had thought she would eventually buy horses for the horse barn and milk cows for the other one. She wanted Whitefriars to be as authentic as possible.

Jody had found a log house not far from Joaquin that the owner had been using as a hay barn. He was willing to sell it, and the local historical association had declared their willingness to help her move the logs and reassemble the building on her land as soon as she raised money to buy it and decided where to put it. That might not be a bad place to put the store.

On the other hand, she didn't want to over-extend herself. She had to stay on the conservative side or risk losing everything.

The cabins out back were the only other possibility, especially the one that sat slightly apart from the others. It would be ideal for the shop because it was hidden from the house and would be near where most of the craftspeople were working.

Jody went into her library and sat at the desk to answer the letter. Everything was going so quickly and so smoothly, she thought she might be able to start operations by Thanksgiving if the rest of the wallpaper she had ordered arrived soon.

She looked thoughtfully at the walls around her. When she had started renovating this room, she had not yet had the idea of keeping the house and actually restoring it to its original condition. The entire house had been wired for electricity decades ago, but that modernization could be circumvented simply by not using it when tourists were in the house. She had already found replacements for the electric lamps and light fixtures, including several authentic replicas of candle chandeliers and a few gaslights that had been modernized for electricity. The wall switches and electrical outlets could be concealed, and the phone could be unplugged and put away in a drawer. She could carry the electric lamps up to a storeroom and save them for use in the next house she renovated (if she ever did it again) or she could sell them and get back most of her investment in their replacements.

She had stripped years of paint from the bookshelves and returned them to their natural color. This made the room much more cheerful, and, in view of the colors she had determined had been used on the other walls, she thought the library must once have looked exactly like this. The shelves weren't filled with books yet, but she received offers nearly every day for books that were wasting away in attics or about to be sold in estate sales.

Jody bent over her stationery in deep concentration. She wanted to keep everyone's interest as high as possible, and prompt correspondence was one way to do that.

She heard a faint noise from across the room and looked up quickly. For a minute she felt disoriented. The walls were darker, and she had an impression of rugs covering the oak floor. The scent of roses and wisteria drifted in through the open windows.

As quickly as this aberration had occurred, the world was right again. The walls were light and the floor bare. The windows were closed against the first strong cold front of the season.

Curious, Jody stood and went to the window. Outside she saw the canes of roses and the huge trunk of the wisteria that covered a trellised garden seat. Autumn had stripped the leaves from their branches and had left them lying golden on the ground. The wisteria had not bloomed since spring and the roses had produced their last blossoms by the end of summer. She touched the rippled glass of the window. Even if everything had been in bloom, she wouldn't have smelled the flowers with the window closed and latched.

The phone rang and Jody jumped. When she answered it, she found Angie on the other end of the line. "I'm fine," she said to Angie's question. "An odd thing just happened, that's all."

"What's that?"

"You won't believe this, but for a moment I smelled roses and wisteria." Jody laughed.

"Do you have migraines? I've heard of people smelling strange things just before one hits."

"No, I seldom have headaches at all. It was nothing. Just a stress-induced special effect. What's going on with you?"

"Not much. I thought if you were free tonight, we might go to see a movie. That new romance with Mel Gibson is playing. It starts at seven o'clock."

"Sounds great. I'll drive by and pick you up. I have a lot to tell you. The quilting ladies are eager to start sewing and I heard from a man who makes beeswax candles."

"Okay. See you at seven."

Jody hung up and finished her letter to the quilting circle. After she put it into an envelope, she called a local plumber. She didn't intend to change many things, but public rest rooms were a must.

"I can get out there tomorrow," the man said.

"I thought I'd put them in the cabin nearest the house. That way they'll be centrally located. That cabin is a little larger than the others and can be divided easily."

The man agreed to come out early in the morning to take a look at it, and Jody hung up. She picked up her desk calendar and counted the weeks until Thanksgiving. If she worked hard, she would be able to finish in time. It would be a propitious time to start. She could begin by taking reservations for a huge Thanksgiving feast with all the foods that would have been served at Whitefriars in the mid-nineteenth century.

She went upstairs and dressed in her work clothes. To save money, Jody was doing as much of the labor herself as was possible. Now that the house was nearly finished, it was time to start cleaning the cabins. Since she wasn't at her best with heights, she had hired some men to put new roofs on the slave quarters, and they were due to arrive at any moment.

Aside from the first cabin, which was larger than the rest, the others were more or less identical.

Jody went to the one that was set slightly apart from the others and looked in the door. Why had it been built away from the others? Its rustic appearance clearly proclaimed it had been used for one of the slaves. She wondered if it had possibly been for a favored house servant. As if mesmerized, she stepped inside. The cabin seemed colder inside than the open air had been. She found herself reluctant to enter farther.

"Hey, lady, are you Ms. Farnell?" a male voice called from behind her.

Jody jumped in surprise, but quickly regained her composure, glad for the excuse to go back outside. "Yes. You must be Orville Wilson."

"Yep. Me and the boys are ready to get started if you'll show us which one you want done first."

"Let's start with that one," she said, pointing to the far end of the row of cabins. "I'm going to have a plumber out tomorrow."

"Okay." With an exaggerated gesture to his crew, he pointed to the cabin Jody had indicated. Several teenagers piled out of the pickup trucks, their backs loaded with the supplies they would need to do their work.

"I'll be in one of the cabins if you need me," she said. "Will it take long, do you think?"

Orville eyed the double row of cabins and rubbed his chin. "They're small. We ought to be able to knock off one a day, maybe two if the rafters are sound."

"Good." Jody went back to the house for her cleaning supplies and returned to the cabin set apart from the others so she would be out of the workers' way. She was determined not to let the oddness of the cabin frighten her.

The floor was grimy with a century and more of dirt, but the boards were sound. She dipped her scrub brush into the pail of soapy water and attacked the walls. Spiderwebs and dust yielded easily, but the harder she scrubbed, the clearer the symbols and pictures became.

Exhausted, Jody stepped back and looked at the walls she had cleaned. Rather than being burned randomly into the wood, the pictures seemed to be telling some story. She could see that the crudely drawn figures of women and men had been depicted pursuing the animals and gathering the leaves. In the center of the back wall was drawn a fire about which men were circled. Inside the men's circle, women, led by a taller figure, danced around the flames.

Suddenly the air inside the cabin again felt stagnant and stifling. Jody hurried outside and bent over at the waist to breathe more deeply. For an instant she had thought she was going to faint. She hoped she wasn't coming down with something; her schedule was too full for her to take time out to be sick.

To her surprise, the workmen had almost finished the roof on the first cabin. She glanced at the sun. How long had she been inside the cabin?

Feeling mildly disoriented but undaunted, Jody stalked back into the cabin. She didn't know what had happened to her, if anything, but she was sure her work there wasn't finished. For a moment, she stood motionless in the center of the room, waiting expectantly, but nothing happened—and nothing would, she reassured herself. It was only a cabin. A peculiarly decorated one, but only a deserted cabin, nevertheless. Jody had never been of a superstitious nature, and she wasn't going to start now.

After surveying the interior of the cabin a few moments, she decided the walls needed a good coat of paint. She went to the house and rummaged through the paint cans until she found one that was nearly full. She hadn't intended to paint any of the cabins' interiors, but this time she was going to make an exception.

Going back to the cabins, she motioned to one of the young men who had just come off the roof. "How are you at painting?"

"About as good as I am at roofing, I guess."

"Good. I want you to paint the inside walls of that cabin. Here's the paint and a brush. Let me know when you're finished."

She went to the cabin at the far end so she would be away from the noise of the workers and started scrubbing. After a few minutes she heard the boy come in the door. Turning, she said, "Surely you aren't finished already."

"No, ma'am. The paint ain't acting right."

"What do you mean?"

"It won't stir up smooth. Maybe it ain't fresh enough."

"That's impossible. I just bought it last week. I used it in the dining room yesterday."

She followed him back to the cabin and looked in the paint can. As he had said, the paint was separating. The pale yellow pigment swirled with an oily streak. Jody took it out into the sunlight and stirred vigorously until it was mixed. Wordlessly she handed it back to the boy and went back to her own work.

Fifteen minutes later he was back. "I sure hate to bother you again, but I'm still having trouble with that paint."

"What this time?" She tried to keep the irritation out of her voice.

"It won't go on the walls. It's like they have grease or something on them."

"That can't be. I just scrubbed them myself."

This time she led the way to the cabin, the boy trailing behind her. As he had said, the paint was beading up on the logs as if he had been painting over a thick coat of grease. Jody touched the logs just ahead of where he had been painting and found the surface to be as porous and dry as an old log should be.

"What kind of drawings are those?" the boy asked.

"I'm not sure. I suppose this cabin belonged to a would-be artist."

"Looks like voodoo symbols."

Jody looked at him sharply.

"I know a boy at school who likes things like that. He showed me a book with stuff like that in it."

Jody was none too pleased at having her suspicions confirmed. "Whatever they are, I want them painted over." She went to the wall and tried to spread the paint evenly. It went on smoothly but began to bead as soon as she quit brushing it flat. "There must be an oily residue in the logs themselves. I have some oil-based paint in the barn. You clean this off while I go get it."

By the time she returned, the boy had removed the paint from the wall. "Here," she said, handing him a gallon of paint. "I didn't particularly want the interior painted barn red, but I guess I'll get used to it."

The boy shook the half-empty can of paint to mix it and started to work. This time the paint stayed put. Jody gave a decisive nod. "See? That was the problem. It just needed oil." She hoped she sounded more confident than she felt. The dark red paint did nothing to chase away the cabin's gloom. She decided to use the barn paint as an undercoat and made a note to buy a more cheerful color the next time she was in the paint store.

Jody spent the rest of the day cleaning and planning. She made notes to put the quilters in the first cabin and the candle makers next to them. She had a lead on a couple of women who knew how to make lace, and she thought that exhibit might be good across from the quilters. The cabin on the end farthest from the house would be good to use to dye wool; there was room to safely build a fire beside it for the boiling pot. Everything was shaping up nicely.

The roofers quit for the day when the sunlight faded toward evening, but they had worked steadily, and she was glad to see they had finished the roof on one cabin and had shored up the next in preparation for the next day's work. The boy who had done the painting stopped to talk to her on his way out.

"I had to put two coats of paint on them walls," he said. "But I finally got that stuff on the walls covered."

"Thank you," she said. "I'll see you all tomorrow."

"If it don't rain," the foreman said cheerfully.

Jody waved good-bye. Before going back to the house to get ready to go to the movies with Angie, she thought she would glance at the red cabin again. She was hoping the paint had dried a lighter shade.

Unfortunately, she discovered the opposite was true. Worst of all, she found the characters were bleeding through in places. It would take at least one more coat. "Damn!" she muttered. "What's it going to take to get rid of these?"

She crossed the room for a look at the opposite wall. When she did, she noticed a loose plank in the floor that shifted when she stepped on it. The loose end had another of the odd marks on it. "Not on the floor, too!" she exclaimed.

She bent for a closer look and found the plank quite loose. Thinking it might be easier to replace the board than to eradicate the mark on it, she worked the plank free and removed it. Underneath the floor was an enclosed space with a dirt bottom. On the dirt lay a wooden doll that had been carved to look like a woman. Spread around it were a fang from some large dog or wolf, a piece of fence wire bent into a knot, a part of a fishnet, and several broken feathers. The arrangement was too symmetrical for the grouping of objects to be accidental.

Jody picked up the doll and sat back on the floor to examine it. The crude doll was clad in a dress made from a scrap of cotton material and was belted around the middle by a vine of some sort. The doll's face was stylized, but the features were recognizable as eyes, nose, and mouth. The smear of white paint on the face flaked off at Jody's touch. On its head was a thatch of dark hair that might have been as dark as Jody's own hair before age and dust had dimmed its color.

Jody's hand began shaking. The red room with its frightening symbols combined with the voodoo doll were too much. She stood and hurried outside, the doll still clutched in her hand. She breathed in gulps of air, but her head still felt light and her eyesight was blurry.

Convinced that she was definitely getting sick, Jody started for the house. It looked impossibly far away. The ground seemed to heave under her feet, and she felt her face to see if she had a fever, though she knew she couldn't possibly judge from her own skin. When she reached the oleander hedge she stopped to get her bearings. The setting sun cast shadows that leapt across the lawn, its brilliance bathing the house with hues of red and orange.

Fright touched her. She had never felt anything like this before. Jody threw herself across the yard and up the back steps. Her footsteps sounded too loud on the porch, and the screen door banged shut behind her like an explosion. She was finding it difficult to think, much less to get to the phone to call Angie for help.

The phone was in the library. She staggered across the kitchen and butler's pantry to the wide hall. Her hands found the door frame of the library and she shoved open the door. As if it were a lifeline, she fastened her eyes on the phone and tried to make her way to it. Her legs had turned to jelly, making it nearly impossible to move. Her knuckles ridged white as her grip tightened on the voodoo doll, the thought never occurring to her to drop it.

She stumbled against the wall, grabbing the fireplace mantel to break her fall. There was a creaking, scraping sound, and the wall beside the mantel swung open. Jody lost her balance, and, with a strangled cry, she fell into the yawning darkness.

Jody opened her eyes, aware that she had apparently been asleep, but even with her eyes fully open, she could see nothing. For an instant she thought she might have gone blind, but then she remembered that she had fallen. Now she assumed she had lost consciousness and now it was nighttime. Still clutched in her hand was the doll she had brought inside to examine. As she turned her head about, straining to see, she was aware that she had never known the night to be so totally devoid of light. She reached out with her free hand, hoping to find some piece of furniture to get her bearings, but instead her hand bumped into a solid object. A wall? Was she inside a closet? No, that couldn't be, for there were no closets in any of Whitefriars' rooms. As she rose to her feet, her cheek brushed against a spiderweb, and she cringed back and batted fruitlessly at the offending object. Her hand hit a wall again, harder than before, and suddenly she could see a thin sliver of light to her right. With claustrophobia quickly setting in, she pushed against the wall beside the crack of light and, to her great relief, the wall swung open easily.

As she blinked against the sudden brightness, her vision blurred and the dizziness returned full force. She had to get to her bed before she hurt herself. Tossing the doll aside and with her hand pressed to her mouth, she hurried from the library. It was not nighttime, as she had thought while trapped within the wall, but judging by the dim light in the hallway, evening was fast approaching. At the bottom of the stairs, she stopped for a moment and listened. As impossible as it seemed, she could swear she heard voices back toward the kitchen. She thought perhaps she had left the radio on, but couldn't remember.

Another dizzying wave of disorientation washed through her as she climbed the stairs. At the top, she swayed, almost losing her balance, then stumbled to the door of her bedroom.

The room was all wrong somehow, yet she was sure it was hers. The various pieces of furniture were more or less where they were supposed to be, but they were different than she remembered. She blinked her eyes, trying to bring things into better focus, but to no avail. With a groan, Jody stripped off her clothes and pulled open the drawer that roughly corresponded to the one where she kept her nightshirts. She put on the first one she came to, noticing that the cloth felt different, but she was too sick to care.

Not bothering to turn on the lights, she climbed into bed. In her disorientation, it seemed that the bed was so high she did indeed have to climb into it. As soon as she lay on the mattress, which should have been firm but instead billowed beneath her, Jody fell asleep.

Hours later, Micah Deveroux came home. The house was lit for his arrival, and his butler met him at the door. "Welcome home, sir," Gideon said as he nodded respectfully.

"Thank you. I don't mind telling you, it was a long trip. New Orleans hasn't changed."

"No, sir. I reckon it never will."

Gideon walked with him to the foot of the stairs, where Micah paused and stepped aside to make room for his driver to carry his trunk up to his room. "There's no need to come up, Gideon. Go on to bed and get some rest."

"Yes, sir."

Micah always loved getting back to Whitefriars. The coming home was almost worth the time away.

By the time he reached the top of the stairs, the driver was on his way back down. Micah bade him good night and, since no ladies were present in the house, removed his coat and brocaded vest as he walked down the hallway to his room, pausing at the hall table near his door to blow out the lamp. After stepping into his room, he closed the door behind him and tossed his coat and vest onto the chair he knew would be there. With the glow of moonlight streaming in through the large windows, and since he intended to go straight to bed, he saw no need to light the lamp.

He was in the process of removing his shirt when he heard a noise that sounded like a soft moan. He froze, and his eyes darted about the dimly lit room as his mind struggled to identify the source. It had been too loud to have come from another room, and besides that, he had no houseguests. The next sound to pierce the stillness was the rustling of cloth. He jerked his head toward his bed, and in the moonlight he caught the movement of the bed covers.

Warily, Micah stepped nearer and craned his neck for a better look. Whatever or whoever it was in his bed had stopped moving. Keeping one eye on the bed, he lit his bedside lamp, and as the flame filled the room with yellow light, he discovered the occupant of his bed was a strange woman wearing one of his best shirts. Tentatively, Micah reached out and touched her shoulder, thinking he would rouse her. But instead, she nestled deeper into the bed. With his second attempt he shook her, but the woman would not awaken. Only the pink of her cheeks and her steady breathing told him she was alive.

Grabbing up the lamp from the table, Micah stalked back to the landing at the head of the stairs. "Gideon!" he bellowed. On his second summons, Gideon rushed into view, still pulling his butler's coat back on.

"Yes, sir?"

"Who the hell is this in my bed?"

Gideon stared up at him. "There's somebody in your bed?"

"Get up here!"

Micah preceded Gideon back to the room and pointed at the sleeping woman. "Who is

61

this woman and why is she sleeping in my bed?"

Gideon stared at her and shook his head. "I don't know, Mr. Micah. I never seen her before."

Micah frowned down at her. "I've tried to awaken her, but I can't get any response."

Gideon poked at Jody's arm cautiously. "Ma'am? Wake up, ma'am."

"See? Have you ever seen anyone sleep so soundly?"

"No, sir. She looks like she's alive, though."

"How did she get in here without you seeing her?"

"I don't rightly know. Looks like she made herself to home, though."

Micah sighed. "I suppose I have no choice but to let her sleep where she is for tonight. I'll sleep in my old room."

"Yes, sir. I'll go see to it that there's fresh linens on the bed for you," Gideon said as he hurried from the room.

As Micah looked back at the sleeping woman, she rolled over and his shirt—now her nightshirt—gaped open, revealing an abundance of flesh and suggesting that she was wearing nothing else. Realizing that he was watching a woman dressed in night attire who was asleep in his house, and who presumably had some claim to his protection, his proper upbringing surfaced and he averted his eyes. After blowing out the lamp and replacing it on the table beside the bed, he backed out of the room and closed the door behind him. There would be questions to be answered in the morning. In the meantime, he could sleep in the room he had not occupied since he had become master of Whitefriars.

When Jody awoke, it was early morning, and her odd dizziness, though abated, had not disappeared. Feeling as if her mind were in a fog, she put on the clothes she had worn the day before and went out into the hall.

Everything seemed different, and she rubbed her eyes groggily. Coffee. That was what she needed. She kept a jar of instant coffee on hand for the rare times when she felt she needed caffeine. Threading her fingers through her disheveled hair to straighten it, Jody went downstairs and headed for the library as a shortcut to the kitchen.

As she entered the library, the sense that something was terribly out of place compelled her to stop. This was Whitefriars' library, but it was not the room as she knew it. The shelves were stained darker and were filled with books in new leather bindings. The oak desk was gone and a walnut one stood on the other wall. There were no green shades on the lamps, and sunlight blazed through windows and onto the colorful rugs on the floor. At her feet was the doll she had dropped in her confusion the evening before. She took another step and swallowed against the hard lump in her throat. Something was very wrong here.

She heard a movement behind her and wheeled to find a man coming into the room from the drawing room. He frowned when he saw her. "You, sir! What are you doing in my house? Who are you?"

She glanced over her shoulder to see if there was anyone else in the room. "Do you mean me?" The man stepped closer to her.

She knew she was staring, but she couldn't help it. "Who are you?" she managed to whisper.

"I'm Micah Deveroux. Who are you and what do you mean coming into my house unannounced? And why are you wearing my bedclothes?"

Dizziness overcame Jody and she stumbled toward a chair. "You can't be Micah Deveroux. Whoever you are, call for an ambulance. I'm sick."

He knelt beside her chair and looked at her more closely. "Gideon!" he shouted over his shoulder.

A black man dressed in an impeccable suit opened the door and stared at Jody. "Yes, sir?"

"Fetch a glass of cold cider and some smelling salts."

"Yes, sir." Gideon was gone at once.

"Who was that?" Jody asked weakly. "What's going on here?"

Gideon was back almost at once with a vial, which he uncorked and handed to Micah. Micah waved it under Jody's nose; the fumes of ammonia from the vial made her cough and sit up so she could fan it away. As Micah was corking it, a black woman came in with a glass of golden liquid.

"Drink this," Micah instructed. "Brandy would be better, but my sisters swear by cider."

"I'd rather have the brandy," she retorted, but she sipped the cider. The taste was better than any cider she ever remembered.

Micah nodded for his servants to leave the room. When they were alone, he stood and went to the chair opposite her. "Now, then, madam.

Explain yourself. Why were you in my room when I returned last night?"

Jody looked around again. The windows were open and she smelled leaves burning on the autumn air. A dog barked nearby, and in the distance were the voices of children playing. The portion of the wall nearest the hall door wasn't covered with shelves as she remembered, but instead was decorated with two hunting prints in ornate frames suspended from the cornice board by gold silk ropes. Two leather chairs of a quality she would never have been able to afford stood where her desk should be. The chair behind the desk was also leather and looked as if it might be on a swivel. The desktop was covered with a blotter mounted in a leather case. Two pens stood on either side of a rosewood inkstand. On closer examination, she noticed the lamp was missing more than the green shade. It was now filled with liquid and had a wick awaiting a match.

"I don't feel well at all," she murmured.

He reached for the smelling salts again. She pushed it away, and with more strength than she felt, she demanded, "Who are you? What are you doing in my house?"

"*Your* house? On the contrary, madam, this is my house. Whitefriars has always been my home, and that of my father and grandfather before me. How did you get in last night without Gideon seeing you?"

Jody opened her mouth, but she couldn't speak.

"Did you hope to rob me? I know you weren't here earlier, because I've questioned the servants."

"I remember falling against the mantel," she said as much to herself as to him. "It gave under my weight, and I must have fallen inside. There really *is* a room in the wall!" She was trying to hold on to whatever remained of her reality and was finding it difficult, indeed.

"I've never seen you before. Where are you from?" Micah's eyes traveled over her figure. "And why are you masquerading as a man?"

"I'm doing no such thing." She glanced down at her jeans, sweatshirt, and tennis shoes and felt her spunk returning under his probing gaze. "And Whitefriars is mine. I bought it months ago. I don't know what you're doing in here, but . . ." She looked around again. This was not her Whitefriars. She felt herself growing faint again.

"You aren't going to be sick, are you?"

"Are you really Micah Deveroux?" The question was rhetorical. Now that she was feeling more herself, she recognized him from the tintype. "How did I get here?"

"That was my question. How should I know how you arrived? On foot, I assume. Surely if there were a strange horse tied out front, it would have been noticed by now. No offense, but you don't look as if you'd own a buggy."

Jody glanced down again at her faded clothes. She looked as out of place in this room as she, indeed, was. "I've got to get back. I . . ." She looked around frantically. How was she to do that? She got to her feet and went to the mantel. "How do you open the panel?"

Micah came to her and pressed a spot on the wall. It swung open silently. Jody could see a small, narrow room that might hold as many as three people if they stood close together, but no more. "As you can see, this is the only way in or out. How is it that you even know of its existence?"

"I told you. I fell against it and somehow . . ." Jody's eyes lifted to his. He was standing closer than she had thought; so close she could have touched him easily; so close that he was almost touching her. Her breath caught in her throat and she felt her lips part.

For a golden instant, time seemed to stand still. His eyes mesmerized her, and she felt a dizziness that had nothing to do with her disorientation. "They're gray," she heard herself saying.

"Pardon?"

"Your eyes. I thought they would be blue, but they're gray."

He seemed unable to stop gazing at her, as well. "I've never seen any woman go about in such clothes. And your hair—it's cut short. Have you been ill long?"

"I'm not ill. I mean, I don't feel great, but I'm not actually sick. I'm feeling better now." She touched her hair, which curved close to her head and ended just above her shoulders. "It's not all that short."

He looked as if he were about to dispute her, then changed his mind. "I think you should sit back down." He closed the wall and the narrow door once again disappeared into the paneling.

"I think you're right." She remembered how she had earlier thought for a minute that this room had changed, and how she had smelled roses and wisteria at a time when none were blooming. "This is all a figment of my imagination. In a minute or two I'll be back where I should be."

"Your words don't make sense."

Jody sat on the leather chair opposite him. "I don't know what happened, but I seem to have stepped back in time for a moment."

"I think maybe you should have a brandy after all." He went to a cabinet and poured a small amount of brandy into each of two snifters. As he handed one to her, he said, "Careful. It's more potent than a lady is used to having."

"I've had brandy before." She tasted it, and it felt like smooth fire on her tongue. She had never cared much for spirits, but now she welcomed it.

"Now," he said as he sat back down. "Are you from Joaquin? I've never seen you before."

"I don't know how this happened, but I'll be gone any moment. I think this is sort of like a déjà vu—but it's lasting longer than I thought possible. It's a time warp or something." He looked even more confused, and she said, "I'm from the future." The words sounded so odd, she laughed. "This is so strange! I mean, I certainly never thought I'd ever meet you! Not even for a minute."

He took the snifter from her hand and their fingers touched. Jody was more affected by physical contact with the man than by the intoxicating effect of the brandy. He said, "The drink is going to your head. I should have known not to give it to you. Do you want more cider?"

"No. There are so many things I ought to be asking you. I mean, you already know which rooms are what color and what furniture was where. I'll kick myself for not having asked you questions when I get back."

"You aren't making any sense. Have you fallen from your horse and struck your head? Have you been running a fever, perhaps? And how *did* you get into my house, and for what reason?"

"Okay. Let's take it from the top." She tried to organize her thoughts. "First of all, this is my house, too. I own it, will own it, in 1993."

"1993? You're saying you're some sort of descendant of mine? That's impossible. I'm not married." He frowned. "It's impossible anyway! 1993 is a hundred and twenty-one years from now."

She hesitated. It seemed cruel to tell him his family would eventually die out and that Whitefriars would be owned by a stranger. "At any rate, I'm restoring it to what it looked like ten years ago, your time."

"My time?"

"I know it's confusing, but can't you at least try to understand?"

"Why would anyone want to make their house look older than it is? And ten years ago Whitefriars looked just as it does now. That makes no sense, madam."

She noticed his accent. It lay soft and cultured on his baritone voice and was not quite like the southern accent of her own day. Of course, she thought, he's never heard television or radio or a voice that's been trained to lose its accent. His speech patterns were original to the area.

"Okay, let's try it again. I don't know how it happened, but I somehow am in your time for a few moments and I . . ."

"You don't sound as if you come from around here."

"I don't. Well, actually, I grew up in Grand Coteau, south of here, but I was born in 1966."

He made no comment, but only gazed at her as if he were wondering what she might do next.

Jody looked around. "I wonder when I'll leave. I should stay close to the mantel, I guess. That may make a difference." She waited. "This is odd. I don't seem to be going anywhere. And I'm not dizzy or sick anymore." She felt her body to be sure she was solid and awake, then felt the chair. "How can this be? I'm still here." She got up and hurried to the mantel. She concentrated on seeing her own library about her. Nothing happened. A sense of dread began to steal over her, and her eyes widened. "This isn't funny. I've had enough. You and your house go back to your own time. I'm ready for this illusion to be over." Nothing happened.

She went to the window. The yard she was accustomed to seeing was altered. The wisteria was much smaller and barely covered the trellis over the bench. Beyond, where her drive should be, there was dirt, not pavement. She could see several black men and women walking about as if they were busy at daily tasks. Jody shook her head. "This can't be happening."

"Come back and sit down. You've had a shock of some sort." Micah touched her elbow, and she turned to find him beside her.

"I can't be stuck here. Why, I have a life of my own to lead. I'm to meet Angie at seven and go to the movies. I have men coming tomorrow to finish the roofing. I can't be here!"

"Please. Sit down."

She went back to the chair and picked up her brandy snifter as she collapsed onto the soft leather. "This can't be real!"

"Obviously it is real. You're here. Not somewhere else. Now, try to tell me exactly what you remember last."

"Don't talk to me like that. I'm not simple-minded!"

"I never meant to imply that you are. I'm only trying to help you."

Jody fought it, but she was beginning to panic.

Chapter Four

Jody sat with Micah Deveroux in his library, thoroughly confused. She had clasped her hands in her lap, but that hadn't stopped their trembling. "I don't know how I got here. Worse, I don't know how I'm going to get back." ˙

"You keep referring to going back. To Grand Coteau?"

"No, no. To my own time."

Micah gave her a thoughtful look and leaned over her.

"What are you doing?"

"I'm trying to see if you have a head injury. That could explain why you are so convinced of something that's completely impossible." He touched her head gently. "Does this hurt?"

Jody dodged away from him. "Stop acting as if I'm crazy and just listen to me. Something happened. I don't know what. I was in my library one minute, and the next here I am, over a hundred years in the past. I know that's impossible, but that's what happened." She pointed at her jeans. "I can prove it! Have you ever seen clothes like these before?"

"No, and certainly not on a woman." His lazy eyes traveled down her tight jeans and back up again.

"And my sweatshirt." She bent over and pulled the label up. "Read what this says. Fifty percent cotton, fifty percent acrylic. Right? Have you ever heard of acrylic?"

Micah read the tag and frowned. "Anyone could make up a word and sew it onto a piece of cloth. But this is printed on. And what does 'machine wash' and 'tumble dry' mean?"

"There! That proves it. Washers and dryers haven't been invented yet."

He shook his head. "It proves nothing."

"Micah, why would I go to all the trouble to make a label, sew it into clothes like you've never seen before, and sneak into your house?"

"Nothing else makes sense. And why are you calling me by my first name when you barely know me?"

In exasperation, she rose from her chair and paced to the window. She felt like crying but was afraid that if she did, she might not stop. "You've got to believe me." Despite her efforts to the contrary, her voice broke and her lower lip began to quiver. The effect on Micah was immediate.

"Please, come sit down. May I at least know your name?"

She felt her tears gathering as she returned to the chair. "I'm Jody Farnell. I thought I had already told you that."

"Jody? That's an unusual name." He shook his head, as if his thoughts had wandered. "Who are your parents, Miss Farnell? I'll send a man to Grand Coteau to inquire. They may be worried about you."

"It's unlikely. They aren't born yet." She saw his expression and said, "Helen and Louis Farnell. They'll live on Elm Drive."

Micah summoned Gideon and met him at the door to the library. Gideon nodded as Micah gave him the names. "We will know in a few days. In the meantime, I offer you Whitefriars' hospitality."

"Thanks, considering it's my own home."

"Miss Farnell, your attitude is making it difficult for me to be friendly toward you."

She sighed and the tears gathered again. "I'm sorry. It's the stress."

"Tell me again exactly what happened."

"I was in the cabin out back, the one that sits slightly apart from the others. I found a doll of some sort under a loose board in the floor." She went to where she had dropped the doll in her shock at seeing him. "See? It was in there with other bits of things. I don't remember what they were now. Anyway, I started feeling sick, so I came to the house. I was going to call Angie or 911 and get help because I felt as if I might pass out. I fell against the wall and here I am."

"Is Angie your servant? And why would you call out numbers? For that matter, what were you doing out in the quarters, of all places?"

"Angie is my friend. I don't have any servants. And in my time, the quarters are empty. I'm restoring them as places for crafters to work once the house is finished."

"You'd have me believe you're a philanthropist? Why would crafters, whomever they are, care to do anything in deserted slave cabins? Are you offering the cabins as homes for the indigent?" He shook his head. "What am I saying? There are people living in the cabins, and all this nonsense about the future is just your imagination."

She held out her foot. "Ever see a tennis shoe?"

Micah looked at it with interest, trying gallantly not to stare at her bare ankle or the shape of her legs. "No, I have not. Did your people make them?"

"You don't believe a word I've said, do you?"

"Surely you can see why I would not. Your tale is—unique."

"It's also true." Suddenly she felt completely exhausted again. "Do you mind if I lie down? I'm not feeling so well."

"Of course. I'll have Bessy take you up."

"Never mind. I know the way." She stood and turned her face up to his. "Which room should I use?" It stood to reason that the large front bedroom she had slept in had to be Micah's. She wondered where he had spent the night.

"I think the front east one will be to your liking. It was my sister Camilla's room."

"The pink one? Yes. I'll lie down there."

"Pink? It hasn't been pink for years." He came to her. "I know you've been upstairs. You must have known that room is green now."

"Is it? I thought pink was correct. Well, when I get back home, I'll repaint it."

Micah frowned as he watched her cross the entry and start up the stairs. Her steps weren't

75

hesitant at all, just as if she knew exactly where she was going. "Miss Farnell, what colors are the other rooms upstairs?"

She paused at the foot of the stairs. "The smaller one is green. I've used an ivy paper in there that's not very different from the one you probably have in it. The one I'm to go to is pink—rosebuds and ribbons in the paper. The one directly behind it is shades of blue. I put a striped paper in it. Your room is also blue, but a darker tone." She paused. She had just left the master bedroom and it was dark green, not blue. Her confusion returned and she rubbed her head.

"You've just given an apt description of the rooms—as they looked when I was a boy. None of them are the same now."

She sighed. "Well, at least my research was close. I have to lie down. I'm suddenly exhausted." She walked slowly up the stairs.

"Gideon," Micah said, knowing the man would be somewhere within hearing distance. "Send Annie up to tend to Miss Farnell, then come into the library."

"Yes, sir."

Micah went back into the library and paused. Bending, he picked up the doll from the floor beside his desk. It looked old. Moisture had spotted the fabric of the dress and the remnants of a cobweb clung to the hair.

When Gideon came into the room, Micah said, "Have you ever seen anything like this before?"

Gideon's eyes fastened on the doll and he backed away. "That's a voodoo doll. Where'd you get it, Mr. Micah?"

"Miss Farnell had it with her."

"She ain't a voodoo woman, is she?" Gideon's eyes were round.

"No, of course not. She said she found it in the quarters. From the description of the cabin, it sounds like Iwilla's place."

"I don't know nothing about that place. No, sir."

"She lives in the cabin beside your parents'. You ought to know if she's practicing voodoo or not."

"No, sir, I don't. We stays away from her, 'less she sends for us special. We don't want to have nothing to do with a voodoo woman."

"Then she is practicing it again?"

Gideon shut his mouth and refused to meet Micah's eyes.

"Do you know what a doll like this means? Look at it, Gideon. It can't hurt you. It's only a piece of wood with cloth on it."

Reluctantly, Gideon gazed at it. "I don't know what she made it to do. Depends on the spell she cast. Could be 'most anything."

"Have you ever seen one like it?"

"Just once. It was when Jobe wanted 'Cilla to be his woman. Iwilla cast a spell on a doll a lot like this one. It was a keep-away spell to make 'Cilla tend to her own business."

"These things don't work, Gideon."

"All I know is 'Cilla married Mars, not Jobe. He couldn't get her to so much as look his way once that spell was cast."

"Do you have any idea who this one is supposed to represent?" Micah turned the doll over in his hand. The fact that Iwilla believed in such things was unsettling, even though he didn't believe in the power of voodoo, himself.

"No, sir. I'd say it's a white woman though."

"Yes." He touched the flaking, white paint on the doll's face. "And this looks like real hair." He didn't know what to make of it, but he was aware of Gideon's discomfort. "That's all, Gideon. And don't mention this doll to anyone." He knew Gideon would talk about it the minute he left the library, but he had to try to keep it quiet. The servants were superstitious, especially when it came to something like this, and he didn't want them frightened.

He studied the doll as Gideon left the library. It was clearly made to represent someone, but who? Neither of his sisters had hair this dark, nor did Emma Parlange, the woman he was courting. For that matter, why would old Iwilla want to keep anyone away from Whitefriars?

He went out the front door, walked down the steps and around the house. Whatever Iwilla was doing, she had to be ordered to stop it.

Iwilla lived just behind the oleander bushes that had been there for as long as Micah could remember. He had often thought as a child that it was appropriate that she would live near the poisonous plants. She had been old from his earliest memories and always kept to herself. His father had inherited her along with the plantation and other slaves and had been too tender hearted to sell her. That consideration had been lost on Iwilla. She hated white people and barely bothered to conceal her feelings. As a small boy, Micah had been terrified of her.

As always, the cabins were humming with activity. Many of the workers were in the fields gathering the last of the sugarcane, but there were older women about to watch the children who were playing in the sand in front of the cabins, and older men who were too far in years to be up to the strenuous effort of cutting the cane. These older people worked at weaving baskets or whittling kitchen utensils on their doorsteps and passed the day in conversation.

Iwilla's cabin was apart from the others by several yards. Micah had always wondered if she had built it there herself as a sign that she would never completely bow to the white man's wishes, or if the cabin had at one time had some other use. At first glance, it seemed much the same as the other cabins, but there were subtle differences. There were no children playing near her door, and the small garden allotted for the cabin was filled with plants that yielded neither vegetables nor kitchen herbs.

As he neared the door, it opened and Iwilla stepped out. She made no sound of greeting, but only frowned at him. Micah held out the doll. "Did you make this?"

Her eyes widened, then narrowed. "Me, I no ever see that doll before. Where you get it?" Iwilla had come directly from Africa and had never let herself become proficient in the white man's language. Micah suspected she could speak English far better than she pretended.

"It doesn't matter where I got it. If you're practicing voodoo again, you'll have to leave. I've given you fair warning. It frightens the other people, and I won't have them upset."

Iwilla drew herself up to her impressive height and gave him a cold stare.

He tried reasoning with her. "I don't know why you're so determined to be miserable. You have a cabin all to yourself and enough to eat and warm clothes in the winter. Why can't you get along with people? I know this is supposed to be a keep-away spell. Who did you want to keep away this time?" He saw a flicker of surprise in her obsidian eyes. Gideon had been right about the nature of the spell. "This is your home, just as it is for all these other people. Why can't you get along with them?"

"My home is Africa."

"Your home was in Africa, but now it's in Louisiana. You've been here at least thirty years. It's not like you arrived yesterday."

Iwilla only looked at him. Her high cheekbones scarcely seemed to reflect the sun and her hair was worn in the type of braids that Micah thought she must have worn in her native land. She wore a knotted scarf on her head, but rarely wore shoes unless compelled to do so, and her clothes were of a style not worn by any of the other women. Heavy earrings of bone and leather hung at her ears, and she wore an amulet bag on a thong around her neck. Her feet were bare and dusty to the ankle. She was so tall she could almost look at him eye to eye.

When she made no answer, Micah sighed. There was no remedy for her hatred. He hadn't been responsible for selling her into slavery. Micah had always detested the practice, and as soon as Whitefriars was his, he had freed the slaves. By the time war broke out between the north and south, there had not been a slave on Whitefriars. It was true he could only pay the workers a small sum, but he provided food and lodging and medicine when they needed it. None of his neighbors had done as much for their people. Iwilla did not care. Her hatred was complete and all-consuming.

"Whoever you have the grudge against, let it drop. I don't want any trouble from you."

Iwilla gave no sign that she had heard or understood, but Micah turned and left. Due to her advanced age, he was reluctant to tell her she had to leave the plantation, but she was pushing him to the point of having no choice.

Unblinking, Iwilla watched until Micah was out of sight, then she went back into her cabin. She was still shaken over seeing the voodoo doll in his hand. Had someone been in her cabin? She knew of no one in the quarters who would dare enter it, much less risk touching one of her dolls.

She went to the middle of the floor, where she crouched and pushed on the loose end of a plank. The other end popped up a fraction of an inch, and with practiced ease she removed the board. Her spell lay untouched in the dirt beneath the floor.

Iwilla sat back and thought. The spell had been built carefully and over several months' time, even down to putting "goofer" dust—which required her to make a special trip to the graveyard to get dirt from a suicide's grave—and the tooth from a mad dog next to the doll. Taking care not to disturb the other objects, she picked up the doll and looked at it in wonder.

The face was freshly painted and the dress was unstained. She had carved the intricate facial features while muttering incantations and had sewn each stitch of the dress in the dark of the moon.

The hair was her only failing. She had wanted hair from the white woman on the adjoining plantation who was the target of her spell, but she had been unable to get any of it and had been forced to make do. The light brown hair she had used was from a pale-skinned octoroon who lived on that same plantation. She figured the octoroon carried some of the same blood in her veins as the plantation's owner, and that would have to be close enough. It had not been all that easy to get that hair either, since the woman had been afraid Iwilla was casting the spell against her personally. The doll Micah had shown her had had darker hair and looked old and faded, but it was fashioned in the unique way she made all her voodoo dolls. She was sure it was not one of her own, but how it had come into being was a mystery.

Iwilla held the doll's ear close to her lips and whispered a word she never spoke aloud, a word she had learned from her own mother far back in her childhood. She put the doll back in place, made the intricate gestures with her hands that would rebind the spell, and dropped the floorboard back into place.

Perplexed, she sat in her chair facing the door. Where had Micah found the voodoo doll? Was someone else practicing in the territory Iwilla had claimed as her own? Impossible. No one would be so foolhardy. Besides, the doll had been identical to the one she had made, except for the hair. No two people could, or would, make identical dolls—that was part of a voodoo woman's strength. It was most confusing.

Iwilla had nothing personal against Emma Parlange. She had never spoken to her and had only seen her from a distance. Iwilla had been a field worker until her advancing age gave her a reason to stay in her cabin. Her hatred for Emma, as for the Deverouxs, was as simple as it was deep. They were white and she hated everyone of that race. It was white men who had trapped her away from the safety of her village and put her in a ship that smelled of fear and sickness and death. It was white men who had put her, the daughter of the most important woman in the tribe, on a platform and sold her to another white man. She would never, could never, forgive them for that.

She could still remember her mother. Iwilla liked to think that she looked a great deal like the older woman, and that when her mother died, as she must have by now, her soul had come to rest in Iwilla. As long as Iwilla lived, so would the power they had shared.

For Iwilla had been no ordinary child. She was the only daughter born of the magic woman of the tribe. Her mother had been held in fearful awe by their tribesmen, and she had been almost as powerful as the chief himself. Her mother had told everyone that Iwilla was a true child born of the gods, because she had first made her presence known when her mother was alone in the forest and talking to the god of thunder and his consort, the goddess of lightning. Thunder had spoken, and her mother had felt her kick for the first time. In her season, she had birthed Iwilla and presented her to the tribe as the next magic woman.

Iwilla's childhood had been spent learning the plants and spells that her mother had learned from her own mother, spells that had been passed down since the earth was new, always by women, always by the keepers of the magic.

Not all her mother's teachings had been applicable in this new land. Iwilla had had to bend the lessons to fit the plants that grew here, but she had done so successfully. Just as she had added new charms and spells to her repertoire.

In truth, Iwilla's memory of her early life was fuzzy and distorted by time. She had been only nine when she was captured. She had no idea how old she was now, for a magic woman never kept count of years, but she knew she was older than most of the men and women who were content to doze in the sun and watch over babies.

She had never taken a husband. When she was young, and taller and stronger than any of the other women, a man had been sent to her cabin, but he had been terrified of her and had not touched her. Iwilla let it be known about the plantation that her magic was so strong, it prevented a baby from coming to her, no matter what man was sent to her cabin. After a few years, the master of Whitefriars decided she was barren and she was left alone. The young men had gladly corroborated her story, each believing that he was the only one who had been too fearful to touch her. Iwilla knew it was her duty to raise a daughter to receive the magic after her, but she refused to bring a life into this foreign land.

So she had vowed as a child of nine that she would never relinquish her hatred, and for seventy years she had detested white men and everything they touched. To Iwilla's mind, this was not unreasonable.

Sometimes her spells had not worked out exactly as she had planned. She had, for instance, cast a barren spell on Antoine's wives. The first had conceived a child, but she and the baby had died in the birthing. Iwilla had rejoiced. Antoine had married again, and Iwilla had cast her spell again. This time the young wife lived and gave him two sons and two daughters, but the youngest son had died in infancy. The wife had died ten years later of a fever that Iwilla was convinced she had brought on, and less than a full year later, Antoine had fallen dead due to heart failure. At least, Iwilla had thought, they had not lived to enjoy their old age.

That was when she turned her attention on the young master. He had freed her, but that meant nothing in her eyes. She was already old and had lost her place in the life she was born to lead. She, the daughter of thunder, had spent her youth chopping cane. She had become determined that Micah would die without issue and that Whitefriars would crumble into dust.

Micah walked slowly back to the house. Who was this young woman in the strange clothes, and where did she really come from? Her story was too fantastic to be believed, but how else had she known what Whitefriars had looked like in his youth? The walls had been repainted the year before his mother had died, and his father, though he had preferred the lighter colors, had left the rooms as his wife had done them. In the years past Micah had been too busy with learning to run the plantation and the war and the ruined markets to worry about what color the walls were.

But the woman had known.

He looked thoughtfully at the voodoo doll. He did not think for a minute that there was any truth in Iwilla's spells. She was just an old woman driven a bit mad by her hatred, and he was not so sure he wouldn't have gone exactly the same way in her place. But how else to explain Miss Farnell's unexpected appearance?

He knew there would be no word of her parents in Grand Coteau. He had not let her know, but he had begun to accept that there was some validity to her story, as unbelievable as it seemed. She did, indeed, wear clothes of a type he had never seen before. True, she could have made them—they were not nearly as intricate as the dresses worn by women he knew—but why would she go to such lengths? And he knew of no one who could make a shoe like that. The sole had been fashioned of something like rubber, with a design imprinted into it. He had never seen white or bright blue rubber. And why would she fabricate a tag in the collar of her top—he could not call it a blouse—with the words *machine wash* and *tumble dry?*

Micah had never washed a blouse in his life, but he knew they were draped on bushes or pinned on clotheslines to dry. Tumbling them about would do nothing but get them dirty again.

She was pretty, this Miss Farnell. Despite her outlandish clothes, she was pretty. Evidently she had recently been sick, since her hair was cut short. Everyone knew a life-threatening fever could sometimes be broken by cutting the patient's hair. She had not admitted it, but she could be embarrassed at it being so short, though he had found it attractive in a foreign sort of way. It had swung about her face in a very attractive style. He looked down at the doll. The hair on it was almost the same color as Jody's hair.

He shook his head in self-chastisement at thinking of her by her first name. That would never do. Perhaps she had stepped over the bounds by calling him "Micah," but he couldn't be so familiar with her. It wouldn't be proper.

He looked up at the windows of Camilla's room. It also was not proper for her to be up there lying down. He was a bachelor, and she had no business being here in the house at all. He decided it would be prudent to send word to Camilla and have her come out. Perhaps in the gentler company of another woman, Jody would confess where she had really come from and why she was dressed so oddly. He gave no thought to summoning his other sister, Claudia. He had enough troubles already with this woman claiming to be from the future.

Why did he half believe her? Even in outrageous clothes, her story was clearly impossible. No one ever traveled through time. He supposed that on a cerebral level it could be argued that everyone was a time traveler, since a person was born in one time and lived to another. He had every right to suspect he would live long enough to see the nineteenth century change into the twentieth. But that was different, and it was a normal progression. Certainly no one traveled from back to front. So why did he find himself believing her?

In Camilla's bedroom, Jody looked out the window and saw Micah coming back toward the house. She pulled back from the window before he saw her. What had happened? How had she done the impossible? Most important of all, how was she to undo it?

She went to the chaise at the end of the bed and sat down. The bed was piled high with feather mattresses and looked too imposing for her to want to climb into it and lie down. Besides, the sick feeling had passed by the time she reached the room.

She looked around at the walls and wrinkled her nose. They were done in paper with a heavy green pattern on a paler yellow background. She couldn't imagine anyone putting such paper in a daughter's room, even if it had been the height of style in Victorian days. She had found a swatch of this paper, mercifully dimmed by age, beneath other paper and had marveled that anyone would have bought it on purpose. It was even worse in its prime, unfaded condition.

Going to the door, she listened to see if anyone was in the hall, then opened the door a crack. No one was in sight, so she slipped out and across to the room she had claimed as her own in her own time.

The walls were a deep green, but here the color was not oppressive. The paper was the shade of pine trees, with a design in lighter green. The woodwork was painted a paler green still. Jody had assumed it would have been left in the natural wood tones. The furniture was much heavier than her own. The four-poster bed, dresser, and washstand were of oak, and the latter two had creamy marble tops. The curtains were a heavy brocade in an unlikely shade of garnet, but they gave the room warmth—and sensuality.

Jody could tell this was the room of a man who was well in touch with his senses.

She heard a sound on the stairs and slipped quietly back to the room she had been told to occupy. Through a small crack in the door, she saw a maid come up, look questioningly in her direction, then turn to the linen shelves. Jody assumed news of her arrival had spread throughout the house. It was no wonder. Company arriving in much more conventional ways than this must be subjects of conjecture with the staff.

Shutting the door silently, Jody went back to the window. Shadows had shifted to show the afternoon was edging into evening. Soon the sun would go down. She did not want to be here after dark. What if she never returned to her own time? Was time on some sort of continuum? It had been autumn in her time, as it was here. If so, it must be close to seven o'clock. What would Angie think when she didn't show up?

Jody pressed her hands to her mouth. She would be declared missing! What would everyone say? Her family would be beside themselves with worry and concern. And her friend Angie, even though they had not known each other long, would surely be upset. They had become good enough friends that Jody would be worried over and missed.

Maybe they would think she had been kidnapped! Concern knotted in Jody's stomach. Some stranger might even be arrested. She had to get back! She closed her eyes to shut out the evidence of her being in the wrong century and concentrated on her ordinary life. No matter how hard she concentrated, or how measured she made her breathing, she stayed firmly put just where she was.

She opened her eyes. Nothing had changed. She went to the wardrobe and opened the door. Dresses hung there, along with bonnets and capes. Camilla's, she assumed. She took a dress down and held it to her. Apparently she and Camilla were about the same size. The dress might fit. In exasperation, she hung it back on the peg. Whether it fit or not didn't matter. She had to leave this place.

Once more she sat down, this time on the floor, reasoning that contact with the furniture might have impeded her first attempt to regress. And, since she didn't own furniture for this room yet, if she were to snap back to her own time, she would already be on the floor and wouldn't be hurt by a fall. Crossing her legs yoga style, she laid her palms upward on her thighs and straightened her spine. It had been months since she had meditated, but she knew how. Slowing her breath and allowing herself to relax, she tried to calm her mind.

"I'm in my own home," she said, as if it were a mantra. "The year is 1993. When I open my eyes, this will all have been a dream." She repeated the words several times. A restfulness came over her. She could feel herself becoming more tranquil and in tune with her vibrations. She let a low hum build from deep inside her and pass through her lips.

All at once a shrill scream shattered her calm. Jody jerked to alertness in time to see the maid back out of the door amid a shower of sheets and pillowcases and slam it shut behind her. Jody got to her feet and called after the woman, but the maid was losing no time in putting distance between Jody and herself.

"I guess she never saw anyone meditating before," Jody said wryly. "That's really great. Now I've started scaring people half to death. I've got to get out of here."

The words sounded good, but they had no effect on her situation at all.

Chapter Five

Jody watched from the bedroom door as the maid dashed down the stairs, obviously frightened by seeing Jody sitting cross-legged on the floor meditating. *I've got to stay calm,* she reminded herself. *A panic attack won't serve anything.* All the same, she felt her anxiety rising.

She went back to the wardrobe and again studied its contents. The dresses were apparently castoffs that Micah's sister Camilla had left behind. In the drawers of the dresser she found a few undergarments that looked to be her size. If she was stuck here for a while, as it seemed she might be, she would need a change of clothes. The hoopskirted dresses and odd underwear were not her preference, but she had no other choice.

As she closed the drawer, the notion that she had no other choice weighed heavily upon her. How could she stay here? She had a niche to fill in her own time, a life of her own to live. She could not afford to do anything that might lock her into the wrong time forever. Somehow, she had to find her way back.

Resolutely, she left the room and went down the hall to the stairs. The house was so familiar to her, yet it was also so different. The banister of the stairs was the same polished mahogany, but the railings were painted a pale cream color, almost a yellow. A chandelier was suspended over the entry, but this one was simpler than the one she knew, and it was rigged to a pulley so it could be lowered for the lamps to be lit. Even as she watched, the man Micah had called Gideon was lowering the light so a maid could put a match to the candles. Gideon saw Jody watching him, and for a moment he forgot himself and stared back. The woman helping him noticed his odd behavior and quickly averted her eyes, motioning for Gideon to do the same.

As the servants resumed the task at hand, Jody went downstairs and turned into the short hall that led to the library. She could feel the servants' stares on her back as she stopped at the library door, but decided it would be best for her to ignore them. This was their time and she was the foreigner, and until something changed, she would have to get used to it. With a perfunctory knock, she went in.

Micah was sitting behind the desk when she came into the room. For an instant he looked startled, then his eyes traveled over her body. "I see you have not seen fit to change clothes," he commented.

"These are all I brought with me. I don't make

a habit of helping myself to whatever I find lying about."

"I must insist you wear Camilla's dresses while you are here. I cannot have you going about in trousers, shocking the servants."

"Is that why they keep staring at me?"

"I understand you gave 'Cilla quite a turn. She said you were sitting on the floor with your legs bent at odd angles and humming."

"I was meditating."

"About what?"

"Not meditating as in thinking, meditating as in centering myself in an attempt to get back to my own time."

Micah closed the ledger book in which he had been writing and said, "I see you are maintaining your original story."

"It's the truth. If I were going to lie, wouldn't I have made up something more believable?"

"One would assume."

Jody went to the desk and sat on the edge of it. Micah stared at her as if he had never expected her to do anything like this. She pretended not to notice. "I want you to think back. Maybe your thoughts somehow connected with mine, and that's how I ended up here."

"How should I know what I was thinking when you were slipping into my house?"

She ignored him. "I was in the library, trying to get to the phone to call for help."

" 'Phone'?"

"I was holding that doll, but I don't recall thinking about it. I was too busy trying to keep my balance. I felt terribly dizzy and nauseated. I leaned on the wall next to the mantel and the door opened and I fell in, I think. The next thing I remember is waking up in what should have been my bedroom, but isn't, and finding you sitting in here."

He looked at her skeptically.

"Damn it, Micah, you've got to believe me."

His eyes narrowed. "Your speech gives you away. First you insist on calling me by my first name, now you swear. And isn't that paint on your eyes?"

"I have paint on my eyes?" She touched her eye. "Do you mean eye shadow and mascara?"

"I should have known you could be nothing else. Who paid you to come here? Was it Will Breaux?"

"Who? No one paid me at all. I'm here by accident." She slipped off the edge of the desk and faced him with her hands in her pockets.

Micah looked relieved, as though he had cleared up a mystery in his own mind. "That explains the trousers and how you're sitting on my desk. You must be one of Madam Agnes's girls."

"What's that supposed to mean?" Jody jumped to her defense and advanced on him. "Are you calling me a prostitute?"

"There! No lady would use that word. You go back to Will and tell him the trick worked. I was beginning to fall for it. I will have to devise an equally good trick to use on him."

"I don't know this Will person, and I'm certainly not one of this Agnes's girls! The nerve! There was no reason for you to insult me." She crossed her arms and glared up at him.

"Will didn't send you?" Doubt was back in his voice.

"No! Are you going to help me find my way back or not?"

"Miss Farnell, you're a most confusing woman. You use words that have no meaning to me, like 'phone,' and you wear scandalous clothes and don't seem to realize they are improper. You swear like a man and sit on floors and on desks. I confess that I don't know what to make of you. If you aren't a woman of loose morals, why are you wearing paint on your face?"

"Because it's the style where I come from." She felt tears welling, and this time was unable to check them. "I don't want to be here. I'm scared stiff that I won't be able to get back home, and you don't believe me." She sniffed and pushed at the tears with her palm. "I don't know what has happened, and I'm sure everyone I know is worried sick about me. I don't belong here, yet I can't seem to leave."

Micah reacted instinctively, moving to her and putting his arms around her. Jody let him hold her as sobs shook her. Being in his arms was the most comforting sensation she had ever known. His arms about her were strong and protective, and the faint scent of soap and cloves and starch from him seemed terribly familiar.

"There, now," he said as he stroked her hair. "I never meant to make you cry."

"You don't believe me," she said in a voice that trembled. "I don't know how to make you see that I'm telling the truth."

"I believe you." His deep voice was tender and gentle, not accusatory as before.

Jody lifted her face doubtfully. "You do? Why

do you believe me now when you didn't two minutes ago?"

"I don't know. I think it's because you're crying, and you let me comfort you."

"And that convinced you when an acrylic sweatshirt didn't?"

"If you were one of Madam Agnes's girls, you would have reacted quite differently once you were in my arms. Your speech is too rational for a deranged person's. There's no other explanation but the one you're giving me."

He reached up and gently wiped away the tears staining her cheeks, then handed her his handkerchief. "Eye paint doesn't hold up well to tears."

She wiped the rivulets of mascara from under her eyes. "Thank you. I'm sorry for crying. I rarely do that. It's just that . . ." She felt the tears gather again but stemmed them by not speaking.

Micah cupped her face in the palm of one hand. "I don't mind if you cry. I just don't want to be the cause of it. I feel like a cad for causing you to be so unhappy by my words."

She looked up to see if he was teasing her. No man she knew would use the word *cad* seriously. But Micah was quite serious. He was also quite close. As she watched, his eyes darkened to a molten silver and he bent his head imperceptibly, as if he were about to kiss her. Jody's tears vanished. She was suddenly more aware of him than she had ever been of any man. He exuded a charisma that swept her breath away. Her lips parted.

A muscle tightened in Micah's jaw and he stepped back, his eyes filled with confusion as well as desire for her. Jody knew her own eyes must look the same. She turned away quickly.

"I'm sorry. I shouldn't have—"

"You didn't do anything wrong," she inter-rupted. "It's okay." Although the fluttering con-tinued in her middle, she knew she should not feel this way about him, because he was practi-cally a complete stranger.

To cover his discomfort over what had almost happened, Micah went to his desk drawer and took out the voodoo doll. "I asked Iwilla about this. Naturally she denied it."

"Iwilla?"

"She's the Negro woman who lives in the cabin you described. I'm sure she recognized the doll, but she's difficult."

"If you have an employee who is troublesome, who goes around making voodoo dolls, why don't you fire her?"

"If I understand your meaning correctly, I could never do that. Iwilla is too old to support herself, and she has never lived anywhere but here since she was brought to this country. It's not a matter of letting her go the way a merchant would rid himself of an inept stock boy."

"She's living here on your charity and she's making voodoo dolls against you?"

"How do you know it's against me?" Micah looked at her sharply.

"Who else? It's obviously supposed to be a white woman. As far as I can tell, you're the only white person living at Whitefriars."

"Actually, I'm not sure who it's cast against. Gideon tells me it's something called a keep-away spell. It's supposed to prevent a person from fall-ing in love with, or even from meeting, the person they would marry."

With a hint of laughter in her voice, Jody said,

"It must not be much of a spell. It drew me here from the next century. I wish it *had* kept me away." She was totally oblivious to the subconscious implication of her words.

"Surely you don't really believe this thing can work," he said with a half smile. "You believe in voodoo?"

"Of course not. I was joking. So how do you explain what happened?" She took the doll from him and carefully studied it curiously. "It's an ugly little thing, isn't it?"

"It wasn't meant to be pretty." He took it back from her. "Since, as you pointed out, I'm the only white person living here, and since the doll is supposed to be a woman, you're probably right in assuming it was aimed at me. As I said, Iwilla is a most difficult woman. I've racked my brain to find a way to send her somewhere else, but short of turning her out on the road, there is none. And I won't turn out any of my people, even if I do sometimes wish I could. I have a responsibility to them."

"Why would she want to put a spell on you?"

"Who knows why one person thinks one way and another in some other way? I have no idea what Iwilla has against me."

"Slavery had to leave some scars on her psyche." Jody looked at the doll in his hands and shivered. "It must have been terrible."

He looked puzzled for an instant, then adopted a defensive posture. "None of our slaves had scars. We were good to them."

She knew there was no point in trying to explain what she had meant.

"As you pointed out, the spell did not work. Not

only did you somehow come here, if indeed that event had anything to do with the spell, but I'm engaged to be married."

Jody's head jerked up. "You are!"

"To Emma Parlange of The Oaks. Do you know her?"

"How would I? I only just arrived. Remember?" she snapped. The unexpected dart of pain she felt on hearing news of his engagement had made her voice sharper than she had intended. "When are you to be married?"

"In the spring."

Jody almost protested that he didn't love Emma but was able to stop herself in time. She felt rather embarrassed at having read Micah's private diary now that she was standing face to face with him.

In a lighter, almost teasing, tone, he asked, "Why are you looking that way, as if you know something you don't want to tell me?"

"Who, me? I don't have anything I want to tell you." She backed away.

"It suddenly occurs to me that if you come from the future, you may know what my life will be. Tell me, Miss Farnell, how many children will I have? What will my sons become?"

"You mustn't ask me things like that."

"Oh? Is there some social etiquette for time travelers?"

"How should I know? I've only done it once. But the future should be kept secret. Personal future, at least. We aren't supposed to know how things turn out."

She remembered the smudged entry in the family Bible. The name of his wife had been

100

illegible. Jody had assumed the names listed below the smudged one had been his children, but she supposed they could have been nieces and nephews. She wished she could remember the names. "Do your sisters have children?"

"Camilla does. She and Reid have a son and two daughters. Claudia and Vincent do not. Why do you ask?"

"No reason. Just making conversation." So there was a nephew to inherit Whitefriars. She knew it was not unheard of for a nephew or cousin to take the mother's name in order to carry the family line forth. That could explain why Deverouxs had lived at Whitefriars for so long.

Micah took a gold filigreed watch from the pocket of his vest and clicked it open. "We'll have supper soon. You should go up and dress."

"I would feel odd in another person's clothes. What's wrong with what I'm wearing if no one will be here but you and me?"

"You have created enough scandal for one day." He went to the library and called out, "Bessy?" In a few seconds a black woman about Jody's age came to the door.

"Yes, sir?"

"Take Miss Farnell upstairs and help her dress for supper."

"Yes, sir." Bessy stood quietly, waiting for Jody to leave the room first.

Jody had no choice but to do as Micah wished. As she went up the stairs, she said, "We haven't been introduced. My name is Jody Farnell."

Bessy was so caught off guard she almost tripped. "Beg pardon, miss?"

"I said, my name is Jody. I heard Micah call you Bessy. What's your last name?"

"Bessy Deveroux. We took the family name when we were freed." She was glancing at Jody with wide eyes. "Nobody ever asked me 'bout that before."

"I'm new here." Jody preceded Bessy down the hall and into the room that had been Camilla's.

Bessy went to the wardrobe and took out a dress and petticoat. "How's this one? It's one Miss Camilla wore all the time."

"It's so pretty. Is it too formal?"

"No, ma'am. I reckon it's a bit outta style, but all these is the dresses Miss Camilla left behind when she married Mr. Reid."

"I don't mind if it's out of style." She waited for Bessy to leave.

"I'm supposed to help you dress."

"Oh." Jody hadn't had or needed help in dressing since she was a toddler. Feeling a little self-conscious, she pulled her sweatshirt over her head.

Bessy was trying not to stare at Jody's underclothes. She had obviously never seen a bra before. "I reckon I better get you out a chemise and corset."

"Chemise, all right; corset, no." Style or no style, she wasn't going to cinch herself into the dresses. "I think it will fit without it." She stepped out of her jeans.

Although Bessy obviously objected, she made no comment as Jody stepped into the whalebone-stiffened petticoat. Jody held it to her waist. "This can't be right." The stays made the petticoat bunch out in front.

"No, ma'am. The fullness goes to the back." It was to Bessy's credit that she managed to keep a straight face. She turned it around and tied it at Jody's waist.

She helped Jody slip the dress over her head and adjusted it around her hips. Jody had never worn a dress even remotely like this, and she touched the fabric in wonder.

The dress was a pale pink with ivory lace and ruffles around the skirt and at the wrist of the sleeves. A silk rose in a deeper pink was sewn at the waist. The neck fit close to her throat and was trimmed with more of the lace.

Jody could hardly wait to see herself in the mirror. "Is that really me?" she murmured as she stared at her reflection in the cheval.

"Yes, ma'am." Bessy glanced at her charge as if she thought the question was a strange one, but as she was determined to humor Jody, she made no comment.

Jody turned to look at her profile and over her shoulder. The dress fit closer in front than it did in back. The petticoat held it away from her hips, and the skirt was gathered to give the effect of a bustle. More of the pink silk roses were sewn on the gathers of cloth in the back. Jody wondered how a woman could sit in a chair without crushing them until she remembered that women in the nineteenth century didn't lean back on chairs.

"It fits like it was made for you," Bessy said. "If you was to sit down on the stool, I could fix your hair."

Jody sat down and watched as Bessy tried, to no avail, to comb hair that was shorter than any she

103

had dressed before. "It's all right. There's nothing that can be done with it."

When Bessy stopped brushing, Jody's hair swung back into place, cupping her neck. "I maybe could put a bow or something in it. Miss Camilla is real fond of bows," Bessy suggested.

"Is there a hair clip or a barrette I could use to hold it back?"

"A what?"

"Never mind. It looks fine." Jody was still amazed at how becoming the dress was. It was more feminine than any she had ever owned, and she was surprised at the way it transformed her. If her hair had been long enough to pile on top of her head, she would have looked as if she belonged in this century.

"Are there any shoes?" Jody asked.

Bessy searched the wardrobe, then shook her head. "No, ma'am. Miss Camilla took all the shoes. There's some stockings in the drawer."

"Do you have a pair of shoes I could borrow?"

Bessy looked thoroughly shocked. "No, ma'am!"

Jody ignored her reaction and stood up, surveying her image. "My tennis shoes won't show under these long skirts. I guess we're ready to go down. Micah seemed to expect dinner to be ready any minute."

"Dinner? No, ma'am. It's nearly suppertime." Bessy was watching her closely. "We had dinner hours ago."

"I meant supper."

"Yes, ma'am."

"Do you have to keep saying *ma'am*? Call me Jody."

"Yes, Miss Jody."

Jody refrained from sighing. She wouldn't win this one. Bessy's people had a century of freedom to get through before she could meet Jody on the grounds of friendship.

When Jody started down the stairs, she found Micah in the entry staring up at her. From the look of amazement on his face, she thought she had done something wrong. "Is this dress all right? Bessy said it would be."

"The dress is perfect."

Jody touched her skirt. "What's wrong? Am I unfastened?"

"Nothing is wrong." He took two steps up the stairs and held out his hand to help her the rest of the way down. "I was about to come up and tell you supper is ready."

Jody put her hand in his, and the physical contact touched her soul. He continued to gaze at her as she drew even with him at the foot of the stairs, and her heart beat faster.

Micah tried to hide his feelings as he ushered her into the dining room. Earlier, even clad in the outlandish trousers and shirt, he had thought she was lovely. But wearing Camilla's dress, she had been transformed into a being of beauty. True, her short hair was a drawback, but the dress accentuated her slender waist and rounded bosom, and the color put pink in her cheeks.

As was done every night, the meal had been set on the mahogany table prior to their arrival. Gideon was standing at the wall, and after Micah helped Jody to her seat, Gideon held Micah's chair for him. Micah noticed Jody was staring at the table. How long had it been since she had eaten?

"Is all this for us?" she whispered.

"Of course."

"We can't possibly eat half this much."

"The servants will eat what we leave."

"They don't eat until we do?"

"Of course not. Are things different where you come from?"

"In every way. You wouldn't believe how different."

Gideon helped them serve their plates by handing around the heavy platters. From the corner of his eye, Micah watched with interest as Jody deliberated over which fork to use, obviously trying hard to avoid doing the wrong thing. Choosing the correct one, she ate with an appetite, but not as if she were starved. He was glad to find her manners were as fastidious as his own. If she was to be his houseguest, it was nice to know meals would not be an embarrassment to either of them.

"I'm not familiar with this meat," she said after she had tasted it. "What is it?"

"It's a dish called *daubes glace's*. Do you like it?"

"Yes, I do."

He took for himself a portion of the meat, served in jelly with spices and mushrooms. "We have it often. I'm glad it suits you."

She chewed for a minute in silence. "Do your sisters look like you?"

He thought for a minute. "I think Camilla does. She's the youngest. Claudia looks more like our American grandmother."

" 'American?' "

"From the States."

"Louisiana is in the States," she said in confusion.

"I know, but we're Creole. We consider ourselves to be French, not American. Grandmother is the reason I have gray eyes and my sisters are blond. Most Creoles are dark."

"I see."

"I thought you might be Creole, too, since your hair is dark brown. I've seen others with eyes your shade of hazel."

"I'm part Creole, part Cajun, part everything else," she said carelessly. "I guess that makes me all American."

He had never met anyone in his circle of friends who was so offhanded about his heritage. Emma and Claudia were adamant about their being French, and referred to the States as if they were a foreign country. He wasn't sure how to respond to her.

"Do you mind if I ask you a personal question?" she asked.

"Not at all."

She glanced at Gideon, who was standing passively against the wall. "Which side were you on in the Civil War?"

Micah decided he couldn't have heard her correctly. "I beg your pardon?"

"I've been baffled by that in my research. If you freed your slaves before the war, I thought you must have fought for the North. That would explain why Whitefriars was unharmed. It would also account for the reason you weren't ruined like most of the other plantation owners were during Reconstruction."

Micah felt his mouth drop open. "I fought for the South, madam! I'm shocked that you would suggest otherwise."

"Then why was Whitefriars not damaged? After all, the South did lose. And why would you fight to preserve a system that you obviously don't believe in?"

"Miss Farnell," he said, as he struggled to control his temper, "I fought to preserve my country, not slavery. There were many issues at stake in the War Between the States."

"I didn't mean to offend you."

"What else can it be but an offense to ask a thing like that?" He looked at her suspiciously. "Which side did your family support?"

"Neither. It was only an issue in history books by the time my parents were born."

"It sounds to me as if the passage of time has biased history in the favor of the North. You referred to the war by the Northern term."

"Everyone does. Maybe it's because the name is shorter. 'War Between the States' is a mouthful."

Micah made no comment.

She glanced again at Gideon. "Does it bother your employees to talk about it?"

"My people know how I feel. Gideon and I fought side by side in several battles."

"You did?" She looked genuinely surprised. "Gideon fought for the South?"

"Of course. He's loyal to me."

"Why was Whitefriars spared?"

"Fortunately, there were no battles nearby. The troops missed us by ten miles on their march to New Orleans. Being off the main road saved us, and The Oaks as well."

"The Oaks?"

"The plantation just east of here. The one owned by Emma's parents. We're so far from New Orleans, no troops were quartered near here. Except for a few carpetbaggers and the like, we were left in relative peace, although my sisters assure me it was terrifying at the time, not knowing if the enemy would arrive at any hour."

"Were you drafted?"

"Drafted? What does that mean?"

"Did you have to go to the war? Did you have to fight?"

"Conscription began in March of '62. Naturally, I had joined up before then. No Deveroux has ever been a coward. I would have been ashamed to be ordered to go."

"I see." She seemed to be mentally comparing this with knowledge she had from her own time.

Curiosity got the best of him. "Tell me, Miss Farnell, have farming methods improved much by 1993?"

Jody laughed. "You'd be amazed. For one thing, we no longer use horses and mules. We have tractors and things with engines in them to do the plowing and harvesting. There aren't many small farmers left, and on the big farms a few men can do the work of hundreds today. And the seed has been improved. More of the crop matures and produces, so there's less waste."

Micah studied her. She seemed to be telling the truth. "Engines? Like the cotton gin? How could that plant a crop and harvest it?"

"I can't explain it. I didn't live on a farm. My father is a banker."

"Who do you live with at Whitefriars if your parents are in Grand Coteau?" He looked at her cautiously. "Are you married?"

"No. I live alone."

"Alone." He wondered how she could utter such absurdities and not blink an eye. "At Whitefriars. Alone."

"It no longer is a cotton and cane plantation. There are only—" She glanced at him and abruptly stopped.

"What were you going to say?"

"Nothing."

"Miss Farnell, this involves my home, even if it is in the future. What are you keeping from me, and how can one person manage to run a plantation?"

"It was no longer a plantation by the time I bought it. There were only ten acres and the house."

Micah put down his fork. "Ten acres? That and the house?"

"And the outbuildings, of course."

He felt more than a little disturbed. "Whitefriars has been in my family for generations. Are you saying that some descendant of mine will be such a wastrel as to lose all I have here?"

"I'm not saying anything of the sort. I don't know what happened, other than that the last of your descendants died, and I was able to buy the property. I had begun to repurchase the furnishings when I landed here."

Micah found he wasn't hungry anymore. He pushed his plate away, and Gideon immediately removed it from the table.

"I knew I shouldn't tell you. I said it wasn't good

110

for you to know the future."

"Is there anything else you're keeping from me? I want to know the worst."

"No, that's everything."

Her face was too open to lie. That was one reason he had begun to believe her preposterous story. "Now that I know about the future, maybe I can change it somehow."

"No, no! You mustn't do that. I may not be able to get back if you do. I left from here in Whitefriars. If the future changes, I may be trapped."

"If I don't do something, my family will die out and Whitefriars will be sold to strangers!"

"I should never have told you!"

"Miss Farnell—"

"Will you stop calling me that?"

"What would you have me call you?"

"Call me Jody. That's my name."

"I can't call you that. It wouldn't be proper, especially with you living in my house."

"I'm going to stop answering to Miss Farnell." She looked as if she were about to cry again.

Micah sat back in his chair. "There's no reason for us to argue. What can I do? All this will happen long after I'm dead and gone. Maybe I couldn't change it anyway."

"Maybe not." Her tone was wary, as if she were afraid she might have to defend her viewpoint again.

"On the other hand, you're here now. Who knows what your coming here will change."

Jody paled. "I never thought of that."

"I've never believed the future is predetermined. I know your being here must have thrown something out of kilter. It's only reasonable."

"Only if I stay here. All I've done is change clothes and eat din—supper. I haven't done anything that would change history. Have I? I mean, nothing has changed. Has it?"

"I have no way of knowing. I've met you. So have Gideon and Bessy. I've sent word to Grand Coteau inquiring about your parents. Tomorrow Camilla will be here, and more people will meet you. How much does it take to alter the future? Do any of us know?"

"Now I'm really worried. Thanks." She looked despondent.

"On the other hand, maybe you were meant to come back here."

"For what possible reason?"

"How should I know? Maybe you were born in the wrong time period to begin with."

Jody looked concerned. "If that's the case, I may never get back. I'll be here forever."

"I think we have to admit that as a possibility," he said gently. "After all, the impossible has already happened."

Jody put her fork on the plate and her hands in her lap. "I had convinced myself that I would be home at any instant, that I would be back when I open my eyes in the morning, at the latest. Now I'm not so sure."

"Neither am I."

"What bothers me the most is that I don't feel dizzy at all now, and that seemed to have something to do with it." She pushed back from the table. "If you don't mind, I think I want to go up and try to get some sleep. I need to be alone with my thoughts."

"Of course." He stood while she left the table, then sat back down. She was an unusual woman. What impact would she make on his life? He rather dreaded telling Emma about her, and decided it would be best to never admit the details of Jody's arrival. Emma didn't have a very open mind when it came to him seeing women other than his female cousins.

If Jody had come back to satisfy some particular purpose in the grand scheme of things, what could it be? For some reason when he looked deep into the dark hazel depths of her eyes, he felt as if he had known her before—had known her, perhaps, forever.

No, it wouldn't do to tell Emma everything about this new visitor to Whitefriars.

Chapter Six

Micah was anxiously awaiting Camilla's arrival when her brougham stopped out front. Even before Gideon got to the door, Micah was through it and on the step to meet his sister. "I'm glad you're here. Claudia isn't coming, is she?"

"I doubt it. I haven't seen her since Sunday. You two aren't having words again, are you?" Camilla's soft accent perfectly matched her appearance. She was blond, in sharp contrast to her dark Creole friends, and her eyes were the same gray as Micah's. She was the more feminine of his two sisters, and far prettier than Claudia had ever been. She was also far more congenial and had always been Micah's favorite.

"I haven't seen Claudia or Vincent in days," he commented as he waited for her to gather up her voluminous skirts, then offered her his elbow to guide her up the steps. Behind them, her carriage driver popped the reins and guided the carriage away toward the stable, where it would await her departure. "I have a guest," he said as they reached the porch.

"Do you? Who is it? Has cousin Christophe come and you didn't tell us? Shame on you, Micah." Camilla looked up at the house expectantly.

"No, it's not Christophe. It's someone you've never met."

"Someone from the War? You haven't invited that terrible sergeant who always had a wad of tobacco in his cheek, have you?" Her laughing gray eyes twinkled at him. "If so, I shall call for my brougham and leave immediately."

Micah laughed. "No, I never expect to see the sergeant again."

"I'll never understand how he ended up in your command anyway. He was simply awful."

"My soldiers weren't chosen for their social graces. He was a good soldier."

"Well, who is it? I've run out of guesses."

"You'd never guess anyway. You've never met her."

Camilla stopped dead still on the porch. "'Her'?"

"Come inside."

Micah could feel Camilla's curiosity bristling all about her, but he didn't speak again until they were in the back parlor. "Her name is Jody Farnell."

"Farnell? I don't believe I know any Farnells. Is she from around here?"

"She's originally from Grand Coteau." He paused. This was harder than he had thought it would be. "Maybe you'd better sit down."

Camilla laughed, but she humored him. "What will Emma say about you having a female houseguest? I'll wager this Miss Farnell is sixty years old and carries an ear trumpet."

"You'd lose your wager." Micah rubbed his thumb over his lower lip. This was more difficult than he had expected. However, Camilla had to be told. There was simply no way around it. "Miss Farnell is quite young. About your age, I'd say."

"You go on," his sister said with a laugh. "As if twenty-six is all that young! No wonder all the ladies consider you to be so dashing, you rogue."

"Camilla, be serious. I'm afraid we have a bit of a problem here."

Camilla's smile faded. "A problem? It's not smallpox, is it? She's not sick!"

"No, no. I wouldn't have allowed you inside if it were anything like that." He frowned at her. "What an idea!"

"Well, what else am I to think? You're frightening me, Micah."

He went to her and knelt beside her chair. "Miss Farnell is a very unusual visitor."

"Unusual in what way?"

"I must ask you to give me your word that you won't tell anyone what I'm about to tell you."

Camilla's eyes grew rounder. "Micah, you haven't done something awful, have you?"

"No, I haven't done anything at all. Now give me your word or I won't tell you why she's here."

"I promise. You know I do."

"Actually, to say Miss Farnell is an unusual woman is an understatement. You'll see that when you meet her. She was here when I returned from New Orleans last night. She was quite a surprise for everyone. It seems no one saw her arrive. I'd have said that it was impossible for anyone to get into Whitefriars unnoticed, but nevertheless she was upstairs and asleep before anyone knew she was in the house." He refrained from telling his sister that Miss Farnell had chosen his bed in which to sleep and that she had been wearing next to nothing when he found her.

"She slipped in without you knowing about it? I'd have sent her packing immediately!"

"No, you wouldn't have. She was feeling ill, she said, ill to the point of fainting. She has told me the most fantastic story." He paused an instant to be sure he had Camilla's full attention. "She says she's from the future."

Camilla looked back. "The future? I don't understand what you mean."

"I mean she will live in Whitefriars in the year 1993."

Camilla let out an uneasy laugh. "That's impossible. There is no 1993. I mean, it hasn't happened yet. Good heavens, that's more than a century away."

"I know."

"Surely you didn't believe that. Micah, next you'll be believing in fairies and elves."

"You haven't met her. As I've said, she's a most unusual woman."

"Where is she?"

"Upstairs." He went to the door and said, "Gideon, have Miss Farnell come down, please."

117

Micah came back to Camilla. "She was wearing the most unusual clothing I've ever seen. She had on tight trousers and a loose, soft-looking top, and white shoes with rubber soles. She had a tag in the neck of her shirt that had wording I still can't understand."

"You saw the tag inside her blouse?"

"Don't look so shocked. She showed it to me."

"Did you say she was wearing trousers?"

"I did. Very tight trousers, I might add."

"Goodness!" Camilla sat down in the nearest chair and tilted her head thoughtfully. "A woman in trousers! She must have looked bizarre."

Micah picked up a paperweight from the nearby table and pretended to examine it. Bizarre was far from the way he would have described Jody. Those tight trousers had figured largely in his dreams last night. "They were scandalous, but not unattractive." He avoided his sister's shocked glance. "She's different, this Miss Farnell. I believe her story."

The door opened, and Jody came into the room. She was wearing one of Camilla's cast-off dresses, a yellow one sprigged with tiny flowers and trimmed in ecru lace. When she saw Camilla, she hesitated.

"Miss Farnell, I'd like you to meet my sister, Camilla Gallier. I was just telling her of your unexpected and most unusual arrival."

Jody came to Camilla and extended her right hand in greeting, as if she were a man. Camilla awkwardly shook hands with her. Jody smoothed her palms over the billowing skirt of her dress. "I hope you don't mind if I wear the dresses you left here. I don't have any of my own, and Micah

118

thinks the clothing I was wearing when I suddenly appeared here is too revealing."

"You're welcome to anything I have." Camilla was trying not to stare at Jody's short hair. "Have you been ill recently?"

"Why does everyone keep asking me that? No, I'm rarely sick. Except for last night, that is."

Micah explained, "It's well known that cutting the hair will reduce fever."

Jody touched her hair. "Aspirin works better, I'll bet."

Camilla was frankly staring now. "Your accent is unfamiliar. It sounds southern, but then again, it doesn't."

"I guess speech patterns and accents have changed over the years. Yours is beautiful." Jody smiled, and Micah felt his heart skip.

To cover his interest, he said, "I was just telling Camilla how you came to be here."

"Do you believe me?" Jody asked Camilla eagerly. "I'm not lying. I know it sounds impossible, and I don't know how it happened, but here I am." Her voice faltered. "I really thought I would be home when I opened my eyes this morning."

"How terrible for you." Camilla shook her head as if to negate her own words. "But it's impossible."

Micah went back to the door. "Gideon, ask Bessy to bring down Miss Farnell's trousers and other clothing, please." To Camilla, he said, "See what she was wearing before you judge."

Camilla walked around Jody to look at her from all angles. "My dress fits you well, but it's rather out of style. I'll have a man bring out some others for you. While you're here, you may as well look fashionable."

"Thank you. I hope you won't think I'm rude, but I hope it *is* only for a visit. I have no idea how to get home again." She laughed nervously. "I found myself saying 'Auntie Em, Auntie Em, there's no place like home. There's no place like home.'"

"You have an Aunt Em?" Camilla asked in confusion.

Jody shook her head and her smile disappeared. "I guess you would have had to be there to understand."

Bessy knocked at the door and entered with Jody's neatly folded clothes. Camilla took them and began a careful examination. "Look at the stitching in the pants," she exclaimed. "And feel the top. It's smooth on the outside and so soft and fuzzy on the inside."

"It's called a sweatshirt," Jody supplied. "A sweatshirt and jeans."

"What an uncouth name for such a comfortable blouse," Camilla said. "I'm amazed it would have such a name, or that people would use it if it did."

"These are my tennis shoes," Jody said as she lifted her skirt and held out her foot.

Camilla leaned down for a closer look. "Amazing! Women wear these?" She realized Micah was in the room and pulled Jody's skirt down to cover her ankles. Jody wasn't embarrassed in the slightest.

"Do you see what I mean?" Micah picked up the sweatshirt, and as he felt its softness, he imagined it soft against Jody's body. "We've never seen clothing like this."

Camilla shook her head. "There would be no need for lacing in a blouse like this. Why, it would hang all about you!" She picked up the pants. "These would fit right against the legs." She blushed and put them back down. "I don't see how you could have brought yourself to wear them."

Jody took no offense. "It's the style where I'm from. All women wear things like this, and no one thinks anything about it. We wear dresses, too, but not like this one. The skirts are short and not nearly as full."

Micah smiled. "If women wear pants, do men wear dresses?"

"No." Jody smiled back at him. "Men's clothing hasn't changed all that much. They wear clothes just like these, as well as suits and slacks."

Camilla caught the look exchanged between Jody and her brother. "Does Emma know about Miss Farnell?"

"Please, call me Jody. Everyone does. I'm not comfortable being addressed as Miss Farnell."

"No," Micah said, "Emma hasn't heard about Miss Jody yet." He couldn't bring himself to use only her first name in front of Camilla. His sister was too perceptive, and Micah's emotions toward Jody were too uncertain.

"I think she should, don't you?" Camilla looked at her brother and his guest. "She's bound to hear about it. You know how word travels."

"I agree, but what should she be told? She would never believe the truth."

Jody said, "What if I have to stay here forever? I'll have to be explained some way."

"I think it would be best if we pass you off as a cousin," Camilla said uncertainly. "One from, say, Tennessee. That could explain your accent."

"I don't have a Tennessee accent," Jody objected.

"Our friends won't know that." Camilla looked at Micah. "What do you think?"

"It's possible. We do have some connections there. No one here has met all of them, so it might be believed."

"Naturally, I think she should come home with me," Camilla continued.

"I can't do that!" Jody shook her head firmly. "If I leave Whitefriars, I may never get back. If I did go back from some other house, what would I tell whoever is living in that house in my time? I might materialize in the air two stories up if the house isn't standing a hundred years from now, or inside a wall that *doesn't* have a secret room. No, it's too risky."

"She has a point there," Micah said. "Whatever brought her here may only work at Whitefriars."

"But she can't stay here unchaperoned." Camilla stared at her brother. "What would people say?"

"Not even if I'm a cousin?" Jody asked.

"But you *aren't* a cousin. Not really. It's not proper."

"Then what do you suggest?" Micah asked. "We can't prevent her from staying where she may be able to return to her own time. We can't risk trapping her here indefinitely."

"No," Camilla agreed slowly. "We can't do that. I suppose she has no choice."

"I can assure you," Jody put in, "I have no plans to seduce your brother. As soon as I can leave, I will."

Camilla blushed prettily. "I never meant to imply that you did. Such a thing never entered my mind. I was only thinking of what would be the proper thing to do."

Micah was surprised that Jody would speak her mind quite so bluntly, even if she was from some other time. "Do all women like you speak their minds so openly?" he asked. "You certainly don't mince words."

"I'm outspoken?" Jody seemed surprised. "No one ever described me that way before."

Camilla patted Jody's hand. "Don't worry. I'm sure this will right itself before long, and you'll soon be back with your Aunt Em."

Jody smiled, but she didn't look convinced. "Of course I will be. I'll never be able to tell anyone, you know. Everyone would think I'm crazy."

Camilla sat on the front edge of a chair and said, "That's exactly why we aren't going to let anyone know where you came from. Sit down and let me tell you about our Tennessee cousins so if anyone asks you, you'll know what to say."

Micah went to the window and pretended to be interested in the view while he listened to the women's voices. He didn't want to admit it, but he wasn't eager to have Jody leave. She was going to be hard to explain, and he knew Emma would have quite a bit to say about it, but he was fascinated by Jody. She knew the future.

He looked back at the women. Jody, unlike Camilla, sat well into the chair, and he could swear she had crossed her legs under her skirt. Yet she had a femininity that was unmistakable. Her short hair was startling, but now that he was becoming used to it, he rather liked the way it swung about her face and gleamed in the sunlight.

The evening before, he had heard 'Cilla and Bessy carrying water up to Jody's room for a bath, so he knew she had habits of cleanliness. That was important to Micah. During the war he had promised himself that if he returned alive to Whitefriars, he would never be dirty again. Too many of his acquaintances, women included, relied on a damp washcloth and perfumed water to see them from Saturday to Saturday.

As Jody concentrated on Camilla's words, committing to memory the names of his Tennessee cousins and the details of their lives, her heart-shaped face was as earnest as that of a child learning her lessons. He had seen her smile so rarely. Would she be unhappy if she had to remain here?

He turned back to the window. Would he be unhappy if she left? That was a question that was more and more on his mind. There was so much he wanted to ask her—not just for the answers, but to hear her voice. He had to remind himself that he was engaged to be married, and that it would not matter if Jody were here or not. He and Emma would be married in the spring, and Jody had no part in his life.

Perhaps, he thought, he was misjudging Emma. She was the soul of sweetness. He couldn't imagine her ever being in a real temper. The strongest words he had ever heard her speak were when she called him a mean old thing for almost forgetting her birthday. Maybe Emma would take Jody under her wing as Camilla was doing. He shook his head. Emma might be as sweet as treacle, but she had a jealous streak. She wouldn't take it well when she heard he had a woman living here, even if the woman were a cousin and it was the most platonic of situations.

"Do you think you can remember all that?" Camilla asked Jody.

"I think so. I have a good memory. Maybe I'll be lucky and not be asked anything I don't know."

"Let's hope so. None of our friends would be so rude as to question you directly, of course, but they could ask about relatives."

"Will I be likely to see your friends? Maybe I should stay here all the time."

"That would definitely raise questions and cause talk. No, to be inconspicuous, you must go where we go. Otherwise people will wonder about you."

"Then you had better tell me about the people I'm likely to meet here."

"First of all, there's Emma Parlange. I'm sure Micah has already told you about her. They're to be married in a few months."

"He mentioned her."

"The Parlanges are from almost as old a family as ours. It will be the marriage of the century around here. Of course, we are distant kin already, but this will make the bond firmer."

"What's she like?" Jody tried to keep her voice neutral.

"She's as pretty as can be and purely sweet," Camilla said, as if by rote. Jody had the feeling Camilla was not all that fond of her future sister-in-law. "She gives the best parties in the entire parish. She is skilled at riding horseback and can do lovely needlework. Whenever anyone hears of a poor family, Emma and her mother are the first to call on them with a basket of food."

"She sounds like a saint." Jody wished she didn't feel a twinge of jealousy. "No wonder Micah wants to marry her."

"Emma has told me that she had been in love with him for nearly a year before they announced their engagement."

Jody glanced at Micah's back. After reading his diary, she knew he didn't return Emma's love. Or was it that he loved her but was reluctant to write about it? Some men found it hard to talk about love even in their private thoughts.

Gideon brought in a tray of coffee and served it up in tiny demitasse cups. As was the custom, the coffee was strong and thick. On the tray there was a sugar bowl but no cream. Jody took her cup tentatively. Coffee had never been her favorite drink, and she always had to drown it in milk to drink it at all. "Is there milk?"

"Yes, ma'am." Gideon went to get it.

"Did I do something wrong?" Jody asked when she saw Camilla glance at her in surprise.

"No, not really. Around here we don't use cream in coffee. You may be able to pass it off as a Tennessee custom. Or you can ask for *eau sucre* instead."

Jody's French was practically nonexistent, but she had picked up a few words from living in Louisiana all her life. "Sugar water?"

"It's something ladies drink," Micah supplied.

"Don't they drink it where you come from?"

"We prefer something called cola. I'd give almost anything for a Diet Coke right now," she added. "Cold, straight from the can."

Micah and Camilla looked at her as if she were speaking a foreign tongue.

"I don't mean to seem ungrateful. If you hadn't been so good to me, there's no telling what might have happened to me. It's just that I'm homesick for my old life."

"I understand." Micah smiled at her. "If I were dropped without warning into your world, I might not behave nearly as well as you have. It must be a great shock."

"You can't even imagine."

"What is it like?" Camilla sipped her coffee as Gideon returned with a small pitcher of cream and left again.

Jody poured a liberal portion of cream into the coffee and stirred in sugar. "I don't know where to begin. There's television, for example. That's a box with a glass on the front called a screen, and moving images appear on the screen. We watch movies and sit-coms . . ." She faltered when she saw their perplexed expressions. "Movies are like stories, only instead of listening to them, you can see the story acted out. Sit-coms are much shorter and are supposed to be funny."

"This box has people in it? Like a puppet stage?" Camilla seemed to be trying hard to understand.

"No, only their images. They travel on electronic waves to the box, and when the set is turned on, you see whatever movie is playing on the air."

"On the air?" Micah was as confused as Camilla.

"Like I said, I don't know how to describe the differences in our lives."

They sat in comparative silence while they drank their coffee. Even laced with cream, Jody found hers too strong and bitter. Camilla and Micah drank theirs as if it were water. Jody knew she had said too much. How could she have thought she could describe television? They didn't even know about electricity yet, certainly not in terms of common usage in a home. She knew she was indeed fortunate that they didn't assume she was out of her mind and have her locked away somewhere. Jody shivered when she remembered that in this time, madness was treated severely and that a fear of witchcraft was not all that far into the past. She had been lucky to have a host who was broad-minded.

When the coffee was gone, Camilla stood up. "I have to be going. I told the children I was only going to come out here for a little while. They would have insisted on coming, otherwise." To Jody she added, "Little Marie Celeste has been sick with the whooping cough, and I'm trying to keep her inside and quiet."

"I'm sorry to hear that. I hope she is well soon." Jody thought of the immunizations that were available to children in her time and hoped her own immunities were still in effect.

"Almost all children get it," Camilla said philosophically. "It can't be helped. At least she wasn't as sick as her brother when he came down with it."

"Tell them all I said hello," Micah said. "And tell Armand that I haven't forgotten my promise to find him a suitable pony. I'm going to look at one tomorrow that may be perfect for him."

"I'll tell him." Camilla turned back to Jody. "I'm glad to have met you. We'll do all we can to make your stay here as pleasant as possible."

"Thank you." Jody noticed that even though Camilla lived in town, she clearly still thought of Whitefriars as her home. "I hope we can talk often." She liked Camilla and already felt a friendship growing. "I'm looking forward to meeting your sister."

Camilla and Micah exchanged a look. He said, "You won't find much resemblance between Camilla and Claudia."

Jody wondered what he meant by that, but neither of them offered an explanation. She made a mental note to be more circumspect when she met Claudia.

When Camilla was gone Micah said, "I'm glad you and Camilla hit it off so well. She and her family are out often. I had to be honest with her about you. Her children are too young to ask many questions. They will accept you as just another cousin. Reid, Camilla's husband, will probably have to know the truth. I don't think she keeps many secrets from him."

"What about Claudia? I have the feeling you aren't looking forward to my meeting her."

"I'm not. Claudia can be difficult."

Jody nodded. Even though she didn't fully understand, *difficult* was the word Micah had used to describe the voodoo woman in the quarters, and its use applied to Claudia sounded ominous.

Looking for a more pleasant topic, she said, "Will you show me Whitefriars? If . . . when . . . I get back, I want to be able to restore it properly."

"I'd be delighted." He gestured about them. "This, of course, is the back parlor. Its use is probably the same as that of back parlors in your own time: a place for informal gatherings of family and intimate friends."

Jody smiled.

He opened the door and motioned for her to join him in the hall. "You'll notice how wide this hall is. I'm sure you appreciate its breezes in the summer, if you've lived in Whitefriars through the warmer months."

"I was there last summer." She didn't tell him that the house would be equipped with air conditioning in a hundred years. "I've noticed that there is always a breeze here."

"It's not as pleasant in the winter, but with the doors closed at either end, it's not drafty. Whitefriars has fireplaces in every room. Not many houses can boast that. I've heard it was because my great-grandmother was particularly sensitive to cold. Whitefriars was built soon after my great-grandfather married her."

"I think it's wonderful that you live in a home that has been occupied by so many of your ancestors. It must give you a great sense of roots."

"Roots?" Micah laughed. "That's a good way to put it. Roots."

As they circled through all the rooms downstairs, many of which Jody had already seen since her arrival, she was entranced by the stories Micah told about each one. "That window there is the one where my grandfather, Lucien, sat for hours as a young man, worrying whether the British would successfully invade Louisiana during the War of 1812 and move this far north.

Look up there, near the ceiling. Can you see the bullet hole?"

Jody studied the area of the ceiling Micah had indicated until she found a small round hole in the plaster. "A battle was fought here?"

"No. My great-uncle was cleaning his pistol one day back in the '20s and it discharged, nearly hitting his sister. His father was so angry at him that he refused to let the hole be patched, as a reminder of what carelessness can do. It's been pointed out to every Deveroux since that time."

"It's a good way to remember," she agreed. She thoroughly enjoyed listening to Micah talk about his home because of his obvious love for it.

He led her into the library. "You already know this room. The secret room in the wall was built when this wing was added. Father wasn't of an adventurous nature, so he wasn't involved in smuggling slaves to freedom, but he didn't mind turning his back while I did it."

"I admire you for that."

"Do you?" His expression and the inflection in his words told her he really cared what she thought about him.

She hadn't intended for their conversation to take such an intimate turn, so she sidestepped his question and guided the conversation back to the house. "Was the secret room used very often?"

"Quite often. Whitefriars saw a lot of traffic before the War, more than anyone in the area ever would have thought possible. Incidentally, even though the War has been over for seven years, I haven't told anyone outside our family about this wall. I would appreciate it if you kept it a secret. My neighbors didn't feel as I did about slavery."

"I promise." Emma was his neighbor. Did that mean she didn't know of Micah's involvement in the Underground Railroad? She would have assumed he would have told his fiancée about that.

"This is the drawing room, as you can tell. A man was once killed in here."

"Really?"

"He was a thief who thought he could slip in unnoticed. My father's first wife, Celina, heard him. She was more or less alone in the house, and he tried to attack her. She hit him over the head with a poker."

"She sounds like my sort of woman." Jody looked with interest at the heavy iron pokers that stood by the hearth. They looked a lot like the set that was still used at her Whitefriars. That would be a wonderful tale to pass on to tourists.

They finished downstairs and went up to the private rooms. "Has the house been changed much, by your time, that is?" Micah asked. "I suppose it must have, if you're trying to restore it."

"The rooms are the same, though they're painted and decorated differently. It seems odd to see so many people around, especially in the kitchen. As I told you, I live alone."

"Whitefriars is too large for one person. You must be lonely."

She glanced at him and found him watching her closely. Her heart quickened. "I get lonely at times," she said. It was an understatement.

"You wouldn't be lonely here."

Before she could ask him what he meant by such a statement, and whether he had intended it as personally as it sounded, he opened the door to the first bedroom and continued the tour. "My sister Claudia had this room."

"It's so dark for a child! All this gold and brown seems oppressive to me."

Micah nodded. "Mother redecorated the house a year or so before she died. She was trying to be fashionable, but I don't think she liked it either. After her death, Father never changed it. He tried to keep her with him in any way he could. They were truly in love. He only outlived her by a few months. Less than a year."

"That must have been hard on you, to lose them both when you were so young." She watched his face to see if he still mourned them.

"It was difficult."

He was as accomplished at understatement as she was.

"I've decided to put the colors back to the way they were. You would have liked it much better. Shortly after Celina and my father married, she had the entire house repainted in light colors. As far back as I can remember, Mother complained that the walls were too pale and that it made the house seem chilly in the winter, but Father argued that it was a waste to paint again so soon. When she first became ill, he relented, and in keeping with her argument, she chose these dark colors. Unfortunately, we have a longer summer than winter here, and the house now seems too warm."

"I see," Jody said in apparent agreement, even though she had studied enough psychology in college to suspect that Micah's mother, Julie, was probably trying to eradicate Celina from the house

133

and thus from her husband's memory. No matter how good a relationship she had with Antoine, she had had the earmarks of a jealous woman.

"I intend to start with the bedrooms. Especially this room and the one you're using. I hope I can remember the exact color."

"I can show you how to find it. I do that all the time."

Although he looked unconvinced, he didn't argue, instead merely leading her to the room at the back of the house. "This was the nursery. It hasn't been used in years, of course. It smells musty now."

"I guess Camilla was the last to use it. That's a long time to remain closed up."

"No, there was a baby after her. His name was Leon. He died when he was two."

"I'm sorry. How terrible that must have been, to lose a baby."

"It happens to nearly every family, unfortunately. Mother took it hard. Leon was her baby, and there wasn't another one after him. I was nine, and I remember him quite well. It's time to air the room out and give it new life."

"And a brighter color. I couldn't decide what this room had been used for. I never guessed it was a nursery."

"My room was originally the one you have. Camilla was in with Claudia, and if Leon had lived, he would have shared my room. After my parents died, I took their room, giving my sisters each a room to themselves." He went to his door and gestured inside.

Jody stepped into the room, a bit surprised, given the mores of this era, that Micah seemed so at ease inviting her into his bedroom unchaperoned. Perhaps, she thought, she had been mistaken about his adherence to the rigid social conventions of the time, or maybe he wanted the intimacy. Suddenly she decided her thoughts had gone too far astray, so she stepped ahead of him to the center of the room and cheerily said, "This is the room I have at home. It's my favorite. I like to look at the river from my window." To put further distance between herself and Micah, she went to the window and gazed down. There below was the familiar Petite Coeur winding through the trees, though now it was considerably wider than the river she knew.

Micah had come in behind her but remained near the door. "It seems odd to see a woman in here. I've never seen anyone here but my mother and sisters."

Jody looked back at him, trying to read more meaning from his expression, but she failed. If she had overstepped the bounds again, it was at his invitation, and if he was suggesting she should leave, he would have to be clearer about it, because she didn't want to go. "The river is wider now," she offered.

"You should have your men dredge it." A faint smile was on his lips as he came closer to her. "Waterways have to be kept up or the silt buildup will prevent boat traffic."

Her heart was beating in her throat, despite her efforts to remain unaffected by him. "We don't get many boats through here in my day," she said. He was so near she could see the dark flecks in his eyes and the lacy shadow his black eyelashes cast on his cheeks.

Micah reached up and touched her cheek with the tips of his fingers. His touch was so light she might have missed it if her heart hadn't responded with so much excitement. "Jody," he said, "why do you confuse me so?"

She didn't know how to answer. "I'm as confused as you are," she whispered. "I've never met anyone like you, either."

He looked as if he wanted to kiss her, but he stepped back, his eyes filled with intense longing. "I'll not compromise you. You can trust me."

Jody wasn't so sure she wanted to. She found she was hoping he would put all that trustworthiness aside and kiss her.

Chapter Seven

"I shouldn't be here," Jody whispered for the seventh time.

"Smile and quit worrying." Micah took her elbow to help her up The Oaks' front steps. "If I had come without you and it became known that you are staying at Whitefriars, there would have been a scandal."

"There may be anyway. Look how everyone is staring at me." Jody glanced around at the strangers who were sitting on the wide veranda and wandering in and out the open front door.

"I see them." Micah was all too aware of them and why they were staring at her. In spite of her strange hairstyle, Jody was a beautiful woman, and she was also a stranger. "We don't see many strangers in Joaquin. Everyone is trying to guess who you might be." He grinned as nonchalantly as he could. He was sure Jody had no idea how important this meeting could be. If she made a slip and referred to something that had not yet happened, or if Emma didn't believe her to be his cousin, there could be a problem.

He led her to where a handsome young man was sitting on the porch rail and sipping the local concoction of cane syrup laced with whiskey. "Miss Jody, I'd like for you to meet my friend, William Breaux. Will, Miss Jody Farnell. She's a cousin come to visit with us from Tennessee."

"I'm pleased to meet you, ma'am," Will said in a soft drawl. "I don't believe I've met the Farnell branch of cousins."

"She's Louis Farnell's daughter," Micah said, giving the first name the French pronunciation. "It's possible you've never met."

Will took her hand and bent to kiss it. "You're a lovely ornament to the family, Miss Farnell."

"Thank you. Please call me Jody." She smiled at Will in a way that gave Micah a twinge of jealousy.

"I'll do that, Miss Jody. It's an unusual name. Is it short for something?"

"No, my parents simply liked it, I suppose." She glanced up at Micah as if to see how she was doing.

He gave her a smile of encouragement. Had it been a mistake to introduce her to Will? Will was known to be a bit of a rogue with the ladies. But he was Micah's closest friend, and it would have been difficult to prevent them from meeting as long as Jody was at Whitefriars.

"Will you be in town long?" Will was saying.

"I'm not sure yet," Jody answered smoothly. "It all just depends."

Will gave her the smile and wink he reserved for sweeping a woman off her feet. "I hope you will be. I'd like to get to know you better."

When she smiled back at him and said, "I'd like that," Micah thought she looked a bit too sincere.

Taking Jody's elbow, Micah said, "There are others I'd like you to meet." When they were away from Will, he said, "I hope you aren't going to let Will turn your head. He's broken hearts from here to New Orleans."

"I can see how he could."

Micah glanced at her sharply, but she seemed engrossed in her surroundings. He reminded himself again that he was spoken for, that he had no business feeling this way about her.

Emma came out onto the porch as they drew even with the door. When she saw Jody, she hesitated. "Hello, Micah," she breathed softly.

"Emma. I was hoping to find you. I'd like for you to meet my cousin from Tennessee, Miss Jody Farnell."

"Farnell?" Emma tilted her head to one side. "I don't recall any Farnells in our family."

He felt, rather than heard Jody's groan. Of course Emma, who was also Micah's distant cousin, would know their relations as well as he did. "Of course you do. Our cousin Helen married a Louis Farnell. He's her second husband," he added.

"I've always been a bit confused about that part of the family. Welcome to The Oaks, Jody." Emma looked at Jody's hair. "My, that's an unusual coiffure." Honey dripped from her voice.

"It's becoming the latest style in Tennessee,"

Jody said with complete composure. "It's called a pageboy."

"Oh, my! I could never wear my hair in a boy's cut." Emma let out a silver laugh. "A pageboy. Fancy that."

Micah thought Emma was taking the introduction rather well, but he saw Jody's eyes narrow slightly. "Camilla and Reid won't be able to come today. They send their apologies. Marie Celeste had a relapse of the whooping cough and they didn't want to leave her."

Emma gave him one of her slightly blank looks, as if she was trying to figure out why a sick child would affect the actions of the parents. At one time he had found her simplicity touching.

Emma turned back to Jody. "I like your dress. It's very similar to one Camilla made for the Breaux ball this past summer."

"This is Camilla's dress. I borrowed it."

"Did you? I guess you didn't think to bring proper clothing for your visit. Well, if you need anything else, just let me know. I have simply tons of dresses and they can be taken in to fit you."

Micah grinned. He shouldn't have worried about Emma being charming.

"I wouldn't dream of asking to borrow anything," Jody said in as sugary a voice as Emma's. "I'm afraid your style would be all wrong on me."

Micah saw Emma stiffen and purse her mouth the way she always did when she was displeased. Had he missed something?

"How long will you be staying, Miss Farnell?"

"I'm not sure yet."

"I assume Micah has told you that we are to be married next April?"

Micah cut his eyes to his fiancée. He didn't recall them setting the date in any particular month. Not that April was not as good a time as any, but he thought Emma should have consulted him before announcing it.

"Yes, he did," Jody lied, and Micah was thankful. "I assume I will have gone home long before that."

Emma laughed again and her blond curls bobbed. "I should hope so. That's nearly six months away. I mean, your family surely didn't mean for you to be gone so long."

Jody shrugged. "We'll see. It all depends on a number of things."

Emma's smile wavered, and she looked up at Micah and back to Jody. "We must get to know each other better, I think. May I call on you?"

"Please do."

Micah had never heard Jody speak in so syrupy a manner. He expected Emma to sound that way, but he suddenly wondered if Emma might be affecting that manner of speech in order to sound more feminine and helpless. When she was a child she hadn't had that babyish and sugary voice. He had assumed it had changed as his own had when his took on its baritone range. Now he wasn't so sure.

"Why don't you come with me and let me introduce you to the other ladies?" Emma suggested. "I know Micah must be bored to death with women's talk." She cast her blue eyes up at him. "Now admit it, *cheré*. You know you want to be off talking with Will and the others about hunting and so on."

Micah had not thought about it before, but now that he did, he was aware that he actually preferred to be with Jody. But to say so now would require an explanation he wasn't willing to give. To Jody and Emma he said, "I'll be with Will if you want me."

Jody watched him go, certain she didn't want to be stranded with this saccharine barracuda, but apparently having no choice.

"I want you to meet my parents," Emma said. "They're inside."

Jody followed her into the house. It was similar to Whitefriars in that it had a wide entry hall and dark colors on the walls. There were no stairs, however. Jody recalled seeing two sets of outside stairs built into the veranda. Was this the only way of reaching the second floor? In bad weather or after dark, that would be most inconvenient, but it seemed to be true.

Susan Parlange, Emma's mother, was in the front parlor, where several of the older women had gathered. She looked like an older version of her daughter, with a more matronly hairstyle and skin that had started to wrinkle.

"Mama, I'd like to introduce you to Micah's guest. This is Cousin Jody Farnell, of the Tennessee Farnells."

"I'm pleased to meet you, Miss Farnell. Micah's guest, did you say?"

Emma laughed. "I meant she came with Micah. I'm sure Jody must be staying with either Camilla or Claudia. Which is it, dear?"

"Actually, I'm staying at Whitefriars. It's nice to meet you, Mrs. Parlange."

"At Whitefriars? With Micah?" Mrs. Parlange

and her daughter exchanged brief looks, and Mrs. Parlange's eyebrows raised slightly.

"It's rather complicated, I'm afraid." Jody had no intention of explaining her presence to anyone. "You have a lovely home, Mrs. Parlange."

"Why, thank you." Mrs. Parlange sounded as if her mind were on a weightier subject. "How long have you been at Whitefriars, Miss Farnell?"

"Not long. Two days."

"Two days? And Micah never mentioned it?" She gave her daughter a telling glance. "We must take him to task. As his intended, Emma should have been notified so she could do her part in entertaining you. It must be terribly dull. Whitefriars is a *garconnier* these days."

Emma emitted her tinkling laugh. "Oh, Mama, whoever heard of such a grand bachelor's quarters? The things you say!"

Jody smiled even though she felt more like escaping. Micah wanted to marry into this family? She tried to be fair. If she were engaged to Micah and learned Emma had been at his house for two days, she might be upset too. She told herself to cut Emma some slack. "I'm hoping my visit will be a short one. That's why Micah didn't tell anyone of my arrival, I'm sure. I didn't even pack party clothes to bring with me. This is Camilla's dress."

"Imagine not packing party clothes," Mrs. Parlange said in Emma's exact tone. "Whatever could have prompted you to leave home so hastily?"

Jody could see they were determined not to like her. "It's a family matter, and I'm really not at liberty to discuss it."

From the look Mrs. Parlange and Emma exchanged, she saw she had made matters worse. They probably thought she was in some sort of trouble or a runaway. She was afraid to try to fix it by saying more. There was no way to explain the unexplainable. As Jody tried to appear natural and at ease, she wondered how she had come to be here, how the impossible had happened.

At Whitefriars, Iwilla was sitting in her cabin, calm on the outside, but seething within. She couldn't understand it, but somehow her voodoo spell had brought a young, pretty, and marriageable woman to Whitefriars. She had sat in her chair all night and pondered over it. The spell had been cast correctly. No chant or symbol had been omitted. She had even used the mad dog fang that had been so difficult to obtain. Why hadn't it worked?

She stood to her full height and went out the door of her cabin. By the furtive glances from her neighbors in the other cabins, she was sure they knew something was afoot. Even the children were watching her as they played in the sand with their corncob dolls and blocks of wood. Iwilla cast her eyes up at the sky. It would serve them right if she brought on rain and made them retreat into the cabins and stop watching her. Not that anyone would dare to ask her questions or interfere in any way.

She had seen the young woman as she was driving away with Micah. She had been prettier than Iwilla had expected. She wondered what his fiancée would say when she saw Jody. To make sure the meeting did not go smoothly, Iwilla had cast a small spell. Not that she thought it would be needed. Everyone knew Emma was overly possessive of Micah's attentions.

There was some mystery about where the young woman, Jody Farnell, had come from. She had received a garbled report about her appearing from thin air and wearing strange clothes like no one had ever seen on a woman before. Iwilla had attributed it to 'Cilla's imagination. Then 'Cilla had said the young woman was seen sitting cross-legged on the floor and humming in a tuneless manner. Iwilla had begun to wonder if Jody was a witch or even a voodoo woman such as herself. If that were true, Jody had to be sent away. There was room for only one voodoo woman at Whitefriars.

Iwilla left her cabin yard, circled around the oleanders, and crossed the lawn behind the house. The white people had gone to a party at The Oaks and wouldn't be back until evening, or later if there was dancing. That gave Iwilla plenty of time to find the voodoo doll and perhaps unravel the mystery surrounding its uncanny resemblance to the one she had hidden under the plank floor in her cabin.

She entered the house through the kitchen. 'Cilla and two other women saw her, and their eyes grew wide with fright. They had never seen her in the house before. Iwilla ignored them. They wouldn't dare try to stop her.

Beyond the kitchen door was the narrow, steep servant stairs. Iwilla went up them as if she traveled them every day of her life. Behind her she heard whispers as the women asked each other what to do. She soon left them behind.

At the top of the stairs was a door that opened into the long hall that served the bedrooms. Iwilla had no idea which room was Jody's, so she began opening doors at random. The third one led to a green room that had a cozy, lived-in look to it. She sniffed and smelled the rose water and talcum that ladies liked to use. This was the room.

In the wardrobe she found an assortment of dresses in rainbow hues. She touched one whose color drew her attention, and for a minute, her face softened as her hand stroked the fine fabric. Then she remembered the dress belonged to a white woman, and that it was not anything she would ever be allowed to wear, so she pulled back her hand.

With her resolve firmly in place, Iwilla searched through the dresses and petticoats. She found nothing that could be considered remotely unusual. Most of the dresses were ones she had seen on Micah's younger sister.

In the top drawer of the dresser she found cotton small clothes and stockings. The next drawer down held nightgowns. In the bottom one, she found the unusual clothing she had been looking for. Slowly Iwilla took them out and held them up. As 'Cilla had said, the top the strange woman had been wearing was of an unusual weave, and the trousers were as heavy a fabric as a field hand would wear. They would have fit her like a glove, from the size of them. Iwilla shook her head in wonder. What manner of clothes were these, and what was the woman who had worn them?

She rummaged through the drawer, but she couldn't find the doll Micah had shown her. A search of the washstand was also fruitless. Iwilla went back to the odd clothes. She couldn't imagine any woman wearing them for any reason.

The door opened behind her, and Iwilla wheeled to find Bessy glaring at her. "You! I knew something was up. What are you doing going through Miss Jody's things!"

Iwilla drew herself up and fixed Bessy with a stare that was designed to dissipate her opponent's courage.

Bessy shook her head angrily. "You put those clothes down and get on out of here. Go on!"

"You know who you be talking to?" Iwilla knew Bessy had known her all her life, and she couldn't imagine the woman daring to cross her. "You better think real careful, girl. You doan want to find gris-gris in your bed."

If Bessy was frightened, she made no show of it. "I'm not afraid of you. You don't have no business messing in Miss Jody's things or in being in this house at all. What if Mr. Micah was to find you here? He'd be fit to be tied."

Iwilla snorted. "You think I be a-feared of Micah Deveroux? There ain't nothing he can do to me. Ain't nothing a-tall."

Bessy crossed the room and glared fiercely at Iwilla. "Don't you make me call the men to throw you out. You better get out on your own steam, you know what's good for you."

Iwilla knew she was defeated for the moment. At the door she paused and looked back. "Hope you been enjoying your food up to now, Bessy, cause I'm going come live in your stomach from now on." Without a change of her stony expression, Iwilla moved away from the door and made her stately way down the hall.

Bessy collapsed on the recliner couch at the end of the bed and pressed her hands to her stomach. She had been terrified of Iwilla for as long as she could remember, and she hadn't been at all sure she could roust the woman from the house. Her heart was racing at the risk she had taken, but she had felt it was something she had to do. Miss Jody was a bit odd, but she had been unfailingly kind and friendly to Bessy. As a house servant, Bessy felt a deep loyalty to the family, and in her opinion, that now included Miss Jody as well.

She looked at the doorway where Iwilla had stood and shivered. Everyone knew Iwilla had fearsome powers. She had said she was going to come live in Bessy's stomach, and Bessy had a pretty good idea what that meant. Bessy's eyes widened with fear, and she moistened her lips. She hoped Iwilla's threat wouldn't come to pass, but she had never known her to speak idly. Bessy groaned and rocked back and forth miserably.

To Jody the party seemed to have lasted forever. She felt like an outsider despite the fact that everyone but Emma and her mother was friendly to her. She had never been good at meeting people and she felt intimidated by so many strangers, all of whom seemed to know the most minute details about each other.

At last the first of the carriages drew around front in preparation for departure. Emma and her parents expressed profound sorrow that their guests had to leave so early. Jody knew that as Emma's fiancé, Micah couldn't be the first to leave, especially not with Jody by his side. She tried to hide her impatience.

Emma had ignored her after the exchange with her mother, and Jody was glad to be rid of her company. But several times, she had seen Emma and one of her particular friends look over at her and turn away as if they were talking about her. Jody was determined not to embarrass Micah and herself by showing them she knew what they were doing. Nevertheless, the afternoon was the longest of her life.

She found herself on one end of the porch with no one nearby but Will Breaux. He came to stand beside her wicker chair and smiled down at her. "You were the belle of the day," he said.

"I was? Surely you're mistaken." She looked around to see if Micah was nearby. He had gone around the house with Emma several minutes before and had not returned.

"No, I'm never wrong about something like that. Everyone was wondering about you and where you've been all these years and why we've never heard of you."

"My branch of the family isn't particularly close to the Deverouxs. I think there was some misunderstanding between them in the past." She had become proficient at embellishing her story during the afternoon.

"Yet you decided to come to Whitefriars for an undetermined period of time."

"We're trying to heal the breach. Think of me as an emissary."

"You're a remarkably pretty one." Will pulled a chair closer and sat beside her. "I'll be amazed if our local girls aren't trying to cut their hair in imitation of you before the week is out."

Jody smiled at his flattering comment despite her desire to remain neutral, if not somewhat aloof. "Do you know the expression 'full of blarney'?"

He grinned. "No, but I can gather its meaning. You know, Miss Jody, there's something I don't understand. I was at Whitefriars only an hour or so before you arrived, and I saw no preparations for your arrival. Micah didn't even mention it to me."

"I'll have to take him to task over that," she said as she thought Emma might have put it. "Maybe he thought my arrival wasn't important enough to be mentioned."

"On the contrary, I think that could hardly be the case. Why did you say you're staying at Whitefriars instead of with Camilla or Claudia?"

"My visit was arranged this way. Whitefriars feels just like home to me," she couldn't resist adding. "No other place could have suited me better."

"I saw Claudia this morning, and she never mentioned you at all. She told me a previous engagement would prevent her from coming here, but she never said a word about a visiting cousin."

"My family is indeed remiss. No wonder our separate branches have had trouble in the past. I can see I have my work cut out for me."

"Do you recall meeting Zelia Ternant?"

"Zelia?" She remembered the name from Micah's diary. It hadn't struck her when she was introduced, but then she had met so many people today.

"She's the pretty one who was wearing a camellia in her hair."

"I remember. So that's Zelia Ternant. Was her husband here?"

"No, Valcour wasn't up to visiting today." By Will's expression, Jody surmised that the couple seldom attended outings together. "Anyway, Zelia mentioned that it was strange that you would stay at Whitefriars when there were two sisters who would be able to put you up."

"Zelia should mind her own business," Jody replied tartly. "What are you getting at exactly?"

"Only that I care a great deal for Micah. I'm to be his witness at the wedding. I don't want him to be hurt, especially not by a beautiful woman who probably has left a string of broken hearts from here to Tennessee."

"Nicely put, but I'm no femme fatale, and I'm not trying to break Micah's heart. If he loves Emma, far be it from me to interfere." Jody could hardly believe how painful it had been to say those words.

"In that case, could I call on you? You've half broken mine already."

"I've done no such thing, and no, you cannot. I don't want any visitors. I only want to be left alone. I'm sure your heart will survive just fine."

Will studied her thoughtfully. "You aren't like anyone else I've ever met. I truly mean that. Perhaps it's a good thing Micah became engaged before you entered into the picture."

"Why?" She stared at him.

"You seem more like the type of woman he would be interested in than Emma." Will smiled too quickly, as if to cover the truth in his words. "But you aren't interested in him, so it doesn't matter. Is that right?"

"Exactly. Even if I were, it wouldn't be possible for me to marry him or anyone else here."

"Why not? Are you engaged to someone in Tennessee?"

She cast him an enigmatic smile. "Now who's stepping over the bounds?"

"As I said, Micah is my friend and I'm protective of him."

Micah came up behind them. "I hope I'm not interrupting anything."

"Not at all," Will said. "I was only trying to convince your lovely cousin to allow me to call on her."

Micah looked at Jody. "And what did my cousin say?"

"I told him no."

"Just like that?" Micah's face lit with amusement.

"She's given me no reason to hope," Will said forlornly as he touched his heart in a melodramatic gesture. "Perhaps you'll intercede on my behalf?"

"My cousin can speak for herself. If she said no, she probably meant it."

"I always mean it if I say no," Jody affirmed.

"I've sent for the buggy," Micah said. "I hope you're ready to leave."

She gratefully rose and Will stood. "It was nice talking with you," she said. "Perhaps we'll see each other again."

Will again bent at the waist and kissed her hand. "I don't give up easily. I'm positive we'll meet again."

Jody was glad to see Micah's black horse and buggy roll to a stop out front. Together, she and

Micah sought out Emma and her parents and thanked them for having her. Emma was so busy smiling and blushing up at Micah that Jody didn't know if she heard her or not.

"You'll be over to see me soon, won't you?" Emma said to him. "We have so much to discuss. I want you to see the silver flatware Papa has bought us, and there is the matter of dishes. I want to send to France for them, but if they are to arrive before the wedding, we really must make some decisions right away."

Micah nodded. "I'll try to come over soon. Whatever pattern you choose is all right with me. Whitefriars has more dishes than we can use now."

Mrs. Parlange put her arm around her daughter. "All brides need their own belongings. We're so pleased Emma will remain so close to us. It will be almost as if she hasn't left home at all."

While the attention of those about them was on Emma, Jody studied her critically. She was pretty enough in a pale sort of way, but couldn't Micah see through the sugar-coating? The way her mouth turned down in a pouting way whenever she wasn't actually smiling should have been a signal to him. Emma's hands reminded Jody of bird talons, but she had to admit to herself that she might be prejudiced against her.

With their farewells concluded, Micah handed Jody down the steps and into the buggy, waved to the people on the porch, and tapped the reins on the horse's back. The buggy moved smoothly away, and Jody sighed with relief.

"Did you enjoy the visit?" he asked her when the horse was well on the road toward Whitefriars.

"Will seems to be a conquest."

"I wasn't there looking for conquests. Emma is . . . pretty. I hope you'll be happy."

"I'm sure we will be. She never has a harsh word to say about anybody. That makes for an amiable marriage."

Jody stared at him in the gathering dusk. Was he so blinded by Emma that he hadn't understood the exchange between Emma and herself? Emma had all but insulted her outright on several occasions. "If you ask me, a marriage needs more than that."

"Yes, children, of course. That goes without saying."

"I wasn't thinking of children. I know childless couples who are perfectly happy. I was thinking of interests two people should have in common. Do your goals match?"

He laughed. "Our goals? What on earth are you talking about?"

"I mean, do you want the same things in life? Twenty years from now, will you be satisfied to watch her bat her eyelashes and giggle, or will you wish you had someone with whom you could talk about meaningful things?"

"There's no reason to insult Emma," he said stiffly.

"I wasn't trying to be insulting. I just don't want to think of you being bored to death. Can she talk about anything deeper than the color of a parasol or the trim on a bonnet?"

"If I want stimulating conversation, I'll go see Will. But that doesn't mean I want to marry him. Wives are for something else entirely."

"What? To ensure that the family name will be

passed down? For what reason? Why does it matter at all whether there are Deverouxs in the next generation? What is your wife supposed to be? Some pretty ornament to keep in the parlor?"

"You make it sound as if I'm buying furniture. Of course a wife is more than that. A wife runs the house and the daily affairs of the family so the husband can see to business."

"Nonsense!"

"What?"

"Where I come from, marriages are expected to be equal. I certainly wouldn't marry someone who wanted no more from me than simpering grimaces and babies."

Micah frowned at her. "I might point out that your attitude may explain why you have never married."

"That's not the reason. I've had my share of boyfriends and men have proposed to me."

"Oh? Then why did you turn them down and become a spinster? You're what, twenty-five or so? You've been too choosy."

"Spinster? Hardly. I'm only twenty-six, and that has nothing to do with my decision not to marry. I simply haven't found the right man yet."

"And how will you know which one is the right one? You said you've recently moved to Joaquin and can't hope to know much about the families in town. You're too far from your parents to take their advice. How will you know when you find him?"

"I'll know because I'll see love in his eyes, and when he kisses me the earth will stop spinning. I won't marry anyone unless I'm in love with him."

"I thought that way once. It's not a good idea, especially in the case of a woman."

"Then you really don't love Emma!" Jody stared at him. His face was barely visible in the fading light of early evening, and she couldn't read his expression.

"Of course I love her. What do you take me for?"

"I don't believe you."

Micah reined the horse to a stop. "You mustn't go around saying things like that. You have no idea how I feel about Emma."

"Don't I?" Jody was all too aware of his nearness. Because of the buggy's narrow seat, her thigh was pressed close to his, and their arms touched from shoulder to elbow. "Micah, don't make a mistake. You're going to live a long, long time, and I don't want you to be unhappy."

His silence told her that she had said too much. Then he turned to her, and she could feel his eyes on her. She wanted to take back what she had said. It really had been none of her business. He had every right to marry whomever he pleased, and it was wrong of her to judge whether the marriage would be happy by her own standards. This was another century, another lifetime. Maybe that was all Emma wanted out of life as well.

Slowly Micah leaned toward her, and before she realized what he was going to do, his lips were upon hers, warm and firm, and she swayed closer into his embrace. Kissing Micah seemed to be the most natural thing she had ever done. Her lips parted beneath his, and as she returned his kiss, she felt her body respond to him. She wanted the kiss to go on forever.

When he released her she put her fingertips to her lips and stared up at him. Whatever he had felt, it had been more than a mere kiss to her. Far more.

"I shouldn't have done that," he managed to say, sounding choked up. Through the darkness of the gloaming, she couldn't see his face at all. "You have every right to hate me. I'm engaged to one woman, I've just left her side, and here I am kissing you."

"Why did you do it?" she whispered. "Why did you kiss me?"

He was silent for a minute. "I don't know. All at once I felt I had to kiss you." His voice broke off as if he hadn't wanted to admit that. "Forgive me, Miss Jody. It will never happen again."

"There's nothing to forgive. I kissed you back. And stop calling me 'miss.' That's really irritating."

She couldn't be sure, but she thought she saw him smile as he signaled the horse to carry them home.

Chapter Eight

Jody sat on the front edge of her chair in imitation of Camilla and sipped her *café au lait*. Several times she had tried to drink the thick, black coffee Micah liked so well but had concluded she would never become accustomed to the taste. *Café au lait*, with its heated milk, was their compromise.

Camilla sat on the sofa beside Reid, their two older children on chairs to either side of them and the youngest, Marie Celeste, in Micah's lap. Reid, like his children, was studying Jody as if he wasn't sure what to think of her.

"Miss Jody," the elder girl said, "why do you wear your hair that way?"

"Hush, Matilda," her mother admonished with a quick glance at Jody.

"It's all right. I wear my hair short because it's less trouble this way. I can wash it and as soon as it's dry, I'm done. Besides that, it's cooler in the summer."

Matilda was thoughtful for a minute. "Mama, can I cut my hair like Miss Jody's?"

Camilla smiled at the idea. "No, darling."

"I may let mine grow out like yours," Jody mollified. Matilda was only eight and was trying hard to identify with her elders.

Armand grinned at his sister. "You'd look funny with short hair, Matty. You'd look like a boy."

"I would not," Matilda disputed, frowning at her younger brother.

Two-year-old Marie Celeste tilted her head up to look at Micah and whispered in a voice heard by everyone in the room, "Is Miss Jody a boy, Nonc Micah?"

"No, cheri. Not in the least." Micah smiled at Jody.

"I think it's time for you children to go outside and play," Camilla said quickly. "Run along now."

"Me, too, Mama?" Because of her age, Marie Celeste wasn't always allowed the same freedoms as her older siblings.

"You may go too. Watch her carefully, Matilda."

The children walked decorously as far as the parlor door, but as soon as it closed, Jody could hear their small feet racing down the hall. "You have wonderful children," she said. "They're well behaved."

"Thank you," Camilla said. "At times they can be more direct than is polite."

"Tell me, Miss Farnell," Reid said as he returned his coffee cup to the silver tray, "how do you come to be here? Camilla told me a fantastic story about you appearing from out of nowhere. I must admit, she had me almost convinced." He smiled, but his dark eyes remained serious.

"I'm not sure myself how it happened. For obvious reasons, I don't want it to become known around town."

"You can trust Reid," Micah said as he held out his cup for Camilla to pour him more coffee as she was pouring Reid's. "I've known him all my life and he's not one to pass on gossip."

Jody gave Reid a brief history of herself, ending with, "The next thing I knew, I was here."

"I'm concerned about this voodoo doll. Micah, if old Iwilla is practicing her witchcraft again, there could be trouble."

"I've warned her not to frighten anyone. There's not much else I can do. She appears to speak so little English, I'm never sure how much she understands of what I tell her."

"I think she speaks more than she lets on," Camilla said. "She's been in the States since she was a girl, from the way our parents talked about her. She's bound to know English by now."

"Probably, but you know how she is."

Camilla shivered. "Yes, I do. She's always frightened me. I wish you'd find another place for her."

"I'm willing. Would you want to take her in?"

"No, thank you," Camilla said quickly.

"Will Claudia, do you think?"

"I see what you mean." His sister picked up the other coffee server and poured more *café au lait* for Jody. "She's older than a rock, but I doubt she will live forever."

"I've never met her," Jody said. "Maybe I should. No, that's silly. I don't believe in voodoo."

"Neither do I," Micah said. "She's just a crazy old woman."

"All the same, I've seen some amazing things," Reid put in reluctantly. "So have you, Micah. Remember when we saw her handling that snake?"

"A snake?" Camilla asked doubtfully. "What sort of snake?"

"A water moccasin. Micah and I had heard there was to be voodoo dancing in a field not far from here, and we slipped out that night to watch. It was on St. John's Eve—that's a night that's supposed to be important for practicing voodoo. Iwilla was there, dressed all in red with a tignon on her head."

"Tignon?" Jody leaned forward with interest.

"That's a way of wearing a scarf," Micah explained. "It's tied in seven knots with seven points."

"They were drinking tafia and were all pretty well drunk by the time we got there. We hid in the bushes and watched. After a while, Iwilla reached into a covered basket and brought out a snake as long as she is tall."

Camilla's eyes widened. "Goodness!"

Micah nodded. "She was doing a dance like I never saw before or since. She was moving all of her body except her feet. After a while I realized this was how a snake might dance if it suddenly became human."

"It was like watching old Marie Laveau to see Iwilla dance. It would be something to see if those two ever got together," Reid commented as he sipped his scalding hot coffee.

"I'm glad the children aren't hearing all this,"

Camilla said nervously. "They wouldn't sleep for a week."

Her husband smiled at her and winked. Jody wondered if Camilla were as lacking in superstition as she professed to be. "It sounds as if Iwilla puts on a good show, but I still don't believe in voodoo. There's a lot of strength in the power of suggestion, you know. If someone believed in it, and Iwilla told him he was going to get sick, he probably would. I, however, came here before I ever heard of Iwilla. No, the doll is just a coincidence."

"I'm inclined to believe Jody," Micah said. "Iwilla doesn't have that kind of power. No one does."

Reid glanced from Jody to Micah and back again. He hadn't missed the fact that Micah referred to her without adding the "Miss" to her name. Jody wondered if Micah had noticed that he had done it.

"However you got here," Reid said, "I hope you'll consider our home as your own, just as Whitefriars is. We have plenty of room if you'd like to stay there instead. We're in town, and it's more convenient for shopping."

"Thank you, but I feel I shouldn't leave Whitefriars for any length of time. I'm still hoping to get back somehow."

"I saw Emma in town yesterday," Camilla told her. "She mentioned that Micah had taken you to her party last week. She was full of questions about you. I told her what we had agreed to say. I could see she was aching to ask more, but I pretended to be in a hurry to return home."

"If I were in Emma's place, I would be anx-

162

ious to know more about you, too," Reid said. "It's not a daily occurrence for a bachelor to have an unmarried woman for a houseguest."

"What are you implying?" Micah asked sharply.

"Not a thing. But I'm not Emma."

"She didn't seem too happy to meet me," Jody agreed.

"Nonsense. She couldn't have been more polite." Micah took a tea cake from the tray and bit into it.

Camilla smiled at her brother. "You wouldn't notice if she weren't." To Jody, she said, "Micah isn't one to pay attention to a woman's subtleties. Once he pledges his loyalty, he becomes blind to any faults."

"I realize Emma has faults," Micah defended himself. "I don't know why you've never cared for her."

"She was always Claudia's friend, not mine. I'm sure Emma is as nice as you say she is."

"Speaking of Claudia, she will be out later on today. I received a note from her just this morning. I wonder if she will believe Jody is a Tennessee cousin."

"If you can convince her of that, my hat is off to you," Reid said. "Miss Farnell bears no resemblance to a single person in your family."

"Please, call me Jody," she said for the third time. "I'm not accustomed to such formality."

"She's right. If she were a member of the family, we would call her by her first name," Micah said.

The clatter of feet in the hall announced the return of the children. "There are puppies in the barn," Armand said with great excitement. "May we have one, Papa?"

Micah smiled. "Those are Sounder's puppies. They will be ready for new homes by next week."

"Sounder? The red hound?" Reid asked.

"That's the one."

"All right, son. You can have one if Nonc Micah doesn't already have a home for them."

"Take your pick," Micah said. "Have Mars daub some paint on the puppy's tail, so I don't accidentally sell the one you want."

Armand ran out to do as his uncle instructed. The girls settled back down in their previous places. Marie Celeste gazed solemnly at Jody. After a while she said, "Do you have any little girls?"

"No, I'm not married. Though I hope to have a daughter someday."

"Girls are nicer than boys, I think," Matilda commented with a nod of approval. "I intend to have only daughters, I believe."

"Be quiet, Matilda," Camilla scolded gently. "You have no idea what you're talking about."

From the security of Micah's lap, Marie Celeste added, "When I grow up, I'm going to have puppies and kittens and ponies all over the place. Nonc Micah will come see me every day, and we'll go for long rides, me on my pony and him on his horse." She thought for a minute, then looked at Jody and said, "You may come too."

"Thank you," Jody said with a suppressed smile. "If I'm still here, I'd like that."

"Is Tennessee terribly far away?" Matilda asked. "I can't imagine what it must look like."

"It has beautiful, rolling hills on one side of

the state and wonderful mountains on the other," Jody said. "Maybe someday you'll go there and see for yourself."

"I'll do that." Matilda decided the matter with a firm nod. "I've never seen a mountain."

Micah was watching Jody with interest. "You've seen both sides of Tennessee? You're well traveled."

"Travel is easier where I come from." She knew the children didn't know about her true background, so she spoke obliquely. "I've been in all the states."

"All thirty-four?" Matilda's eyes grew round. "I've never known anyone who has traveled that much. Is that why you're not married?"

"Matilda!" Camilla reprimanded, then said to Jody, "Please excuse my daughter. She seems to have lost her manners on the way out here."

"It's all right. Yes, Matilda, I've been busy." She was glad she hadn't said she had seen fifty states. That would have been hard to explain.

"Do you know any stories?" Marie Celeste asked. "Nonc Micah always tells us a story when we come out, but Mama said he may be too busy to tell us one since he has company."

Camilla rolled her eyes as if she were completely exasperated with her children.

Armand bounded back into the room wearing a triumphant smile. "Mars and me marked the puppy, Nonc Micah."

"Mars and I," his mother corrected.

"I'll see that he's kept for you." Micah hugged Marie Celeste. "I always have time to tell you a story. Jody may not know any."

Marie Celeste turned a scandalized face toward

Jody, who quickly said, "As a matter of fact, I happen to know a lot of stories. And what's more, I can guarantee you've never heard a single one of them."

"Really?" Armand's interest was piqued.

As Jody stood and held out her hand to Marie Celeste, she said to all the children, "Let's go sit on the porch so the others can visit. I'm going to tell you about a family called the Brady Bunch."

As they left the room, Reid said, "What did Emma think of Miss Jody?"

Micah was thoughtful for a minute. "She seemed to like her. You know Emma. She never says a cruel word about anyone."

Reid only smiled.

Throughout the remainder of their conversation, the subject of Emma was avoided. When they were ready to leave, Camilla said, "Ride into town with us, Jody, and we'll buy you some gloves. We'll bring you home in time for Claudia's visit.

"I don't need any gloves. Not really," Jody said.

"Of course you do. Mine won't fit you properly and no lady can go without them."

Jody looked at Micah. "She's right," he said. "I'm sure there are other things you need as well. I'm remiss in not taking you shopping before now."

Camilla laughed at her brother. "As if you know the first thing about shopping with a lady. Jody needs me at a time like this."

Jody knew they were right. She was having to wash out her underwear every night, and at this rate it wouldn't last long. "I don't have any money," she admitted reluctantly.

"Have them send me a bill," Micah said. "I know every shopkeeper in town."

"I couldn't do that."

"Then consider it a loan." He smiled down at her. "If you're to pass as a Deveroux cousin, you must look the part."

"Whatever you say. But only if we consider it a loan." She had no idea how she would manage to pay it back, but she had her pride. If she were to be here forever—and only time would tell—she would have to find some way to support herself. Surely, she thought, there would be something she could do to earn a living.

Stay forever. The words formed so easily in her mind. She had tried not to think of never returning to her familiar world, but she was too much of a realist to ignore the fact that her chances of going back might be growing slimmer every hour.

As she climbed into the brougham, she noticed she showed more of her ankles than Camilla or even Matilda. There were so many things she needed to master if she was to be here long, she silently reminded herself, all the while struggling to keep the word *forever* from creeping into her mind again.

The ride to town seemed to take forever, as she was accustomed to getting there by car in only ten minutes. It took the brougham that long to reach the main road. In time, however, they entered the sleepy town of Joaquin, which proved to be far different from what Jody had expected.

Although the streets were laid out more or less the same as the Joaquin of her day, the stores were entirely different. She realized a great deal of face-lifting and change would occur in Joaquin during the century to come. Not too surprising to her, as she had always had a special pull to the past, she preferred these original storefronts. Each of them had special touches—a medallion here, a pressed tin column there. The display windows had smaller panes of glass and were darker, but that lent them a certain mystery or intrigue that piqued her curiosity. As they rolled slowly down Joaquin's main street, she craned her head and looked closely so she could see the dresses and bonnets displayed in the various stores. It was like stepping onto a movie set.

"I'll take the children and go home," Reid said as the driver pulled to a stop in front of a store. "I'll send the brougham back for you."

"That will be fine," Camilla said as the driver came around to hand Camilla and Jody out of the carriage.

Jody held her skirts in one hand and tried to keep as much of her legs covered as Camilla did while exiting the carriage. The driver helped her onto the boardwalk as if she were made of delicate glass. Then he latched the door and climbed back onto his seat. Jody and Camilla waved to Reid and the children as they drove away.

The dry goods shop was filled with things that made Jody's eyes widen. The right side of the store was devoted to men's needs, the left to women's. Lining the countertop were countless bolts of fabric ranging from calico to satin. The walls were covered with measuring tapes, pincushions, hat forms, and ribbons. A large counter display was filled with thread. Jody picked up a spool and noted that it was all cotton. Curiously, she examined a bolt of fabric. "There's not an inch of polyester in the place," she said to Camilla.

"What's polyester? A color?"

"It's a type of synthetic fabric." She touched a fold of silk velvet. "Beautiful!"

"I think we should get you some material while we're here. I'm sure you'll be wanting to sew dresses for yourself."

Jody didn't know how to tell Camilla that she had never made a dress by hand in her life. "Are the patterns easy to follow?" She looked down at the dresses they wore. Lace and ruffles and braiding covered most of the material.

"Of course, Bessy will put the dress together. She's a wonderful seamstress. I'll help you put in the embroidery and add the trim. I like to sew. Matilda can already do rather nice embroidery. I guess she will take after me in enjoying needlework."

"I've never been very good at it myself," Jody confessed. "You might say I know next to nothing about it all."

Camilla looked momentarily surprised but said nothing. "The gloves are over here."

A sales clerk met them at the glove counter and began taking gloves out of the narrow drawers beneath the case to display them on the glass countertop. Jody picked up a pair of white lace gloves for a closer look. She had never seen such delicate work and was half afraid to ask their price.

The clerk was a young man with a moderately handsome face and an overly eager expression. He seemed to be trying so hard to please that Jody felt sorry for him. When he told her the price, Jody was amazed at how little it was. "I wish I could take this whole store back with me," she whispered to Camilla when the clerk went to get more gloves from the stockroom in back. "I'd make a small fortune in resale."

"Prices are higher where you come from? That's hard to believe. I've heard people say this place values everything it sells too dearly. Micah will want you to have the best, though, so I brought you here."

"Where are the bras and panties? I need them more than anything."

Camilla blushed. "Do you mean undergarments? We'll have to find a woman to help us with those." She paused. "I know about pantalets, of course, but what's a bra?"

"I have a terrible feeling they haven't been invented yet."

The clerk returned with a new box of gloves and opened it with a flourish. "These are the latest in fashion. Look at the stitching and the cut of the fingers."

Camilla turned a glove inside out to examine the seam. "They are nice."

"They would be lovely on you ladies, if you don't mind my saying so." His unusual accent branded him as being from outside the area.

"I suppose I'll take a pair," Jody said doubtfully. She had no idea how to buy gloves.

"She'll have six pair and so will I," Camilla said. "You know where to send my bill?"

"Yes, ma'am, Mrs. Gallier. You're one of our best customers." He bowed to Jody. "I don't believe I've seen you in here before."

"I'm staying at Whitefriars," Jody said. "It's the colonial about two miles out of town." At once she felt foolish. Half the houses in town were what she would term colonial, and she wasn't sure the style had been named yet.

"I know Whitefriars. Yes, ma'am. Mr. Deveroux." He actually bobbed up and down at the waist as he tried to convince her that he knew the place. He counted out six pair of gloves in both their sizes and put the others away. "I'll have these sent out to your carriage."

Jody smiled and commented to herself, "We don't have to carry our own packages." She glanced to see if Camilla was as amused at the man's obsequiousness as she herself had been.

Camilla had already turned away and was fingering some ribbon. "This color would look good on you. Don't you think it would be nice with that blue kerseymere over there?"

They wandered through the fabrics, choosing enough for two dresses, and the man in that department carried the fabric to the cutting table. "Don't look now, but the glove salesman is staring at us," Jody whispered.

"I know. He does that. Pretend not to notice."

"It's irritating. Why is he doing that?" When she glanced back at him he noticed and beamed at her.

"I suppose it's his way. No one has much to do with him. He came here just after the War. I'm sure you could tell by the way he talks that he's a Yankee." Camilla dropped her voice lower. "He's a *carpetbagger.*"

Jody's eyes widened. "He is?" She risked another look back. "I always pictured them as being older and more aggressive."

"Yes, well, he wasn't very good at it. Most of the

others have long since gone on to New Orleans or Baton Rouge and are making a fortune by taking advantage of people too poor from the war to protect themselves, but we seem to be stuck with George Percy forever."

"He must have a pound of pomade on his hair. I'll bet his head slips off the pillow at night."

Camilla laughed and covered her mouth with her fingertips. "Shame on you, Jody. How risque."

Jody smiled and thought how shocked Camilla would be if she could see a television show.

Camilla's next stop was at the corset counter, where a matronly woman greeted them. Jody gave a firm refusal to the idea of buying a corset. "I'm not about to put on one of those things."

Camilla was astounded. "You're not wearing a corset?" she whispered.

"No, and I'm not going to. It's not healthy. Even if it were, I wouldn't put myself through that misery." She looked at Camilla's waist. "Are you?"

"Of course I am. All women do."

"Not me." She said to the woman behind the counter, "Do you sell bras? You know, brassieres?"

"I never heard of anything like that," the woman said doubtfully. "I've sold women's garments for years and no one ever mentioned those words to me."

Jody frowned. "Maybe I could make my own." She thought about explaining to the women what purpose a bra served, but decided against it. There was no point in shocking Camilla further. "I'll make them myself somehow."

Neither was she too pleased with the selection of lace-trimmed drawers, or pantalets, as Camilla called them. They were made of cotton and looked as provocative as flower sacks to Jody, who was accustomed to bikini panties. With no choice, she gave in and bought six pair, reasoning that no one would see them anyway.

By the time they left the store, Jody had also bought two pairs of shoes. The saleswoman had exclaimed over the oddity of her tennis shoes, but Jody had offered no explanation. Camilla helped her pick a pair of shoes to wear outside and another for inside the house. The house shoes were slippers, and Jody was relieved to find they were actually comfortable. Although the saleswoman tried to convince Jody to buy a pair of walking shoes that were too small in order to make her foot seem smaller, Jody stood firm. Finally she was fitted with a pair that didn't crimp her toes and she was satisfied.

As they left the store, Camilla glanced at the sky. "Oh, dear. It's later than I thought. You'll have to hurry back to Whitefriars if you're to see Claudia. I had hoped you could come by my house for some tea first."

"Next time I will." Jody smiled. She genuinely liked Camilla. "I hope to see you soon."

To the driver, Camilla said, "I'm going to walk home. Will you take Miss Farnell back to my brother's house?"

"Yes, ma'am." The driver helped Jody into the carriage.

Jody dreaded meeting the formidable Claudia. For a moment she considered telling Camilla that she would love a cup of tea, but she knew the meeting was one that couldn't be postponed forever and that the sooner it was over with, the better.

When she arrived at Whitefriars she didn't see a buggy out front and began to hope that Claudia already had gone and she would have a reprieve. But her hopes were dashed as soon as she walked into the parlor. Micah was sitting with a woman who didn't smile when Jody entered.

Jody went to her and held out her hand automatically. "Hello. We haven't met. My name is Jody Farnell."

Claudia looked at Jody's outstretched hand and made no move to shake it. "Emma sent me a note that we had a cousin down from Tennessee. I thought she must have lost her mind."

"I should have told you," Micah said smoothly, "but Jody hasn't been here very long."

Claudia jerked her head around. "Miss Farnell has been here at least a week. Emma said she met her at the party."

Micah looked as if he was determined to smile in spite of his sister. "I apologize, Claudia. It was thoughtless of me."

"I'd expect no more from Camilla. With that brood of hers, it's a wonder she gets anything done at all. You, however, have disappointed me."

Jody knew immediately that she wasn't going to like Claudia. She went to a chair and sat down. "I've been shopping. The packages will arrive soon, I assume. I hope I didn't buy too much. Camilla seemed to be happy with what we found."

Claudia wasn't interested in hearing about a shopping trip. "Your name isn't familiar to me. Tell me, Miss Farnell, how are we kin?"

"I'm Helen and Louis Farnell's daughter. My father is her second husband," she added, as had been decided to make the relationship more difficult to follow.

"We don't have any Helens in the family. Not a single one as far as I've ever heard."

Jody smiled. "There's at least one. We've lost touch with our Louisiana branch."

"Who are your mother's parents?" Claudia pursued. "How are you kin to the Duprees?"

Jody had never heard of the Duprees so she looked at Micah for help.

He smiled disarmingly. "No one understands the family tree the way you do, Claudia. You know I've always been hopeless at remembering how we're kin to whom. Jody is the same way."

"Why are you calling the young woman by her first name, as if she were a child or your sister? And you, Miss Farnell, why are you allowing it?"

"I asked him to do it. 'Miss Farnell' is so formal and 'Miss' Jody makes me sound as if I'm a hundred years old."

"Everybody calls me Mrs. Landry or Miss Claudia and I would insist on it if they didn't. It's only proper."

"Claudia, I'm surprised at you," Micah said in veiled warning. "Jody is a guest in our house and you're taking her to task as if she were a disobedient servant."

Claudia immediately changed her tack. "I certainly never meant it to sound that way, goodness knows. At times I may sound more outspoken than I really am."

"Think nothing of it," Jody said. No, she thought, she would not like Claudia a bit.

175

Elizabeth Crane

Physically, Claudia was tall, with the gray eyes that seemed to be a Deveroux trademark, but hers were like pewter to Micah's silver. Her hair was brown but not nearly as dark as his. Although she and Jody had to be about the same age, Claudia looked years older.

"I suppose Micah has told you that he and Emma Parlange are to be married in April?"

"Yes. He did." Jody recalled that Claudia was a friend of Emma's, and she tried to think of something nice to say about the woman. "She's very pretty."

The compliment mollified Claudia. "Yes, she is. Emma is considered to be the belle of the parish. Micah is a fortunate man."

Jody managed to smile. "It's so difficult to get to know anyone at a party. I didn't have much opportunity to talk to Emma."

"She was too busy talking with Will Breaux," Micah put in. "She made a conquest there."

"Will should get married and settle down. If his brother has no children, the family place will go to Will."

"Perhaps he hasn't found anyone to love," Jody suggested. "I can't see why anyone would want to marry for less." Her eyes met Micah's, but she couldn't read the expression in them.

"There are many reasons for marrying, surely." Claudia's tone was stiff, as if she had married for other reasons herself. "Love is transient."

"It's also of great importance," Jody said firmly. Now that she knew Micah, she hated to think he would marry for any other reason, and especially that he would marry a woman as two-faced as she suspected Emma to be. "If I had a brother,

I'd counsel him to be sure there was love on both sides before he married."

Claudia turned away. "That may be well and good, but if the brother was the master of a grand place like Whitefriars, that would be foolish counsel. There is too much at stake here to wait and see if love comes into the picture." She picked up one of the tea cakes. "Vera is putting too much sugar into Mama's recipe again. You must speak to her, Micah."

Jody managed not to grimace at Claudia's attitude. She could easily see what Claudia and Emma had in common, but in Claudia's case, she didn't try to hide her claws. She hoped Claudia wasn't as accustomed to coming to visit as Camilla was.

Chapter Nine

"I'm telling you, Vincent, it's scandalous," Claudia said as she ate her buttered muffin. "Micah has that woman living under the same roof, in the house where my own parents lived!"

Vincent, who was accustomed to his wife's tirades, only nodded and held out his coffee cup for the butler to refill it.

"I couldn't sleep at all last night." Claudia fingered the lace on her morning wrapper. Over the past few years, she had developed the habit of postponing getting dressed until well into the morning hours. "I was too busy worrying about poor Emma."

"Micah is an honorable man. He wouldn't move a mistress into the house where he plans to bring his bride next spring."

"Of course you would say that. Men always stick together. I'm telling you, Miss Farnell is scandalous. You should see her hair!"

"What's wrong with her hair?"

Claudia frowned at her husband. "Don't you ever listen to me? I told you all about it at supper last night. It's short. As short as a man's!"

Vincent's pale blue eyes gazed out the window. "That must look rather remarkable. Perhaps there's some reason. I can't imagine a woman cutting her hair short unless she had to for some reason."

"Last night it occurred to me that it could have been a punishment."

"Pardon?"

"I've read about it before. I've heard of women being caught in a compromising position with a man and of her family cutting her hair as a punishment."

Vincent shook his head. "I've never heard of anything like that. Not around here."

"She's not from around here, you dolt. She's from Tennessee. And that's another thing. After you went to bed last night, I stayed up and went through my family records and found no reference whatsoever to a Jody Farnell in our family. Whoever heard of a woman being named Jody in the first place?"

"It's probably short for Josephine or something like that."

"You didn't see her. She's much too young to be living alone in a bachelor's house. And she's passing herself off as our cousin. My heart goes out to Emma."

"I hate to run, but I'm to meet a man about that roan colt."

Vincent stood and dropped a kiss on his wife's cheek. Claudia managed not to flinch. She hated

179

for him to touch her, but she suffered it in front of the servants. As he left the room, she glared after him. He had not heard a word she had said. She shoved the empty plate toward the butler. "More muffins," she snapped.

As he took away the plate, she leaned back in her chair and tapped her fingertips on the white linen tablecloth. She hadn't been happy in her marriage and had turned to food for solace. Her figure was beginning to show it, but Claudia didn't care. Now that she was a wife, she no longer had to starve herself and remember to simper in order to attract a man.

She stood and threw her napkin on the table in disgust. Emma had to be warned, and who else should do it but Emma's closest friend. Not caring that she had sent for more muffins, she stalked from the room and went up to dress.

In an hour's time, she was at The Oaks, accepting a blueberry muffin from the Parlanges' laden table. "I hope you'll forgive me for coming at this time of day," she said as she spread a generous pat of butter on the muffin. "I had to talk to you."

Emma smiled at her friend. She was wearing a wrapper not unlike the one Claudia had worn earlier and her hair was still disheveled from the night. Claudia, who was several years older and beginning to develop tiny wrinkles, was rather glad to see that Emma didn't look as pretty early in the morning as she did later in the day.

"I'm always glad to see you," Emma said as she sipped her hot cocoa.

"I've met Miss Farnell." Claudia made it sound as if the experience had been most harrowing.

"You have my deepest sympathy."

"What do you mean?" Emma paused with a muffin half to her mouth. "Sympathy in what way?"

"You don't have to pretend with me. I know she's living at Whitefriars."

Emma put the muffin back on her plate. "She's still there?"

"I saw her there only yesterday afternoon. She had been shopping and returned to the house as if she owned it."

"I had assumed she had gone to stay with Camilla. She's still at Whitefriars? With Micah?"

"She's simply awful. And that hair!" Claudia covered her mouth as if she were shocked all over again. "I thought I would fall off my chair when she came in! She had made no effort even to pin it back from her face. And she didn't sit like a lady. Granted, she may have been tired from shopping, but that doesn't give a person license to loll about in a chair like a man."

"Did she happen to mention when she plans to leave?" Emma said, then began nibbling at the muffin in a way that reminded Claudia of a rabbit.

"Not a word about it." Claudia leaned closer. "I don't want to further alarm you, but I don't think we're any kin to her at all."

Emma frowned, her face pinched and waspish. "I thought she might be one of Cousin Amos's granddaughters. You know he had a dozen children, and by now the grandchildren would be about Miss Farnell's age."

"I thought that as well, but I looked in some family records, and Cousin Amos never named one of his daughters Helen. Miss Farnell said that is her mother's name."

Emma's frown darkened. "If she isn't one of our cousins, then who is she, and what's she doing at Whitefriars?"

"Those were my questions exactly. I have the address of one of Cousin Amos's daughters, and I intend to write her and ask if they have ever heard of Miss Jody Farnell." Claudia spoke the name as if it were a plague.

"You must word it carefully. If she is a cousin, we don't want to offend the family."

"If she's a cousin, I'm a billy goat."

"What must I do?" Emma pleaded. "If she's there under false pretenses, I can't allow her to stay." Emma's eyes widened. "She could be after Micah and doing goodness knows what at this very minute! I haven't liked her since I met her at my party. I thought at the time it was odd of Micah to bring her and not Camilla, but since Camilla had a sick child, I told myself there was nothing to worry about."

"Men can't be trusted. I ought to know. I've been married several years now. Once the ring is on your finger, you're safe. Until then, you can't trust their word in anything."

"My sentiments exactly." Emma bobbed her head firmly. "Even Micah is suspect, evidently. I thought since we became engaged he would behave himself, but I guess I was wrong."

"The engagement is the most precarious time of all!" Claudia drew herself up as if she were amazed that Emma didn't know that. "They sense the end of their freedom, and we have to try ever so much harder to be sure they do as we wish."

"You're right, of course. Mama said I should ask him questions about Miss Farnell, but I thought she would be gone by now. Micah knows I don't like her. He must have noticed that I didn't make any effort to talk to her at the party or to invite her to the wedding."

"Men never notice anything. Vincent lives in the same house with me and he never hears a thing I say."

"Miss Farnell must leave. I'll tell Micah she has to go. I know! I'll tell him I want to start decorating whatever room she is using as my own bedroom so it will be ready for me when we marry."

"No, no. You shouldn't tell him you'll want separate rooms until after you're married. Don't you listen to a word I say?"

"I remember now. You did say that. But surely he won't really expect me to sleep in his room. You and Vincent don't have to share a room, and neither do my parents."

"Men can be particularly obstinate about that. He will expect it."

"Then what excuse can I use to make Miss Farnell leave?"

Claudia tried not to show her impatience. Emma was pretty, but she was short on intelligence. "Go to him and demand it as his future wife. Not in a brash way, of course, but firm enough that Micah will understand what you mean."

"Yes. That's exactly what I'll do! I'll tell him I won't be happy until she's back in Tennessee."

"Good. When you leave Whitefriars, come and tell me all he said."

*   *   *

Micah smiled when he saw Emma in his parlor. "Gideon said I had a visitor. I didn't expect you to come by. I'm afraid neither of my sisters is here." He knew Emma set great store by proprieties and that she would not want to stay without a woman in attendance.

"I know," Emma said in her little-girl voice. "I want to talk to you alone. We *are* alone, aren't we?" She looked around the room as if she thought someone might be lurking there to eavesdrop.

"Yes, we are." He had almost said that Jody had gone riding, but realized in time how rather domestic that might sound to Emma. "You look beautiful today. That's my favorite color on you."

Emma smiled and blushed. The feather of her pink hat curled flirtatiously about her cheek. "There's something we must discuss."

"Oh? What's that? I thought you had decided on the china pattern and flatware."

"This is something almost as important. At least it is to me. I'm unhappy."

"You are?" He looked at her in surprise. He had thought she was so deep into their marriage plans that she had no room in her head for unpleasant thoughts. "Unhappy with me?"

"Yes, indeed. I understand Miss Farnell is still here at Whitefriars." She contrived to look like a wounded puppy as she batted her eyelashes up at him.

"That's right."

"A certain little bird told me that she looked as if she had moved in to stay."

"That little bird wouldn't be named Claudia, would it?" He had known his sister was upset,

184

but he hadn't expected her to go to Emma.

"I'm not at liberty to say. I gave my word." Emma stepped nearer to him and began toying with the silk fringe on her reticule. "How long does Miss Farnell expect to stay?"

"I have no idea. It would be rude of me to ask a thing such as that." Micah had tried not to think of her leaving at all. Jody fascinated him beyond reason, even though he was engaged to be married to someone else. Micah tried to turn Emma's mood with a smile. "You wouldn't ask a guest when she expected to leave. Now would you?"

"I've never had a guest like Miss Farnell. I don't think she's in our family at all." Emma pouted prettily. "Mama asked me how we're kin after you left my party and I didn't know what to tell her. Is she one of Cousin Amos's granddaughters?"

"Possibly. I'm not that good at sorting out family relationships." He had hoped no one would question Jody's exact place in the family. "We have so many cousins, who can keep up with all of them?"

"Claudia can. She's going to write Cousin Amos and ask if there's something about Miss Farnell that we ought to know. There's just something about her that doesn't seem right." She gazed up at him beseechingly. "Do you know what I mean?"

"She's an extremely unusual woman." He had found himself thinking about Jody far more than was proper for a promised man, but he couldn't stop himself. She was, indeed, unusual.

Emma let her eyes fill with tears. "Oh, Micah, I feel so awful about this."

He went to her in concern. "Are you crying? Has something happened that I don't know about? What did Claudia say to you?"

She put her hands on his chest and let her cheek and part of her hat rest against him. "It's breaking my heart that you are here with her. You have no idea what people are saying about it."

Micah automatically put his arms around her. "Who else have you been talking to?"

"After you left the party everyone was speculating about Miss Farnell. The men even winked at each other when they said her name. They thought I didn't see, but I did." She lifted her head to look up at him with confused innocence. "What did they mean by that, Micah?"

He frowned. "I have no idea." The thought that people were saying things about Jody angered him. She had done nothing to harm anyone. "Who was still there? Will Breaux and who else?"

"No, Will left just after you did. I was talking to the Theriot brothers and James Mouton."

"I see." Those men had never been particular friends of Micah and were known to be rather wild when they were away from the gentling influence of the ladies. "I wouldn't worry about what they say."

"But I have to. I'm to be your wife and I don't want a scandal to be attached to you."

"A scandal? Because of Jody?" He had told himself that her posing as a cousin would prevent gossip.

Emma drew back. "You call her by her first name? As you do me?" Her chin quivered delicately.

"Emma, be reasonable," he said with a calming smile. "She's a cousin!"

"Even Mama doubts that, and you know Mama never has a bad word to say about anyone." Emma lowered her eyes. "Papa even suggested that she might have come here looking for a husband and that she might have you in mind."

Micah let his arms drop and turned away from her. "I can hardly believe my ears. All this has been said behind my back about a houseguest at Whitefriars? I've a good mind to pay your father a visit." He felt the anger building and tried to defuse it. If he was to marry Emma, it would not do to call out her father.

Emma stamped her foot, her curls jiggling. "I want you to send her away. Today!" She bent at the waist as she buried her face in her hands and sobbed. "Oh, Micah! See what discord she has caused?"

Micah went back to her and took her in his arms. He had never seen Emma exhibit anything approaching a temper, and what he saw brought a smile to his face. It was like watching a kitten spit and pretend to be ferocious. "There, now. Don't cry. You sound as if your heart is breaking, and I can't have that."

She raised her face, and her eyes were drier than he had assumed they would be. "Then you'll send her away?" Her dewy eyes sparkled with hope.

"No, Emma. I can't do that and remain a gentleman. You wouldn't have me be rude, surely."

"She could go to Camilla's house. They must have plenty of room for her. She needn't stay here

187

Elizabeth Crane

at Whitefriars." She drew a quivering breath. "I had hoped to send some of my things over in a day or so. You know, my linens and flatware—things like that." She lowered her head and toyed with a button on his vest. "It would be like starting our marriage, almost."

"You can do that with Jody in the house."

"Please don't keep referring to her in that informal way. It troubles me."

"Emma, I believe you're jealous." The realization struck him. "That's why you're so upset! You're jealous of Jody!"

"I have every reason to be. If Papa is right and she's come here to find a husband, what better man could she find than you?"

"If that's all it is, I can reassure you. Jody—Miss Jody—didn't come here to find herself a husband. She has no intention of marrying anyone in Joaquin or of staying here at all."

"She told you that?"

"In a roundabout way. She doesn't want any ties with us, and she isn't looking for a permanent place in my home." He managed to hide from Emma how difficult it was for him to admit that.

"I wish I could believe you. I hate to say it, Micah, but some women, well, they lie." She made her eyes round and innocent. "I know it's hard for you to believe, but it's true."

"I'm not as gullible as you seem to think. I've heard lies before. I have reason to believe Miss Jody is telling me the truth."

Emma's eyes again brimmed with tears. "What on earth would I do if I were to lose you?" she asked in the smallest of voices.

Micah held her close. He didn't feel the emotional swell that he had once felt when holding Emma close. If anything, the emotion he now felt was more akin to pity. He frowned and tried not to breathe in the feather on her hat. Emma was the most logical choice for his wife, and he had honestly believed that, in time, love would develop between them. Occasionally he had even thought that love was flowering. Now, however, he felt no more toward her than he would toward one of his sisters. Should he not be more excited to embrace the woman he intended to marry, especially since she had braved censure and come to his house unchaperoned?

Jody had left the house with the intention of going for a ride. She was accustomed to leading a more active life than she had found at Whitefriars, and she was looking forward to being alone for a change. Whitefriars was filled with people and she had begun to feel claustrophobic. Managing to convince the stable hand that she should ride astride and not sidesaddle hadn't been easy. He had argued, but she had been firm. The last thing she needed was a broken arm or leg from falling off a horse. Before mounting, however, she had remembered she had forgotten to tell Micah she would be home in time for dinner and stopped to do so.

As she went into the house, she was aware that the servants were watching her in their covert way. She knew they must all be speculating about her, wondering where she had come from and whether she was someone to fear. Bessy had apparently lost her fear of her, but she was resisting all the efforts Jody made to befriend her. Jody tried to remember that Bessy had clear memories of being a slave and likely had psychological scars from it, but Jody had hoped to plant the idea of equality in the woman. In her own time, she thought, she and Bessy would have become friends.

She went down the hall and looked in the library, but Micah wasn't there. She started to call out to him, but something stopped her. Instead, she went to the parlor and looked in the open door.

Micah was there, embracing Emma. He was smiling down at her, and Emma was gazing up at him as if he were the only man on earth. All the breath left Jody, and she heard her pulse pounding in her ears, but she couldn't turn away.

"There now," Micah was saying gently. "Do you feel better now?"

Emma nodded, her face as innocent and as blank as a child's. She managed a tremulous smile.

Jody stepped back to avoid being seen. Pain coursed through her. In the past few days Jody had found herself watching Micah and listening to the cadence of his voice, wondering what it would be like to kiss him again, to have his arms around her, to have him look at her as if she were the only woman in the world for him. She had tried to stop the thoughts, but they had refused to leave her mind.

What she felt wasn't jealousy; it was searing pain. She couldn't be jealous when she had no right to him. This pain was deeper than such a petty emotion. She knew now why the poets called this feeling brokenhearted. That was exactly how she felt.

Suddenly she became afraid someone might see her and know what she was thinking. Blindly she ran back the way she had come and out of the house toward the barn. She kept her face stiff to stem the buildup of tears, but as soon as she was handed onto the horse, she felt the tears winning. She nudged the animal into a canter and rode away from the barn before the stable men could see how upset she was.

She had no idea where she was going. All she wanted to do was to put distance between Micah and herself. The horse carried her around the trees and toward a stream that wound behind Whitefriars to join with the Petite Coeur River. Jody let the horse go where he pleased.

Trees closed around her and she welcomed the shield they provided. No one from Whitefriars could see her here. She let the horse slow to a walk and reined him in beside the stream. Dismounting, she led him to the water and let him drink as she sat on a mossy rock.

She was being foolish. She couldn't fall in love with a man who had died half a century before her own birth. But here she was in his time, apparently here to stay, and she had fallen in love with him. Jody bit her lower lip and tried to tell herself it was simply a biological urge. Micah was handsome and virile in a way that sent tremors of excitement racing through her. But that was not all it was. She had found herself listening to the way he talked about Whitefriars as if it were a beloved person, and she had seen the respect in

Gideon's eyes when he spoke to Micah.

Their minds seemed in tune. She remembered coming downstairs one morning and seeing a lemon yellow stream of sunlight making rectangles of gold on the parlor floor. Micah had come into the room at the same moment and had noticed the same thing. He hadn't commented on it, but their eyes had met. He had smiled, and they had watched the sunlight together in silence.

Jody had never known this kind of togetherness with a man. There had been men she had cared for, but none of them had understood her thoughts so thoroughly that no words were necessary between them.

She touched a trailing of pale green Spanish moss that hung like a beard from the tree. All this was gone in her own time. The stream had dried up or been diverted, the trees had been cut, and a parking lot had been put in its place. Work had been started on a discount store that would stand in about the same spot where now stood a magnificent old magnolia with glossy leaves. Most of the pastures remained, but they were no longer a part of Whitefriars. There were fewer conveniences in Micah's time, but his presence made up for the loss.

Jody stood and walked along the stream, the horse following docilely behind her. Since coming here, she had felt no pressure of paying bills, no worry about making a living or having her investments pay off. Although she was still reluctant to admit it, she was beginning to hope she might stay here.

But in her mind, staying in Micah's time meant staying with Micah. If he married Emma that would be impossible. Not only would Emma never welcome her in the house, but Jody wouldn't be able to stay anyway. Not and feel about Micah the way she did.

Did Emma love him? What if he loved Emma? Jody had been convinced that he didn't until she saw him embracing Emma in the front parlor. He had looked as if he had been about to kiss her. Tears rose again at the memory. Jody knew she had no right to him, but that didn't matter in the way she felt.

How long had she loved him? She couldn't remember when it had begun, but she also couldn't clearly recall a time when she hadn't. It was as if when she came here, she had settled in a place where she already belonged and had picked up a strand of life where she had left off. She neither understood it nor could she deny it. Loving Micah was the easiest thing she had ever done.

But Emma evidently loved him, too, or at least she wanted him for her husband. Micah wanted Emma in return or he wouldn't have proposed marriage to her. Jody told herself that the sooner she faced the facts, the sooner she would be able to accept what had to be. She had too much principle to try to win Micah away from his fiancée. But she had too much love for him to simply go away and let matters take their course. If only, she thought, he didn't love Emma, it would be different.

Maybe Micah was supposed to marry Emma. Maybe it all fit into some grand scheme far beyond what human thought could conceive. Maybe Jody's arrival had truly been no more than an accident and she would be ruining the divine plan if she made a life for herself here.

On the other hand, how could Micah love a featherbrain like Emma? Jody hadn't heard Emma say anything of intelligence during the party at The Oaks. Emma was like a little girl playing dress-up, acting as if she were an adult only for the time being. She couldn't imagine Emma being clever enough to engage Micah in a conversation about anything that really mattered.

She stopped walking, and the horse draped his head over her shoulder in a bid to be petted. As Jody rubbed the velvety skin of his nose, she said, "Be glad you're a horse. It's not easy being a person. Especially not when you know how some things are going to work out."

If Micah married Emma, as he evidently would without Jody's intervention, his line of descent would be gone by the time Jody bought Whitefriars. What if he didn't marry Emma and married Jody instead? Might they not have children who would be of different stock? Children who might have more children who would love Whitefriars as much as did Micah and Jody?

She walked back to the meadow and gazed across the field at Whitefriars. A lone rider was heading in the direction of The Oaks. No doubt it was Emma, and Jody was glad to know she had left. From this distance, Whitefriars looked so peaceful and serene. As she watched, Micah came out of the house and crossed to the blacksmith shop. She was too far away to see his face, but she would have recognized his walk anywhere.

She wished either that she had never come or that she could be sure of staying. Knowing that would have a great influence on how she handled her love for Micah. If she were destined to leave him, it would be a tragedy for him to love her as much as she cared for him.

Chapter Ten

Will Breaux sat down beside Jody on the porch steps and gave her a lazy smile. "I can't tell you how glad I am that you've come to Joaquin. Once Emma was spoken for, I thought I'd have to remain a bachelor forever."

Jody smiled, unable to refrain from being amused by the man's tactics. "I'm not interested in marrying anyone, especially not a man who proposes to me twice in less than a week. What would you do if I said yes?"

"I'd proclaim myself the happiest of men and ask Micah to be my groomsman."

"You've got quite a line, as we say where I come from." Jody gazed down the drive toward the main road. Early autumn had turned the sweet gum trees to vivid shades of gold and red, but the rest of the woods remained deep green. "Tell me, Will, what do women do around here if they decide not to marry?"

"They stay with their families and become doting aunts."

"What if they have no family?"

He thought for a minute. "I suppose those who don't enter the convent live alone, earning their living as needlewomen or as clerks in stores. Why do you ask?"

"Just curious."

"You're the last one to need to worry about becoming an old maid. Why, you're still in the bloom of youth. Besides, I'll marry you and save you from a lonely old age."

"I have a good mind to take you up on that and see how fast you wriggle out of it." She looked down at her lap and pleated the lace that trimmed a ruffle of her dress. "What are people saying about me?"

Will glanced at her, then smiled. "They say you're putting life back in the parish. We had grown dull until you came here."

"Be straight with me." At his blank look, she said, "Tell me the truth."

"A few wonder if you're really Micah's cousin and speculate as to why you've come here."

She nodded. "I thought there must be talk about me. Why is everyone so eager to mind other people's business?"

"No one around here ever met anyone like you. There's something mysterious and foreign about you. Not just because you come from the States—it's something more. I can't quite put my finger on it."

"I understand." She stood and walked the length of the porch, then leaned on the rail to look out over the pasture. Where she had once become accustomed to seeing a neighboring farm and storage shed, she now saw grasses waving beneath the wind and horses grazing. Beyond the pasture were fields of cotton. She knew cane was planted past that, and that all of it was a part of Whitefriars. "Did you ever go to a place you've never been before and feel as if you belonged there?"

"Never, but then, I haven't done much traveling. I don't count my days in the army. We were too busy watching for the enemy to pay attention to the scenery."

"Was Micah in your company?"

"I was in his. Micah was the commanding officer. He was quite a hero. If we had had more like him and more horses of the caliber he raises now, we might have won the war."

Jody made no comment.

"Micah doesn't talk about himself much," Will went on to say. "Maybe that's because he had so much responsibility at such an early age. He was master here at eighteen, you know. He was responsible for not only managing Whitefriars, but for seeing that his younger sisters made good marriages."

"I hadn't thought of that. Camilla must have been only fourteen, and that would have made Claudia sixteen. They would have been at the most difficult age."

"I don't know how difficult they were. By then they were almost old enough to be married."

Jody tried to imagine herself having been ready for marriage at fourteen or sixteen. At that age, she had been more interested in planning slumber parties with her girlfriends than in boys. "I haven't met Vincent yet. What's he like?"

"He's a good man. He's a bit older than Claudia, but that's not unusual. Personally, I think she chose him because she knew she would be able to train him the way she wanted him. Vincent's first wife died soon after their marriage, and he's so afraid of losing Claudia that he's given her more rein than most men would have."

"I can see how that would be true of Claudia. She was here the other day and made it clear that she doesn't like me. I suspect she's putting pressure on Micah to get rid of me."

"Micah is a gentleman. He won't have you cut your visit short. How long will you be staying, if I might ask?"

"I wish I knew. It could be for quite a while." She turned and leaned back on the rail. "I hope I don't wear out my welcome. I know Micah has his own life to lead."

"Micah isn't complaining."

She looked up at him. "You've talked to Micah?"

"Of course. We often meet for coffee in the afternoon at my house. He often talks about you." Will gave her an oblique glance. "If Emma were to know, she'd be jealous."

"He talks about me? What does he say?"

"It isn't so much that he told me things about your childhood or your plans for the future, as it is that he seems to punctuate every sentence with 'Jody thinks' or 'Jody said.' I don't believe he is aware he does it."

Jody felt a warm glow build in her and she smiled. "He does?"

Will moved closer to her. "Miss Jody, please

don't think I'm too forward, but as Micah's best friend, I have to remind you that he's engaged to be married, and that you could very easily break his heart."

"No, I couldn't." Her smile faded. "Emma was over yesterday and I saw them embracing in the parlor. He loves her. I'm not trying to come between them."

"I never implied that you were doing it intentionally. Micah never says what Emma thinks."

"It seems to me that he would if he cared for her. Is it possible that he doesn't love her? As his best friend, you're in a position to know."

Will sat on the rail beside her. "Why do you want to know?"

"It's none of my business. Forget I asked. I only want him to be happy."

"And you don't think he will be with Emma?"

"Do you?"

Will shrugged. "Emma is pleasant and she's pretty. Her name is as old as the Deverouxs'. Her land borders on Whitefriars."

"That doesn't have anything to do with a happy marriage. Do they have anything in common?"

Will laughed. "What do you mean? They love their homes and the South, and each knows what is expected of him in life."

"Is that enough? Does he love her?"

Whatever Will might have said was interrupted by Micah's stepping out onto the veranda. "I thought I heard voices out here. Hello, Will."

"Hello, Micah. I thought you'd be riding the fields by now. I noticed the cane was being cut."

"I just came from there. Harvest is going well." He looked at Jody. "I left so early, I didn't have a chance to see you today." He smiled at her, and she felt it all the way to her heart.

Jody felt she should break eye contact with him but couldn't bring herself to do so. Instead, she said, "I had thought I might ride out and see the harvest after a while. I've never seen cane being cut before." Although she tried to keep the conversation impersonal, her voice came out softer and sweeter than she had intended. With great effort she made herself look away from him.

Will gazed from one to the other. "Maybe you'd like for me to send some of my men over to help. My cotton is finished for the year, and they don't have much to do until we plow again."

"Thanks. I could use the help. I'm shorthanded this year." He was still looking at Jody.

"Sometimes I miss the old days," Will said. "When it was time to harvest the cane, the slaves worked in shifts around the clock. Cane doesn't get fully ripe here; we have to let it stay in the field as long as possible, then cut it before the first frost."

"Cotton prices are still dropping," Micah said as he went to the rail and sat beside Jody. "I'm wondering if I should plant it again next year."

"I wonder if you're too far north to grow rice," Jody said. She could feel Micah's eyes upon her and it was making her nerves tingle with excitement. She didn't dare let Will see how Micah's presence was affecting her.

"Rice?" Micah asked.

"Grow rice as a crop?" Will looked past her thoughtfully at the field. "I never heard of growing rice."

Jody knew she had made a mistake but saw no

way of correcting it. "It's grown in level fields that can be flooded. I've seen rice fields, and someone somewhere must know how to do it."

"Rice," Micah said, as if he were turning over the possibility in his mind.

"You must be remarkably well-traveled," Will said. "Where did you see these rice fields?"

"South Texas. Joaquin may be too far north. Forget I said it."

"I never heard of rice being grown in Texas," Will said.

"Jody has seen more than most young women," Micah replied. "If she saw rice fields, it must be possible. I think I'll look into it."

"You do that. I'm going to stick to cotton. Prices may not be good now, but if we hold out long enough, they'll rise. They have to. Cotton is still in demand, and it's always been a safe crop."

"What do you do with the cane once it's cut?" Jody asked.

"We make molasses and sugar and sell it in Shreveport."

"You make it here? Could I see how it's done?"

"You care?" Will stared at her. "It's a messy business. You wouldn't enjoy it as an outing."

Micah studied her face. "If you want to see it being done, I'll show you." He stood and took her elbow as they went down the porch.

Jody was beginning to enjoy being treated as if she might fall down at any moment. She also was beginning to notice this was an acceptable physical contact in a time when holding hands in public was generally forbidden. She could feel Micah's warmth through the thin fabric of her sleeve, and she no longer felt the urge to say she could manage on her own.

The syrup barn was behind the one used for horses. There were several people milling about, most of them children. One of the older women was tying shelled pecans to strings and letting the children dip them into a cup of hot cane syrup. The children were crowding close for a taste of the rare treat.

Inside, the noise was greater. At one end of the barn Jody saw a mule walking about a millstone that was pressing the liquid out of the cane. A half-grown boy with a switch was keeping the mule on the move as the adults fed the purplish stalks of cane into the press.

The liquid was gathered in the largest size of the various kettles being used. When the kettle was full, men carried it to the women outside, who stoked the fires to boil it down. The aroma wasn't the most pleasant Jody had ever smelled, but she was fascinated by the process. The cane pulp was tossed to one side.

"What happens to that?" she asked Micah.

"That's called bagasse and we use it for fuel." He pointed to the kettles. "As the syrup boils down, it crystallizes into sugar. The molasses that's left is put into jars. As with the sugar, we sell what we don't intend to use. The sugar will be packed into barrels."

"It's a brown sugar," she said as she went closer. "I expected it to be white. I had wondered why we always have brown sugar for tea."

Will had been watching her. "I don't believe I've ever seen a lady so excited by watching cane being rendered into molasses and sugar. My sisters don't have any interest in it at all, and I doubt they know or care where their sugar comes from."

"I do. I'm interested in everything." Jody leaned forward to watch several men straining to lift a heavy pot onto the iron arm over the fire. "I love to learn." Just past the fire, a tall woman was standing apart from the others. When Jody noticed the woman was staring at her a chill shivered through her. She nudged Micah. "Who's that?"

He followed her gaze. "Iwilla. She's too old to do strenuous work like this, but she always comes out to watch."

Iwilla stood tall and straight, her gray hair hidden by the tignon she wore, and her arms circled by woven bracelets. An amulet in a beaded bag hung from her neck, and there was another hanging from her belt. Even though she wore the same type of nondescript dress as the other women, on Iwilla it looked distinctive. Her skin was dark but had a reddish sheen to it, and her face was almost unwrinkled even though it was the face of an old woman. The hatred within her was expressed from her widespread feet to her flaring nostrils.

Jody took a step backward. "I think I've seen enough."

Micah hesitated, as if he were considering giving Iwilla a sharp word, but since the woman was doing nothing but staring, he turned away. "I think we all have."

Jody heard Will talking as they went back to the house, but her thoughts were elsewhere. Iwilla was more fearsome than Micah had led her to believe.

*   *   *

That same afternoon, when Emma entered Simpson's Dry Goods, she headed, from long habit, toward the bolts of cloth. She wanted to buy a length of material to make a new dress for the cooler weather ahead. Claudia had planned to accompany her, but at the last minute had changed her mind. Emma sometimes wondered if she and Claudia were as close as she usually assumed. Because Emma seldom thought for very long on any given subject and because she rarely thought for any length of time about a subject that was unpleasant, she quickly put it from her mind.

The lighter weight cottons had been moved to the back of the store and the more conspicuous shelves now held the heavier bombazine, kerseymere and worsted. The salesman George Percy, who usually sold the gloves, was helping the saleswoman lift and stack the large bolts. Emma knew George from previous trips and she ignored him as she always did.

She went to where the lace was displayed on paper cards and chose a cream variety that would be pretty with her blond hair. Moving slowly down the row, she held the lace to first one bolt, then another.

"May I help you, Miss Parlange?" George said as he scampered to her side.

"No, thank you. I'll wait for Miss Baker." She never gave him so much as a glance.

George shifted his weight to the other foot. "Miss Baker said for me to see to you because she was busy."

Emma's head jerked up. "She's too busy to wait

on me?" Ice could have formed on her voice.

"No, no. I never meant it that way. I mean she has her hands full. Since she's head of this department, she has to sign in the new material. It's being delivered at the back door now."

Emma looked around. Miss Baker was nowhere to be seen. "What sort of material is being delivered? I'm looking for something to make a dress."

George ducked his head a couple of times and tried out a grin or two. "There's some beaver wool."

"I said I'm making a dress, not a cape. I couldn't stand up in a dress made of such heavy material." She automatically gazed up at him as she did at every man over the age of twelve. "I'd be absolutely smothered by it."

George blushed scarlet all the way to his starched collar. "Yes, ma'am. I wasn't thinking. You're such a little slip of a woman. We have some nice bolts of poplin." He lowered his eyes and added shyly, "There's some blue just the color of your eyes."

Emma regarded him thoughtfully. She had never liked him, but she was impressed by anyone who knew the color of her eyes. "I'd like to see that."

George made a jerky bow and hurried off to get the cloth. Emma continued down the aisle comparing the color of the lace to material. She found a pale yellow worsted and she put her head to one side to debate whether or not it would look good on her. The color was perfect with the lace, but sometimes yellow made her skin appear jaundiced. She wished Claudia was there to give her advice. She always relied on Claudia's instincts.

In no time George was back, a bolt of clear blue in his arms. Emma had to admit that if her eyes really were this color they must be pretty indeed. George laid the bolt on the top of the others and unwrapped a length. "Feel this. It's as soft as kitten fur."

Emma pouted her lips and looked up at him. "Is it really the color of my eyes?"

George swallowed and nodded vigorously. "It is indeed. It couldn't be more like them if it was made to match."

Emma smiled and made a dimple appear in her chin. She was beginning to like George better than she had thought possible. If only he would stop bobbing up and down like a toy on a string, he would be rather nice looking. She fingered the cloth. The silk strands in the wool gave it a soft feel and the corded surface was prettily done. She tried the lace beside it. The combination wasn't pleasing.

"Here. Let me. If I may?" George bowed as he took the lace from her and trotted back to the lace display. He picked up a card with a silvery hue and came back. "Look at this. Isn't it pretty?"

Emma was doubtful. "I never wear gray. I'm too young and I'm not in mourning."

"Yes, ma'am, but this isn't exactly gray, it's more blue. It would be too bright for mourning. Look how pretty it goes with this blue."

"I have to admit it's not bad." She glanced at him from the corner of her eye. He was only a bit taller than she was, not like Micah, who towered over her and made her feel half scared at times.

She held up the material and the lace beneath her face. "How would it look on me?"

George seemed speechless for a moment. "Magnificent," he breathed at last. "Simply magnificent."

"Good." Emma smiled with satisfaction. "I'll take ten yards of the poplin and twenty of the lace."

"If I might offer a suggestion, we also have new gloves. I have a pair that will exactly match this lace."

"I must have them." She followed him to the counter. "Do you think you have a pair small enough to fit me?" Her tiny hands were her pride.

"Your hands are delicate, but I think I do." George bent to search in a drawer. "Yes, indeed. Your hands are scarcely larger than a child's."

Emma warmed to the compliment. "I sometimes have to wear children's gloves to get a proper fit."

George found a small pair and put them on the counter. Emma pulled one on. She hated to admit that they were rather too snug. "A perfect fit. I'll take two pair."

"When I saw how tiny these gloves were, I thought to myself, 'If Miss Parlange doesn't buy them, they'll go to waste.' That's what I said to myself."

Emma arched her neck so her face was set off to the best advantage. "I believe you're flattering me, Mr. Percy. You do know I'm engaged to be married." She pretended to look miffed.

"So I've heard. I had heard you were." For an instant he looked crestfallen. "I never meant offense."

"None taken." She turned to go. "My buggy is at the corner, if you'll see that the parcels are sent there."

"Yes, ma'am. I'll do it myself."

Emma didn't pause. She had other stops to make. When George carried her purchases to the buggy she wouldn't be there. While it was pleasant having him admire her, she had a position to uphold. It wouldn't do to have him think she cared whether he admired her or not.

It had been over a week since Jody's unexpected arrival at Whitefriars, and still she had no clue as to how she had gotten there or whether she would ever get back to her own time. Micah had been a wonderful host; he was trying to make her as comfortable as he could by including her where possible in his normal routine. But even as desperately as she tried to fit in, she often felt out of place, and at the time, she was a bit edgy, fighting the temptation to be out of sorts.

"You're doing that all wrong," Jody said as she looked over Micah's shoulder at the notes he had made about repapering the rooms. "The pink should be in the room I'm using and the yellow in the one across the hall. And if you use this huge sunflower print, the room will be as oppressive as it is now."

"I've planned houses most of my life," Micah said with some impatience. "That room is on the north side and needs a warm color. Otherwise it will freeze anyone who tries to live there."

"I agree, but the sunflowers are too awful for words."

"Don't they teach tact where you come from?"

"They teach good taste. I had several decorator courses at college, and huge sunflowers are out."

"College." He looked at her as if he didn't believe her. "You attended college."

"Of course I did. I thought I had mentioned it."

"No, you haven't. What college did you attend?" He smiled at her as if he were humoring her.

"Louisiana State. Which one did you attend?" she challenged.

"Notre Dame. Perhaps you've heard of it?"

She looked at him in surprise. It had never occurred to her that he had gone to college, let alone a northern one. "Is that where you got your progressive ideas about slavery?"

"No, I'm able to have some ideas on my own."

"I wasn't trying to offend you. We're only having a discussion."

"If you were a man, we'd be having an argument. Need I remind you that Whitefriars is my home and that I may paint the walls purple if it pleases me?"

"That would be an improvement over sunflowers."

Micah gave her an exasperated look. "What would you suggest?"

"Early in the twentieth century someone will put pale yellow paper with a design of pink roses in that room. When I was stripping the walls, I particularly liked that paper."

"Has it occurred to you that the paper you are referring to may not have been designed yet?"

Jody came around and sat on the edge of his desk. "I never thought of that."

"The latest fashion is for darker colors and

larger prints. I had to look at dozens of samples before I found anything better than what's in there now."

Jody crossed her arms and tapped her heels against his desk as she thought. "What if I draw the design? Will someone be able to copy it onto wallpaper?"

"That's possible. If I can't find anyone to print it in Shreveport or New Orleans, I can send to Paris."

"You'd send to Paris, France, for wallpaper?"

"Of course. That's where this came from." He gestured at the library. "My parents bought most of their things from Paris. I haven't been there in years, but I know who to contact."

"I'll need paper and paint to create the example."

"Emma has paints you could borrow."

"I doubt Emma will be willing to loan me anything." Jody sometimes couldn't believe how obtuse Micah could be. "I'm not exactly her friend."

"You should be. You may be seeing a great deal of each other." At the stubborn expression on her face, he added, "Camilla has paints as well."

"They both paint?"

He looked puzzled. "All ladies are taught to paint, just as they are taught to sew."

"I'll ask Camilla if I may borrow hers. Now about this back room . . ."

"The nursery? There's no reason to change it as yet. It's bad luck to set up a nursery before the wedding."

"Since when are you superstitious?" She

sounded angry because she had not been prepared for him to mention his wedding to Emma. Lately she had found she had to steel herself for a discussion about Emma and his future.

"It's not so much superstition as it is common sense. Why do a nursery when there are other rooms that need attention more urgently? Now that I've decided to put brighter colors in the house, the dark ones bother me more than ever."

Jody was still upset. "Shouldn't you consult your bride before making all these changes?"

"I have. Emma prefers the rooms as they are now. If you'll recall, The Oaks is also dark."

Good manners prevented Jody from saying she had found The Oaks to be unpleasant in every way. "Then why are you making these changes?"

"Emma is my fiancée, not my ruler. I want to please her, but not when she's wrong."

"Micah, there's something we have to discuss. I've avoided saying anything about it for days, and I know you must have, too, but what happens if I never get back to my own time?"

He was silent for a moment. "You'll always have a place at Whitefriars. There's no reason why you can't continue to live right where you are from now on."

"Yes, there is," she said softly.

Micah rose and came to stand in front of her. "There are some things we can't discuss. My life was already patterned when you came here. I have commitments that I'm not at liberty to alter."

"I admit that my being here changes things, but there aren't many decisions in life that can't be changed. If you no longer want a particular future, you can change it."

"No, Jody, I can't. This is a matter of honor, mine as well as Emma's."

Her breath caught in her throat. "What are you saying, Micah?"

He paused, as if he were searching for the right words. "I've said too much already."

"You haven't said anything at all. Not really."

"If you leave, I can't stop you any more than I could have prevented your coming."

"Would you if you could?" She knew she was overstepping the boundaries again, but she couldn't continue speculating as to what he felt. She needed to know.

His gaze met hers. She could see the misery and confusion in the silver depths of his eyes. "If I could prevent you from leaving, I would," he said at last. "I'd keep you here at Whitefriars with me. But I have no way of controlling that. I keep thinking that I could be talking to you and have you simply disappear, or that I may wake up one morning and find you've gone."

"I know. I have no way of promising that it won't happen that way. But we all face that risk. Loved ones die or leave without warning. We never have a guarantee."

"How do you feel? If you had a choice, would you go or stay?"

Jody didn't know how to answer him. He was, after all, engaged to marry someone else, and she was trespassing in his life. "I think I would stay. I miss my friends and family and all the conveniences of my modern life, but I would want to stay here."

"Why?"

She turned her face away. "I'm not going to answer that."

"You see? You have principles, too. That's why we can't discuss this."

Jody gazed up into his eyes. "Not discussing it won't make it go away."

"No, but it's all we can do."

"Micah," she whispered as he leaned closer. He hesitated, as if he knew he should never do what he was about to do, then put his hand under her chin and lifted her face for his kiss.

The instant Jody felt the warmth of his mouth on hers, she opened her lips beneath his. She had told herself in days past that she had imagined how wonderful it had felt when he had kissed her in the buggy. Now she saw she had not given the memory full credit. She swayed toward him and put her arms about his neck. Micah pulled her to him, and his kiss deepened from chaste to passionate. Jody met his desire with an equal measure of her own.

When he pulled back she nearly fell off the desk. He backed away, then turned on his heels, but not before she saw the aching need on his face. She sat for a moment, looking at the broad expanse of his shoulders, then silently slid off the desk and left the room.

Chapter Eleven

Jody was finding it difficult to occupy her time. Everyone at Whitefriars seemed to have chores or interests that kept them busy, but she often found herself with hours when she had nothing to do. She had memorized every inch of Whitefriars and had even begun a diary, positive that if she managed to get back to her own time, she could perfectly restore Whitefriars to its present elegance. That activity, however, didn't serve to occupy her idle time now, or her thoughts.

For days she had successfully avoided being alone with Micah, hoping to avoid a repetition of the intimacy they had shared, which was neither right nor good for either of them. They, of course, had meals together, but servants were always present, and as soon as a meal was finished, Jody made herself scarce. Although Micah showed no signs of intentionally avoiding her, he also made no obvious attempt to seek out her company. Fortunately, he was pleasant enough in their conversations during mealtime that Jody was convinced he was not angry with her. Logic and reasoning assured her that a cooling off of their relationship was the right thing to do, and even though it was painful, she was doing her best.

Shortly after the evening meal one day, Jody went to the library in hopes of finding another book to read, and in her haste, she was upon Micah and he was aware of her presence before she could turn back. Not wanting to appear conspicuous, she nodded a greeting and approached his desk. "What are you doing?" she asked as casually as possible.

"I'm drawing up some plans for a house a friend of mine intends to build."

"May I see?" Her interest was piqued immediately. House plans were something she understood perfectly, and the subject of architecture seemed to be a safe topic for conversation.

"I doubt you'd be able to make heads or tails of it," Micah said with a smile. "I haven't drawn the outside of the house yet."

"Don't be so condescending. I may surprise you." She pulled the drawing around so she could see it better. "Two rooms up and two down?"

"It's called an 'I' construction. My friend is planning to marry and, as he's the younger son, he has no inheritance, nor will his bride. After their family grows he can build an addition on the back, here." Micah drew imaginary lines to indicate a wing behind the original house.

"It seems rather plain."

"It's what he can afford to build."

"Why not do it all one story? Is it a small lot?"

"I don't know what you mean. He has bought thirty acres."

"If he has that much space, I'd draw up a one-story. It would be more attractive than piling the rooms on top of each other like blocks."

"I rather doubt my friend and his wife would prefer a dog-trot cabin to this." Micah sounded as if he were trying to be polite, but it was clear that she was disrupting his thoughts.

"Not a dog-trot, a ranch-style." She took a pencil and a fresh sheet of paper and began to draw. "I'd put the living room in front and behind it, the dining room. That leads to the kitchen. Back here, I'd put a den if they can afford it. Then I'd put a hall with bedrooms opening off it. Like this. See?"

Micah leaned forward. "What did you call this? A living room? A den?"

"In my time, those are the names we use for what you call the parlor and the back parlor. As the family grows, the den could be added and maybe a playroom for the kids or more bedrooms if the family is large."

Micah picked up the paper and studied it. "How is it you're able to draw plans for houses and can't sew?"

"I'm an architect, not a seamstress. No one ever taught me to sew."

He pondered the house plan. "I've never seen anything like this house. Where are the stairs? Is there no upstairs at all?"

"One isn't needed. A one-story will be easier to build, since the men can work at ground level. I assume it's to be pier and beam, not slab?"

"I don't know what you're talking about."

"It doesn't matter. This plan is very adaptable. If the lot slopes, the living room or den could be lowered a step or even two. Then it would be a split-level," she added rather smugly.

"If I were to show this to Marcel, he wouldn't know what to think. Neither would Sally. The carpenters wouldn't know how to go about building it."

"I could show them. It's no different than building the first floor of the house you drew, only it needn't be so reinforced to support the second floor."

"And there are no stairs."

"They can have an attic if they want stairs. The steps could be put in a closet."

"What about air flow? My 'I' house has good ventilation. This central hall would block the movement of air."

Jody studied the plans. "What if we do away with the hall and have the bedrooms open off the den? The children can live in these two rooms and the parents' room can be built over here, off the living room."

"And have the mother so far from her children? No one would want a house like that. Where would the house servants sleep? Where is the governess's room?"

"That can be added after the children are old enough to need one. The house servants could live in rooms in the attic, I suppose."

"Then it will have a second story after all."

"Or they could live in separate units out back."

"That's more building. In mine, the rooms are in the attic and fit under the eaves."

"If you aren't willing to be flexible, forget I said anything." She tossed the pencil down. "I was only trying to help."

"I wasn't trying to make you angry." Micah leaned back in his chair as she perched as usual on the edge of his desk. "I'm intrigued. You say you've drawn up house plans before?"

"Yes, believe it or not, I'm rather good at it."

"And men followed your plans without question? You must have drawn them under a male pseudonym."

"Not at all. I was also on the building site along with the construction workers, hard hat and all."

"What do hats have to do with it?"

"The roles of the sexes won't always be as rigid as they are now."

He grinned. "Too bad."

She shot him a quick glance and decided he hadn't meant it as a double entendre, as a man of her time would have. He meant only that he liked knowing what was expected of him, and his sisters were comfortable in their roles as well.

Micah picked up the drawing again. "I'm not challenging your expertise, but I see another flaw. There are no fireplaces, and with the kitchen practically surrounded by the dining room and the den and the parents' bedroom, it would be dangerous in the event of fire."

"Someday there won't be a need for fireplaces and air currents to keep a house warm or cool."

"No? You expect people to automatically adjust to temperature like animals? I have to say I doubt that will happen."

"We use central heat and air conditioning," she countered. "The windows need not be opened all year round, and no one has to buy firewood unless he likes the looks of a fire."

He laughed, his white teeth flashing. "I love to talk to you. I never know what you will say next. No wonder my nieces and nephew love your stories."

"I'm not telling stories. It's true. They will be cooled and warmed by gas or electricity."

Micah still chuckled. "I've seen a demonstration of electricity. It's a pretty toy and can be dangerous, but as for making a climate, it's useless."

Jody sighed. "There's no use explaining to you. You've already made up your mind that I don't know what I'm talking about. Where I come from, you'd be considered a chauvinist and the bane of all women."

He rose from his chair and sat beside her on the desk. "Is that true? Women would really shun me?"

The twinkle in his eyes and his nearness had an immediate effect on her nerves. She knew she should move, but she couldn't and still stand her ground in this argument. "I know *I* would. Chauvinists make me see red. I know as much about houses as you do, probably more. I'm positive I know more in terms of my own century."

"It's an easy argument. How can I dispute it?"

He was much too close. She knew he was teasing her, and that her body was answering in exactly the way he had intended. She should have turned and left the moment she realized he was in the library. "You might at least give my plan some thought. Just because it's different doesn't mean it wouldn't work. If your friend needs an inexpensive house, mine may suit him better than the cracker box you drew."

"Now who's being insulting? I think you're a chauvinist as well."

"Women can't be. Only men."

"Who says? What is the proper term for a woman who thinks she knows better just because she's a woman?"

Jody frowned. "There isn't any such word as far as I know."

"There. You see? You *are* a chauvinist. I've proved it."

"You've proved nothing. I didn't make up the language."

"No? Someone did. If men are off building houses and women are teaching babies to talk, who do you think invents new words for the language?"

"I never thought of it that way before." She struggled to find a flaw in his reasoning but couldn't. She wasn't used to complicated twists and turns in conversation. Micah and his generation were masters when it came to the art of debating. "You confuse me."

"Do I? I didn't have that in mind. I was only giving you a different view of the same conversation. Don't people talk where you're from?"

"We'd rather watch TV or play games."

"I like games, too. What's TV? That magic box you told me about?"

"Yes. Only it's not magic, it's electrical."

"Electricity again. You seem obsessed by it."

"If you'd listen to me, you could learn a great deal," she snapped to quell the urge to touch him. She slid off the desk and went to the window.

"You could be ahead of your time. I could make you a wealthy man."

"I'm already wealthy." He came to stand beside her. "I own the land as far as you can see in every direction. Whitefriars is the most prosperous plantation in the parish. I don't need electricity." He reached out and brushed her hair back from her face. "Although I have to admit I enjoy learning about it."

His touch sent fires racing through her and her breath quickened. Jody couldn't understand why she felt this way every time he was near. No, he didn't even have to be near. She could get the same reaction from hearing his voice in the next room or by seeing him ride across the fields on one of his horses.

Trying to find a safer path for her thoughts, she said, "I'm still amazed that the Civil War didn't ruin Whitefriars. You could have lost everything."

"I know, and it's the War Between the States, not what you called it. That's the term the Yankees use for it. We had already seceded; therefore it was *not* a civil war."

"So how did you manage? It wasn't just that no troops found it. The markets were ruined and taxes were levied on everything."

"I know, but my trade was always primarily with France. As soon as the blockades were lifted, I resumed shipping as usual. I was even able to lend money and some of my hired hands to my neighbors—The Oaks, for instance—who might not have been able to harvest crops otherwise. It was a matter of careful planning and being willing to have some lean years in order to reap larger benefits. Also, I had a good overseer while I was gone to war and he carried out my instructions to the letter."

"Is he still here? I haven't met anyone who fits that description."

"No, he's dead now." Micah's voice hardened and he looked past her out the window. "It happened after the war was over and I was on my way home. He was in the forest and some bushwhackers found him. They shot him down in cold blood and left him in the woods."

"Were his killers ever punished?"

"By whom? After the war all the law and government was run by men who would have found in favor of the bushwhackers. After all, they only killed a former slave who was, I'm sure they thought, trying to rise above himself."

"He was black?"

"Why are you surprised? All the white men were fighting in the war, along with a number of black ones like Gideon. He was Gideon's father."

Jody nodded slowly. She was having to re-evaluate all her preconceived notions about the South. "Were you different from the usual slave owner, Micah?"

"Quite different from most. By the time the war broke out, I didn't own any slaves, you'll remember. Gideon and his father were loyal first to me and then to the cause I fought for."

"Even though that cause supported slavery." Jody still couldn't believe this. It went against all she had ever heard.

"I learned that a person will fight to keep a thing he knows and is familiar with over something he doesn't understand. It's impossible to

223

explain, but even slaves on plantations where they were constantly mistreated seldom tried to escape. I've never been able to make sense of it. That's why I participated in the Underground Railroad. If some of them found the courage to escape, I wanted to aid them. Otherwise they were almost certain to be recaptured."

"The more I learn about you, the more I admire you," Jody said in a soft voice. "It's a shame you didn't become a psychologist. You're making observations that won't be thought of for decades, until Freud's work becomes accepted, and even some that won't be popular ideas until Carl Jung comes along almost a century from now."

"I'm not sure just what observations you are referring to, but I accept your compliment."

As she gazed up at him, she tried to keep herself from touching the sunny pattern the lace curtains made on his cheek. Not touching Micah was becoming harder and harder.

"Jody, you're different from anyone I've ever known." His voice was soft and tender, as if he were feeling the same emotion she was experiencing. "We can talk about so many things. I've never told anyone how I felt about my former slaves and about helping others to escape. Even now I wouldn't want my neighbors to know about my work in the Railroad. Yet I tell you and it seems right to do so."

"For two people who are so different, we have a lot in common," she replied. "I can't explain it. Just when I think I have you pegged as a self-serving chauvinist, you say something that's so gentle and so empathetic that I want to . . ." She broke off. There were some things she couldn't say, not even to Micah.

"Come with me," Micah said. "I want to show you something."

Jody was glad to escape from the intimacy, but at the same time she regretted the break. When Micah was near she was filled with inconsistent emotions.

He escorted her to the stable, and soon they were riding across the fields in a direction Jody rarely took. When they reached the fence surrounding his property Micah leaned from his horse and unlatched the gate. After they had ridden through he fastened it again.

"Where are we going?" Jody asked as they rode away from town.

"I want you to see where Marcel will build his house."

She smiled. Micah might pretend to be amused at her house plan, but he was willing to prolong their discussion of it.

Marcel Howard's land lay along a ridge and was flanked all around by trees. At the base of the rise a small stream splashed and gurgled toward the Petite Coeur River, several miles away. Micah rode to the top of the ridge and dismounted, then helped Jody from her horse. He walked to the center of a clearing and stopped. "The house will be here."

Jody studied the spot with a practiced eye. "It's a good location. I'd put the den facing west. The sunsets will be spectacular from here."

"No, no. You can't put the main rooms facing east and west. What have they taught you? The narrow end of the house goes to the west."

"But then they'll have to leave the house to see the sunset. It would be so much nicer to watch it from inside."

"Jody, think. Where does the sun rise and set? We want to give it as little surface as possible to heat. The summers are worse here than the winters. The house must be positioned for coolness."

She frowned. What he said made sense, but it wasn't the only possible solution. "A tree could be planted to shade the house from the sun."

Micah laughed. "A tree would also obscure the sunset you're so determined to see. Knowing Marcel, he will be in town watching over his emporium until sunset and will see it on the way home every night. He won't expect to see it from inside as well."

"Where would you put the house?"

He paced off a rough square. "I'd put it here. With the main rooms facing south. There will be more light than on the north side, and in the winter it will be warmer."

"But that faces the house away from the road."

"You can't see the road from here. I would wind the drive around to approach the house from the south."

"That will mean more work."

"True, but it will be best. There will always be a breeze here, just as there is at Whitefriars, you'll notice. No trees are close enough to the house to obstruct it."

She turned in a slow circle. "If the house is built in an 'I' plan, the new wing will go that way, right?"

"That's right."

"You have a steep slope to the ridge there. I think my plan is better for this location." She paced off one side of her proposed house. "The living room and front bedroom will start there and end here. That makes an 'L' shape going in that direction. It will catch every breeze."

"You don't want breezes in the bedrooms."

"Why not? I've slept with my window open every night so I will be cool."

"I've heard night vapors are harmful to ladies." He looked at her doubtfully.

"Do I look as if I've been harmed? Why would 'vapors' hurt women if they don't hurt men? You were in the army. You must have slept outside most of the time. It didn't hurt you any either."

"It wasn't pleasant in the winter," he retorted. "Besides, men are made of stronger stuff than women."

"You just don't want to admit that my house is a better plan than yours. I'll bet Marcel's fiancée would like it better. She would have fewer stairs to climb during the day, if any at all."

Micah looked thoughtful. "She will have servants to do that."

"For now, maybe, but I can tell you, those days aren't going to last much longer. Eventually whoever lives in this house will be doing her own housework and tending her own children and doing whatever it takes to keep the house running."

"You paint a dismal picture of your time. Are women so hard worked where you come from?"

"We have more conveniences. Automatic washers and dryers, vacuum cleaners, electricity, telephones. If I wanted to go into town, I had a car,

227

and I could be there in a matter of minutes." She paused. "It's hard to believe I always took all these things for granted."

"And there really will be such a thing as air conditioning?" Micah said the words as if he were trying them out in his mouth. "It will keep the house cool?"

"And in the winter central heat will keep it warm."

Micah shook his head in amazement. "I sometimes wonder if you're telling me stories. I can't imagine such a world. And in only a hundred and twenty-one years. The last century and more haven't seen anything like that much change."

"You haven't heard the half of it. Man will go to the moon. A satellite will be sent deep into outer space and will take photographs of the planets as it passes by them."

He laughed. "Now I know you're pulling my leg." He came to her and caught her hand. "Come look at the stream. It's almost as pretty as the one behind Whitefriars."

Micah hadn't exaggerated. He pointed out trees that he said were dogwood and wild plum. Huge grapevines draped from the other assorted hardwood trees. "Muscadine grapes make the best jelly you've ever had," he said. "Camilla always puts up a supply for me each year, as well as wild plum. They have a flavor the cultivated trees can't match."

She walked beside the stream, her feet whispering in the leaves that lately had begun to fall from the trees. "It's a pretty place. I don't recall what's here in my time. I'm not sure I've ever come this way." She smiled back at him.

"Wouldn't it be something if I had, and found a century-old ranch-style house? I wonder how it would have been explained."

"Maybe that means Marcel will choose my design."

"Or maybe the house simply won't last that long."

He shook his head. "Houses are built to last nearly forever. Even cabins are sturdy enough to last centuries."

"True, but sometimes houses burn or are moved away."

"Moved away?" He grinned. "What do you think they would do? Pack it on a horse's back and carry it closer to town?"

She looked back at the rise. "I would still build the house I designed. I would be more than willing to draw up the blueprints for you."

"You can really do that?"

"I told you I can."

"I can tell Marcel and Sally about your idea and see what they say."

"You don't have to say it was my idea. I don't care about getting the credit, I only want to have something to do to occupy my days."

"You're bored?" He came to her, and together they walked farther downstream.

"I'm not unhappy, but I'm used to staying busy. Bessy won't even let me make up my own bed. I'm being pampered to distraction."

"Emma likes to be pampered," he said, as if he were thinking aloud. "I can't imagine her wanting to lift a finger around the house in any menial task. She would rather be sewing or painting."

"I'm not Emma," Jody pointed out more sharply than she had intended. "On second thought, you'd better tell Marcel that I drew the house plan. I may have to find a way to earn a living after you and Emma are married, and it won't hurt to have people know I have some talents."

"You can't go off on your own as if you were a man or had no one to take care of you." Micah looked offended at the very idea.

"I certainly can't live in the same house with Emma. We don't get along."

"How do you know? You barely know each other."

"I can tell. Take my word for it." She hadn't meant to say anything against Emma. Naturally Micah would have to take up for the woman he intended to marry. "Tell me one thing, though. Do you really love her?" She turned to face him.

Micah frowned down at her. "You have no right to ask me that."

"You don't have to answer. I only want you to think it out before your wedding and see how you really feel."

"Why do you dislike Emma? She has never said she dislikes you." Then his frown deepened, as if he were thinking of an instance when she might have hinted at such.

"No? Then she's more circumspect than I would have thought. That, or you wouldn't recognize the truth if it bit you."

"I'm not quite so dense as you seem to think." He scowled at her, but she could also see hurt in his eyes.

"I didn't mean to insult you. I shouldn't have said anything at all about Emma." She looked away. "Please forgive me."

"Of course," he said stiffly.

"All the same, I don't think Emma and I can live under the same roof. I can't impose on Camilla and her family, so that only leaves me the alternative of earning my own living. I'm trained to design buildings. It's how I've earned my living since I graduated from college. That's the most logical course for me to take."

"I'm not sure people around here would like to have a woman plan out their houses and stores. It doesn't seem quite proper for you to do a man's job."

"Then what do you suggest?"

"You could teach school. Or maybe work as a clerk in one of the stores, if you're determined to have a job."

"Wouldn't I earn more as an architect?"

"Only if people would hire you."

Jody turned away and started back toward their horses. "I don't fit in here, Micah. Maybe I never will."

"Or maybe you'll wake up tomorrow in your own time."

She glanced at him. "Do you still think that's possible?"

He shook his head. "Not anymore. I did for the first few days, but the longer you're here, the more certain it seems to me that you'll stay. On the other hand, how can we ever be sure?"

"I guess we can't be," she said reluctantly.

In silence, they returned to the horses. Jody caught her reins and stirrup and started to pull herself up onto the saddle, but Micah stopped her. "If you're here to stay, I'll take care of you.

I know you don't want to live at Whitefriars if Emma is mistress there, but I can buy you a house in town and pay your bills."

"I could never let you do that."

"I have to insist. No gentleman would do less."

She looked up at him. A breeze stirred his black hair and the sunlight looked warm on his skin. She had an almost irresistible urge to put her arms around him.

"What are you thinking when you look at me like that?" he asked softly.

Jody lowered her eyes. "Nothing. Never mind."

He put his fingers under her chin and lifted her head until she met his eyes again. "I have a feeling you're thinking something that could change both our lives."

"If I was, I could never tell you, could I?" She hoped he wouldn't insist. She had to be at least as honorable as he was and not force him to hear something he might regret.

"It's like a child making a wish for something and never telling. Sometimes such wishes can't come true. Some secrets shouldn't be kept."

She tilted her head to study him. "What are you saying, Micah? Do you really want me to tell you what I was thinking?"

For a moment he looked as if he would say yes, but then he stepped back. "As you say, some things are meant to remain a secret. Some wishes can't be fulfilled and therefore should never be spoken."

"You keep me confused," she said. "I never know what you want from me."

"I'm confused myself. I have been ever since you came here."

"I'm sorry if I confuse you. That wasn't my intention." She swung up onto the horse.

"I wasn't complaining." Before she could see his face and try to discern his meaning, he turned away and mounted his own horse, then reined toward Whitefriars.

Chapter Twelve

"Micah, I hope you won't think it presumptuous of me, but I must speak my mind," Claudia said as she accepted a cup of steaming coffee from Gideon.

"I was under the impression that you always did," her brother said with a smile.

"Don't be flippant. As the elder of your sisters, I feel it is my duty to instruct you as poor Mama would have."

"What have I done this time?" He tried to keep his tone light and not to frown. He hated it when Claudia took it upon herself to run his life. They never agreed on what he should be doing.

"You know exactly to what I am referring. It is Miss Farnell. Her being here in this house is a scandal."

Micah couldn't keep the displeasure he felt from his expression. "I have to remind you that she's a guest in my house."

"Exactly! The two of you will become the sensation of the parish. She cannot stay at the home of a bachelor and not expect people to talk. You know how gossip is around here."

Micah nodded to Gideon, who left and closed the door firmly behind him. "Jody is out riding now, thank goodness, or she might have overheard what you said. You've all but impugned her character!"

"I never did. I implied that if she is not that sort indeed, she ought to comport herself more decorously."

"You think Mama would have given me this advice? She never would have. All visitors were made welcome at Whitefriars, even the destitute ones. Don't you remember the time Cousin Alcide arrived with four of his children and stayed for nearly three years?"

"That was different. His wife had died and he had fallen on hard times. Besides, there were plenty of people about this place, serving as chaperons, and it was entirely different from your being here alone with Miss Farnell." Claudia jerked her head in a nod. "If I were Emma, I would never stand for it. That Emma is a saint!"

"There is nothing for her to be saintly about. Nothing is happening between Jody and myself that she couldn't know about." That was not strictly true. He remembered the kisses he and Jody had shared. Those kisses had touched him in a way Emma's chaste pecks never had.

"No one cares if you are innocent or not. Appearances say the opposite and that is what matters. I am constantly amazed that Miss Farnell's family countenances what she is doing.

Incidentally, I don't think she is really related to us at all, and if she is, it is not close enough to count."

Micah smiled, but it didn't reach his eyes. "Neither is Cousin Alcide. That doesn't keep him from being family."

"But we know *how* he is kin to us. No one has ever heard of this Miss Farnell before. Her name is not even Creole. How can she be our cousin?"

"Neither is my name, but I'm as Creole as you are. Mama happened to prefer American names. Maybe Jody's mother did, too."

"Stop calling her by her given name as if she were your sister or wife! Micah, if you speak of her this way to other people, what else can they think except the worst?"

"I don't really care what other people think. She prefers to be called by her Christian name."

"And that's odd, too. Have you ever heard of any lady who would prefer that? I certainly haven't."

"So what do you suggest I do? Drive her from my house and let her fend for herself on the roads?"

"Don't be ridiculous. If she is determined to stay in this area, she can go to Camilla's house. Or even mine, for that matter. I only mention Camilla's because it is known they have become friends, though I have no idea why."

"I can see Jody would be welcome at your house," he said dryly. "Thank you for the invitation."

"Why won't you listen to reason, Micah? It is not like you to be so stubborn. Not about something like this." Claudia lowered her voice even though they were alone in the room. "You are not falling in love with her, are you?"

Micah was silent. The soft noises of the house seemed loud by comparison. "No, I'm not falling in love with her," he responded, but the words felt false on his tongue.

"Then why did you hesitate? Micah, you have to keep your wits about you. Why, you are engaged to be married to Emma in April! You can't go off after some other woman!"

"I'm not." His voice was curt. "I'm not going to sit here and have you insult my guest. What if Jody walked in and heard what you're saying?"

"You said yourself that she is off riding somewhere. Besides, any woman who would listen to private conversations deserves to hear the worst about herself."

"If you were a man, I'd ask you to leave."

Claudia drew herself up. "If I were a man, I would take you to task even more harshly. I only wish Vincent would do as he should in this instance."

"This is even less Vincent's business than it is yours. I won't send Jody away and that's final. Did Emma send you?" he added suspiciously.

"No, that angel does not know I am here. You don't seem to realize what a treasure you have in her. A man would be fortunate to have such a wife, yet you seem ready to cast her aside."

"I'm not casting her anywhere." Micah sighed and rubbed his temple. Claudia could give anyone a headache. He disliked himself for wishing it would be so easy to rid himself of his promise to Emma as to simply cast it off. "I know what's expected of me. I knew it when I proposed marriage to her. It's not a thing a man does lightly."

"You couldn't prove it by your actions." Claudia finished her coffee and put the cup down with a clink. "I am afraid I have to insist that she leave. If you like, I will talk to Camilla about taking her in."

"You'll do no such thing. Jody stays. Claudia, does it ever occur to you that you may be wrong or that you might not have all the facts? I'm neither a fool nor a libertine. Jody is here for a reason and it's not something I'm at liberty to discuss."

Claudia drew herself up. "I hope this reason is not something you couldn't tell your sisters." She lifted her head high until she was looking down her nose at him.

"Good-bye, Claudia. It's too bad you have to cut your visit so short."

She glared at him, and for a moment he thought she would refuse to leave. Then she jerked herself to her feet and walked toward the door as if she had been starched. When she opened it she turned to give him a withering look, then exited, banging it shut behind her.

Micah went to the sofa and sat down. Slowly he leaned forward and rubbed his face with both hands. Claudia had always had a knack for getting under his skin, and she was worse lately than ever before. Or was it his guilty conscience that made her seem that way?

He was afraid he was falling in love with Jody—more than afraid, because he wasn't fighting it all that hard anymore. He enjoyed the sight of her at his table, the sound of her odd songs as she played with his nieces and nephew, the way her eyes sparkled when she laughed. Jody was more alive than any woman he had ever known. She didn't seem to care a fig about recipes or sewing and could talk about any subject as cleverly as any of his men friends. Micah had never been of the opinion that education spoiled a woman, but he had never met one as well educated as Jody. Even if she was exaggerating a bit—he couldn't name one woman who had attended a university and learned to be an architect—she was smart enough to carry it off.

He found himself wanting to know her opinion about everything or even to hear her talk about nothing at all. Even her silence intrigued him. He no longer doubted that she was from another time, and that meant she could tell him things that were beyond his, or any man's, comprehension. He couldn't fathom the sights her hazel-gold eyes had seen or the knowledge that was in her brain. He thought it might take the rest of his life to learn all there was to know about her. And that the years would be well spent.

Micah stared at the pattern in the carpet. What was he thinking of? He couldn't spend the rest of his life with her, or even another year. In April he would be married to Emma, and he knew the two women would never be content under the same roof. From what he was able to glean from Jody's conversation, she was not accustomed to households that included grandparents, aunts, and cousins, as he was. Emma was, but she didn't believe Jody was their cousin at all.

Worst of all, he knew Claudia was right about this. People would talk and probably already were.

He might not care for himself, but he would not have loose talk about Jody. Yet how could he ever bear to let her go? Or even to send her as far away as Camilla's?

Jody left her horse at the barn and walked up the path toward the house. To her right she caught a glimpse of the quarters and her steps slowed. Jody had never been one to run from her fears, and Iwilla was both a fear and a fascination. Taking a deep breath, she walked toward the double row of cabins.

As soon as she rounded the oleander bushes, she saw Iwilla sitting on the tiny porch of her cabin. Not allowing herself to hesitate, Jody walked directly to her. "Nice day, isn't it?"

Iwilla blinked. Jody had a feeling that was more surprise than the woman had registered in fifty years. "I was out riding and I thought I'd drop by and get to know you."

"I no talk to folks," Iwilla said coldly. "White folks not come here."

"Then you must be lonely." Without being asked, Jody sat down on the porch and leaned back on the support. "How are you feeling? Are you well?"

"Why you here?" Iwilla shifted uncomfortably on the wooden chair. "You come to see what I up to?"

"No, just being friendly." Jody knew she at least had Iwilla at a disadvantage. From the corner of her eye she could see the occupants of the other cabins collecting in small groups and glancing her way as if they were talking about her. Jody noticed the symbol painted over Iwilla's door.

"That's interesting. What is it?"

Iwilla stared at her, then at the bloodred symbol. "That sign of *Papa La Bas*. The devil. He protect me."

Jody didn't let her gaze waver. "Very interesting. So you really are into voodoo?"

"You no speak like I understand. You make fun of Iwilla?" The old woman drew herself up and gave Jody a regal glare, obviously calculated to make her run away.

Jody stood her ground. "Not at all. I just never knew a voodoo person before. Have you ever heard of Marie Laveau in New Orleans?"

Iwilla put her head to one side. "You know Mamzelle Marie?" Her black eyes flickered over Jody's face. "You know of Papa John?"

Jody had never heard of the man's name and only knew Marie Laveau by reputation. "Not personally."

"Marie Laveau not name to say out loud."

"So what do you do? Make spells and do dances? Things like that?" Jody knew she was pushing her luck, but she also knew she was putting Iwilla off balance and weakening her confidence. "Could I see one sometime?"

"*Fe Chauffe* not for white eyes! How you know about it? You not voodoo. White woman no can do voodoo!"

"How do you know? Maybe no white woman ever tried." Jody looked around. "I like the way you wear your head scarf. How on earth do you manage to tie it so it has seven points? Could you show me how to do that?"

Iwilla jumped to her feet. The people clustered in front of the other cabins drew back. Jody smiled

241

as if she were perfectly at ease. "You go!" Iwilla
commanded.

"Have I overstayed my welcome? I didn't mean
to tire you." She stood and casually dusted her
skirt, as if she had all the time in the world and
wasn't wanting to run away as fast as she could
go.

Iwilla stepped into her cabin, but she left the
door open. Jody's curiosity was stirred. The old
woman was fascinating, even if she was scary.
Iwilla emerged holding a black wax ball. "You
take!"

Jody hesitated. She wasn't eager to touch the
thing. "No, thank you. I couldn't accept a gift."

Iwilla tossed it to her and Jody caught it by
reflex. Iwilla smiled in a frightening manner.
"Now you go."

"See you later." Jody forced herself to amble
away.

As soon as she was around the oleander bushes and out of Iwilla's sight, she looked at the
ball. It had smears of a rust-colored substance
on its surface, and a crude likeness of a woman had been drawn on with some sharp object,
along with some of the indecipherable symbols
she had seen before. Jody wondered what it was
and what she should do with it.

Before she reached the back porch, Bessy came
running down the steps to meet her. "Miss Jody,
Miss Jody! You haven't really been to Iwilla's cabin, have you?" Bessy looked terrified.

"How did you know that? Word certainly
spreads fast here."

"'Cilla saw you, and she come and tell me."
Bessy saw the black ball and backed away.

"What's that you got in your hand?"

Jody looked at it again. "I don't know, actually. Iwilla tossed it to me after she told me to leave. Would you like to see it?" She held it out.

Bessy jumped back. "Throw it away, Miss Jody! Throw it as far as you can heave it! That's a conjure ball!"

"A conjure ball? I never heard of that. What's it supposed to do?"

"It brings death! If it even touches the lawn, it will bring death to somebody in the house. Lord, Miss Jody, get rid of it in a hurry! If you was to bring it inside, there's no telling what could happen."

Jody wasn't feeling nearly as brave as she pretended. The ball was the ugliest thing she had ever seen and seemed to radiate a malice all around it. Still, she could not let Bessy see her fear. "It's just black wax with markings on it."

"No, it's not. My granny told me about things like this. It's a black candle what's got a curse on it. Iwilla melts it and shapes it into a ball around a piece of human skin and floats it in blood. Then she writes who she wants the curse to be against and finds a way to get it into that person's house. You were about to take it right inside."

"Now, where on earth would Iwilla get human skin?" Jody asked reasonably, but the rust-red streaks did look uncannily like blood.

"She might have used something else just as bad. Please, Miss Jody. Don't stand there holding that thing."

Jody went to the fence that marked the border of the yard and threw the ball as far into the pasture as she could. "There. Is that better?"

Bessy wiped beads of sweat from her brow even though the day was quite cool. "Yes, ma'am. Some better. Maybe you ought to wash your hands before you go in, just in case something rubbed off on them."

Jody looked down at her hands. "I'd love to. The wax ball had a dirty, ugly feel."

Bessy walked with her to the outside pump and worked the handle while Jody held her hands under the stream of water. "I never heard of nobody going to old Iwilla's cottage before. Not without she sent for them. Weren't you scared?"

"She's only an old woman and probably half crazy. She just has a good act, that's all." But Jody couldn't shake the feeling of trepidation. "It's no wonder voodoo spells work at times. I don't believe in it and I still feel shaky." To explain she added, "You have to believe in them for them to really work, as I understand it. Your mind is marvelous at bringing about whatever suggestion is planted there."

"I don't know nothing about that, Miss Jody, but I've seen voodoo work when the fellow didn't even know it had been cast on him. It's not nothing to fool around with." She suddenly realized she was talking to Jody as if she were an equal and clamped her mouth shut and lowered her eyes.

Jody noticed and understood her sudden deference but refused to acknowledge it. "Which cabin is yours, Bessy?"

"I live in the one nearest the oak tree. The one with blue-and-white checked curtains in the window."

"I noticed the curtains. They're pretty."

Bessy smiled shyly. "I made them from a skirt I wore out."

"Camilla has told me how beautifully you sew. She said you might make some dresses for me. I bought some material at the dry goods store."

"Yes, ma'am, I'd be happy to. Of course I don't do none of that fancy embroidering like Miss Camilla or Miss Claudia do, but I can make clothes and things like that."

"Will you teach me?"

Bessy looked at her as if she thought Jody was making fun of her. "Teach you to sew?"

"I never learned and I'm embarrassed to tell Camilla or Claudia." That was nearly true. Camilla would understand in a fashion, but Jody doubted anyone here could ever realize the difference between Jody's culture and his own.

"Your mama didn't teach you to sew?" Bessy put her hand on her hip and stared at Jody. "Not a stitch?"

"Will you teach me? I have some material, but I don't know the first thing about cutting out a dress or how to put it together."

"Sure. I could teach you." Bessy was still looking at her as if she were wondering if she was being teased.

"Thanks. Maybe this afternoon we can get together." As she walked to the house Bessy was still staring after her. Jody looked at the pasture over the fence and shivered.

"I did exactly as we decided," Claudia said to Emma as they sat in the back parlor at The Oaks. "I told Micah in no uncertain terms that she must be sent away."

Emma put a seashell in place on the box she was decorating and placed another dot of mucilage beside it for the next. "What did he say?"

"You know how Micah is. He won't ever say what he's thinking. I made it plain, however, and he has to do something."

As she nudged a pink shell into the glue, Emma said, "I don't know. He can be so stubborn. Sometimes I think he acts that way just to try my patience."

"All men are like that. That is why we have to watch them so closely to be sure they do what is right."

Emma glanced up. "People aren't really talking about him and Miss Farnell, are they?"

"Not yet, but it is only a matter of time before they will. Micah should know this without having to be told. I think you are right. I doubt we are kin to Miss Farnell at all."

"You haven't heard from Cousin Amos?"

"No, but surely we will soon. If someone asked me a question about a stranger who is posing as a member of the family, I would reply quick enough."

Emma put her hands in her lap and pouted her lips. "What if Miss Farnell isn't kin at all? That means Micah is sharing his house with some stranger. I don't like that. Not at all."

"That is why it was important for me to tell Micah that we won't stand for any nonsense. However," she said loyally, "I am sure Micah wouldn't have let her in if he was not convinced that she has a right to be there. It is just that men are so gullible and they seem quite unable to see the consequences of their actions. Just the other day Vincent tracked mud onto my new hooked rug and couldn't seem to understand why I became so upset."

"It did clean, didn't it? That's such a pretty rug."

"Yes, it did, but it took Bertha all day and she had other things she needed to be doing." Claudia pushed a finger through the box of shells. "You always seem to be making something pretty. I wish I had your talents."

Emma smiled and blushed. "Thank you, but I'm not good at this at all." She paused to arrange the next shell. "I went into the dry goods store the other day and you'd never guess who waited on me. It was that awful George Percy."

"No! I do wish they would get rid of him. It is all I can do to speak to him in a civil manner." Claudia sniffed as if she could smell his pomade at that very moment. "He didn't try to talk to you, did he?"

"Of course he did." Emma made her eyes round and drew herself up straighter. "He actually suggested a certain lace for the dress I was buying and had gloves to match." She was thoughtful for a minute. "They went quite well together."

"What difference does that make? I can't stand to be around the man."

"Neither can I, goodness knows. I've a good mind to tell Micah that Mr. Percy has been bothering me."

Claudia leaned forward with interest. "He did not become impertinent, did he? If he did, your father should talk to his employer."

Elizabeth Crane

"No, not really. I mean, he paid me some compliments, but one can hardly call that impertinent, can one? He has such an awful accent, I declare I can hardly understand half he says."

"I know exactly what you mean." Claudia smiled and hid her lips behind her fingertips. "Wouldn't it be too funny if he developed a passion for Miss Farnell and her for him?"

Emma laughed right out loud. "How delicious! Oh, Claudia, you do say the cleverest things. I could never think of half you do!"

Claudia sighed. "It is idle wishing, however. They are both insufferable, but in opposite ways. No man would be attracted to Miss Farnell, with her strange hair and her hoydenish ways."

"You don't think Micah is attracted to her?"

"Absolutely not. He's in love with you," Claudia said as if it were impossible for her brother to find anyone else attractive now that he was promised to Emma. "I never meant that she is nice looking. Far from it. You know, from the way she moves, I don't think she even uses lacing."

"No corset?" Emma's mouth dropped open. "Only her chemise? That's scandalous!"

"I could be wrong, mind, but the last time I saw her, I was struck by the way she moved."

Emma touched her own tightly cinched waist. "I would feel absolutely naked without my corset. And she goes about in front of Micah without one?"

"That's one reason I say she could not be attractive to him. A woman's waist simply will not nip in properly without help."

"Goodness." Emma seemed thoroughly shocked. "I had no idea she was that . . . loose.

248

I'll just die if I find out she's really kin to us."

"We have to get rid of her whether she is or not. She is too much of a distraction and a temptation to Micah."

"But how are we to do it?" Emma had a thought and laughed as she tilted her head. "We could have old Iwilla witch her away!"

Claudia chuckled. "Remember how frightened we used to be of her?"

"I have to confess that I still am, a little. Once I'm mistress of Whitefriars, I shall have to insist that Micah send her away. She could mark a baby." Emma blushed demurely. "I shouldn't have said that."

"Nonsense. There aren't any men about. If we can't talk about these things among ourselves, we can talk about them to no one."

"That's true." Emma looked as amazed as if this were an impressive insight on Claudia's part. "Do you suppose Iwilla really can work magic?"

"Nonsense," Claudia scoffed as she handed Emma a particularly pretty shell to glue to the box. "She's just a crazy old woman."

"I've heard she has been able to do some strange things. The time she was given the wrong change for her eggs and butter, she made the Theriots's cow dry up."

Claudia looked uncertain. "That was just a coincidence. I don't believe in her charms."

"Neither do I. At least not entirely. Still, you know someone cut a piece off old Mr. Johnson's shroud. Zelia said she saw it and was the one to call attention to it. Who else would want to do such a thing other than Iwilla?"

"I think the seamstress just sewed it wrong or was clumsy in cutting it out. How could Iwilla get into the mortuary?"

"They say she can get in anywhere." Emma whispered, "When those graves were disturbed a few years back, it was Iwilla's name that was bandied about."

"Emma, that is impossible. She must be seventy or eighty years old. How could she even dig up one grave, let alone several? No, it was burkers hunting bodies to sell to physicians, just as the sheriff said."

"Maybe he said that because he couldn't prove it was Iwilla and he had to say something."

"Will you stop it? You're giving me the shivers." Claudia rubbed her arms. "What a morbid conversation."

"I'm sorry. It was awful of me to talk about such disgusting things." Emma went back to her gluing. "I hate to talk about ugly things. Why can't everything be pretty and sweet?"

Claudia glanced at Emma. Sometimes Emma's act of purity and chastity was difficult even for a friend to swallow. She knew for a fact that Emma was adept at gossiping about the most sordid occurrences. "It's more important that we decide how to get rid of Miss Farnell. I can't see why she is here in the first place. It is not as if she is returning a family visit. None of my family has visited the Tennessee relatives in years. I've never met more than a handful of them."

"If I were a guest, I'd not stay where I wasn't wanted," Emma said with pious conviction. "I couldn't bear to be an inconvenience."

"We aren't all as genteel as you."

Emma smiled prettily. "You say the sweetest things, Claudia. Truly you do. I've never had a better friend. If anyone had asked, I'd have said I would have been more likely to be friends with Camilla since we are nearer the same age. Isn't it amusing how things work out?"

Claudia, who was becoming sensitive about her age, said rather tartly, "Isn't it? One never knows what to expect."

"It's like that odious glove salesman. Before the War, there was no one like him in Joaquin or anywhere else in this parish. Now carpetbaggers are everywhere. Do you think Mr. Percy will ever pack up his carpetbag and move on?"

"I have no idea. I can promise you, I have far more to think about than George Percy."

"So do I. I think he's simply awful. Would you hand me that pink shell? Thank you."

Claudia jiggled the tray of shells in her search for more pink ones. "If I were you, I'd spend more time with Micah and less making pretty things, at least until after the wedding. Afterward, there isn't that much to do, but men can be willful before a wedding. Not that Micah would jilt you. He would never be so cruel. But he might be tempted to indulge in a flirtation. Especially since Miss Farnell is right under his nose."

Emma looked as though she were weighing a heavy subject. "I know you're right, but I can't follow him about all the time. I never know what to say to him once I've discussed all the recent parties. Men can't carry on a conversation about anything interesting, like the cut of a dress or the trim of a bonnet." She put her head to one side. "I've told him how I feel. Or at least I made it plain enough he ought to be able to figure it out."

"We can't rely on that. Micah can be so obtuse."

"Maybe I really should go to old Iwilla."

"Emma!"

"I've tried everything else."

"No, you haven't. You have to tell Micah that unless he sends Miss Farnell away, you will be too angry to forgive him."

Emma's eyes filled with tears. "I can't face an unpleasant scene. Micah can be so frightening when he frowns."

"If you are afraid of a little frown, how will you ever be able to control him once you are married?" Claudia reasoned. "You would be wise to take my advice, Emma, and learn how to do it now before he grows accustomed to doing exactly as he pleases. If that happens, your life will be miserable!"

"You're right. I'll try to do exactly as you say." Emma nodded her head as if she were a child learning a lesson.

Claudia smiled. It wasn't easy training Emma in the ways to manage a husband, but she knew Emma would thank her for it someday.

Chapter Thirteen

"I'm so worried, Camilla. I'm no good at meeting people."

"It's not like you've never spoken to them before. You must have met every one of these ladies at The Oaks when Emma had her party."

Jody paced the width of Camilla's parlor. "In that case, I can tell you now that they don't like me. I don't mean to speak badly of your friends, but they were scarcely polite to me."

"That's because they were surprised to see you arrive with Micah. Now they all know you're our cousin and that you will be here. They will all welcome you. You'll see."

"I still think I shouldn't have come. What can I talk to them about? You know how terrible I am with a needle. Why did I ever agree to come to a sewing bee?"

"It's not a bee, exactly. We meet every Wednesday to sew for the poor or for the church bazaar. It's not a real party."

"Camilla, they'll know I'm a fake as soon as I thread my needle. Assuming I can. Bessy has been trying to teach me to sew, but I just don't have the knack for it."

"That's just because you got such a late start on it." Camilla shook her head. "I still can't imagine why you never learned. Did your servants make all your clothes?"

"I've never had a servant. I bought all my clothes ready-made from a store."

Camilla gave her a look of compassion. "I'm so sorry, Jody. Well, now you can have some really pretty things. With Bessy teaching you the basic stitches and me showing you how to do the fancy work, you'll have a lovely wardrobe in no time."

Jody opened her mouth to say she couldn't possibly make clothes as nice as those she bought, but stopped. Camilla had seen only the faded jeans and sweatshirt that Jody had kept for working around the house. She would never believe that Jody owned anything nicer, since she didn't know what to think of the ones she had seen. "I'll try not to embarrass you."

"As if you could." Camilla smiled with genuine friendship. "If you're to stay here, you have to learn the things we all know or you won't fit in."

"Do you think I really will stay here? It no longer seems so fantastic to me. In a way that's scary. I've adjusted so easily. Too easily, it seems. On the other hand, I can't possibly stay. Can I?"

"I wish I knew. The children would miss you terribly. Matilda was singing that song you taught her about Aphrodite . . . no, Venus. 'Venus in Blue Jeans.' And Armand has named his puppy Lassie."

"It's an old song, but it's easy to sing. Well, I guess it's not so old from this angle, is it?"

"The children love you. Even little Marie Celeste was excited when she heard you were coming today. It was all I could do to keep them out of the parlor. Of course, since Matilda is eight, she's old enough to sew for the bazaar, but she has lessons today. She made it clear that she would rather be here with her Tante Jody."

"She calls me Aunt?"

"That seemed to be the easiest. You don't mind, do you?"

"No, I like it. Before I go, I'll tell them another story."

"Armand says no one can tell stories like you do. He's the envy of all his friends."

"I'm glad we decided not to tell them where I'm really from. I can't have too many people know."

"No, that might not be safe." Camilla took out her sewing basket and unfolded the linen napkins she had marked off for a cut-work design.

Jody decided she didn't want to know what Camilla meant by that last remark. She had heard of witch hunts, and she didn't want to be the object of one. "You know, it seems funny, but I used to think this would be such an easygoing time. No pollution or nuclear bombs or terrorists. Well, there is the Klan. Women don't have to leave their children and go to an office to work all day and fight traffic jams, and divorce is all but unheard of. But I never realized how much work there could be in a life like this. You're busy from dawn to dark."

"That's what it takes to run a house properly." She put her head to one side. "You must have been as busy, too, if you lived at Whitefriars all alone. How could you manage? I'm surprised no one offered to help you."

"It's not unusual for a woman to live alone in my time. I've lived alone all my adult life."

Camilla's gray eyes widened. "How sad. It's a good thing you came to us, so you'll be properly cared for."

Jody smiled. "I've never been anywhere that felt more like home. Not even in the house where I grew up. I was never much like the rest of my family, and we aren't close."

"I know. You said you're from Grand Coteau."

Jody started to explain she had meant an emotional distance, not a physical one, but she knew Camilla wouldn't understand. She had been raised with the premise that families are indivisible and encompassing for all their members. By common decision, Jody and her own family saw each other only at Christmas and other occasional holidays, not on a regular basis. In retrospect, it occurred to Jody that the emotional distance between herself and her other family members had made it easier for her to accept what might prove to be a permanent separation.

A soft knock on the door drew Jody's attention. Camilla's maid opened it, and three ladies came into the room. Jody fixed a smile on her face and let Camilla remind her of the women's names. Jody, who had never been good at either names or faces, tried hard to commit these to memory.

These could well be her friends and neighbors for the rest of her life.

They sat and began unpacking the sewing baskets they each carried. Although they were trying not to stare at Jody, she felt their eyes on her every time she turned her head. She pretended not to notice. The pillowcases, tablecloths, collars, and the like the other ladies were getting ready to resume work on were already beautiful examples of handwork. Jody was hesitant to take out the table runner she was sewing.

"That's lovely," the woman called Katie said to Jody. "Is this a pattern Camilla drew? It looks familiar."

Camilla nodded. "It's the one I used for the tablecloth I did last year. I'm showing Jody how to make Battenberg lace."

Katie glanced up in surprise. "She doesn't already know?"

"Jody had a terrible fever last year and it caused her to forget some things, like needlework," Camilla improvised.

"How awful," Katie said. The other women nodded their agreement. "It must have been some kind of brain fever. You know, Luther Harrison had that, and he forgot his wife's name and how to add columns of figures."

"It was sad," Nanine said. Camilla had spoken of her as being a close friend, and she seemed perfectly at home in the Galliers's parlor. "Opal Lou told me their eldest son had to take over the family books."

"We never value our own health until we see someone less fortunate," Katie said in agreement. "Opal Lou isn't too well herself these days. I doubt she will be able to come today."

"That's too bad," Camilla said. To Jody she explained, "Opal Lou is our priest's sister. Father Graham, not the younger one."

Jody nodded. She attended church with Micah and the Galliers every Sunday, but she had been too engrossed in not making any mistakes in the unfamiliar service to notice much about the priests.

Nanine said, "I'll help you in any way I can, Jody. You're to think of me as another cousin." She laughed. "Camilla and I are together so often, I feel like part of the family."

"You are," the older woman said. "I remember distinctly that your grandmother married one of the Deveroux cousins thrice removed. That gives you family ties."

Jody wondered how anyone could sort through the tangle of cousins and near-cousins and figure out the relationships. "When I was growing up, I didn't live near any of my cousins. I wish now that I had. You all seem so close."

"Not live near family?" Katie said. "How can that be?"

Camilla stepped in quickly. "Tennessee is full of mountains. That must make travel difficult. Is that right, Jody?"

"Yes. Travel was difficult." She reminded herself not to say anything about her past that could trip her up again.

"Look," Nanine said as she peered through the lace curtain at the street. "It's Emma. I knew she would be late."

"She always is," Katie chastised.

Apparently, they were not all as close as they

had first seemed. Maybe Emma was not so well-liked as Jody had assumed. Her estimation of Camilla's friends rose.

Emma came breezing in the door as if she were in her own house. "Hello, everyone. I do hope I'm not too late, but I had to go by the dry goods store and the emporium before I could come. You just can't trust them to send out exactly what you want anymore." When she saw Jody she stopped, then offered a tentative word of greeting.

"Hello," Jody responded with more enthusiasm than Emma had shown her. She had known Emma would be invited, but she had hoped she wouldn't come. It made her decidedly uncomfortable to be in the same room with Micah's fiancée. "That's a pretty dress," she said as a gesture of friendliness.

"This old thing?" Emma looked down as though she were surprised to see what she was wearing. "I ought to give this to my maid, but I haven't had the time." To the others she said, "I'm simply buried in details about the wedding. The dry goods store hasn't got a single bolt of satin in the right weight, and their selection of lace is deplorable. Mama says we will have to send to France for it. One can't get really nice things here."

Jody turned away. She didn't want to be reminded of the wedding. She picked up her cloth and the needle. Camilla had shown her how to draw the pattern on the cloth and to cut out the open work. Jody was attempting to stitch the raw edges.

"What are you working on?" Emma came to her and looked at the cloth. "Is this something Matilda is working on?"

259

The women exchanged a look. "No," Camilla said. "Jody is doing that."

"Oh." Emma let it drop back into Jody's lap. With a tinkling laugh, she said, "I had thought Matilda already knew how to do lace. Will Claudia be here today?"

"No, she sent word that she has a headache and won't be able to come this time," Camilla said.

"Such a pity," another of the ladies put in. "Claudia seems to have so many headaches."

Jody tried not to glare at Emma for her comment about the lace and was too proud to offer the brain fever explanation the others had accepted. Had she met the other women after Emma had arrived, she would have assumed their silence in her defense was because they agreed with Emma. Now she saw they could be silent simply because none of them cared that much what Emma thought. Jody felt her confidence rising.

"Papa has ordered a new buggy for me," Emma went on. "I told him that Whitefriars has perfectly good buggies already, but you know how he is. Nothing is ever good enough or new enough to suit him when it comes to me." She laughed again. "I'm perfectly spoiled, I admit it."

"Would you like some tea?" Camilla asked. "Or maybe some iced lemonade?"

"It's much too cool for iced lemonade. I was chilled just coming here." Emma pressed her hands against her thin stomach. "Mama says it's because there just isn't enough of me to keep warm. Isn't that silly?"

"Extremely," Katie said, deftly throwing a barb and not missing a stitch.

Oblivious to Katie's affront, Emma sat down and fluffed her skirts around her, then took out a small bit of cloth. "I'm making collars this year. I've been so busy planning the wedding and seeing that my trousseau is ready that I've hardly had time to turn around. It seems so odd to me to think that I will soon be a married lady like all of you." Her pale eyes lit on Jody and her smile held no humor. "Well, like most of you."

"Could I have some iced lemonade?" Jody asked. She didn't care whether the day was cool or not. She only wanted to silence Emma.

"Of course." Without raising her voice, Camilla said, "Sukey, will you bring Miss Farnell iced lemonade, please?"

Jody leaned forward to see Sukey pass the parlor door to do as Camilla had asked. She thought she would never get used to the battalion of silent and near-perfect servants in these houses, or the fact that no conversation was ever entirely private if a door was open.

"Have you been feeling well?" Nanine said to Katie.

"Pretty well except in the mornings. It won't last much longer."

Emma made her eyes round. "You're expecting again?"

Katie nodded. "In early summer, I think. Most of mine come then, it seems."

Jody looked at her. Katie was about her own age. "How many children do you have?"

"This will make six."

"Six children?" Jody knew families were large here, but she was always surprised.

"We hope to have another one someday,"

261

Camilla said softly. "You know, it was about this time of the year that we lost little Andre. I was thinking of him only this morning."

"You lost a child?" Jody asked. "I'm so sorry. I didn't know that."

Nanine nodded. "It's so sad when that happens. Father Graham says it means there's another angel in heaven, but it's still sad."

"He would be four by now," Camilla said. She shook her head. "I'm sorry. You'll have to forgive me. Sometimes melancholy affects me."

"I should think anyone would be depressed over losing a child," Jody said quickly. "It's only natural."

"Still, it happens all the time." Camilla smiled. "Marie Celeste asked yesterday if she would ever have a baby brother or sister."

"I hope you cautioned her," Emma said. "She mustn't talk like that around anyone. It's not proper."

"Marie Celeste is only two," Jody replied more sharply than she should have. "She's just a baby."

"Neither of us has any right to talk at all," Emma answered. "We aren't married and we really don't know what we're talking about, now do we?" Her eyes dared Jody to take the bait.

Sukey came in with Jody's lemonade, cups of hot tea for everyone else, and a platter of tea cakes.

"These are delicious," Katie pronounced as she bit into a cookie. "I wish my cook had this recipe."

"I'll give it to you before you leave." Camilla sipped her tea before continuing to sew. "I hope the bazaar is successful this year. Last year we hardly raised any money at all."

"I heard of something new," Nanine said. "Zelia told me about a custom she saw when she was visiting in Shreveport a few months ago. The women took a large basket and each made something to go into it. Then the basket was sent to each house in the congregation and the women bought items from it and made others to take their place. Isn't that a nice idea?"

"It is indeed," Camilla said. "I've never liked the idea of buying things from booths at the bazaar. It feels like shopping at the market for vegetables. It would be much nicer to be able to buy from a basket in the privacy of your own home."

Katie nodded. "That way you're not beholden to buy what you know your neighbor or cousin made. No one knows who bought what unless they see it at someone's house. Let's do that here in Joaquin."

Jody listened to the women plan where to get a suitable basket, but that didn't seem to be as important to the women as the idea that it would be a new undertaking. For the first time that day, she relaxed and enjoyed herself and didn't pay Emma any attention at all.

After the other ladies departed, Jody told the promised story to Camilla's children, then left to go home. All in all, she thought it had been a good day. While she still felt unsure of herself, she thought she would become friends with Katie and Nanine. Her confidence was up for having tried to fit into this world, and she thought that with Micah and Camilla behind her, she would be able to pass herself off as being no more than eccentric.

In light of her achievement, Jody decided to try to make friends with Claudia as well. She reined her horse toward the street where Micah had said she lived.

Claudia's house was near the edge of town, set prettily in behind some elms. It was a smaller house than Whitefriars, and knowing Claudia as she did, Jody wondered if that bothered her. Perhaps, Jody thought, that was why Claudia always referred to Whitefriars as if she still lived there.

She left her horse out front and was taken into the house by a butler who was more stern and forbidding than Gideon at Whitefriars. The house was beautiful, but Jody didn't think it looked as if anyone really lived in it. She had seen other houses of this sort that looked as the furniture was part of a stage setting and as if nothing was ever out of place or worn from use.

Claudia had not expected visitors and she still wore a shapeless wrapper, though her hair was pinned up in the bun she always seemed to wear. She didn't look too pleased to see Jody.

"Hello. I hope you don't mind my dropping by, but I was in town at Camilla's. I heard you have a bad headache. Is it better?"

"No, they last for days." Claudia didn't look as if she felt bad at all. "Did you send your card around? I wasn't expecting callers. I hope you'll forgive the way I look." Her words lacked sincerity.

"You look just fine." Conversation threatened to lapse into silence. "Camilla and the others were concerned about you."

"It's so nice to have friends. Tell me, Miss

Farnell, was Cousin Amos in good health the last time you saw him?"

Jody wondered if this was a trap. "Pretty well, I'd say. I haven't actually seen him for quite a while, however."

Claudia studied her face. "He hasn't answered my letter. I thought perhaps he's sick. I was under the impression that you live near him."

"No, there's a mountain between us." She thought it might be best to stick with the story Camilla had invented. "Travel is difficult."

"He must be getting on in years. How old would you say he is now?"

"I have no idea." Jody could see it had been a mistake to come here. "I've never been a good judge of age."

"Would you like some coffee?"

"No, thank you. I can't stay. I only wanted to stop by and see if you are all right before I went back to Whitefriars. May I give Micah a message?"

"No, I'll see him myself tomorrow or the next day. Speaking of Whitefriars, don't you think it would be a good idea for you to move into Camilla's house? It would be so much more convenient to town and she loves having guests."

"I'm quite comfortable where I am. You might say Whitefriars feels just like home to me."

"It shouldn't. Forgive me for speaking bluntly, Miss Farnell, but I'm afraid people will talk about you staying there with no chaperon. Naturally I'm not implying anything, but Emma is hurt that we may begin hearing gossip about Micah and you." Claudia sat ramrod straight in her chair and frowned at Jody. "Nor would I like to see gossip attached to you as our cousin either."

"I understand. However, nothing is going on at Whitefriars, and I see no reason to impose on Camilla's hospitality when I'm already in Whitefriars." She stood. "Perhaps it was a mistake for me to come. I should be going."

Claudia rose. "Perhaps it was. You should know, Miss Farnell, that Emma Parlange is my particular friend, and I'm very protective of my friends."

"I understand. It's an admirable trait—when there is a need to protect them. Good day." Jody turned and walked away. She felt her cheeks blaze in embarrassment, but she refused to show her emotions. Jody couldn't recall a single time anyone had ever felt the need to upbraid her for a moral reason. Claudia made her feel like a disobedient child.

At any rate, she thought as she led her horse to the mounting block by the front steps, she had tried to make friends. She had done all she could.

Micah was waiting for Emma when she returned from the sewing circle at Camilla's house. When she saw him, she smiled brightly and waved. He met her at the steps to hand her out of the buggy.

"We got ever so many things started for the church bazaar," she bubbled as she went up the steps and onto the porch. "It will be our best sale ever."

"Will it?" He looked down at her and tried to remember what he had found so attractive in her before Jody came. Emma was as pretty as ever and as daintily feminine, but she never touched a part of his soul.

"We're going to make something called a church basket and send it around to everyone's house. It's going to be simply wonderful. I wish it had been my idea."

"Was Miss Jody there?" He was glad he remembered in time to use the more formal address.

"Yes, she was." Emma pouted, but made it look pretty and childish. "I don't like her any better now than I did before. Poor Micah. Maybe she'll go home soon."

"Now, Emma, we've been all through that. I didn't come here to argue about Miss Jody."

"Why did you come?"

Micah was at a loss. He couldn't say he had come in hopes of rekindling his love for her. "I only wanted to see you."

Emma smiled and her dimples appeared. "Did you? Just to see me? I like it when you flirt with me. I've heard some men stop flirting when they convince a girl to give them her hand. Will you promise to flirt with me forever, Micah?"

"Forever is a long time." He watched her sit on one of the porch chairs, then he settled on the railing.

"Camilla is sewing the prettiest napkins. She does such beautiful work. Not at all like me." She waited for the compliment.

"You sew as prettily as she does. Maybe better. I'm not much judge of such things."

"You never seem to pay any attention to anything but horses and crops and so forth. It must be so dull to be a man." She smiled up at him from the corners of her eyes. "I could never make heads nor tails of ledgers and boring things like that."

"Fortunately, you'll never have to." He was thinking of Jody and how she seemed as familiar as he was with columns of numbers. She could even draw house plans like he had never dreamed possible. "I've started work on Marcel Howard's house. Would you like to hear about it?"

"I saw Sally yesterday, and she said her trousseau is almost finished. She was choosing a bonnet of the oddest shade of yellow. It will make her look as sallow as a gourd. You don't suppose she actually has a dress that will match it, do you?"

"I have no idea. The house will sit on the little hill just back from the road. The place where we gathered persimmons last fall. Remember?"

"I certainly do. I tore my best lace gloves on that bush under the persimmon tree. And after all that, the persimmons weren't ripe. I guess the frost wasn't heavy enough."

"This house will be different from any you've ever seen. The rooms are all downstairs except for the children's rooms and the ones the servants will use. Even the room Marcel and Sally will use and the guest bedrooms are downstairs."

Emma turned away, and as he watched, she held her breath until she blushed. "You mustn't talk to me about bedrooms. What on earth are you thinking of?" She glanced back at him. "Marcel and Sally won't share one, surely."

He laughed. "Of course they will. They will be married."

"My parents don't share a room, and neither do Claudia and Vincent."

"My parents did and so will we." He expected

her to blush, but she frowned instead.

"I wouldn't be too sure about that. I don't recall you having asked me if I want to share a room with you or not."

Micah stared at her. "Why should I have to ask? I assumed that you would prefer it."

"Well, Micah, you can't go through life assuming everything. I have some opinions, you know. I may not be as smart as you are, but I have opinions."

"What does this have to do with intelligence? Husbands and wives sleep together."

"Hush! Don't talk so loud. Do you want Mama to overhear? She would die if she knew what we were talking about. I should go straight in the house if you're going to keep talking about this subject. I really should."

"You brought it up. I think we should talk about it." He wondered if the signs had been there all the time. Now that he thought about it, Emma never wanted him to do more than hold her hand. If he kissed her, she pressed her lips together tightly and held her breath, as if she were afraid of being contaminated. "Emma, look at me."

"No. I won't. You're being beastly and you're just trying to make me cry." Her voice trembled, and he saw color flame in her cheeks.

"I don't want you to cry. I wouldn't do that to you. Are you serious about us not sharing a bedroom?"

She held her breath as if she were exasperated beyond endurance. "I know we have to *some* time or we won't have any children. I do know that much."

For the first time, it occurred to Micah that she

might not know exactly how children were conceived. If she didn't want to so much as sleep beside him, how would she take that news? "I think you should talk to your mother and ask her to explain some things to you."

"I'm sure she will tell me all I need to know on the day of my wedding. I never should have mentioned it to you. Claudia said I shouldn't."

"You and Claudia discussed this?"

"Not exactly, but she tells me things, like how to be a good wife and how she manages to run her house."

"In what way?"

Emma smiled. "I can't tell you. Some things are meant to be women's secrets."

Micah didn't like the sound of that. He had seen Vincent Landry go from being a personable and friendly bachelor to Claudia's husband. The change hadn't been pleasant. Vincent rarely smiled in his wife's presence, and even when he was away from her, he had a reserve that had never been there before. "I'm not so sure Claudia is the best one to give you advice. Ask Camilla. She and Reid are completely happy."

"She's not my friend. At least, not like Claudia is. Camilla likes that Miss Farnell." Emma wrinkled her pretty nose. "I couldn't be so open with her."

"Emma, I don't know how to say this, but I'm concerned. We don't seem to be growing fonder of each other."

Her eyes widened. "Not growing fonder? How can you say that? I love you to distraction. Of course I do. Did someone tell you I don't? Was it Miss Farnell?"

"She hasn't mentioned you to me at all. Not really." He found it telling that Emma thought of everything only as it directly affected her. She never even questioned that the lack of fondness could be on his own part. He looked at her and she smiled. He looked away.

"Mama and I bought such a pretty piece of velvet the other day. We're going to embroider it for my best Sunday dress, and I'll wear it the first Sunday after our wedding. Don't you ask what color it is, now. I won't tell you."

Micah felt as if he were sinking into a mire. Emma was so childlike and innocent. How could he tell her he loved Jody and not her? She had said she loved him. A woman who was in love was not likely to call off a wedding, and Micah couldn't do it and still remain a gentleman. He felt trapped, and there was not a thing he could do about it.

Chapter Fourteen

Jody tied her horse to a bush and walked along the edge of a pond on Micah's land but some distance from the house and secluded by a nearby woods. She needed to be alone, and even the horse was a distraction. Her feelings for Micah were growing at a rate she found alarming, especially since he showed no signs of calling off his engagement to Emma.

As a girl, Jody had had crushes from time to time, but she had weathered them, and they had eventually disappeared. What she felt for Micah was nothing like that. Instead of growing fainter over time, it was becoming stronger every day and had far more depth than a mere infatuation. She was in love with him.

Because the day was unseasonably warm and her clothing seemed to be choking her, Jody loosened the collar of her blouse and rolled up the sleeves. She wanted to cast off her restricting clothing and find a pair of shorts and a cool blouse to wear, but of course, that was impossible. And poor Micah must be even hotter than she was, since he was constrained to wear not only a starched, long-sleeve shirt, but a coat as well.

Jody plucked one of the remaining leaves off a nearby tree, and as she twirled its stem between her thumb and forefinger, she was aware that this leaf looked no different than any of the autumn leaves she had seen all her life. It seemed strange to her that so many things about her should be so familiar when her situation was so drastically changed. She let the leaf flutter to the ground. In the grand scheme of time, was she no more important than that leaf, so that her appearance or disappearance meant no more than it might have if that leaf suddenly disappeared? No, she thought. She didn't believe that. She was here for some reason, but she had no idea what that reason was. And if she were to figure it out and fulfill that mission, would she return to her own time?

What if she stayed here in 1872 for forty years, then returned to her own time? Would she return at the age she had been when she left, or at the age she had become? She had no way of answering any of these plaguing questions.

She stared out at the pond as if the answers might be there, but saw only the blue sky reflecting off its placid surface. As she watched, a gentle breeze rippled the water, causing it to sparkle in the sunlight. The scene reminded her of the pond she had swum in as a young girl, one not far from her home, although this one was much larger.

That had been a happy time, a carefree time. The breeze subsided and again the air became still and ever so warm, yet the water looked cool and inviting. A glance around her assured her she was completely alone, and the seclusion of this place was not likely to be invaded by a casual passerby.

Without hesitation, she removed her clothes, laid them carefully on a bush near the water's edge, and waded in. As the water sloshed about her ankles, she discovered it was colder than she had anticipated. For a moment she stopped, then decided it would be even more refreshing than she had first thought. A school of minnows swam toward her to investigate the intruder, then scattered as she resumed her progress, going deeper with each step. Jody had rarely gone skinny-dipping, and she felt a delicious sense of excitement as the water rose higher on her thighs, then circled her hips.

She dipped her hands beneath the surface and splashed water over her upper body to cool her skin and prepare it for the drastic temperature change to come. The drops ran down her skin and dripped back into the pool like beads of silver. She waded deeper.

With her eyes on the far side of the pond, she pushed off into the water and swam with clean, sure strokes. The water toward the middle was colder still, bringing even more relief from the day's heat. Relishing the sensation, she drifted onto her back and floated in the sun, letting her pale body bob in the water. Her dark hair floated about her head like a halo, and the sun warmed her breasts and stomach in sharp contrast to the chill on her back and buttocks.

What would become of her? She had been here several weeks already; she had to face the fact that she might never get back where she belonged. She had heard stories of people disappearing without a trace. Were they all alive and well in some other time, just as she was? Remembering it was dangerous to swim alone, especially in an unfamiliar place, she rolled over and began swimming toward the bank with the long, smooth strokes of a strong swimmer. The ripples she created strummed her body, and her breasts floated buoyantly beneath her in a sensuous rhythm that she had never noticed in a swimsuit. Although the chilly water cooled her skin, the sensuousness of the water flowing over her naked body stirred a passionate need in her, and unbidden, her thoughts returned to Micah.

What if Micah married Emma? There was no thought she tried more desperately to keep from her mind, but it always seemed to crop back up. And it wasn't one she could simply ignore. Emma was all wrong for him. Jody didn't understand why he couldn't comprehend that fact when it was so obvious to her. He would be bored with Emma in a matter of weeks, maybe days. Jody had become bored with her in minutes, but she had to admit that as a man, Micah undoubtedly looked at Emma in a way Jody could not.

She remembered the times she and Micah had sat in his library or on the veranda and talked. They talked about everything from building houses to philosophy. If there was one thing this generation knew how to do, she had observed, it was to talk. To them, conversation was indeed an art. What would Micah find to discuss with Emma? Even as broad as Micah's interests were, she couldn't imagine him engaged in conversation about the best way to trim a fashionable bonnet or what ladies were wearing in Paris that year. Emma seemed capable of discussing nothing else.

Jody swam faster and harder, splashing a great deal in an effort to work off her frustration. As she neared the marshy end, she curled under the water and headed back. Realizing it wasn't wise for her to exhaust herself in the water, she slowed her strokes and focused her concentration on making her body as streamlined as possible and to swim as silently as she could.

Not far away in the woods, Micah heard the muffled sound of splashing and reined in his horse to listen. Could it be a horse in trouble? One of his ponds was only a short distance away through the woods, and sometimes his horses waded out too deep, became bogged in the marshy mud, and had to be roped and pulled out. Agitated, but knowing the animal might need his help, he turned about and headed for the pond.

Only a few yards from sight of the water through the dense vegetation, he saw the red horse Jody usually rode tied to a bush, and he drew his mount to a stop alongside the animal. When the horse saw Micah it whickered softly in recognition. Micah dismounted and threaded his way through the underbrush to the edge of the pond. As he looked around for Jody, finding no one, he noticed the water was rippling. When he saw Jody's head lift from the water several yards away, then disappear again, his heart almost stopped.

He was yanking off his heavy boots and preparing to dive in after her when he realized she wasn't drowning.

Micah paused, one boot in his hand, the other lying in the leaves. To his total amazement, Jody was swimming, and now that he took the time to watch her, he could see she was doing it as proficiently as he could himself. And she was doing it naked.

Slowly Micah pulled his boot back on and reached for the other. He had never seen a woman swim before. As children, his sisters had occasionally splashed around in one of the ponds, but they had always worn their chemises and a sort of shift they sometimes slept in. They would never have considered stripping down to the skin like a boy and jumping in over their heads.

He looked around. No one was likely to come this way. There were no crops planted in these fields, and even if there had been, no one would be tending them at this time of year. No one was likely to see her. All the same, he was reluctant to go away and leave her unattended.

Logic told him to go. She was as good a swimmer as he was and in no danger. And there were few places in the pond that were much over her head at this time of year. Still, he lingered. He rarely was able to indulge his need to look at Jody, and this seemed to be a priceless opportunity.

Her body was, for the most part, hidden by the water and reflections of sky and sparkles of sunlight, but he was sure she was nude because her slim arms flashed out of the surface and he caught a glimpse now and then of her bare shoulder and her buttocks. She swam as she did almost everything—swiftly and efficiently. The water churned about her, but she made little sound. Had she been swimming this silently as he rode by, he would never have noticed anyone was in the pond.

Telling himself he was staying because she might get a leg cramp and need assistance, he sat on a mossy log and watched her. She was so different from every woman he had ever known. Who else would ride so far from the house and swim alone? What other woman would even want to do such a thing? He couldn't imagine Emma in any water deeper than a bathtub. Jody definitely shared his sense of adventure.

Where and how had she learned to swim? She occasionally told him about her world. A world of electric boxes that talked, of carriages that required no horse to pull them, and houses that stayed warm in the winter and cool in the summer as if by magic. He wasn't sure he believed all her stories, but they fascinated him nonetheless. Jody had a way of telling a story that riveted his attention as surely as it did that of his nieces and nephew. But in spite of the unlikeliness of some of her stories, he knew she had seen and taken for granted things beyond his wildest dreams.

She said she had traveled all over America, and alone, without even a chaperon or a family member in attendance. He would have thought this to be a tall tale, except that she had accurately described states he had seen as a soldier, and besides, she had given him no reason to think she was given to lying. He recalled stories he had heard of wagon trains and how long it had taken them to reach the western coast, and he concluded this must be the reason Jody had never married. Having traveled so extensively, she wouldn't have been in any one place long enough to have been courted.

He had seen Camilla the day before, and she had told him how her sewing circle had gone. Camilla didn't like Emma, though she had never again mentioned that fact once he told her that he had proposed marriage to her and she had accepted. But Micah knew Camilla would never be as close to Emma as was Claudia. From what Camilla obviously did not say about the ladies' gathering, Micah concluded that Camilla thought some of Emma's comments were rather sharp and that she was upset that Emma had teased Jody about being less skilled with a needle than most women, or even most girls. Micah couldn't imagine sweet, gentle Emma doing such a thing, but he had no reason to think Camilla would lead him to believe something that wasn't true.

As he watched Jody he tried to think about Emma, but it wasn't easy. They were as unalike as two women could be. Jody could be as forthright as a man and still be utterly feminine. She liked to debate almost any issue and had a quick mind. He had to be on his toes around her or she would get the better of him. Micah liked the challenge.

Emma, on the other hand, was sweetness personified, as genteel and as delicate as any lady could be. She was so refined that a harsh word was enough to make her dissolve into tears, and she blushed if he spoke of anything pertaining to marriage and their future living together. He frowned. She still refused to discuss the slip she had made concerning whether they would share a room. He was at a loss as to how to get that point across to her. He couldn't just move her into his room and bed when he knew she objected, yet he didn't want his wife to live down the hall from him, either.

Micah watched Jody roll underwater and come up swimming in the opposite direction. He had never discussed it with her, nor could he, but he knew instinctively that Jody wouldn't insist on separate bedrooms when she was married.

That brought up another dilemma. If Jody stayed, what was he to do with her? Emma had made it abundantly clear that she was to be the only woman at Whitefriars. Camilla had offered to take Jody into her house, but how long could she stay there? It would be best for Jody to marry, but whom?

He thought of Will Breaux and frowned again. He liked Will, but for some reason he detested the idea of Will courting Jody. She wasn't suited to him, no matter how Will insisted that she was. She had given him no encouragement, but that seemed to fire Will with more determination. Micah supposed it was because so few women had ever turned away Will's courtship. He was from an old family that was already regaining the prosperity it had enjoyed before the War Between the States. But Micah didn't want to see Jody marry Will, nor did he want to see her marry anyone else.

Micah was rarely unreasonable, and he knew these thoughts were highly illogical. He couldn't marry her and he couldn't keep her under his roof after he was married, so it was best for Jody to find the best husband possible and marry him. That way she would be cared for and protected. She would have children who would tend to her needs in her old age, should she survive that long. She would have a life of her own. It would be a life apart from his, but that was necessary in any case. She could do a lot worse than Will, and Micah knew Will would be a kind husband to her.

Jody put her feet under her and waded slowly toward the shore. First, her shoulders emerged from the water, then her breasts. Micah knew he should look away, that he should leave, but he found it impossible to move. He knew that if she glanced in his direction, she would probably see him, but that didn't matter.

As he continued to stare, transfixed, she waded into shallower water. Only her lower hips were covered now, and her exposed skin gleamed like wet marble. Her wet hair was flattened against her head and neck like fur, making her seem even more naked. Micah felt his desire rise rapidly, but he couldn't tear his eyes away.

Jody half-turned and looked back at the pond as if she had heard his thoughts and wondered if she was still alone. Micah didn't move. He couldn't hide from her like some boy peeking at his first nude woman. She didn't see him. The sunlight was silver and gold on her skin and her nipples beaded hard and rosy. Micah found it difficult to breathe. Jody put one arm across her breasts as if she felt his gaze and realized her nakedness, but she made no effort to hurry into her clothes. Instead she walked onto the shore as if she had no reason to feel ashamed of her nakedness.

Using her chemise as a towel, she blotted the water from her skin, then pulled the undergarment over her head. The wet cloth clung to her damp curves and was almost transparent. Micah's pulse quickened as she turned toward the pond again. Her nipples were clearly budding under the fabric, and he could see the tantalizing curve of her hip, as pale as alabaster and as smooth as a work of art. Turning her attention back to the task at hand, Jody pulled on her bloomers and tied the ribbon at her waist. The bloomers were made of the same thin cloth as the chemise and were trimmed in the same lacework. Like the chemise, the bloomers became sheer due to the contact with her damp body.

Jody seemed to be in no hurry to finish dressing. She ran her fingers through her hair and shook it to sling off the excess water. The movement caused her breasts to sway seductively. Micah swallowed against the lump in his throat. He couldn't have moved if his life had depended on it. Jody tilted her head back and stood in the sun in a way that reminded Micah of stories he had read of Greek goddesses of forests and lakes. Instead of hiding her skin from the sun, she let it dry her more thoroughly, tossing her hair about to dry it as well. Her tresses fell in a smooth curve that cupped her head.

At last she seemed satisfied that she had done all she could with her hair and got her dress off the bush. As she slipped it over her head and began fastening the buttons, Micah knew he had to leave. She couldn't drown on dry land, and no one was around to threaten her. If he stayed where he was, she would know he had seen her and that he had watched her as if he were the most callous of voyeurs. No, he thought as he stood. Not callous. Not when she affected him the way she did.

He slipped into the woods before she could notice he was there and went to his horse. He led it away from the surrounding trees before he mounted and galloped home.

Jody looked up when she heard the noises in the woods, but she saw nothing. After a while the noises stopped and she thought it must have been a deer or perhaps an armadillo. Nevertheless, she felt more alone than before, and she hurriedly dressed and went back to her horse.

After supper that evening, Jody and Micah went out onto the veranda. He had been unusually silent all afternoon, scarcely speaking even during the meal. "Are you upset with me about something?" she asked as she gazed at him through the gathering twilight.

"No." He didn't elaborate.

"Yes, you are. Usually you talk my ears off. You act as if your mind is a thousand miles away. I get the feeling you're avoiding me."

"That's ridiculous. I haven't been rude to you. I'm not four yards away."

"You're not yourself."

Micah didn't answer. She studied his profile against the soft lamplight coming from the window. He might not admit it, but something was bothering him. "Did you see Emma today? Did you argue?"

"We never argue. No, I didn't."

Jody sighed. "If you decide to talk about it, let me know."

He made no comment.

Beyond the porch the night was unusually still. Not a single breeze stirred the leaves or the garlands of Spanish moss. Jody thought of her swim and wished the cooling effect had lasted longer. Already she felt sticky and hot again. She glanced back at Micah. He always seemed to be so self-contained. "You don't even sweat," she said aloud. "As hot as it is, you aren't sweating."

He glanced at her. "When it gets hot enough I do. Everyone does."

"Even Emma?" she couldn't resist asking. "Sorry. That was uncalled for."

"Emma is human, just like us."

She wondered if his voice affected her so deeply because of his southern accent, lightly touched with a French twist, or because of its timbre. When he spoke, especially when the night was closing around them, his voice seemed to caress her and to suggest an intimacy that she knew he didn't intend. "You have a beautiful voice."

As he looked at her, she wondered if her features were visible in the light from the windows and whether her desire for him showed. She lowered her eyes to protect her privacy. He looked away. "Thank you."

Jody stood and walked to the railing. "It's so hot. I don't remember it being this hot when I first came here."

"It's Indian summer. We often get warm spells like this before winter settles in."

"It's so still. I can't even hear the crickets."

"A storm is brewing. I can feel it."

Jody leaned on the railing and looked up at the night sky. There were no stars. "When I first came here I was surprised how black the sky is. At home there's always light from somewhere."

"Where would light come from out here except from inside the house?"

"Joaquin will be larger then. My neighbors have security lights that come on at dusk. I can sit on my porch and see the lights on either side of me."

He was silent for a while. "I don't think I would like that."

"At the time it seemed safe. I was even planning to install security lights of my own. At home we tend to be afraid of the dark."

His voice sounded amused. "You come from a confusing time. I don't think I would fit in there at all."

"No, you probably wouldn't. No more than I fit in here."

"I think you fit here just fine."

Jody shook her head and glanced back at him over her shoulder. "There's no place for me here."

He didn't respond.

"I have to make plans for my future." She put her hands around one of the veranda supports and leaned her cheek against the cool wood. "I can't stay here, and I don't know that I should go to Camilla's house. Not permanently. I have to make my own way and not live off someone else. You're both too polite to shove me out, but I have to be reasonable about this."

"You're welcome to stay with either of us."

Jody smiled sadly. "No, I can't stay at White-friars."

"You could marry."

Jody held her breath. "Who? Who could I marry?" She turned and faced him and waited for him to answer.

"You could marry Will Breaux. I could speak to him for you, I suppose." His voice was reluctant in the extreme, but Jody didn't notice.

"Marry Will Breaux! You're proposing for him?"

"I can't speak for Will, but we've been friends for so long that I know him well. He will propose for himself if you give him the least encouragement."

"He proposed the first day he met me. I can't take him seriously. You want me to marry him?" Her sharply spoken words revealed the depth of her pain. She had known he couldn't have meant himself, but she had let herself hope.

"I'm not trying to convince you to marry anyone, but you could do worse than Will. He's a gentleman to the core and would never mistreat you. His family fortune is almost back to what it was before the bottom fell out of cotton prices, due to his trade with France and England. His family would accept you."

"I want more from marriage than acceptance. Being a gentleman isn't enough to recommend a man to me. I want someone I can talk with about all sorts of things, and I want someone I can love."

"You could love Will." His voice sounded strained, but the darkness kept her from reading his face. "He's already half in love with you."

Jody felt as if a cold hand were squeezing her heart. "I can't be content with crumbs of affection. Will isn't capable of returning the kind of love I have to give. He would be better suited to Emma."

Micah's voice snapped with his rare anger. "I don't want to hear any more about what you feel my fiancée's shortcomings may be."

Indignation flashed within her. "You don't want to hear anything that might upset the neat little world you have mapped out, do you? Not even when it would be in your best interest. You'll never be happy with Emma. You may not want to hear it, but someone needs to get that through to you before you make a huge mistake and condemn yourself to a life of utter boredom!"

"And you think I would be better suited to you perhaps?" he lashed out. "Is that what you're saying?"

Jody bit back her words. She had said too much. For a minute she tried to find a way to take back what she had said, but she couldn't. Instead she lifted her skirts and ran back into the house.

As Micah had predicted, a storm was building. Jody lay on her bed and tried to imagine a breeze into being. Beyond the French doors that led onto the upper veranda, she saw flashes of lightning and heard low rumbles of thunder. The storm was still miles away, and with it the cooler air it promised.

She sat up. Perspiration slicked her skin and made her nightgown cling to her in a most uncomfortable manner. With disgust she put her feet off the side of the bed and slid to the floor. Barefooted, she padded over to the open doors. The night air beyond was slightly cooler, so she stepped out onto the veranda. Lightning flickered to the north. After a moment thunder answered. Jody lifted her hair off her neck and prayed for even the least stirring of air.

The creaking of a floorboard beside her made her jerk her head around. Micah was standing a few feet away, cloaked in the darkness. "I didn't mean to startle you," he said.

She turned away. Even though her nightgown was concealing, she felt bare after becoming accustomed to the multiple layers of material in Camilla's dresses. "I didn't know you were out here. I couldn't sleep."

"Neither could I."

He stepped closer to the railing and a flicker of distant lightning shimmered over him. He was in his shirt sleeves, and as she had rarely seen him without a coat, she noticed, even during that brief moment of illumination, how narrow his hips were and how the shirt hugged close to his lean ribs. She had once heard him say that he had his shirts made by a French tailor in New Orleans, and she could see they fit him perfectly.

She looked away. "I shouldn't have said what I did about Emma. That was rude of me."

"I forgive you. You must be under a terrible strain." He hesitated. "What with finding yourself here and not being able to go home. I keep forgetting that you don't belong."

"So do I, sometimes." She put her hands on the rail and looked over the distant treetops to where the storm was gathering its force. "Do you think it will turn cooler?"

"I'm sure of it. I can feel change coming."

"Is that what I feel?" she asked in a whisper. "Change? I feel it all through me."

"Change comes in many shapes."

She waited, but he didn't elaborate. "I did something I probably shouldn't have done today. I went swimming in that big pond in the horse pasture."

He was silent for a long moment. "Did you?"

"It was so hot. The water felt good. Later I realized that it might not have been safe. I was always told not to swim alone, but I didn't think much about it at the time."

"Why are you telling me this?"

She sighed. "I'm only trying to make conversation so we can get past being angry at each other. I didn't mean anything by it."

"You shouldn't swim alone. Maybe Camilla could go with you if you decide to do it again."

"Can Camilla swim?"

"No."

"Then she wouldn't be much help, would she?"

"I don't know any woman who knows how to swim. I guess you shouldn't go there again. You could drown, even though that pond isn't all that deep. I once saw a man drown in only a few inches of water."

"You did?"

"It was during the war. Sometimes we fought beside creeks. I saw a man who was shot and couldn't get out of the water. We couldn't get to him because of Yankee bullets. He drowned in water a kitten could have waded through." Micah's voice was filled with remembered anguish. "He was a soldier in my command. I don't think I'll ever forget what I felt, not being able to get to him." Micah was silent for a moment. "He probably would have died anyway, but that doesn't make any difference."

"You almost never talk about the war."

"It's not a fit subject for ladies to hear. You can't imagine anything like that, Jody. It's quiet for days—you don't know for sure where the enemy is and you don't want to call attention to yourself. Then you're face to face with him, and it's as if all the noise in the world is suddenly turned loose. When a man is shot he'll scream for a while, then get quiet. The horses scream until they die. You can't forget sounds like that." He came to stand beside her and they looked out at the approaching lightning. "Nights like this bring it all back to me. That's what a battle looks like at dusk. You see flashes from cannons and rifles, and the sounds come later, just like the thunder."

"I never thought of a storm being like a battle."

"Maybe they don't have wars where you come from." His voice was hopeful.

"We have wars. Just not any fought on American soil. I've never seen a battle, not even from a distance."

"I hope you never do."

"I won't." She had made it a rule never to tell him such things about the future as would have a direct effect on him, but she couldn't let him think war might break out again in his lifetime. "Not if I stay here."

He looked at her and nodded. "Thank you."

She knew he had understood. "I never see you without your coat," she said to fill the silence. "Don't you get tired of being so formal?"

He turned as the lightning flashed again, and his face was gilded for an instant. "I'm not used to seeing you in a gown, either. As a gentleman, I feel I ought to remind you that you forgot to put on a wrapper."

"I didn't forget. It was too hot." She waited for him to digest that. "And I didn't know you would be out here."

"Jody, I can't let myself care for you. I can't."

She heard the anguish in his voice. It told her that, permissible or not, he did care. "Where I come from things are less complicated. Engagements can be broken without there being any shame to either person."

"That's there, not here."

"Or is it only in your mind that you can't change your decision? Any man can make a mistake. In my opinion, the sin would be in following through with something after a person knows it would be wrong."

"To follow through with what I'm thinking right now would be wrong. Wrong for everyone."

"How can you be so positive?" Through the darkness between them, she could feel him straining to keep apart from her. "Are you so sure that this isn't exactly what you should do, Micah? How do you know that I didn't come here to prevent you from making the mistake of marrying Emma? I know I shouldn't say these things or even think them, but how can I sit back and not try to prevent something I know is wrong?"

A growling noise rumbled from Micah's chest, and he backed away. "I can't let you tempt me like this. Damn it, Jody, I can only take so much!" He turned and strode toward the doors that opened into his room and was swallowed up by the night.

Jody waited until she knew he wouldn't be back, then went to her own bed. She could sense him on the other side of the wall, the veranda and open doors linking them across the darkness. He wanted her; she had no doubt. He might be determined to marry Emma regardless of whether he loved her, but she didn't have to make that choice easy for him. She smiled with her decision as the storm overtook Whitefriars and rain poured from the dark sky. It was good to know Micah wanted her, possibly as much as she wanted him.

Chapter Fifteen

Emma instructed her servant to put her paint box down on the grass, then she waited as he unfolded the canvas chair he had brought for her to sit on. The storm the evening before had turned the air decidedly cooler, and she thought this might be her last opportunity to capture the fall colors in the sweet gum trees just beyond the clearing. "That will be all I need for now, Marcus. I want you to return for me in about an hour."

"Yes, ma'am." Marcus went back to the road and climbed into the buggy.

As the buggy creaked into motion behind the horse, Emma studied her subject. She had always found autumn colors difficult. There were so many variations. Her style was much better suited to the pastel shades of spring. That was why she had chosen April for her wedding month. By then everything would be in bloom.

She opened her paint box and poured a bit of water from a bottle into the tray. Resting the paint tray on a cloth on her lap, she began to block out the painting. She was so busy, she didn't hear the horse approaching until George Percy was right behind her. When he spoke she jumped so, she almost spilled the water. "Mr. Percy! How dare you sneak up behind me like this!"

George blushed red from head to toe. "I didn't mean to startle you, Miss Parlange. I thought you heard me coming."

"When I didn't acknowledge you, you should have gone on. My goodness! Don't they teach children manners where you come from?"

"I'm sorry," he repeated.

"What are you doing here anyway? This is my family's land and you're trespassing."

"I was just riding down the road and thought I'd stop to speak to you. I live just down there."

She squinted up at him, shading her eyes from the sun. "You do? Down this road?"

He grinned. "Yes, ma'am. I just bought the old Hubbard place."

"Then you're planning to stay in Joaquin?" She didn't bother to keep the displeasure from her voice.

"It's my home now." His grin broadened. "I reckon that makes us neighbors."

"Only in a geographic sense. Are you going to sit there on that horse blocking my light? If so, I can move." Her sarcasm was biting, and she thought Claudia would be proud of her.

George didn't take the broad hint. Instead, he dismounted. "What are you painting? I don't see anything but a meadow."

"I'm trying to capture the fall colors. After that storm last night all the leaves will be gone in a week's time." She frowned at the trees. "They're already past their peak."

"You should see the autumn leaves in Minnesota."

She looked up at him. "Is that where you're from? Minnesota?"

"Yes, ma'am. I sure do miss it this time of year."

"It's a pity you can't go back there." Emma wished he would ride on and leave her alone. She always found it difficult to concentrate on more than one thing at a time.

"I don't miss the winters, though. No, ma'am. It gets cold enough to freeze the . . . I mean, it gets real cold."

Emma glanced at him. "I do hope my intended, Mr. Micah Deveroux, doesn't happen along this road. He might just decide to take a shot at you for talking to me all alone like this."

George looked back at the road. "If I hear a horse coming, I'll ride on."

She sighed. He just couldn't take a hint. "If you're going to stand there, at least step to one side. You're putting a shadow on my paper."

George obliged hastily. "Sorry, ma'am." He squatted down beside her in the grass and studied the paper as she put paint on it with careful dabs. "My sister can paint. She's real good at it."

"How admirable." Her voice was distracted in her concentration. "She must be a blessing to your parents."

"That she is. There's just the two of us. My sister and me. And my parents. They're still alive. She lives with them."

Emma saw no reason to comment. She couldn't have cared less where his sister lived.

"Maybe Hortense will come down and visit me someday and you two can meet and paint together."

She turned to face him. "Hortense? You're French?"

"Yes, ma'am. French Canadian, to be exact."

"Oh. Imagine that." He had risen somewhat in her estimation. Emma was proud of her own French heritage and thought no other was worth having. "My family originally came from France. Avignon, to be exact."

"No! They didn't ever? Really? Mine came from Marseille."

"I thought you said your family was from Canada."

"Not originally. First we came from Marseille."

Emma put down her paintbrush. "What a remarkable coincidence! Our ancestors were practically neighbors."

"And now we're neighbors in fact." He grinned so wide his back teeth showed. "My father can speak French to this day!"

She turned back to her paper, pretending to ignore him. "So can I. Everyone around here can." She dabbed her brush into the red paint. "Of course, being Creole is far different from being French Canadian."

"I guess so. French is French, I thought. Hortense and I call ourselves American."

"That's the difference." She touched the brush to the paper and studied the effect. "Watercolors are so difficult. You can't paint over your mistakes. I really prefer pastel chalk."

"I don't know one end of a paintbrush from the other," George said with what sounded like pride. "I'm practically color-blind."

"You are?"

"Just about."

Emma frowned. "You can't be nearly color-blind. Either you are, or you aren't."

"Then I guess I'm not."

"I hope I'm not keeping you from something," Emma said hopefully.

"Not a thing. I don't work today. It's my half day off."

She started to point out a half day was not the same as not working, but refrained. She thought that he might ride on if she ignored him.

"We've got a new batch of gloves in. There's a pink pair that you'd just love. They're about the color of that material you bought the other day."

"I have gloves to match that dress already."

"There're some blue ones, too."

"Blue?" She thought for a minute. "I have that blue poplin. Are they that shade of blue?"

"Identical. Should I put a pair back for you?" He ducked his head and pulled the top off a weed to examine it. "I don't mind riding into town and getting them for you if you want them today."

"I don't need them today. The poplin is part of my trousseau. It's my second-day dress."

"You have the prettiest clothes in town. Maybe it's because you're so pretty yourself."

Emma blushed. "You shouldn't say things like that, Mr. Percy. It's not proper. I'm practically a married woman."

"I'm sorry." He looked so crestfallen Emma felt sorry for him.

"Well, I suppose you can't help your opinions." She tried to match the yellow on the trees beside the red one. The result was not pleasing. "I declare I think there's something wrong with these paints. No matter how hard I try, I can't seem to get it right."

George studied the paint on the paper. "I never saw a tree quite that red nor quite that yellow. Not in real life. I reckon you're right. Something must be wrong with the paints."

Emma glanced at him to see if he was making fun of her. He was not. "I suppose there's no point in my trying to do anything with it. I'll just have to try again some other day." She looked in the general direction of The Oaks. "I don't suppose you saw my man coming this way? Seems like I've been here at least an hour."

"I could go get him."

"He'll be along directly, I suppose." She started packing her paints back into the box. "Does Miss Farnell ever come in to shop?"

"Not real often. Sometimes I see her with Mrs. Gallier. She doesn't seem to care much for gloves."

Emma smiled. "Her hands will be as speckled as guinea eggs. You wait and see." She looked at her own hands. She wore a pair of fingerless gloves to protect the backs of her hands from the sun; her wide-brimmed hat shaded her face. "I saw her outside one day without a hat, too!"

"Imagine! That's probably why your skin is so much paler than hers."

Emma liked that. "Well, I am a blond. Sometimes dark-haired people tend to have swarthy skin. Like Miss Farnell, for instance."

"I wouldn't say she's swarthy," George said judiciously. "Just not as pale as you."

"And she can't sew worth a flip. She was at Camilla's last sewing meeting, and she can't sew any better than a child. You should see her stitches!"

"It's hard getting them just right. I know because sometimes I stitch seams on gloves that are pulled apart."

"You do? I assumed Miss Baker did that."

"No, she only sells the cloth. I mend the gloves. That's my department. I'm hoping to add hats to my counter before long. It's not to be known around town yet, but Mrs. Simpson says she will retire soon. She's nearly sixty, you know."

"Is she really that old? I would never have guessed. What will we do when she isn't there? I'll have to go to Shreveport for my hats!" Emma let her eyes widen at the idea of such a tragedy.

"No, ma'am. I'll do the hats as well as the gloves."

"You!"

"I've been trimming hats most of my life. My mother is a milliner." He smiled with pride. "I don't mind saying that I'm rather good at it."

"You actually trim bonnets?" Emma couldn't keep from staring. "I've never known a man who could make a hat. I thought only women did that."

"I'm older than Hortense. I suppose Mother thought she would have to hand her expertise on to me. Anyway, she taught me all she knows. Hortense is really better at beading purses."

"Imagine! I can hardly wait to tell Claudia." Emma laughed. "She says men can think of nothing but dogs and horses and crops."

"I'm no good at any of those things. I always lived in the city before I came here to make my fortune."

She shook her head and her curls bobbed. "You picked a strange place to earn a fortune. Joaquin is so small even the Yankees didn't want it." She suddenly remembered she was talking to a man from Minnesota and apologized.

"That's all right. I don't mind being called that. It's what I am, a Yankee. Back home we're proud of it."

"I suppose it takes all kinds." Emma closed her paint box and put it primly aside. "It's not considered a compliment around here."

"Miss Parlange, maybe you don't know, but I never saw any fighting in the war. I was in uniform and all, but I was never in a battle. I carried bandages and mail and things like that."

"You did?" She had never thought of George as a soldier, but now that he mentioned it, he could have been.

"I just wanted you to know I never fired a shot at one of your soldiers. At the Rebels."

"The Confederate," she corrected. "I'm glad you told me, Mr. Percy. That will ease my mind, as well as that of my friends. We have had hard feelings toward Mr. Simpson for hiring you, if you must know."

"I was afraid you might think that. Well, I just wanted you to know."

The rattle of an approaching buggy drew Emma's attention. "I hear Marcus coming to get me. You should ride on before he sees you. It wouldn't do for us to be seen talking out here alone like this."

"Yes, ma'am." He made an awkward bow and lifted his foot into his stirrup.

By the time Marcus and the buggy rounded the corner, George was well down the road in the direction of his new house. Emma watched him thoughtfully. She didn't really care whether he was in the Yankee army or not, but she was deeply impressed to learn he could trim hats and sew the seam on a glove. What a pity, she thought, that he was so socially unacceptable.

"No, no," Jody said as she hurried up onto the wooden flooring. "Measure the studs. Don't put them wherever you feel like." She matched the man glare for glare.

"Mr. Deveroux knows I always do it this way. I put the studs so they come out even on the wall, more or less."

"You're doing it wrong."

Micah heard the argument and came to see what was happening. "What's the trouble?"

"She wants to tell me where to put the studs," the man complained. "Ain't no woman born that knows more about building than I do."

"Except me," Jody snapped. "Look how much lumber you'll waste doing it your way." To Micah she said, "The studs should be on sixteen-inch centers. That way you always know where they are."

"Who cares where they are once the wall is up?" the man argued. "My wife don't even know they're there, much less care how far apart they are."

"If you're going to do a thing, you should do it right." She was mad enough to throw something at him.

"Do it her way," Micah said. "Put them in at sixteen inches. She has a reason."

Jody let him take her elbow and lead her off the platform. When they were away from the men, Micah said, "What difference does it make where they put the studs?"

"What if Marcel Howard decides to put in a new door or window some day in the future? He will know what studs he will saw through before he ever starts. Besides, it's easier to insulate the house if you know where they are."

"Insulate?"

She stared at him. "You don't insulate the walls and ceiling? No wonder houses are so drafty. I never realized there was no insulation."

"We're using thick lumber. That's insulation enough." He frowned, as if he wasn't sure he was right.

"No, it's not. Wood's R factor is about zip."

"Pardon?"

Jody drew in a calming breath. "That means it doesn't do much of anything toward keeping a house warm in the winter and cool in the summer. You need something in the walls and ceiling that slows the exchange of heat."

"We don't have anything like that."

She bit her lip. "There must be something we can use. What about cotton?"

Micah grinned. "You want to stuff the walls with cotton? My men will be laughing so hard they won't be able to hammer in the nails."

"All right, not cotton. Help me think." She

looked up at the trees. "Spanish moss! It won't help much, but it will be better than nothing."

"Jody, I can't tell my carpenters to stop work and gather moss to put in the walls."

"It will help the house be more comfortable." She racked her brain to think of some other substance that would do better.

"It wouldn't be safe. If the house caught on fire, it would be filled with kindling. Marcel wouldn't be able to put it out before the whole house burned to the ground. No, we can't use moss."

"I'll think of something."

"Honey, sometimes you have to give in and let things go the way they want to go."

Jody looked at him sharply. Did he realize what he had called her? She was never sure what he meant as an endearment and what was simply the way he had of speaking. She decided it would be best not to call it to his attention. "I caught that redheaded man not using a level again," she said darkly. "I told him to level the walls or I would make him take them down and do it all over again."

Micah put his hands on her shoulders. "Do workers do all these things where you come from, or are you just trying to drive my men crazy?"

"Micah, these men seem to think a house can build itself. They use strings and ball bearings for levels, and one man was doing nothing but gathering up bent nails."

"If the nail bends or breaks, we don't throw it away. We save it and melt it down and make new ones. Now who's wasting material?"

She shook her head. "I keep forgetting that wood isn't the most precious commodity, that

303

we can't simply go to the store and buy a keg of nails."

"You could, but it would cost you dearly. It's cheaper to make them yourself, and that way you know what quality you're getting. The same with lumber. I know that the lumber I get from the sawmill here in town measures true. You don't have to measure each piece."

"I'm not used to two-by-fours that are actually two inches by four inches."

He looked puzzled. "If they weren't, they wouldn't be two-by-fours."

"Everything doesn't get better as time goes on. Heartwood costs a small fortune where I come from."

"Your houses won't be as steady if you don't use it. All the supports in Whitefriars are of heartwood."

Jody looked back at the house. "It's going up slow. We could speed it up if we had the power tools I used to take for granted."

"What's the rush? Marcel and Sally aren't married yet. The house will be ready when they need it."

She smiled. "I still forget that everything doesn't have to be finished yesterday in order to meet some deadline." She gazed up at him. "We can learn a lot from each other."

"I think we already have. What if we pack the walls with adobe?"

"Adobe?"

"I saw it done in Texas once. They were mixing mud with leaves and straw to make a wall. It wouldn't burn and would make the walls stronger."

She laughed. "Perfect. Why didn't I think of that?"

"I think I'd better be the one to tell the men. They'll take it better from me."

"They don't like me, do they?"

"It's not necessary that they should. They are our hired men, not friends. They would be against taking orders from any woman, not just you."

"That's going to take some getting used to."

"Men are accustomed to having women bosses in the future?"

"It happens. There's not such a strict division of who does what work. I know couples where the wife works and the husband stays home and takes care of the house and children."

Micah grinned as if he thought she was teasing him. "You come from a remarkable time."

"Will you walk down to the outbuildings with me? I want to ask you something." She matched her steps to his as they circled the house. "Why is that man building a shed over the stream? I asked him and he wouldn't answer me. I was coming after you when I saw how they were putting in the studs."

"He's building a spring house. Marcel wants that instead of a root cellar like Whitefriars has. The water runs through the shed and will keep butter and milk fresh longer."

"Interesting." She watched the man work for a while. "I thought maybe he was doing it to irritate me."

"Your skin is too thin. These men know what they're doing for the most part. It may be different from the way you had it done before, but they're still good at their jobs."

"Sometimes it's hard," she confessed. "I want to boss them around and have them do things that I know I shouldn't make such a fuss over." She crossed her arms and looked back at the house. "Maybe I'm more trouble than I'm worth."

"I wouldn't say that, exactly. Not always."

She had to smile. "What does Marcel think about the house?"

"He says he can't wait to move in. He never heard of putting the bedrooms on the ground floor in a house this size. Once he got used to the idea, he was all for it."

"I wish I had driven down this road before I came here so I would know if this house will still be standing a hundred years from now."

Micah nodded firmly. "It will be. I make houses to last."

"Did you build many of the houses around town? I never realized that you did this except for friends."

"I have friends all over town." He smiled down at her. "Are you getting hungry? It's almost time to quit."

She glanced at the sun. "I hadn't realized it was so late. I guess we may as well call it a day."

After the workmen had gone, Jody and Micah mounted their horses and rode toward White-friars. "I'm glad you let me help you with this house," she said. "I feel as if I'm not pulling my weight around here. Do you think I could design and build houses for other people and earn my living that way?"

"Not a chance. No one would hire you."

"Because I'm a woman." She made a face. "I have to think of something. I can't live off Deveroux charity all my life. And I'm not going to marry Will Breaux," she added. "Don't even suggest it."

"I wasn't going to."

Jody knew time was slipping by. The days were settled into autumn now, and spring would come all too soon. With spring would come his wedding. "I'll race you to the house!" She kicked her heels against her horse's sides and it leaped forward. She had to do something to keep herself from thinking about Emma and Micah together.

Jody sat on the steps and pulled her shawl closer about her.

"Are you cold? We could go inside."

"I'm okay. Soon it will be too cold to sit out here after supper. I want to enjoy it while I can. This is my favorite time of day." She looked up at the stars. "Do you ever wish on stars?"

"I did when I was a boy."

"What did you wish for?"

"The usual. A horse fast enough to outrun my friends' horses, a new toy, a good report from my teacher. What did you wish for?"

"I wished for blond hair as pretty as Mary Jean Fraser's. She was the prettiest girl in school and I thought I wouldn't stand a chance against her where the boys were concerned." She laughed. "I was right. I never was as popular as she was."

"She must have been a rare beauty indeed." His voice was surprisingly gentle. "You're beautiful."

Jody looked at him. "Don't tease me. I know I'm

307

not." He didn't dispute her, though she had hoped he might. "You really think I'm pretty?" she asked when he didn't comment.

"No, I said you're beautiful. Katie Neston is pretty. There's a difference."

"Does it bother you that she married Elwin instead of you?"

"How did you know I used to court her? No, it doesn't bother me. I wasn't as eager to be married as she was. Elwin is paying for his haste."

Jody leaned back against the porch railing and hummed a tune from a movie she had seen the last week she was in her time. "Do you ever get a tune stuck in your mind and not be able to get it out? That's been running through my head all day."

"It's pretty. What is it about?"

"It's from a movie called *Winter Love* and the song is one the leading lady sings when the man she loves tells her he is about to marry someone else." Until she said it aloud, Jody hadn't realized why she was stuck on that song. "It's a catchy tune. That's all."

"Sing it to me."

She stood up. "I can't sing. I think I'm too cold out here."

Micah uncoiled from the chair and put out his hand to stop her. "I would change things if I could."

She hesitated. She never knew if his words meant what they seemed to mean. "If you want to change something that hasn't yet happened, you can. There aren't many exceptions to that rule."

"It's not that simple. Give Will Breaux a chance. He could make you happy."

Jody lifted her chin. "Could he?" Before she could stop herself she put her arms around his neck and drew his face down to kiss him. Her lips moved beneath his, and she ran the tip of her tongue over them until Micah parted his lips. He pulled her body tightly against his and kissed her in a way that left her no doubt as to what he had meant. And even more doubt that Will could ever make her happy.

When she released him and stepped back she said, "Think about it, Micah. Do you really believe Will can make me feel like that? Maybe you're right." She went inside and left him standing on the porch.

Micah was still stunned by the way her kiss had affected him. His head was spinning. He wanted to sweep her up and carry her up to his bed and let convention be damned. He had never met anyone who could make him feel this way. The thought of Will having her made his blood race hot with jealousy. He went to the railing and looked up at the cold stars. He was on fire with wanting her. He could not sleep nights for knowing she was only steps away. During the day she was his friend and his confidante; in the evening she was a temptress who lured him away from all propriety. Worst of all, he wasn't at all sure she knew what an effect she had on him. If she did, surely she wouldn't have kissed him like that.

He put his hand on the rail to steady himself. He wasn't going to let his emotions and his needs rule his head. If every man did that, all civiliza-

Elizabeth Crane

tion would eventually crumble. All the same, he couldn't help but remember how warm her lips had been on his and how her body had molded itself to his. A muscle ridged in his jaw as he tried to enforce his logic.

Chapter Sixteen

"How nice to see you again," Emma said cordially, but her eyes were like slivers of blue ice. "When Micah sent word he was bringing you I was so excited."

Jody smiled uncertainly. "Thank you. I told him it would be an imposition, but he insisted."

"An imposition? To have guests at The Oaks?" Emma's silvery laughter tinkled. "What nonsense."

Micah smiled at Jody. "There. You see? I told you Emma wouldn't mind." He felt a surge of relief himself. Lately he had begun to wonder if Jody's assessment of Emma might have been more objective than his own. He was glad to see Emma was as gracious as ever.

"What a lovely dress," Emma purred. "Did you make it yourself?"

"No, I'm no good with a needle. Bessy made it."

"Ah, yes. Bessy is good at sewing, isn't she? I've always been surprised that Camilla didn't insist on taking Bessy with her when she married Reid."

"Perhaps Bessy didn't want to go. Besides, Camilla sews beautifully in her own right."

While the ladies were speaking, Micah went to the tray on the side table and poured them all cups of coffee. He knew Jody disliked the strong Creole brew, but as a guest, she would have to drink what they were served. He could have sworn that Emma knew, from a previous discussion of the subject, that Jody didn't like strong coffee. But as there was no *cafe au lait* on the serving tray, he concluded he must have been mistaken.

"Look at me!" Emma exclaimed. "I'm just sitting here and letting you pour the coffee as if I had no more manners than a field hand." She looked over her shoulder. "Where has my butler gone to?"

"We don't need him. The coffee is poured." Micah handed each of them a cup and saucer and got one for himself, then sat opposite Emma.

"Ever since Emancipation, they have become impossible." Emma sipped delicately. "I declare, if I were a man I would join the Klan."

Jody shot her a quick look but refrained from comment.

"The Klan has become nothing more than a pack of rabble-rousers," Micah said. "They have lived out their usefulness and should be disbanded."

"How can you say such a thing?" Emma protested, her eyes round. "If it wasn't for the Klan, think of all the atrocities that would be committed."

"The war missed Joaquin. The Klan has caused most of the trouble here," Micah countered.

"They could rid Joaquin of carpetbaggers," Emma protested, "if they only would. There's a need for that, and I'm frankly astonished that it hasn't been done."

Micah shook his head. "We only have one carpetbagger, and that's George Percy. There's nothing threatening about him."

"I wouldn't say that." Emma lowered her eyes and brushed imaginary crumbs from her lap, then folded her hands demurely. "He's made advances toward me."

Micah stiffened his back. "What sort of advances?"

Jody lifted her coffee cup and tried to drink the black liquid without flinching. "He seems harmless to me."

Emma flashed her a glance. "He rather frightens me."

Jody laughed. "George Percy from the dry goods store frightens you?"

"What has he said to you?" Micah demanded.

Emma pouted her pink lips and tilted her head, as if she were a reluctant child asked to recite a lesson. "He said I'm pretty. He came to where I was painting and tried to strike up a conversation with me. Naturally I sent him on his way immediately."

"Maybe I should have a talk with him." Micah scowled. "I can't imagine George Percy being so cavalier."

"Perhaps you misunderstood him," Jody suggested. "He's overly friendly, but I can't see him as being a threat."

"I don't know what it's like in Tennessee," Emma said, "but around here, a woman has to guard her honor. Especially against Yankees. Tennessee being a border state, perhaps you're less stringent there about who is acceptable and who is not."

Jody's eyes became guarded. Micah did not notice.

"Besides," Emma continued, "I have to be extra careful that no scandal is attached to me since I will soon become Micah's wife." She smiled at him. "No Deveroux wife has ever had the least bad thing attributed to her character."

"They must spend a great deal of time in nunneries," Jody observed. "I don't know any family that doesn't have its share of black sheep."

"I never said there are no family members to be ashamed of," Emma explained sweetly, "only that Deverouxs don't marry them."

Jody replaced her coffee cup in its saucer.

Micah repeated, "Do you want me to have a word with Percy?"

"Would you?" Emma raised her eyes to his and smiled so that her dimple deepened. "It would be such a relief to me."

Jody couldn't help but speak. "If I was confronted with a man who was being a pest, I would tell him to leave me alone. Did you try that, or did you leave doubt in his mind about your feelings?"

Emma laughed again and seemed to be encouraging Micah to laugh with her. "I could hardly be rude to the man, now could I? Goodness! You sound as if you handle yourself like a man! Micah, can you imagine me calling George out?"

"Jody wasn't suggesting you should challenge him to a duel. She merely meant you could have handled this yourself."

"Why, Micah!" Emma's eyes filled with tears, and she looked as if her face might crumple. "I thought you would want to take care of me now that I'm to be your wife."

"I'll speak to him." Micah didn't like Emma when she was so clinging. Neither of his sisters had their husbands look into matters like this, not when it involved a mere conversation or two. He knew George Percy by reputation, and he doubted it could have constituted more than that. "Besides, Emma, you know you like it when someone says you're pretty." He hoped to cajole her into a better mood. "Surely we didn't come over here to talk about Percy."

Emma brightened. "I wanted you to come to go over our wedding plans."

"I thought we had already done that." He was reluctant to discuss the wedding with Jody there; his feelings were too stormy.

"We haven't even talked about where to go on our wedding trip. I thought we might go to Paris."

"Paris, France?" Jody asked. "For a honeymoon?"

"All our friends have been to Paris on theirs," Emma said, ignoring Jody. "I'll be the laughingstock of the parish if I have to go anywhere else."

"I doubt that would be the case," Micah said. He didn't want to talk about the honeymoon at all. "Jody can't be too thrilled to hear us planning the wedding. She hardly knows anyone here."

"Nonsense! All women love to discuss weddings." Emma smiled at Jody. "Next to babies, that's the most important subject there is to talk about. Isn't that right, Miss Farnell? Maybe you could suggest a place for us to stay in Paris. I'm sure you've been, and you may know of some delightful inn where Micah and I can hide away from the world." Emma blushed.

"I really ought to go." Jody stood and looked at Micah. "I have a terrible headache and I can be no help in planning your honeymoon."

"No?" Emma's face was as disappointed as a child's. "I had hoped you would give us some guidance. Micah has no older sister to confide in, and Claudia and Camilla know only the places we know."

Micah wondered if her emphasis on *older* was his imagination. "You didn't mention having a headache earlier, Jody. We can leave at once."

"Micah, you wouldn't just run off!" Emma reached out her small hand, pleading for him to stay. "Not when we have so much to discuss. Miss Farnell can go upstairs and lie down." She called out for her maid.

"No, really. I need to be going. You stay, Micah. I know the way home."

He didn't like the idea of her leaving alone, but she seemed determined, and Emma was imploring him to stay. He hesitated, and Jody slipped out.

"What an odd woman," Emma said pensively. "She's positively peculiar. I never knew a woman who didn't relish wedding plans."

"She has a headache." Micah spoke more abruptly than he had intended.

Emma buried her face in her hands. "Now you're angry with me. Micah, what can I do?

I try so hard to include Miss Farnell in all our plans, and she refuses to be friends with me. I don't think she had a headache at all. I think she just wanted to be mean."

"That's not true." Micah went to Emma and sat beside her. "There now. Don't cry. You know I can't stand it when you cry."

"I'm trying not to, Micah. I don't want to do anything that would displease you."

He tried to see her face, but she kept it lowered so he was unable to look into her eyes. He told himself he was a cad for not believing her.

Jody rode home with real tears streaming down her face. Every time she saw Emma, and especially those times when Emma manipulated Micah, she disliked her more. Couldn't he see what she was really like? Even given that men expected women to behave differently from the way Jody had been brought up, she found it hard to believe he could fall for Emma's obvious tactics. Micah wasn't a foolish man, nor was he dense. She had to think he did it because he loved Emma. Jody's tears flowed faster.

She let the horse find its own way across the pastures. She didn't want to meet anyone and have to explain why she was crying. None of Emma's insults had gone unnoticed by Jody. How could Micah be so blind and deaf?

There was only one answer, and that was that she had to stop loving him. If she no longer loved him, she wouldn't mind that he was marrying a woman like Emma. No, she thought, that wasn't true. She wouldn't want even a casual friend to make such an obvious mistake. Micah would never be happy with Emma. Jody felt foolish for having been convinced to visit her in the first place. She had only agreed because Micah wanted her to go with him and because she wanted to be with him as often as possible before he was lost to her forever.

As much as she disliked the idea, she had to reconcile herself to accepting his engagement to Emma and his approaching wedding. Winter was already upon them and spring wouldn't be that far away. The days were passing at a speed she could scarcely believe possible.

She had to decide where she could go. To simply move in with Camilla went against her grain. Jody had never been the type to sponge off her friends, and she wasn't going to start now just because it would be easiest. Somehow she had to find a way to support herself. For a moment she considered leaving Joaquin altogether. If she was away from Whitefriars, she would never have to see Micah and Emma together. At once she threw out the idea. As hard as it was to pass as a normal woman here, where she had Micah and Camilla to help her, she would never make it on her own in another town. Besides, she didn't think she could survive without so much as a glimpse of Micah now and then. Not even if he had Emma at his side.

Perhaps, Jody thought, she could get a job as a clerk. She had seen some women working behind counters in women's sections of stores in town, although they were usually the wives or spinster daughters of the store owner. Earning a living with her needle, as Camilla might have done under similar circumstances, was out because she had no ability as a seamstress, and Micah had been adamant that no man would hire her as an architect, even though she was trained in the field and talented at the work.

Brushing the tears from her cheeks, Jody told herself she would feel better once she had a definite plan. When she knew she had a place to go and a job to support her, she would feel more confident. Micah would never understand, but then, he didn't see what a shrew Emma was under the layer of saccharine.

Whitefriars came into sight as Jody topped the rise, and she looked at it in anguish. She should never have bought that place at all. She had known it was too large for her, and if she hadn't been at Whitefriars, she might never have landed here in 1872. She would still be living in her own time and planning her life the way she had intended to live it. And she would never have fallen in love with Micah or known the heartbreak of seeing him marry someone else—or known the soaring thrill of hearing him laugh or speak or seeing the way he moved or the feel of his lips on hers.

The feel of his lips on hers. Jody touched her fingers to her lips. Micah had only kissed her a couple of times. Once she had kissed him. Each time they had kissed, his eyes had been tormented with more than guilt, but he had never followed up on the kisses. Could she be mistaken about how he had been affected? No, she thought, that wasn't possible. She had kissed a number of men, though they were nothing compared to Micah. No, she knew how to read a man's emotion. Micah had felt what she had felt. He had never spoken to her of love, but he wanted her. She was sure of it, just as she was sure his longing for her was more than mere physical desire.

She rode nearer Whitefriars. There were subtle differences in this house and outbuildings as compared to her own house. The trees were smaller, for one thing, and the buildings were newer. In her time there was no row of sheds for corn, furniture and wagon repair, blacksmithing, and the overseer. The barn where sugar and syrup were made from the cane would be a car garage in her own time. Yet the place was surprisingly the same. She was struck by the similarities every time she rode toward it. Most of the differences were visible from this angle, but from the front drive, Whitefriars seemed timeless.

If only, she thought for a minute, it was truly timeless, she could slip back into her own time and that would be that. But a niggling doubt assailed her. Would she go back if she could? It would be a simple solution to her dilemma. She would never have to see Emma as Micah's wife. But she would also never see Micah again, never hear his voice or see his smile. Did she really want that? Adding to her sadness, she had to admit that she didn't. Staying here, even with the hurt of knowing he would marry another woman, was preferable to never seeing him again. In her time, Micah and everyone she had met here were dust in the churchyard and all but forgotten. The thought was extremely hard to bear.

She rode to the barn and left her horse to be cared for by the stable boy. Slowly she walked up the path toward the house. She felt hurt and angry that Micah couldn't see through Emma's syrupy sweetness. He wasn't a dense man; why couldn't he see that she was as false as hair on an egg?

Jody went into the house through the back door and made her way around to the wide front stairs. When she had first come here she had made the mistake of using the servants' stairs and had shocked the entire staff. Since that time, she had made the longer trip and gone up the stairs intended for her. There were more rules in this time, she reflected. Some of them seemed silly in the extreme; others seemed better suited to a fantasy world. Bessy always laid out her clothes, for instance. Every morning when she awoke, Bessy asked what she wanted to wear and put it out for her on the bed, as if Jody were a child. At first this had irritated her, but now she looked on the ritual as an opportunity for her to talk to Bessy without anyone else around.

Jody was trying to sow seeds of independence in Bessy. So far the seeds had fallen on rocky ground. Bessy seemed unable to consider working as a clerk at the emporium or going to college and learning some profession, even if a college would have allowed her to enter, being neither white nor male. Jody knew she was intelligent and could read, though Bessy had denied that she could. After some probing, Jody had discovered that Bessy was afraid of reprisals if it became known that she was able to read. It hadn't always been legal to teach her people any skills that would equip them for a better life, and she was fearful of the Klan. Jody had convinced Bessy that her secret was safe, but it had been days before Bessy seemed confident again.

As she went down the hall to her room, Jody reflected that she could make a difference here, whereas she probably couldn't have in her own time. She could start a school, for instance. She was far better educated than the teacher at the Joaquin schoolhouse. Maybe she could even start a school for the former slaves. Of course, if she did, the Klan would try to run her out of town on a rail. The question was whether she should take the risk. She had never been much of a rebel before, but she had always been strong on equality issues, and here the issues had never so much as been thought of. Slavery itself had only recently become illegal.

Going to her window, Jody looked out in the direction of The Oaks. There was no sign of Micah, nor had she really expected to see him. No, he would still be helping Emma decide where to spend their honeymoon and whether she should make white napkins or ivory ones for her hope chest, and whether her going-away bonnet should be trimmed in yellow flowers or pink ones. Jody knew she was being sarcastic, but she didn't care. In her opinion, any woman could make decisions about silk flowers and napkins, and she had no patience with anyone pretending she couldn't. That the woman who feigned such ineptitude was Emma only made the irritation greater.

She crossed to the French doors and stepped out onto the veranda. Down below she could hear the sounds of 'Cilla sweeping the porch and the happy shouts of some children playing out of sight behind the oleander bushes. In this time,

Whitefriars never seemed lonely. Every inch of it was alive.

Jody went to the rail and put her hands on it. The paint, now a whitewash instead of the exterior enamel she had used, felt different, chalkier, under her fingers. There were no hanging plants where she had suspended baskets of ferns and begonias. But the air was too cold for them to live now anyway. Maybe in the spring, she thought, she could make up some hanging pots and . . . Her thoughts stopped abruptly. In the spring Emma would be mistress here, and Jody would be living somewhere else.

She went back inside and wandered to the window again, this time not bothering to brush aside the curtain. As she looked down, she saw a black woman standing beside the oleander bushes looking straight at her. It was Iwilla. Jody involuntarily stepped back. Even though she knew Iwilla couldn't possibly see her from where she stood, the old woman seemed to be making eye contact.

A cold chill swept over Jody. Reason told her that Iwilla must have seen her on the veranda and knew she was in the room, but it appeared as if the woman had somehow divined that she was there. Iwilla wasn't looking at the house in general, but straight at the window where Jody stood hidden by the lace curtain.

Jody stepped away from the window and backed toward the bed. Iwilla frightened her more than she was willing to admit. She felt behind her for the mattress and was glad when she touched its reassuring bulk at her hips. She wrapped her arm about the thick foot post and drew in a steadying breath.

"Miss Jody? You all right?"

Jody jumped, then saw Bessy. She had forgotten the door to her room was open. "Yes. Yes, I'm fine."

"You look like you been seein' a ghost." Bessy's arms were loaded with a stack of Jody's folded undergarments, and as she spoke, she crossed the room and deftly opened the dresser drawer and began putting them away. "If you're feeling sick, I could get some hot tea for you."

"No, thank you." Jody went back to the window. Iwilla was gone.

Bessy was watching her. "I seen Iwilla looking up here a minute ago. She was looking like she was full of trouble, if you ask me."

"I know. I saw her."

Bessy paused as she tucked sachets between the chemises in the drawer. "Miss Jody, there's something that's been troubling me. I shoulda told you at the time, but I was scared to."

"What?"

"Iwilla was in here."

"She was? Iwilla was in here?" Jody turned and looked at Bessy. "When?"

"It was quite a spell back. That's why I said I shoulda told you at the time, but I didn't know you all that well, and I was scared you'd say I shoulda been keepin' a closer eye on her."

"I think you'd better tell me all of it."

Bessy smoothed her hand over the lace of the chemises. "There's not much to tell. I come up and she was standing here and looking in the drawer where you keep those clothes you was wearing when you arrived. Iwilla was looking at them. I sent her away."

Jody went to the drawer and opened it. "Nothing is missing."

"If there had been, I woulda come to you right then."

"Why are you telling me now?"

Bessy didn't meet her eyes. "I've been feeling poorly ever since that day. Not real sick, just poorly. I've got an ache in my middle. I think Iwilla put it there for me sending her out of the house."

Jody opened her mouth to say that Bessy's assumption was ridiculous, then thought better of it. "Have you seen a doctor?"

Bessy glanced at her. "No, ma'am. It's not that bad. She said she was gonna come live in my stomach, and I thought it was gonna be much worse than this."

Jody didn't press the issue. She wasn't so sure the doctor would be much of an expert, even if Bessy could afford to go and even if the doctor gave her his attention. She had noticed none of Bessy's people went to the doctor unless they were positive they had something seriously wrong. "Do you think Iwilla has been in here since that day?"

"That's what worries me. I don't think so, but I can't be sure. I don't see how she got by me and the others at all. Any of us woulda stopped her. It was like she made herself invisible or something."

"Iwilla can't do that. Nobody can."

Bessy didn't look convinced. "I've seen Iwilla do things that I never thought nobody could do."

Jody wanted to ask what the things had been, but she knew she shouldn't encourage Bessy's fear of the woman. "I'll put a lock on the door. That will keep her out."

"There's already one and Mr. Micah has the key, but I don't think you ought to use it."

"Why not?"

"'Cilla and me come in and out up here all day. If we had to lock and unlock the door every time, it would be hard to get all our work done. And we would both have to have a key, as well as one for you."

"You have a point there. What do you suggest?"

"Maybe you could get Father Graham to bless the room or something. That ought to keep Iwilla out."

"What reason could I possibly give the priest to convince him to do such a thing? He would think I'm crazy. Father Graham already wonders about me, I'm sure."

"Then I reckon there's nothing else to do but to watch real close and hope she don't try anything bad."

Jody put confidence in her voice and said, "I'm not afraid of her, Bessy, and you shouldn't be either. She's just a senile old woman."

"Yes, ma'am." Bessy didn't even try to sound as if she believed Jody.

"If you see her or if you suspect she's been back in here, come tell me or Micah right away."

Bessy nodded and left the room. Jody wished she hadn't found out Iwilla had touched her things and stood in her room. She had a feeling she would have nightmares about it.

Iwilla walked from the moonlit meadow into the darkness of the woods. Her steps were as sure as if she could see perfectly, and she moved with the grace of a woman half her age. Iwilla was as familiar with the forest as she was with her cabin, and she knew exactly where she was going.

For the most part she gathered her herbs during the dark of the moon, but this time she was after a special one. This was an herb that had to be picked when the moon was completely full and when the signs were exactly right; otherwise its strength would be diminished.

Iwilla brushed aside the leafy branch of a live oak and ducked under a limb, but it touched her loose hair, so Iwilla bent even lower. She wore the red dress she saved for all such important occasions, like the ceremony on St. John's Eve. Before leaving her cabin she had drunk tafia, a strong, raw alcoholic concoction that would have dizzied a weaker head. The brew had braced her for the cold and that had been necessary since she couldn't wear a wrap. The moon had to see her red dress and her loose hair so it would know for a fact that she was Iwilla and show her where to find the herbs she sought, especially now that cold weather was upon them and the herb was getting scarce.

She carried a pouch made from a goatskin, and in it were several Johnny the Conqueror roots that she had found on the way to the woods. She usually used these in spells that involved fertility or love, but tonight she had a darker need for them.

In the shadows ahead she heard the sound of the stream. Iwilla smiled without humor. Soon she would be there. The woods thinned and she stepped into a tiny meadow that was so closely surrounded by tall trees that almost no moonlight filtered into it and it was like a well of blackness, with trees and bushes forming the sides. Iwilla reached in her pouch and drew out a small, white sheet, which she spread carefully on the ground. At each corner she placed a black candle, and when all four were in place, she lit them. A dull glow illuminated the sheet and made the forest seem even darker by comparison.

Singing softly, Iwilla reached into a pocket of her dress and took out several packets of dried herbs and balls of black wax. These were the *congris* that she had made especially for this occasion. She arranged the packets and balls of wax on the sheet in a way she had learned years ago. This was more ceremony than she usually went to in her preparation of herbs, but she wanted this spell to be particularly powerful.

Taking a small knife from her pouch, Iwilla went to the edge of the water and squinted into the darkness. As her eyes adjusted, she saw the plants she sought. Increasing the volume of her tuneless song, she stepped onto the soft mud and felt it cold and giving beneath her feet. She knew she had read the signs correctly.

The special plant was growing in a bend of the stream where a rotting log made the water form a stagnant pool. Past the log, the water flowed like ink in the darkness, its song muffled by her own chant. The chant had no real words, just sounds Iwilla fancied she recalled from her girlhood in the jungle, a combination of her first language and the noises made by animals that roamed at night. It was a chant no one but Iwilla had ever used, and that made it powerful.

In the dark, she felt among the razorlike blades of leaf for the base of the plants. She had to have a large one. There was no rush. Iwilla continued to probe in the mud until she was sure she had selected the right plant. With a quick stab of her knife, she cut the roots and drew the bulb out of the mud. She held it high, as if it were an enemy's scalp, and let her spirit go out to it.

After a while she lowered her arm and carried the bulb back up the bank to where the black candles guttered on the sheet. Iwilla stood in the middle of the sheet and studied the root. It twisted about itself and formed a shape vaguely suggestive of a person in torment. That was how she knew the plant—torment root. If it had another name, she had never heard of it.

As carefully as if it might bruise, she laid the root in the exact center of the sheet, then stepped away from it. For a while she watched it in the flickering light. The flames from the black candles made it seem to be moving with a life of its own, as if it were indeed in torment. Satisfied, Iwilla began her dance to honor the plant and to placate it into giving her its strength when the time came.

Faster and faster she danced, until her heart thudded in her chest. Suddenly, Iwilla stopped and swayed in the darkness as the candles burned themselves out and darkness returned. Then she rolled the black wax into warm balls and put them into her pocket. In time they would be used in other spells. Not touching the torment root, she gathered the sheet around it and put it all in the goatskin bag.

Feeling great satisfaction, Iwilla started toward home.

Chapter Seventeen

As Christmas drew near, the stores in Joaquin saw more customers than at any other time of the year. And in keeping with the holiday spirit, some of the shopkeepers had decorated their stores with red and green ribbons and pine boughs on banks of cotton batting in their display windows. At first Jody missed the sounds of Christmas carols being piped throughout the stores and the excessive glitter she was accustomed to, but she found herself adjusting quickly. Christmas was eagerly awaited, but everyone was most excited about the approach of New Year's Day.

On Christmas Eve Jody dressed in her best dress, a dark green velvet trimmed in a froth of ecru lace, and rode with Micah to the church. All of Joaquin was there, even the people who only saw the inside of the church once or twice a year. Jody walked with Micah to the Deveroux pew and sat beside him on the oak bench. At her feet was a brazier of coals, and she was glad for the warmth.

Just before the service was to begin, Emma arrived with her family and sat on Micah's other side. Jody had known she would be there, but she had been pretending that she wouldn't, and she felt a stab of resentment when she saw her. After nodding a greeting to Emma, Jody looked straight ahead and tried to keep her face composed. From the corner of her eye, she watched as Emma put her gloved hand in the crook of Micah's arm, and he responded by giving Emma a quick smile. Jody's eyes stung, and she told herself she was being foolish in the extreme to care so much for a man she couldn't have.

At exactly midnight the bells in the tower began to toll and a hush fell over the congregation. The children who were old enough to attend the midnight mass turned excitedly in their seats and their mothers gave reproving shakes of their heads. Jody's fingers tightened on her prayer book, and she was sure she felt almost as much excitement as the children.

The entire church was glowing with the soft light of candles. Tiny flames were reflected on the polished silver and greenery that had been placed on the main altar. The scents of beeswax and fir and pine filled the air. Something truly magical seemed about to happen.

As the last bell tolled, the organ began to play and the choir joined it in song. The priests, wearing their gold and white vestments, seemed to glow in the candlelight. The acolytes, swinging their lighted censers, filled the church with a

pleasant fragrance that masked the more subtle
scents.

A man stepped forward from the choir and
the organ strains lifted in the traditional *Minuit,
Chretien.* Jody wanted to put her hand on Micah's
arm, but she knew she couldn't. She had no right
to him. Yet the music moved her so deeply, she
felt tears come to her eyes. The soloist was magnificent, and she wondered if he might be a professional singer who had come in to visit relatives
for the occasion. Although he sang the song in
French, she understood enough of the words to
catch its meaning. Though not of her own traditions, she felt the song's special significance for
all those around her.

After the last note of the mass died away, the
congregation sat for a moment as if they were all
reluctant for it to be over. Then fresh excitement
flowed into them as they rose to return home to
the *reveillon,* the breakfast that traditionally followed the midnight mass.

Emma stood and smiled up at Micah. "Next
year I won't have to go home with Mama and
Papa," she said, her eyelashes flirting with him
even though they were in church.

"No," he said. "You won't."

Jody couldn't tell what emotion was behind
Micah's words. He was adept at keeping his
thoughts secret. Emma dimpled as if he had
given her a love sonnet. "Am I shameless to
say such a thing? Especially here in church," she
whispered.

"I would never describe you as shameless." He
took her elbow and turned her to join the crowd
that was pressing out of the church.

Elizabeth Crane

Jody felt as if she were surplus baggage. She didn't belong here. This was not her time, the Creole traditions were not her own, and most of all, Micah was not hers to love, no matter how much she might love him already.

As they joined Emma's parents, Micah said, "Will you come back to Whitefriars and have breakfast with us? You're more than welcome."

"No, no, we have our own breakfast waiting," Richard Parlange said with a smile and a clap on Micah's shoulder. "Enjoy your solitude while you can. Next year you'll have a wife of your own."

Micah's smile never wavered.

"Nonsense," Emma's mother said with a quick glance at her husband. "Micah's to come home with us. We'll have more than we can possibly eat. And Miss Farnell, too, of course," she added.

Micah was already shaking his head. "My cook would never forgive us. She will have everything ready by now. Perhaps next year."

"Well, certainly we will next year," Emma said with a roll of her eyes. "I couldn't have a *reveillon* anywhere but at The Oaks." She laughed, as if she thought Micah was teasing her.

Micah didn't reply, but Jody thought she saw a quickly veiled distaste in his eyes.

"You'll be a Deveroux by then," her father admonished. "Naturally you'll always be welcome at our table, but you'll have a table of your own. Perhaps even a baby."

Susan Parlange's blue eyes cooled. "I hardly think that's possible, since they won't be married until April."

Richard coughed in embarrassment but winked at Micah. Jody had rarely felt so out of place.

Behind them, Camilla said, "I thought you would already be on your way home."

Micah turned and smiled at her. "Not without wishing you a happy Christmas." He shook Reid's hand and bent down so he could be eye to eye with Matilda. With a broad grin, he said, "How did you like your first Christmas mass?"

Matilda grinned back. "I loved it, Nonc Micah. Will you come eat at our house? Jody could tell us more stories," she added hopefully.

"It's too late for stories," Camilla said firmly. To Jody she said, "Please come. We'd love to have you."

"We can't," Jody said. "Everything is all ready at Whitefriars." To Matilda she said, "I'll have a special story ready for you tomorrow. It's called 'Rudolph the Red-Nosed Reindeer.'"

Matilda bounced in her eagerness. "Did you know, Mama, that Papa Noel has a sleigh pulled by magical deer? Jody told me all about it. They can fly!"

Camilla looked at Jody in surprise. "No, I never knew that. Imagine!"

"Flying deer?" Emma laughed. "How silly."

Jody frowned at her. "Not at Christmas it isn't. Magical things happen then. Especially for children."

Emma shrugged. "I've never been fond of deceiving people. Not even children." The words were said so softly, Jody was pretty sure Micah couldn't hear them.

"If Jody says deer fly at Christmas, I believe her," Micah said seriously for Matilda's benefit. "She seems to know a great deal about such things."

Matilda nodded. "Jody tells better stories than even Cousin Christophe."

"That's high praise indeed," her father said in amusement. "Christophe will be amazed at being replaced as family storyteller."

"Will he be, do you think?" Micah asked.

"I have it on good authority that he will." Reid winked at him.

Jody wondered what that exchange meant. The crowd was thinning, and she could feel a cold wind blowing in from the open doors. She was looking forward to Whitefriars' welcoming fireplaces.

"We have to be on our way," Micah said to everyone in general. He put his hand on Matilda's shoulder. "I wouldn't want Matilda to be so sleepy tomorrow that she dozes through Papa Noel's visit."

Matilda's eyes sparkled. "I wouldn't do that."

Camilla guided her daughter toward the doors. "We'll see you tomorrow."

To calls of "Merry Christmas," Jody and Micah went to the buggy, and she climbed onto the seat as he pulled the blanket from the animal. The horse snorted in its impatience to return to its warm stable.

As they drove through town, Jody felt Micah's thigh against her own, and his elbow touched her as he held the horse in check. They passed other buggies and horseback riders as they drove down the quiet streets. Everyone nodded a greeting or spoke to them as they passed.

"Everyone is so friendly," Jody said. "Even complete strangers."

"Christmas makes us go beyond ourselves,"

Micah said. "It's a shame it doesn't last the whole year."

"Everyone seems happy. At home Christmas is always touched at least in part with unpleasant nostalgia. Families are so spread out. I could be with my parents and one set of grandparents, but the other set lives in Washington. Even with airplanes, the distance was too great. I had to alternate years, and wherever I was I missed the other half of my family."

"We tend to live closer to each other than that. Christophe travels the farthest, and he comes from New Orleans."

"He will be here? Matilda often speaks of him."

"He's playing the role of Papa Noel. He's with cousins in Shreveport tonight and will come tomorrow. Matilda is old enough to recognize him and so is Armand, but they pretend not to. Marie Celeste will think he's Papa Noel in person."

"We call him Santa Claus."

"And as a child you believed he came in a sleigh drawn by flying deer?" Micah smiled at her.

Jody smiled back. "Will everyone come to Whitefriars tomorrow?"

"Yes. We all go home on Christmas."

She thought about that. Even though Micah was the only Deveroux still to live at Whitefriars, all the clan still claimed it as their home. She had heard Camilla, who had a house of her own, refer to Whitefriars as if she still lived there, and so did Claudia. Now it seemed the cousins thought of it in the same way.

Breakfast was waiting for them in the dining room. Although it had been prepared for only

337

the two of them, there were two egg dishes, bread thick with currants, a braided loaf, and several kinds of wine. Jody thought she would never become used to the enormous amounts of food served at Whitefriars. When they finished the meal, a cake was brought in and placed before Micah. He cut into it and put a slice of the jelly-filled cake on Jody's saucer. The butler topped it with a large dollop of whipped cream from a silver bowl. She tasted the cake and found it flavored with rum and rich beyond her expectations. "Terrific!" she said.

"It's one of Whitefriars' best traditions."

After they ate, they went into the parlor, where Micah had put the tree. "This surprises me," she confessed. "I didn't think you would have a Christmas tree." He had chosen a native pine that filled a large portion of the room.

"It's a fairly new tradition. We had the first one at Whitefriars nearly twenty years ago. I was still a boy, and I was amazed when I saw it. I couldn't stop looking at it. The children now expect it, but you can't imagine how I felt when I saw that first one. It was covered with tiny candles and looked as magical as a unicorn."

Jody opened the box of ornaments she had made. She and Camilla had worked on them for weeks, and the box was full of pretty shapes cut from paper or cloth. Most of the decorations were of Jody's design. "I may not know much about sewing, but I can do crafts," she said as she hung a stuffed wreath the size of her palm on the tree. "I even surprised Camilla. I think she assumed I couldn't do anything at all along these lines."

"I don't know how you thought of some of these," Micah said as he picked up a snowman made from balls of cotton. "You have a good imagination."

"Since I told the children about Frosty the Snowman, he had to show up on the tree." She held up a reindeer with a red nose. "Here's Rudolph."

"I have to admit, I've enjoyed hearing the stories as much as the children did. You'll make a good mother."

Jody looked up sharply and their eyes met. Micah gazed at her, his desire for her plain on his face. After a time she looked away. "I doubt I will ever be anyone's mother."

"You're still young enough to have a house full of children."

"Only if I marry. And I won't marry except for love," she said as she hung a paper snowflake on the pine tree. "I don't fall in love all that easily."

"No?"

"It's only happened to me once in my life. Real love, I mean. I don't think it will ever happen again."

"What happened?" His voice sounded strained, and she wondered if there was jealousy in his undertone. No, she decided, it couldn't be.

"Nothing. Nothing at all." As she took a padded bell from the box, she tried to keep her fingers from shaking.

"Did he know how you felt?"

Jody glanced at him. In some ways Micah could be so perceptive, and in others he couldn't see what she thought must be obvious to anyone. "Evidently not." She hung the bell on the tree more forcefully than was necessary.

*   *   *

Early the next morning the family began to arrive. Jody had expected a crowd, but she had no idea there were so many Deveroux cousins. In an hour's time the back parlor, drawing room, and library were filled with Deverouxs, Landrys, Galliers, Biernes and Robichauxs, all talking at once. Many of them had come from Shreveport or from the towns surrounding Joaquin, and all were surprised to find Jody there.

"She's some sort of cousin," Emma said as she greeted newcomers in the hall. "She's from Tennessee, Cousin Amos's branch of the family."

Jody pretended not to hear the unconvinced tone of Emma's voice and greeted the guests as if she were indeed a long-lost relative.

With the adults still full from the *reveillon* only hours before and the children too excited to eat anything, breakfast was a small meal of brioche, butter, and the thick black coffee that seemed to be part of any gathering. Marie Celeste was too young to know what to expect, but Matilda and Armand were filled with impatience, as were their young cousins.

When everyone had eaten Micah called to the children and opened the doors to the front parlor. The tree stood there in all its glory, every tiny candle brilliant and flickering. Beneath it was the creche Micah had brought down from the attic. Jody prayed the tree branches wouldn't catch on fire as the children crowded about in awe. Marie Celeste's eyes were so round they looked like shoe buttons. Jody and Camilla exchanged a look of amusement.

Micah pretended to hear someone in the back of the house and said, "Who's that? Did you hear someone?"

Christophe Deveroux, dressed as Papa Noel, bounded into the hall at that moment, and his merry laugh rang out. The children rushed to him. Jody looked on with interest. He resembled the Santa she had known as a child, but was far more worldly in his attitude. Papa Noel was winking at one of the pretty young cousins, who blushed and smiled.

Emma called out, "Gideon, bring wine for Papa Noel." Her attitude was clearly that of mistress of Whitefriars.

"Have you been good, Armand?" Christophe was saying. "What about you, Marie Celeste?"

Marie Celeste nodded, her face solemn and her eyes still wide. "Did you fly in with your deer?" she asked in all seriousness.

"Fly in with my deer?" Christophe drew back in surprise.

"Jody says that's how you can get to all the houses in time on Christmas," the child explained. "She says deer pull your sleigh and that they go so fast they fly."

"If she says so, then it's true."

Marie Celeste smiled. Jody hid her laughter behind her fingers. Children were the same everywhere, she thought. They were all eager to believe in magic at Christmas. She was glad Christophe was able to think so quickly.

"And you must be Jody Farnell from Tennessee," he said as he drew near to her. "Our Tennessee cousins are prettier than I remembered." He winked at her and went into the parlor.

341

Jody was as intrigued as the children. Papa Noel had advice for everyone, and seemed to know even the youngest children by name. When he had exclaimed over the tree and examined the ornaments he called for Gideon to bring him his bag of gifts.

Each child received a gift and a hug. Jody knew the main presents would be received on New Year's, but there were dolls for the girls and toy soldiers for the boys. As soon as the bounty was dispersed, the children were bundled up and let out onto the veranda to play.

Jody saw Vincent, Claudia's husband, across the room. He was gazing after the children with an expression that plainly spoke his disappointment in not having children of his own. Claudia barely gave the brood a glance and was in conversation with Emma on the other side of the room. Emma seemed no more interested in the children than Claudia had been. Jody wondered if this disinterest would continue into Emma's marriage. If so, Micah would be miserable indeed, because he loved children and wanted several.

Papa Noel stole away and soon returned as Christophe. Jody let him kiss her hand, his white beard now but a small black mustache. He was older than Micah but he was unmarried, his wife having died a few years before. Jody could see why the young women had blushed when he complimented them. Christophe was clearly a ladies' man.

"I didn't know Cousin Amos had such a pretty granddaughter," he said when he released her hand.

"Thank you." In keeping with an earlier decision

she had made, she volunteered no information, especially in this gathering where there might be someone who knew more about Amos and his family than could be beneficial to Jody. "I understand you're the storyteller of the family."

"Not when it comes to complimenting young ladies," he said gallantly. "Cousin Camilla says you've taken over my position as storyteller and her children follow you about asking for stories."

"I like children. I never thought of myself as a storyteller before, but they like what I tell them."

"Flying deer?"

"It's a long story." She smiled up at him.

Micah came to them and said, "Coffee, Christophe? There are breads on the sideboard if you haven't eaten."

"I had a plate in the back room as I was putting on my red suit. I would rather talk to Cousin Jody."

Micah looked from one to the other. He didn't look all that pleased. Jody thought it was amusing that Micah would encourage her to let Will Breaux court her and not extend the same encouragement toward Christophe. Could it be because he knew she was not attracted to Will except as a friend? She tried not to read more into his slight frown than was intended.

"I would love to have coffee with you," Jody said sweetly. "Gideon makes *cafe au lait* for me."

Christophe took her elbow, nodded at Micah, and guided her toward the dining room. She felt Micah's eyes on them until they were separated by the crowd.

Once they had gotten their steaming coffee and had found a window seat where they could sit together, Christophe said, "Now where do you really come from?"

Jody jerked her head around, almost spilling the hot coffee. "I beg your pardon?"

"I know Cousin Amos and all his children and grandchildren, and none of them is named Jody Farnell."

"I'm from a second marriage."

He only smiled at her over his coffee cup.

"All right. I'm not his real granddaughter. Are you going to tell anyone?"

"No. I think I know how we're really related. Through Cousin Theodule. Am I right?"

Jody did not know how to reply so she made no comment.

"I thought so. Theodule was always so wild as a youth. Cousin Amos must have been quite amazed when you showed up, but you aren't the first baby to be left on the doorstep, so to speak."

Jody saw what he meant but didn't correct him. If he thought she was the illegitimate daughter of some remote cousin, that was fine with her, especially since there was apparently some precedent. It could also explain why she had no clear tie to that branch of the family. "You've found me out, but please keep it quiet."

"Don't be embarrassed. It happens." He sipped his coffee. "What does Micah think of you?"

"He accepts me as a cousin. What else could he think?"

"What I'm really asking is, what does Emma think?"

Jody wondered if Christophe missed anything at all. "She doesn't like me very much."

"That's understandable. Perhaps you'd like to

come visit me in New Orleans when you leave here. My home will always be open to you."

Jody rose. "If you mean what I think you mean, no thanks. There is nothing between Micah and myself. Nothing at all. Even if there were, it wouldn't include you." She drew herself up and glared at him.

He chuckled as he stood. "I didn't mean to insult you. I've always been too outspoken. Everyone in the family expects it of me. Claudia thought there was more going on than there apparently is."

"Claudia is wrong about a great number of things." So that was how he knew so much about everyone. Claudia must be keeping him informed about all that happened in the family. Her dislike for Micah's sister doubled.

"She means well. Claudia loves her brother and is afraid you might not be a good influence on him. Now that I've met you and we've talked, I can reassure her."

"Don't bother on my account. She wouldn't believe you anyway. Now if you'll excuse me, I have people to greet." As she walked away, her anger seethed.

In the parlor she heard Emma say in a clear voice, "I've never seen such odd ornaments on a tree. Have you? They're quite unlikely."

The oldest woman of the group spoke up, saying, "If you ask me, Christmas trees are an abomination. It's unnatural to bring a tree into the house. It can't be good luck."

Jody went past the door and into the library, where Camilla and some of the younger women were gathered. She joined the group and listened to them discussing babies and who was to marry whom and which cousin had done what in the past year. None of the names made sense to Jody but it gave her a reason to be away from Emma and Claudia, as well as from Christophe. She laughed when the others did and offered nothing of herself, trying in vain to convince herself that this form of socializing was good enough for her.

In no time the New Year was upon them. The cousins from more than thirty miles away had stayed for the rest of the holiday season, and Whitefriars was filled with people. Christophe had gone to stay with Claudia, as had several of the other older cousins. Jody was so tired of seeing faces and hearing voices, some of which spoke only French, that she was more than glad to see the holidays drawing to a close.

There was another midnight mass, followed by another *reveillon*, but this time everyone gathered at Whitefriars, and after breakfast there was dancing. Micah had arranged for music, and the rugs and furniture had been cleared away in the front parlor and drawing room. With the double doors between the rooms opened, the space served quite well as a ballroom.

Jody tapped her toe to the music and watched the couples whirl about on the polished floor. She had always loved dancing, but she didn't know the first thing about these steps. They seemed to be comprised mainly of bounding about the floor as quickly as possible. She was amazed the dancers didn't run over each other.

Christophe came to her and held out his hand. "Will you dance with me?"

"No, thank you. I would rather not." She hadn't liked him since he suggested that she might be interested in more than a cousinly relationship with him.

He chuckled. "You're still angry with me."

"Yes, I am. Go away, please."

"Not until you've forgiven me. I was wrong to assume what I did. I can see now that I was entirely mistaken."

She looked at him. "Is this true?"

"Upon my word as a Deveroux."

She didn't know if this carried much weight or not, but she saw Micah watching them and nodded. "All right. I'll forgive you."

"It's just that with Theodule's reputation and you being his natural daughter, well, you can see how I could come to that conclusion."

"Don't press your luck," she snapped, then smiled for Micah's benefit. "I still don't want to dance with you."

"Will you walk on the veranda then?"

She glanced at Micah. "Yes. I would like some air."

They went out onto the porch. The air was crisp and cold, but after the heat of the house, she welcomed it. Squares of yellow light illuminated the porch boards beneath the windows, but the furniture was black in the shadows. Jody went to the nearest window and looked at the dancers inside. "I've enjoyed my visit at Whitefriars," she said to make conversation.

"Where will you go after Micah and Emma are wed?"

"Not to New Orleans," she said tartly. Then,

"I'm not sure. Camilla wants me to live at her house."

"It would be better than to return to Tennessee."

"I can't go back there." She knew no one in Tennessee at all.

"I want to offer you a place at my house—this time as any cousin would to another. We Deverouxs stick together, you know. Regardless of your birth, you're a cousin, and we'll treat you as such."

"How does Claudia feel about that?" She had wondered if Christophe had confided her "past" to Claudia. Jody had a feeling Claudia had sent him to talk to her for the very reason of finding out more about her.

"She agrees with me, but thinks it would be . . . awkward for you to remain here after Emma and Micah are married."

"You may tell Claudia that I have no intention of doing that." She wrapped her arms about her. "Let's go inside. I feel chilled."

As they joined the others, Jody was aware that Micah had been watching her almost from the moment the door shut behind them. It heartened her to know he cared enough to wonder where she was and what Christophe had been saying to her on the dark porch.

The next day was filled with visiting. All the younger members of the family were expected to visit with all the older ones. Since most of them were at Claudia's house, Jody and Micah drove there. After Claudia's they went to several other houses, and Jody was thoroughly confused by the multitude of cousins she met.

"How do you remember them all?" she asked as they drove back to Whitefriars, where more cousins would come to pay calls for the remainder of the afternoon. "I can't remember half their names."

"You would if you had known them since birth. In time you'll get everyone straightened out."

"That last couple, for instance. Tante Burdette? I could hardly understand her."

"She speaks very little English and she was wondering why you speak no French. You may want to learn it. We all speak it from the cradle. English is our second language."

"What was she saying to you as we left?"

Micah looked away. "Nothing. Nothing of importance."

She didn't believe him. She might know very little French, but she had picked up enough to know the words *unwelcome* and *uninvited*, and she had heard the name of the infamous Theodule. "I gather Claudia and Christophe were here before us."

"We all visit on New Year's Day." He made no comment, but she could see he had been upset by whatever the elderly aunt had said to him. Jody let the matter drop and nodded to a couple passing in a brougham, who were calling, *"Bonne annee, bonne annee!"* She was not at all sure it would be a happy new year.

Chapter Eighteen

No matter how hard Jody tried to forestall it, winter passed. With deep despondency she noted the dogwood blossoms floating like snow in the woods, soon to be replaced by wildflower blooms. Jonquils alongside narcissus and hyacinth filled the flower beds with color. April was approaching fast.

These days, Jody was spending a lot of her time with Camilla, who was teaching her all she would need to know to take care of her own house since Jody continued to refuse to move into the Gallier home. Jody felt as if her head would burst with all the things she had to remember, things she had taken for granted in a time when washing machines and dryers and vacuum cleaners were common.

"You have to beat the dust from the rugs every spring," Camilla said as she strained to put a large rug over the clothesline. This was a task normally done by one of her servants, but for the sake of demonstration, Camilla was doing it herself this time. "And you need a strong line or it will all end up on the ground." She straightened the rug and pushed a stray tendril of hair back in place.

Jody examined the curly wire rug beater she was holding for Camilla. "Can't I just sweep them?"

"Not if you want the rugs to last. Dirt will get imbedded. It's bad enough at the end of winter. If you have servants, they do this hard work, but even so, you'll have to oversee them. The only way to know what they should be doing is for you to know how to do it yourself."

"I doubt I'll be able to afford a servant. I may not even have a rug."

"Don't talk like that. Here. Hold the beater like this and hit the rug as hard as you can."

Jody got a good grip on the beater and swung at the rug. A puff of dust flew in her face. She coughed and stepped back.

"That's the way." Camilla took up the other beater and together they attacked the rug. The cloud of dust they generated made conversation difficult until they had finished and the dust had blown away.

"I'm exhausted. You have to do this to every rug? Every spring?"

"You'll get used to it." In a lower voice, Camilla said, "What did you use? You know, where you come from?"

Jody smiled. Camilla rarely asked questions. "We have electric brooms called vacuum cleaners. You just plug them into the wall and guide them over the floor. The rugs don't even have to be moved."

"Imagine!" Camilla took out her handkerchief and patted the sweat from her face. "That sounds a lot easier than beating the dust out by hand."

"You can't even imagine how much easier. I used to vacuum all the floors in my apartment every other day. I didn't do spring cleaning at all because it never got that dirty."

Camilla shook her head in amazement. "You've had to get used to such a different life. It's no wonder you don't take to housekeeping so easily."

Jody had to laugh. "That's the most tactful way it could be put." She sighed. "Maybe I should accept one of Will's proposals and settle for servants and never having to lift a finger unless I want to."

"Don't you do any such thing."

"It would probably scare Will half to death if I did. He doesn't mean it when he asks me to marry him." She helped Camilla take the rug from the line and carry it back into the house. She saw Will often at church or at parties and almost every time he proposed, usually in a flamboyant manner that no one could have taken seriously, in spite of what Micah believed about his intentions.

As they rolled up the next rug to carry out, Camilla said, "Micah needs to be shaken up good. April is right around the corner."

"You don't need to tell me. Emma is at Whitefriars every time I turn around."

"She is? That's hardly proper." Camilla frowned.

"It's no more improper than for me to be living there. I guess she sees me as a chaperon."

"Micah talked to Reid yesterday, and Reid says he thinks Micah is getting cold feet."

"It doesn't matter. He's determined to marry her."

"He doesn't have any choice. Especially not with the wedding dress finished and the wedding guests invited."

They carried the rug out into the sunshine and draped it over the line. Filled with frustration, Jody put all her heart into beating the dust from the fabric. She pounded the rug until her arm ached, then stepped back to get some fresh air. "He can't marry her, Camilla. He just can't. He doesn't love her."

"There are a lot of reasons to get married. Love is just one of them."

"But you love Reid. You married for love."

"I was lucky. Claudia and Vincent weren't in love. Oh, I think he loved her, but she didn't feel the same way about him. She never pretended that she did, really. They assumed love would grow."

"Evidently it didn't."

"Sometimes it happens that way. Claudia isn't unhappy."

"Is Vincent?" Jody retorted.

Camilla didn't answer. They both knew Vincent wasn't happy.

"It's not so much that I want Micah only for myself. It's really not," Jody continued. "If he were in love, I would manage to accept it. But he's not. I've seen the way he looks at her when he thinks no one is watching. It's the way you'd look at a stranger. At night he sits staring off into space when he's pretending to be reading, and I know he must be worrying about the future."

"There's still nothing he can do about it." Camilla gave the rug a last whack and let her arms drop. "Jody, please don't think I'm too inquisitive, but do you love him?"

Jody looked away. After a while she said, "Yes. Yes, I love him. I can't bear the idea that he will be unhappy."

"Have you told him?"

"Of course not. I can't do that. He hasn't given me any encouragement. Not really."

"How can he? He can't court you while he's engaged to another woman. Micah is a gentleman."

"Would a lady just blurt out that she loves someone? I don't think so."

"You don't have to come right out and say it. There are ways of making it known to him."

"How?" Jody listened with interest. She had never mastered the art of flirting.

"Well, I don't know how to explain it." Camilla frowned slightly as she tried to figure out just what she would do. "It's a way of listening to whatever he says and of making yourself available for his notice. Not by any overt action, of course, but by how you stand and how you smile."

Jody shook her head. "I don't have any idea how to do that."

"You must have had older cousins to observe. Do what they did."

"I have few cousins of any age. Even if I did, I doubt I could learn anything from them. Flirting must have changed drastically over the years. We aren't as subtle where I come from."

"Maybe you're being too subtle. Put yourself in

Micah's place. If you give him no reason to know how you feel, how is he ever to know? At times one has to be rather obvious with men. They don't seem to think the same way we do."

Jody smiled. "What good will it do? You've said he has to marry Emma. There's no reason to embarrass myself if there's no hope anyway."

"There's always hope until his wedding ring is on her finger. Maybe Micah isn't as gentlemanly as we've always assumed. Maybe he doesn't know he has a chance with you."

"That's a thought. Perhaps I could appeal to the cad in him." She grimaced at Camilla. "You're right, you know. If he were going to break off the engagement, he should have done it months ago before everything was ready for the wedding. Now he would be looked down on by everyone."

"All I know is that April will be here in three days and the wedding is set for only a week away. If you're ever going to do anything, now is the time."

Jody helped Camilla remove the rug from the line and carry it back in. Camilla's children, just released from their lessons, hurried in to the room where their mother and Jody were putting the rug back in place.

"Tell us a story, Tante Jody," Armand pleaded. "We haven't heard a story in days."

"Jody will tell you one later," their mother said. "We're busy now."

"Tante Jody, will you come live in my room when Nonc Micah marries Miss Emma?" Marie Celeste asked. She was too young for lessons and had been feeling lonely for several weeks while her brother and sister were with the tutor.

"I can't live in your room, honey," Jody said tactfully. "I have to find a place of my own. You can come visit me there."

"We have an extra room," Matilda said. "We've all talked about it and we think that would be best."

Jody smiled and hugged the children. "Thank you, but I'll have to think about it. I may stay here for a few nights. It all depends."

The children's faces lit up. "You'll be here that long? And you'll tell us stories?"

"You children run along. It's not polite to insist like that." Camilla gently pushed her son on his way. "Go outside and play in the sunshine. It will rain soon enough and then you'll have to stay inside."

As the children did as they had been told, Camilla said, "They don't mean to pester, but they love you and can't understand you have a life of your own."

"I love having them want me. It makes me feel wonderful."

"You should marry and have your own children. I don't think Will is serious, either, but that doesn't mean someone else might not be."

"If you had loved Reid and knew you couldn't have him, would you have been eager to look for someone else?"

"I see what you mean. So what will you do?"

"I wish I knew."

When Jody returned to Whitefriars, Emma's buggy was parked out front. She considered riding past the house and into the fields until Emma was gone, but she was tired and needed to wash up and rest. Camilla owned a great number of rugs. Jody didn't think she would ever be able to walk across a rug again in the same carefree way.

She left her horse with a boy who was eager to ride it back to the stable and went inside. Because she had been riding, she was wearing the full culottes she had made so that she could ride on a man's saddle. Camilla had learned to take Jody's divided skirt in stride, but Jody could tell by Emma's face that she was shocked.

"You were riding astride!" Emma exclaimed as Jody came into the front parlor.

"I always do. I don't like sidesaddles." She looked around. "Where's Micah?"

"He had to speak to a man out back." Emma was sitting on a chair with her skirts spread about her like the petals of a flower. "It will give us time to talk."

"Oh?" Jody was immediately on her guard. "What do we have to talk about?"

"The future, of course. In just over a week I'll be the mistress here."

"Yes, I know."

"I was wondering what your plans might be."

"So have I."

Emma frowned and put her head to one side. "Surely you aren't expecting to stay on here? Not that I am trying to put out a cousin, but it really wouldn't be proper."

"Not proper?" Jody felt like goading Emma, but with great effort managed to refrain. "I can assure you, there is nothing improper going on."

"I know that. Micah is a gentleman, after all." Emma's sharp eyes belied her words. She quite obviously thought something was amiss.

"I assumed cousins always had a place at Whitefriars. That's what Micah said."

"He probably meant elderly cousins who have no place else to go. You could go back to wherever you came from. Cousin Amos would have to take you in, as you are his granddaughter, even if your father *is* Theodule."

"Christophe has a loose tongue," Jody observed wryly. "Who else did he tell that to?"

"I have no idea. Claudia told me. At least it explains why Cousin Amos never answered our letters about you."

"You wrote and asked him?" Jody stared at her. "You didn't take my word? Micah and Camilla never doubted me."

"No, but they can be so naive. Claudia and I were curious. I suppose you can't help having been born on the wrong side of the blanket, but it does relieve us of some duty toward you. After all, it's only an assumption that your father is part of our family at all."

Jody didn't know what to say. She couldn't argue the issue without telling Emma more than she should. She had to bite back the words.

"I see you have no defense. I thought not. At any rate, you must be thinking of some other place to go. If Camilla doesn't object, I suppose you could go there. You do seem to have formed a friendship of sorts with her."

"Believe me, I have no intention of staying at Whitefriars after next week." Jody fought back the tears that threatened to flow. She refused to let Emma see she was hurt.

"I can hardly wait to move my things over here,"

Time Remembered

Emma said in a conversational voice. Micah's footsteps could be heard in the hall. "I don't know what possessed Micah to paint the walls such pale colors, but I will take care of that."

"I like these colors."

Emma smiled and her lips puckered. "All the more reason to change them," she said in a low voice. Micah entered before Jody could reply.

"Jody! I didn't know you were home." Micah smiled at her. "Would you like for Gideon to bring you some tea?"

"No, thank you. I was about to go up and freshen up. I've been helping Camilla with her spring cleaning."

Emma wrinkled her nose prettily. "I had wondered. You're all dusty, aren't you?"

Jody glared at her. Micah apparently didn't notice. "You look fine," he said. "Have some lemonade then."

To irritate Emma, Jody sat down. "Thank you, I will. After all, I ought to be with you if I'm to be your chaperon."

"I never thought of it that way," Micah said, "but I expect you are right. Gideon," he called out. When the man came into the room, Micah said, "We'd all like some iced lemonade."

Gideon left the room. Emma brushed at her skirt with tiny movements of her hands. "I do hope Mama's pink roses are in bloom by next week. I've always wanted my bridal bouquet to be made of those roses."

"They always bloom in the spring. I'm sure they won't disappoint you." Micah went to the window and looked out. "The crops are already coming up."

"How do Marcel and Sally Howard like their new house?" Jody asked. "I was hoping to see them Sunday and ask if they were pleased."

"They like it a great deal." Micah smiled at her, and Jody felt warm all over.

"It's a most peculiar house," Emma said. "I rode by it the other day and was positively startled. It seems to ramble all over the hill. What on earth possessed you to make it such an odd shape, Micah?"

"It's a new style." He grinned at Jody. "It's called a ranch-style house."

"I think it's very peculiar. Of course, Sally has always been an odd sort, hasn't she? Remember when she tried to paint pictures on those turtles and her brother let them go? They went to the creek behind old Mrs. Wallace's house and scared her half to death. She didn't know what to think of turtles with pictures on their shells."

"That was a long time ago."

Jody said, "Sally sounds interesting. I think I'll get to know her better."

"You'd be great friends. I know it." Emma gave Jody her simpering smile. "She's such an unusual person."

Jody refused to be baited. She had seen Emma play this game before. The object was to make Jody look bad in front of Micah. To Micah she said, "I think you should help me look for a place of my own."

"A place of your own? You're welcome here for as long as you want to stay."

Jody saw Emma's quick glare. "Thank you, but that won't be possible. Do you know of a place I could rent?"

"Not offhand. If you won't stay here, you should go to Camilla's. The children would love that."

"I know. Marie Celeste asked if I would move into her room." Jody smiled fondly at the memory. "They are so sweet, all three of them."

"Camilla lets them run about all over the house as if they were wild Indians," Emma said. "She shows no restraint over them at all."

"I think they are exceptionally well-behaved," Jody protested. It was one thing for Emma to toss darts at her, but quite another for her to find fault with someone Jody loved.

"Children are lively," Micah agreed. "It's a sign of health and intelligence."

"They can be healthy and intelligent in the nursery," Emma said with a toss of her curls. She dimpled and looked up at him obliquely. "Our children will be better behaved, if I have anything to do with it."

Micah's brows knitted, but he made no comment.

Gideon arrived with the lemonade on a silver tray. Jody sipped it gratefully. She could still taste the dust from the rugs.

"I was just telling Miss Farnell that I'm amazed at your choice of colors," Emma said. "I would like for the men to start on my room right away. I've decided to paint the wood a deep brown and I've found some wallpaper that I simply love. It's a maroon leaf pattern that will wear simply for years."

"Your room?" Jody asked.

Micah shifted his weight. Emma nodded emphatically. "I've decided to take the room at the top of the stairs and to the right. I believe it's the room you're currently using."

"You aren't going to use Micah's room? You'll have one of your own?" She looked at Micah for clarification.

Emma looked puzzled. Jody realized Emma had expected her to object to having to give up her room to the painters before she had intended to move out, not that Jody would question the sleeping arrangements.

"It's an idea Emma has," Micah said. "We haven't decided it will be that way. Emma, I just had that room painted. It doesn't need more paint and I like the colors the way they are."

Jody stood abruptly. "I think I should go freshen up." She had no intention of letting them argue about Emma's bedroom in her presence. "Let me know who wins," she couldn't resist adding.

Micah watched her go in exasperation. "Emma, you shouldn't have said that. In the first place, Jody is using that room as you well know, and you all but told her to move out of it. In the second place, we have never agreed that you will have a separate room."

"I assumed we had. You know I feel quite strongly about it."

"I feel equally strongly about you sharing my room. We'll be married. You're supposed to live with me then, not down the hall."

"But my parents and Claudia—"

"I don't care what their sleeping arrangements are. In my opinion Claudia and Vincent might be fonder of each other if they had to sleep in the same bed every night. But that's neither here nor there. My wife will sleep in my bed and that's all there is to it."

Emma let tears rise to her eyes. "You're trying to frighten me. That's mean."

He drew a steadying breath. She was so fragile and innocent. "I'm not trying to frighten you. But I have to insist on this."

Emma turned her face away and assumed the posture of a wilting flower.

"You aren't crying, are you?" he asked suspiciously.

"No," she said with a sniff.

"You are. You're crying. I didn't want to make you cry."

"Well, I can't help it. You're so big and strong and you say such shocking things. Whatever will happen to me when we're married and you have complete say over me?" Emma's voice was so small and quivering that Micah had to listen closely to hear what she was saying.

"If you're so afraid of me, why do you want to marry me?" he asked in exasperation.

"I love you. I can't help it if you're so overpowering, too. You don't know how overwhelming you can be." Emma drew in a wavering breath. "I don't mean to be so fearful, but I went to the dry goods store today and that awful man spoke to me again."

"George Percy? What did he want this time?"

"He wanted to talk to me. I was trembling by the time I left."

Micah rubbed his hands over his eyes. "I'll have to speak to him. I can't have you afraid to go to the dry goods store."

"I told him you'd call him out if he persisted in his attention toward me."

"You didn't really, did you? Emma, dueling is

illegal. I don't want to shoot anyone."

"Not even for me?" She looked up at him, and her eyes were dewy with tears. "Not even to protect my honor?"

"Don't do this to me," he said. "I'll talk to him and tell him to leave you alone."

"Everything is just so difficult when a person has to grow up and be a lady. You can't imagine, Micah. At times I feel quite unequal to the burden."

Micah studied her bent head. He was beginning to wonder if anyone could be as delicate as Emma and never be sick or unable to do the things she pleased. It was almost as if she were pretending. He shook his head impatiently. Emma wouldn't do that. What could a person gain by pretending weakness? "I'll take care of you, Emma. You'll be fine."

"I suppose I'm high strung because of the wedding," she admitted. "I want everything to be just right, and I'm afraid something will go wrong. I've dreamed of this day all my life. I don't want it to be less than perfect."

Micah went to her and put his arm around her. He wished he felt something from the contact. Now that he thought about it, he hadn't felt anything when he touched Emma for a long time. Unbidden, the thought of Jody came to his mind. The evening before, their fingers had brushed when she passed him the salt at dinner and he had felt that touch all the way to his toes. Trying to put Jody out of his mind, he hugged Emma.

As usual when he held her, she folded her arms against his chest as if she didn't want too much of their bodies to touch. He hadn't noticed this habit of hers until lately, but once he had, it had irritated him in the extreme. "Emma, put your arms around me. Hold me."

She pulled away. "I can't do that. What if Gideon were to step into the room? Or worse still, Miss Farnell? There will be time for hugs after we're married and it's proper."

"At times I get the feeling that you don't like to touch me or to have me kiss you," he said in concern. "Am I right, Emma?"

She turned away and went to the window where he had stood earlier. "I'm not loose in my morals, if that's what you mean. Mama says she will tell me on the day of my wedding what my duties will be as your wife. I'll fulfill my duties to you. Never fear."

Her reassurance sent more trepidation through him. "I had hoped you wouldn't consider our life together as a duty." He stopped. There was no use discussing it with her; she had all but told him she had no idea what a man and woman did together in bed.

Upstairs Jody had stripped off her dusty riding habit and was washing her body with water from the washbasin. She was still upset from seeing Emma. She looked around the room and tried to imagine it done in dark browns and maroon leaves. "Terrible," she muttered. "Just terrible!"

Emma expected to have this room rather than share one with Micah. Jody still couldn't believe she had heard her properly. If she were in Emma's place, she wouldn't even consider such an arrangement. Evidently the proposition was not new to Micah, but she couldn't imagine him agreeing to it—although it gave her a tiny feeling of happiness to think that he might.

Emma's wanting to have her own room more than proved that Jody was right in her assessment of whether they would be happily married. Micah had to be saved from himself.

As she rubbed the damp cloth over her arms and neck, Jody thought about her options. She had to do something that would leave no doubt in Micah's mind that she loved him. Merely to say so wouldn't be enough. Not when people in his circle seemed to toss the word about so lightly. No, she had to do something that would prove her love to him, and she had to do it as quickly as possible.

Only one thing came to mind. She had to seduce him. Jody sat on the stool beside her bed to think. She couldn't hope to compete with Emma when it came to flirting. Jody knew she could never bring herself to attempt simpering and mincing the way Emma did. Nor would it get his attention if she were more natural and open. She had tried that for months. He seemed to regard her as one of his cronies when she did that.

She looked down at the chemise she was wearing. It was fine lawn and much lighter weight than the heavier cotton one she had worn all winter. A delicate blue ribbon was threaded through the lace and her bloomers matched it perfectly. In her time, the chemise would be considered utterly feminine and seductive. Would Micah think so?

She knew his routine perfectly. After supper he would pretend to read in the library, while his thoughts ranged to who knew where. When the clock chimed ten, he would announce he was tired and go up to his room. Jody usually went upstairs at the same time in order not to keep Gideon and the others up late. She would read in bed and listen to him pace in his room or on the veranda. Micah had followed this same routine every night of late.

Tonight would be different. Jody smiled as she hurried to the dresser to brush her hair.

Chapter Nineteen

Jody waited until she heard Micah moving about in the next room, then slipped off her wrapper. She had left the library before Micah this evening so she would be prepared for him when he went to his room to go to bed. Nervous, but determined to follow through with her plan, Jody went to her mirror and brushed her hair until it gleamed. Earlier she had washed it under the pump in the kitchen, and now it was smooth and soft. Taking a deep breath, she stepped out onto the veranda and crossed to the doors to Micah's room. She hesitated for an instant. If this didn't work, she would look worse than foolish. She opened the doors.

Micah was in his shirt sleeves and the front of his shirt was open, revealing his chest. His trousers molded to his lean hips and muscled thighs like a dark skin. He had been running his fingers through his hair and it was tousled over his forehead. Jody had never seen him look so sexy.

For a moment he didn't speak. "You couldn't sleep?" he said at last.

"I didn't try."

As she stepped into the light, he noticed she was wearing only her chemise and pantalets, and his eyes darkened to the hue of a stormy sky. "You shouldn't be here," he said hoarsely.

"I think I should be. I think I should have come here long before now." She went to him and put her hand on his chest. "There are things between us that need to be said."

"Some words should never be spoken." He didn't pull away from her and looked as if he were struggling not to kiss her. "In good conscience I can't hear them."

"Then your conscience is going to be troubled, because I'm going to say them. I love you, Micah. I can't remember when I didn't love you. I have no idea when it started or how it will end, but I can't stop feeling this way about you."

"Jody." He made her name a caress. "Don't tell me things you will regret in the light of day. Leave now. Go back to your room."

"Only if you can say you love Emma and not me." She waited. He made no reply. "You see? We belong together." She ran her fingers across his chest and the hairs tickled her palm.

He caught her hand and held it beneath his. "You have no idea what you're doing. Go now. You tempt me too much."

"That's exactly what I had in mind. In fact, I intend to do far more than tempt you." She tiptoed up and kissed his lips, then moved away.

She knew his eyes were on her and she made her

movements slow and seductive. As he watched, she made her way around the room, blowing out every other candle, leaving the room in a dim glow. She didn't extinguish them all because she wanted him to see her, and she wanted to see him.

Jody went to his bed and pulled out the stool that was used to climb to the top of the feather mattresses. Micah hadn't moved, but his hot gaze followed her. A thrill of excitement filled Jody, and she smiled at him as she climbed up onto his bed and sat with her legs curled to one side. She reached up and ran her hands through her hair and watched his reaction.

"Don't tempt me so." He sounded as if the words were pulled from his soul. "You don't know what you're doing to me."

She didn't answer. Instead she caught the end of the ribbon that held the neck of her chemise and slowly, ever so slowly, untied it, allowing the neckline of her loosened chemise to fall lower on her breasts. A low groan rumbled from deep within Micah, and he slowly but deliberately strode toward her.

"Don't send me away," she whispered when he reached the side of the bed. "Give me tonight."

She could see the war being waged within him in his eyes. He wanted her, but he knew he shouldn't have her. To put an end to his doubts, she lifted her arms, put them around his neck, and drew him to her lips.

The kiss was gentle at first, a tasting and a sampling. Then, as their desire grew, it became much more passionate. Jody felt the world whirl about her as Micah put his arms around her and drew her up to him. He was so strong, he had no difficulty lifting her up and pulling her against his body. Jody kissed him with all the abandon of her dreams.

When he released her his eyes were dark and hot, his breath ragged. Jody ran her hand over the familiar planes of his face and threaded her fingers through his hair. "I love you," she repeated softly. "Whether you love me or not doesn't change that."

"I do love you," he said at last. "God help me, but I love you more than I ever thought possible. I think about you every waking moment. You're in my dreams. I hear your voice and I forget what I am saying. When you laugh, I feel unreasonably happy and I want to hear you laugh again and again. I feel as if you've possessed me, body and soul."

"Make love with me," she murmured. "Let me stay in your bed all night. Let me sleep in your arms afterward. I want you so much."

As Micah ran his long fingers through her hair, it fell back over his hands like dark silk. "Jody, do you know what you're asking?"

She nodded. "I want to make love with you. I want to give myself to you and to love you in return."

Micah straightened and began unfastening the remaining buttons on his shirt. His eyes never left her face. Jody watched in fascination as his skin appeared inch by inch. He was more tanned than she had expected, and she surmised he must have been working without a shirt whenever she wasn't around. He tossed the shirt aside, and she ached to touch the firm muscles that lay just beneath his smooth skin. Without a word or any change in his expression, he unbuttoned and removed his trousers.

Jody smiled when he stood naked before her. He was built like a Greek god, well muscled, but graceful and lithe. "You're beautiful," she whispered.

"I don't frighten you?" He seemed surprised that she was eager to see him, and that the sight of his naked flesh didn't alarm her.

"You could never frighten me."

He sat beside her on the bed and reached past her to pull down the covers. Jody rolled her legs over and knelt on the smooth sheets. Her chemise slid lower and all but exposed one of her breasts. Micah reached out and drew her to him for a lingering kiss. Jody shifted so that she lay beneath him, her body molded to his.

"Jody," he whispered again. Her eyes met his as he began to move his hand over her sides and stomach.

When he touched her breasts through the thin fabric of her chemise, Jody closed her eyes and sighed in ecstasy. His fingers sent thrills racing through her. When he pulled away the fabric and touched her bare skin she thought she would explode with desire for him. "Yes," she whispered. "That feels so good."

He had evidently expected her to be quiescent, because he gave her a searching look. "I want to please you. I want you to enjoy this as much as I will."

She smiled. "I want to please you, too." She placed petal-soft kisses along his cheek and jaw. "I love you, Micah. I love you so much." When she reached his ear, she caught the lobe between her lips and kissed it.

Micah eased the chemise down to her waist and leaned back to look at her. Jody felt her excitement build as she saw the desire flickering in his eyes. She had never felt so seductive or so beautiful. She let him look at her as long as he wanted. After a few moments he drew her chemise and pantalets off over her hips so that she was as naked as he.

Although the air in the room was cool on her skin, Jody felt hot all the way through. In the candlelight, Micah's skin was a deep gold and his hair was as black as the night. The expression in his eyes spoke of his love for her as well as his desire. Slowly he lay beside her, lowering his body until it touched and shaped against hers. Feeling all his body at once made Jody draw in her breath sharply. He felt so good!

Micah brushed her hair back from her face and gazed deep into her eyes. "I love you," he said. "Never forget that I love you."

He kissed her again, long and deep. She parted her lips and touched her tongue to his. Her passion was soaring and she could scarcely keep from rushing him in her eagerness. As if he could read her thoughts, he said, "I want this night to last as long as possible. I want to love you so thoroughly you will never forget me or how much I love you."

She knew what he meant, but she refused to think beyond the moment. Tonight he was hers, and she wouldn't share him even in her thoughts.

He touched her breasts, teasing her nipples to aching desire, then lowered his head to take them, one by one, into his mouth. Jody closed her eyes and arched her back, offering herself more fully to him. She had never been loved as thoroughly as he was doing, and her body had never before responded so completely. She laced her fingers in his hair to hold his lips to hers and let her soul merge with his.

Micah caressed the curve of her hip, then pulled her against him and cupped her buttocks in his palm. Jody pressed her body to his and moved against him seductively, slipping one leg between his.

Micah explored her body with timeless patience, savoring each touch and kissing her as his hands discovered all her secrets. Jody did the same. His body was hot and firm, and she felt the leashed strength of his muscles beneath her hands. He was so large he made her feel delicate and smaller than she was. She reveled in his strength and in the way he held himself back so she would enjoy every moment possible. She ran her tongue over the swell of his shoulder and nibbled at the base of his neck. "I love the way you taste," she said. "I love how you smell and how you feel."

Micah lifted his head to look at her, and in his eyes she saw the need he felt for her. She knew he saw the same in hers. Wordlessly she touched his beloved face and lifted her head to kiss him again.

When he at last eased himself between her thighs, Jody was more than ready. She ached for fulfillment, wanted him with every atom of her body. When he entered her she cried out in ecstasy. At once he stopped and looked deep into her eyes. Jody began to move beneath him, and he saw that she was wanting him and not hurt or fearful. Slowly and thoroughly, he began moving her toward her pinnacle. Jody had never known such lovemaking, and her body responded to his as if it had been designed especially for his loving. She moved with him and felt his passion build in perfect unison with hers.

Suddenly she felt as if she had exploded into brilliant lights and colors, and pure pleasure pounded through her. Micah caught her to him as her completion triggered his. Together they topped the summit of pleasure and flew as one.

After long minutes Jody opened her eyes and found him looking at her, his head pillowed beside hers. Their eyes held, and she experienced a togetherness she had never known possible. It was as if their souls still touched and the love between them was pure and endless.

"I love you," he said. "I thought I loved you before, but it was nothing compared with what I feel for you now."

"I know," she whispered. "It's as if we are part of one another. Can you feel that?"

He nodded. "I'll never stop loving you, Jody. I could stop breathing easier than I could ever forget you."

"You need never forget me. I'll be with you forever if you want me."

He took her hand and kissed each of her fingers. "I want you more than I want my soul. But that doesn't change anything. We have to do what we have to do."

Dull dread settled in Jody's middle. "You're going to marry Emma even after this? You'd marry her knowing you love me?"

"Darling, let me explain. If I call it off to marry you, not only will it be an insult to her, it will be one to you as well. Everyone knows you are living here, and if it becomes known that we are in love, your reputation will be ruined. You would never be able to hold up your head in town again. You would be shunned by ladies who now hold you in respect. I can't do that to you."

She stared at him. "I don't care what people think about me. All I care about is that I love you."

"That's easy to say now. We're here together and no one knows there is anything between us. But I've seen something like this before. The marked woman was unable to buy so much as a pound of sugar because the storekeeper wouldn't serve her. She couldn't go to any of the parties because no lady would invite her into her house. The man involved fared slightly better, but only until he married her. After that, neither was asked anywhere and both were avoided as if they had the plague."

"What happened to them?"

"In the end they moved away. I understand they went far enough away that they could start all over again without anyone knowing they had once been lovers."

"I would follow you to the ends of the earth. Don't you know that?"

He cupped her face in his hand. "I know it. But it's more than I can do to you and still love you. I would never see you shunned without doing something about it. If we left quietly, it would mean leaving everything I am, everyone I know. Forever."

She nodded slowly. She had been thinking only of herself. To leave Whitefriars would be unpleasant to her, but the depth to which the house and its surrounding land was a part of Micah and him a part of it hadn't occurred to her. It was more than land to him. It was his birthright and his future. In many ways he was the patriarch of the widespread family. At Christmas and New Year's the family came to Whitefriars and to him. If Micah left it all for her, one of his sisters might move here and Whitefriars might continue, but the change would be cataclysmic.

"I don't want to understand," she said at last. "I want to argue and convince you that I'm right and you're wrong. But I can't do that when I love you so much."

"That's why I have to marry Emma next week and why I can't marry you even though I love you more than life itself. We have a niche we must fill and a role we must play. Even if we might choose to change roles and move to another niche, we can't always do so."

She put her arm around him and held him close. Beneath her ear she could hear the steady beating of his heart, and her arm rose and fell with his breathing. He was so alive to her, she had forgotten she might not be able to stay with him forever. "It's so unfair," she said in a tight voice.

"Yes. I've been thinking that for quite a few weeks."

Now she knew why he paced far into the night and why he had to go through with his marriage to Emma. "But what if I stay in this time forever?" she whispered. "What if we could be together?" She lifted her face to look at him.

"That's what I've been asking myself. What if you somehow came here to be with me? If somehow we were meant to fall in love and to be together for all time?"

"If that's true, you can't marry Emma."

"But we could be wrong. I don't know what I should do. I only know what I must do.".

"At least we have tonight."

"Tonight is all we have. If you come to my bed after this, I may not be strong enough to do what's in everyone's best interest."

"I may not be strong enough to resist," she said. "I love you and I'll lose you in a week. Why can't I spend every possible moment with you?"

"What if you become pregnant?"

Jody hadn't considered that.

"What if someone learns we've become lovers? If I'm already married to Emma—and I would be by the time you learn if this coming week left you with child—I would be unable to protect you without making matters worse than if I abandoned Emma for you from the beginning."

"Your time is too complicated," she said. "I wish you had come to mine instead. I would turn my back on anyone to be with you, and no one would think the less of me."

He smiled. "I doubt it would be that easy."

Jody knew he was wrong, but it didn't matter. All that really mattered was that he was right about their not being able to be together now.

"I've thought of something else," he added. "If you came back here because we were meant to be together, something will happen to make that possible."

"I can't wait around and hope for something that nebulous."

"What else can we do?"

Jody had no answer. "The real problem is that you're a gentleman and it seems that I'm a lady. If you were a rogue it would be so much simpler."

He rolled so that she lay half-beneath him. "I'll never stop loving you. Surely such a great love isn't meant to be wasted."

"So we wait and we hope?"

"Tonight we make love. Enough love to last us both a lifetime in case I'm wrong and the world is run on chance."

Jody kissed him, and this time there was an urgency in her desire. How could she possibly love him enough in one night to stay with her for the rest of her life? She was close to tears, but she didn't let him know.

"I have simply got to get that woman out of Whitefriars," Emma said to Claudia. "Can't you talk to her?"

"I've tried. She refuses to move to Camilla's. She did say something about moving into a house of her own."

"She didn't!" Emma's eyes grew round. "You know what that might mean."

"Surely it couldn't mean that or she wouldn't have said anything about it to me."

"Married men often set their mistresses up in houses. You know that as well as I do."

"Micah is more gallant than that. He's the most honest man I know."

"Honesty has nothing to do with it," Emma insisted. "I should never have told him beforehand that I want my own bedroom. Do you think that's what drove him to this?"

"We don't know that he's done anything at all. If he and Miss Farnell were—forgive me—lovers, surely he wouldn't continue letting her stay at Whitefriars. He has a standing in the community."

"I hope you're right. But why else would she want to live alone? I can't imagine wanting to do that. I'd simply die if I didn't have all my friends and relatives about me. I've rather dreaded moving all the way to Whitefriars, if the truth be known. It's necessary, however. Mama laughed at me when I said as much to her."

"Personally, I wish I were living there instead of where we are. I hate it in town, and our house isn't nearly as nice as Whitefriars. I'm practically embarrassed to have people in."

"You shouldn't be. You have a lovely home."

Claudia looked mollified. "Thank you. You're kind."

"That's what friends are for. To make one another feel good." Emma put another stitch on the bed cap she was embroidering. "Micah is making quite a fuss over the bedroom issue. What if I marry him and he refuses to let me sleep where I please? Did Vincent try to talk you out of it?"

"Of course. They all do. You just have to be firm. After all, you'll be the mistress of the house and your word should count for something. You can bet you won't have a say over whatever goes on outside of the house, but inside is your domain."

"It sounds so simple when you put it that way."

Emma sewed for a few minutes, but her brow was wrinkled in thought. "Claudia, can I ask you something? Have you ever thought what it might have been like not to marry Vincent? I mean, what if you had chosen someone else instead? How did you know that you loved him enough to spend the rest of your life with him?"

"I never gave it much thought, really. He was a good catch. All the Landrys are wealthy, even after the war. I decided during the war that I would do whatever was necessary so that I would never have to worry about anything again. Don't you remember what it was like? We couldn't get pretty material or coffee or much of anything. There were times when it seemed as if the Yankees were coming in this direction and we had to hide all the silver and anything else of value to prevent it from being stolen."

"I remember. There were no shipments from France or word from our cousins there. I hated the war."

"I resolved that when it was over I would marry the best choice, and I didn't care if I loved him or not. I thought for a while I might love Vincent, but that wasn't why I married him. He promised me that if another war breaks out, we will go to France until it's over. He promised me that the night I agreed to marry him."

"You'd leave Joaquin?"

"If another war starts, yes. I'd come back as soon as it was over, but I'd leave. I hate deprivation."

Emma tilted her head to one side. "I used to think I would marry anyone at all for love. I just wanted to be adored and petted the way I always have been. Wouldn't it be terrible to have a husband who didn't care for you? I'd just die."

"So would I, but I don't have to worry. Vincent may not love me, but he's a gentleman, and as such will never mistreat me. We have an understanding."

"I hope Micah and I can reach one soon. I don't like it when he frowns at me. At times he can be so frightening."

"You're not afraid of Micah, surely!" Claudia put down her own sewing and stared at her friend. "He would never hurt you."

"I know. It's just that he is so . . . powerful. I feel small and weak when I'm around him."

"Good. Men like that."

Emma bent her head over the nightcap. She didn't know how to tell Claudia that she was often truly frightened of Micah. Not as often as she pretended to be, of course, but still more often than she preferred. Emma liked feeling tiny and fragile but not weak. When Micah had first started courting her she ruled him with a teardrop. Lately he was becoming less alarmed when she cried. What if her feminine wiles lost all their power? How could she rule him then? The idea was unsettling.

"Do you recall the conversation we had about old Iwilla?" Emma asked. "We were discussing whether or not she could really cast spells."

"I remember. We decided she couldn't."

"Did we? I thought we decided the opposite. I was thinking she might be able to help me get rid of Miss Farnell."

"The best thing is to marry Micah and not to worry about it," Claudia counseled. "She will have to go then. If he sets her up in a house for clandestine reasons, Vincent will know and I'll make him tell me."

"But by then won't it be too late? I mean, if she's already his lightskirt, I will have waited too long. I have to get rid of her before anything happens."

"Men aren't as monogamous as we are. Micah has probably been with a woman. I know I shouldn't have told you this, but as a wife, you have to know what to expect."

Emma let her sewing drop. "He has? I won't be his first?"

"Men don't care about that and neither should we. The important thing is that we get what we want—a nice house, plenty of spending money, and servants to take care of everything. If a man has dallied around, so be it. It means nothing to them and we should feel the same."

Emma frowned. It had never occurred to her that Micah would want another woman. "I guess it must be more pleasurable to them," she said aloud. "You know, The Act."

"I'm sure it must be or the human race would have died out long ago." Claudia stabbed at her cloth with her sharp needle. "You'll learn to endure it. We all do."

Emma nodded. She had only a sketchy idea what lovemaking entailed, and it seemed to her that she would never be entirely complacent about it. The mere thought disgusted her. All the same, she didn't want her husband doing it with anyone else. "I have so much to learn," she said seriously. "Sometimes I feel as if my head will fairly burst. Mama has been drilling me on how to rotate linens and how to prepare menus until I feel as if I'm whirling on the inside."

"You'll soon get the knack of it. It's easier in your own house. You may run it however you please."

"Mama will be sure to come over and see how I'm doing. If I don't have Whitefriars running as smoothly as The Oaks, she'll know it. I'd be so embarrassed."

"Emma, you've been taught all these things since you were a small child. You must know how to count linens and when the mattresses should be turned and when to make jelly and so forth. It's not all that difficult."

"Maybe not for you, but sometimes servants make me nervous. Especially the ones who know more about something than I do. I'm sure the ones at Whitefriars will take advantage of me and I won't even know it."

"Just be firm with them. Make notes if necessary, to help you remember what your mother says should be done. She need never know you had to write it down."

Emma put the sewing to one side and crossed her arms petulantly. "I don't want to do all that. I just want to be able to paint all day if I want to and to read poems and be a lady. I don't want to run a big old house and have to wonder if my husband is seeing some trollop on the side."

Claudia shook her head. "You have to grow up, Emma. It's not pleasant, but there it is. We all have to eventually. Even Camilla did, and I never thought she would manage."

"I think she does beautifully."

"She does now, but you know how she was as

a girl. I thought she would never learn to sew a fine seam or learn a recipe."

"Maybe it was becoming a wife that did it. Mama says that makes a person grow up fast. Maybe once Micah and I are married I'll find all this easier. Maybe I'll even want to have children."

"I don't. Thank goodness I was able to move into a bedroom of my own. Otherwise I might have a houseful by now."

Emma sighed. She still hadn't made the connection between being a wife and becoming a mother. That part would be told to her on her wedding day by her own mother. She admired Claudia, however, and if Claudia didn't want to have a baby, Emma was pretty sure she wouldn't want to either. Besides, she disliked being around children. They were so messy and loud, and they moved so fast. No, she thought, she wouldn't want to have any children. Micah would just have to understand.

Chapter Twenty

Emma rode up to Whitefriars along the back way that took her to the stables before the house. She had never before bothered to take her horse to the stables herself, and she noticed the stableman's surprised expression when she dismounted and handed him the reins. Emma, however, ignored him as she did most servants. Whether a servant noticed she was doing something out of character or not didn't particularly bother her.

She had come this way for a reason. Gideon, who was too adept at noticing a person's arrival out front, would be unaware that she had come, and Emma would be able to move about unnoticed for a while. She had learned long ago that she could find out more of what went on at Whitefriars by arriving unexpectedly, and this time by being both unexpected and unnoticed, she would be able to go to the cabins out back without Micah knowing.

She knew exactly where the cabins were. She knew Whitefriars nearly as well as she did The Oaks. But she had rarely seen them after she had become an adult and had outgrown playing games behind the main house. The cabins were older and smaller than she remembered and were better cared for than their counterparts at her home. Not a blade of grass grew in the packed dirt of the yards, and as always in such places, the men and women who were too old to work sat in the sun, watching the children who were too young to work. Emma ignored them all, as she had the stableman, and headed for the cabin that sat slightly apart from the rest.

From the outside, Iwilla's cabin didn't look out of the ordinary, but nevertheless, Emma approached it with trepidation. All her life she had had a superstitious fear of anything suggestive of witchcraft or voodoo, and old Iwilla was known by everyone to be the local voodoo queen.

Emma lifted her skirts out of the dust and crossed the open area in front of the cabin. Although Emma made no sound, Iwilla must have sensed she was there, because the ominous black woman stepped out onto the small porch as Emma neared. Emma's steps faltered, and she wanted to run away. Only thoughts of her rival gave her the strength to continue.

Iwilla fixed Emma with her steady gaze, her dark face displaying no emotion at all. Emma tried not to show her fear. "I've come to talk to you," she said. She could feel the eyes of all those who were outside their cabins watching her, and she wanted to turn and peevishly tell them to mind their own affairs. But she couldn't look away from Iwilla's eyes.

After a moment Iwilla said, "Come inside."

Emma didn't want to go in that dark little cabin, but she seemed to have no choice. Iwilla stood aside for her to enter and waited patiently for her to do so. Emma stepped up onto the porch and edged her way into the house.

The interior was cleaner than Emma had expected, and it was not as dark. The walls had grotesque scribbling all over them, and she wondered with a deep fear if the reddish coloring on the walls might be blood.

Iwilla drew the two chairs she owned toward each other and motioned for Emma to sit down. Fastidiously, Emma perched on the front edge of the chair, holding her skirts close about her. Although there was only one entrance to the cabin, she wanted to look behind her.

"Why you have come?" Iwilla said at last in her broken English. Her voice was deep and powerful for all her years.

"I . . . I want a spell." Emma tried to conjure up more courage. Iwilla had frightened her all her life.

"What kind of spell? One to bring death to enemy?" Iwilla looked as unperturbed as if they were discussing the weather.

"No! I mean . . . not a death spell. I only want something to chase someone away."

"Someone is Miss Jody?"

Emma's eyes rounded. Iwilla was so perceptive! "Yes! How did you know?"

"Iwilla know everything." Iwilla seemed to be thinking for a minute. "I can do spell." She held out her large hand.

For a minute Emma didn't know what she wanted; then she realized Iwilla was waiting for payment. She hadn't brought money—she thought it would be a bad idea to tempt the former slaves by having actual money—but she had brought a pair of gloves for barter. The gloves weren't completely new, but she had worn them only a few times. They were a pair of pale blue ones that she had bought to go with a certain dress, only to find the colors weren't a perfect match once she got them home. She thought Iwilla would never know the gloves weren't new.

Iwilla took the gloves and turned them over as if she were examining them to see if they would be enough to pay for the spell. Emma noticed a tiny snag in one finger that she had thought would never show. Iwilla rubbed her hand over it, but she nodded.

"When will you cast the spell? Will it be soon?"

The old woman laid the gloves in her lap and folded her hands over them. "I cast spell when signs right. Dark moon is two nights away. I cast then."

"Two nights? I'm to marry Micah in only a week. Will you be able to get rid of Miss Farnell that quickly?"

"She not be stronger than Iwilla's spell. No one is." She spoke simply and with complete confidence.

Emma felt a shiver travel down her backbone. She was eager to get far away from the woman as soon as possible. Once she was mistress here, she would be sure Iwilla found another home.

"Need a bit of your hair."

Emma's heart jumped. "My hair? Why do you

need it?" She raised her hands to touch her perfectly coiled hair. Her hair was her pride.

"To make welcoming spell for you as bride."

"Oh." That didn't sound too bad. "How much do you need? A strand or two?"

Iwilla reached into a pocket and brought out a knife, the blade of which glinted in her hand. Without answering, she stood and walked around behind Emma. Emma felt the hairs on the back of her neck bristle, and she was about to leap from her chair and run when she felt a pull at the back of her neck and heard the sound of her hair being cut. Iwilla went back to her chair, a severed curl in her dark hand. The knife had already disappeared. Emma reached up and touched her neck where the stray curl had been. "You might have asked first," she said testily. "Can you see where you cut it?" She was proud of her curly hair and thought the tiny curls on her neck were pretty.

"No one will know."

Emma stood and hurried to the door. Iwilla remained seated, paying little or no attention to her leaving. The shiver coursed through her again. A thin sound formed on Iwilla's lips and rose in volume as she began to chant. Emma's courage deserted her altogether.

Iwilla waited until she was sure the woman was gone, then broke off her chant and laughed softly and without humor. She had enjoyed frightening her. She looked down at the blond curl and smiled in triumph. This, along with the gloves Emma had worn, were enough to finish her spell against her marriage. Iwilla couldn't believe the woman had been so foolish as to give her a personal belonging and to let her cut a lock of her hair.

Iwilla would have thought anyone was smarter than that.

Moving carefully, because her knees weren't as young as they had been, Iwilla knelt on the floor and worked the loose board free. From inside the hole she took the doll she had made months earlier. She studied the doll, then shook her gray head in confusion. Try as she might, she couldn't understand how Jody had had one so much like this one. Iwilla had searched Jody's room more than once and had been unable to find that doll or any other evidence that would indicate Jody was working spells on her own. Iwilla shook her head. No white woman knew enough magic to work a true spell.

Clutching the doll, she got to her feet, but not without some effort. She had been working on this spell for months, and it was sapping her energy. At times she worried about that, but she reasoned that it was worth losing her strength if it would rid Whitefriars of anyone who would bring happiness to the master there. Her old hatred rose to sustain her.

She put the doll on top of her small table, along with a black candle she got from the tin box on a nearby shelf. After pulling the octoroon's hair off the doll, she lit the candle and began mumbling half-remembered words from her childhood. Once the candle wax was molten, she tipped the candle so that the hot wax dripped onto the doll's head. Before the wax had time to cool and harden again, she pressed a curl of Emma's blond hair into it, then dripped more wax on top of it to be sure it stayed in place. With pursed lips, Iwilla blew out the candle, then returned it to the box before finishing the spell.

Finally, she wrapped the gloves around the doll, and as she said the magic words, she tied the gloves tightly with bindweed she kept for the purpose. When she was sure Emma's gloves and hair were a part of the doll, she stopped chanting. A slow chuckle rumbled deep inside her. Before now the doll could have been anyone, but now it was undeniably meant to be Emma. Iwilla shook her head at the white woman's stupidity. It was almost a shame to keep her away. She might make Micah miserable without any spell to aid her.

Iwilla went back to the hole in the floor and lowered her bulk to her knees. The winter had been hard on her, though she let no one know it. Iwilla never let a soul know she wasn't impervious to pain or sickness. She had doctored herself with her dark herbs and felt certain that she would feel better now that the weather was warming. She patted the doll, then made some magical gestures over it to gather the spell around it. "Love be broke," she said in first her native tongue, then in English. "Love be gone from here." She put the doll back in its place and straightened the objects she had placed around it so long ago.

Carefully she pulled the floorboard back into place and sat back on her heels to rest before trying to get up. It still troubled her that Jody had had a doll that looked so much like the ones Iwilla made. No two women made voodoo dolls that were exactly alike. How that could be, she didn't know. Slowly, painfully, and with the aid of the nearest chair, Iwilla pulled herself to her feet. This might have to be her last spell, she

392

thought uneasily. She would have to make it her best.

She went to where she kept her food and took out the cornbread and beans she had intended for her supper. Going to the porch, she called to one of the stray dogs that always lay about near the children. It came to her, wagging its tail uncertainly. Iwilla gave it the food and watched for a minute while it ate. She would center her strength by fasting until the dark of the moon. A fast always sharpened her and made her powers more potent. When the animal finished wolfing down the food, Iwilla took the bowl back inside to wash it and put it away. She had much to think about and to plan in order for this spell to be the most powerful she had ever cast—a spell to keep Emma away and to send Jody back to wherever she had come from.

Emma hurried to the house by a circuitous route that took her away from the cabins and along the fence behind the house. She was rewarded by finding Jody alone on the side porch. Jody looked surprised to see Emma approaching from that direction, but Emma didn't explain her presence there. As the future mistress of Whitefriars, she felt she owed no one any explanation about anything. Slowing her pace considerably, she went up the steps and strolled directly to Jody.

"Have a seat," Jody said without getting up. She had needlework in her hands, and Emma noticed regretfully that her stitches were improving.

She sat and studied Jody a moment before she spoke. "Have you done something to your hair?

You look different somehow."

Jody looked up, her eyes startled. "No, my hair is the same." She touched her face and averted her eyes.

Emma shook her head. Whatever the change was, it didn't matter. "I'm glad to have the opportunity to talk to you alone. We so seldom see each other without Micah or Camilla about."

"What did you want to talk to me about? I would have said we have nothing to discuss at all."

Emma was glad Jody wasn't going to pretend they were friends, though she would have if she were in Jody's place. This was better, because she didn't know how quickly Micah would learn she was out here, and she didn't want him to overhear this conversation. "I'm going to speak to you plainly, Miss Farnell. It's time you left."

Jody gave her a steady look. "Why are you saying this now? I've already told you I will be gone before the wedding."

"I know, but that's an entire week away. People are talking about you, and I don't like this gossip attached to my future husband."

"What are they saying?" Jody's eyes didn't waver.

"I'm a lady, Miss Farnell. I couldn't possibly repeat what I've heard about you." This was not true. Emma had heard no gossip at all about Jody and Micah, but she reasoned that she was unlikely to know what might or might not have been said, for no one in her circle would have the audacity to tell her to her face that they thought Jody was Micah's mistress.

Jody was quiet for a moment. Then she said, "Actually I was sitting here thinking that it's time I left."

"You were?"

"I'm going to move to Camilla's until I can find a place of my own."

Emma wanted to ask her if Micah was intending to set her up in a house of her own, but she couldn't bring herself to form the words. She hated to admit she knew anything at all about sex. It was a shame, she reflected, that she had already given Iwilla the gloves, since Jody was leaving without a spell having been cast. "I think we should understand some things," Emma said to strengthen her position. "I won't welcome you at Whitefriars, no matter where you may live. Once this is my home, you're not to come here again for any reason."

Jody's face held only scorn. "I have no desire to visit in any house you may have claim to. I don't like you, Emma. I probably dislike you at least as much as you dislike me, for all you pretend not to in front of others. We understand each other perfectly."

Emma drew herself up. She had expected Jody to dissolve into tears and to run into the house to pack.

"I'm leaving for Micah's sake, not yours. If he's determined to go through with this wedding, I don't want to cause him any unhappiness. I've already sent a note to Camilla to let her know of my decision." She lifted her chin. "Until my trunk leaves the house, however, this is my home. Good day, Miss Parlange."

Emma had never been dismissed so summarily before. She flounced from her chair and walked angrily down the porch in search of Micah. Jody watched her go. She had almost enjoyed that.

She picked up her sewing and studied it without seeing it. Last night had been like a visit to heaven. She had lain in Micah's arms all night and they had made love until dawn. Leaving his bed was the most difficult thing she had ever had to do. He hadn't come down that morning, and she had learned later that he had ridden out early into the fields. This wasn't unusual for him to do, but she knew he was doing it today in order not to see her. Too much had passed between them the night before. Neither would be able to see the other and not let their love show.

Jody stood and walked to the steps, where she sat on the top one and clasped her arms about her knees. She had always thought love would be a pleasant sensation, but this hurt with a physical pain. Not to live under the same roof with Micah would be like leaving a part of herself behind. Emma had made it plain that she would never be welcome here again, but Jody had expected that. Not that she would want to visit once Emma and Micah were married. Jody wouldn't be able to bear it.

She tried to think of somewhere else she could go. If she stayed with Micah's favorite sister, she was certain to see him frequently. Now that she knew the depth and breadth of their love she wasn't sure she could see him ever again without it showing. She was positive she didn't want to see him with Emma on his arm. She was equally positive Emma would make sure Jody never saw him in any other way. Emma had won, and she was the sort to flaunt it.

To stay under this roof another night was courting disaster. She knew she couldn't sleep in her bed, separated from him by only a thin wall, and not go to him. Even if she could be so strong, he would come to her. He hadn't needed to tell her this; her heart knew it without words.

From inside the house behind her, she heard muffled words, and shortly Emma came back out. She glared at Jody as if she were to blame for Micah being gone, then flounced away in the direction of the stables, not even wanting to remain in Jody's presence long enough for a boy to fetch her horse. Jody watched her go. Emma had dropped her pretty child act long enough to insult Jody and to tell her to leave Whitefriars, but Jody knew she would never let Micah see that side of her. Not before they were safely married.

Jody rested her chin on her knees. Micah was an intelligent man in all other ways. Why did he have to be so blind when it came to Emma? It was the way he had been brought up, she decided. He had been taught that women were sacrosanct; Emma had been raised to fill that image. They were products of their time, just as Jody was a product of her own. She couldn't blame Micah for not having been trained to have her insight, though she did blame him for not having developed it on his own, whether it was fair of her or not. Lately she had noticed that a lot of things were unfair.

All her life Jody had believed in happy endings. Her friends had termed her an incurable optimist. This was the first time she had been

touched with a true depression, and she felt inca-
pable of pulling herself out of it. The depression
was warranted. The man she loved was to marry
a woman she detested, and she was powerless to
do anything about it.

Feeling miserable, Jody stood and went back
inside. All around her she could hear the sounds
of Whitefriars, the hush of long skirts touching the
floor, the half-heard voices from the kitchen, the
movements of women cleaning and straightening
and going about their daily activities. She wondered how she had ever lived here alone. The
house seemed to come alive with people under its
roof. She heard 'Cilla say something and Bessy's
quick answering laugh. Whitefriars would go on
without her; the waters of its daily life would
scarcely be ruffled.

That wasn't entirely true. Micah would miss her
more than he had been able to admit. So would
Bessy. They had formed a friendship of sorts, and
Jody would miss her as well. In time she thought
she might have encouraged Bessy to find some
job more challenging than cleaning Whitefriars.
Jody sighed. That might not have been entirely to
Bessy's benefit. The Klan was still all too active,
and any talk of civil rights was far in the future.

Slowly she mounted the stairs. Had her coming
here done any good at all? Micah was now unhappy about marrying Emma, and Bessy had tasted
more of equality than would allow her to live her
life in the safest way. Camilla and Claudia's relationship was rockier now that they had had to
choose sides because of Jody. What had her coming here accomplished except to make everyone

involved more unhappy? Tears gathered in Jody's eyes, and she didn't try to stop them. Some tears needed expression.

An hour later she heard a knock on her veranda door. It was neither Bessy nor 'Cilla, for they would have used the inner door. Jody went to open it for Micah. They looked at each other for a long minute. "You've been crying," he observed.

"I'm all right." She turned away and went to the middle of the room.

He stepped inside and closed the door so they wouldn't be overheard. "Gideon says you're leaving."

She nodded. "I think that's best."

"Don't go."

"I have to. Don't ask me to stay. It's hard enough as it is."

"We only have a week."

"We decided last night that it would be better this way. That if I stayed it would be too hard on both of us."

Micah came to her and gently drew her around to face him. "It will be too difficult in any case."

"If I were to stay, I couldn't keep myself away from you." She gazed up at him, her heart in her eyes. "I couldn't sleep in here knowing you were in the next room."

"If you stayed, I wouldn't be in the next room. I'd be in here."

"How can I bear to see you married if we have more than one night together?"

He put his arms about her, and they held each other close. "My heart is breaking already," he admitted softly. "So is yours."

There was no reason to deny it. Jody held him tightly, breathing in his clean scent and feeling the texture of his clothing against her cheek, and trying to store every moment for when she would no longer be able to get this close to him again. "I wish I had never come. What has it done but make us all miserable?"

"You've taught me what love really is."

She lifted her face to study his. "Do you regret it?"

"No. I regret only that I can't have you for all eternity."

"You mustn't say things like that." She looked away as more tears gathered. "How can I be strong enough to leave you when you say such things?"

"We always have the strength to bear the things we must." The tightness in his voice told her he was hurting as much as she. "I went for a long ride this morning. I had to sort out matters, to try to find some way of changing the inevitable."

"Did you find a way?" For a minute Jody let herself hope. His silence ended the tenuous thread. "I thought not."

"If only we had more time!" Micah went several paces away and ran his fingers through his hair. "If only we had time to work this out. There must be some way for us to be together without ruining your name and making Emma the laughingstock of the parish."

Jody refrained from saying she thought Emma deserved anything she got. It would accomplish nothing to sink to Emma's level. "I've thought all morning and there isn't any way. I've sent word to Camilla that I want to move there today. I'm waiting for a reply."

"You know she will welcome you."

"I think I should find a place in some other town. I just can't think of any way to earn my living." She tried to smile. "Can you imagine me as a needlewoman?"

"No, but as I suggested to you once before, you could be a schoolteacher."

"Well, I suppose I could." Jody's spirits rose slightly. "Would I need a teaching certificate or anything?"

"No. Only an education. But I don't want you to leave Joaquin."

She looked at him from across the room. "I don't want to leave you, but I couldn't handle seeing you and Emma together at all the family gatherings. I couldn't sit in church and have you and Emma right in front of me, or tolerate listening to friends discuss what you and Emma are doing or planning. It would be too much."

"I know. Can you bear for us never to even see each other again?"

"No. I don't know. What other choice do I have?"

He shook his head. "If only you weren't a lady. I could buy you a house and come to see you as often as I could get away. We could be together. And your reputation would be destroyed, and it would be worse than if we eloped."

"If only you weren't a gentleman, I could convince you that our names in this town aren't as important as our love. But I love the part of you that is above tarnish and that will protect my reputation whether I will it or not."

"We are what we are. I only wish it could be different."

"I know you can't turn your back on all you are and if you did, you might someday come to resent me for taking it from you. That's why I have to get as far away from you as possible. I'm not sure I can be so altruistic indefinitely. I'm not as lady-like as you seem to think. Love is more important to me."

He smiled. "Then why aren't you staying and doing all you can to break my engagement? Why aren't you badgering me and insisting that I run away with you and let all the rest go hang?"

She managed to return his smile. "Maybe I'm more upstanding than I give myself credit for. I've never tried to break up a relationship, and it seems I can't do so now."

"Then you're really going to leave." It was a statement rather than a question.

"I have to."

"My heart will go with you."

"I'll keep it safe. Mine is staying here with you."

Although several feet separated them, she felt as if she were in his embrace. At the same time, she felt as if a world were between them. Tears gathered and spilled down her cheeks.

Micah came to her and put his arms around her. Silently they held each other, and she had a feeling that his own eyes weren't all that dry, either. After what seemed to be a long time, he lifted her chin and kissed her. The kiss was gentle and full of love. It said good-bye in a way their voices couldn't manage.

Without a word, he turned and left. She wrapped her arms about her as if that would prevent her heart from breaking. A deep ache started in her middle and spread throughout her, and she knew Micah was feeling the same pain. It was the sensation of a heart breaking. Because there was no other alternative, Jody began to pack.

Chapter Twenty-one

"I was so hoping Micah would see reason," Camilla said as she helped Jody unpack her things in the guest room. "I know it was a futile hope, but I really did. You two are much better suited than he and Emma."

"I had hoped so too." Jody felt perilously near tears and was glad of something to occupy her hands. "If they loved each other, it would be different. It really would. I'd never try to break up two people for my own selfish reasons. You know that, don't you?"

"Yes, I do. Reid has seen it, too."

"He has?" Jody knew Reid had been reserved in his acceptance of her. It was one reason she had hesitated to say she would move into Camilla's house.

"Last night after the children had gone to bed, we talked. He said Micah obviously loves you and that he's a fool to throw away his happiness just because of a promise he made before he met you." Camilla smiled. "At times Reid can be quite the rebel."

"I wish the same were true of Micah." She sat down on the fainting couch by the window and gazed down at her hands. "Micah said he loves me."

Camilla stopped putting blouses in the drawer and came to sit beside Jody. "He did? He actually told you?"

Jody nodded. "Then he explained why we can't be together. It's not just because of his engagement to Emma. He doesn't want to hurt her, but it's also that he doesn't want to tarnish my reputation. He also said he had considered leaving Joaquin so we could be together."

"Leave Whitefriars?"

"But you know how I got here. What if I skip back to my own time as unknowingly as when I came? He would be in a town where he doesn't belong and Whitefriars and all the people he has known from birth would be lost to him. He would be willing to take the risk, but I'm not. Not when I might leave again at any moment."

"Jody, I hate to say this, but I don't think you're ever going back to the time you came from, not after having been here so long."

"But we don't know, do we?" Jody brushed away her tears. "He said something else that I hadn't considered. He said no love is ever wasted, that it's enough to have loved at all."

"That may be true, but I should think it's small comfort."

"In a way it is. At least I don't think this has all been some random fall of the dice, that I came here for no rhyme or reason, and that all our lives have been turned topsy-turvy by some freak accident. I love Micah and he loves me. Surely some good will come of this."

Camilla patted Jody's hand. "If it's any consolation, the children are thrilled to have you under their own roof. You must be sure and tell me if they become too bothersome. They seem to think you exist only for them. They all love you, you know."

Jody managed to smile. "I love them, too. They could never be a bother to me." She stood and went back to the trunk she was unpacking. "I can't stay here forever. This is only until I find a job and a place of my own. Micah suggested I might try teaching."

"You'd be so good at that! But you'd have to be careful not to tell the children stories about rocket ships and automobiles. Their parents wouldn't be as understanding as Reid and I are."

"I know. I'll have to watch every word I say, even more than I do now. Still, I like children, and I would enjoy working with them."

"Let's consider that for a while and not be in too much of a hurry to move you to your own home. This house is quite big enough for all of us."

"We'll see. I don't want to be a burden to anyone, and I like my independence."

"I know, but that's another thing you'll have to be careful of. A woman living alone sometimes draws gossip even when she's entirely innocent."

Jody nodded. "I understand." She felt so alone without Micah and without the protection and familiar surroundings of Whitefriars.

*   *   *

Iwilla didn't know what possessed her these days. She had become absentminded. In her youth she had been able to remember all the spells she had ever learned and to devise new ones whenever necessary. Now she found herself confusing one spell with another, and although she would never let anyone else know it, she was not as good at her voodoo as she had been. She hated to admit it, but she was growing old.

She looked across the packed dirt yard to where old Achille sat in the sun with children playing at his feet. She could remember when he was young and virile, when he had walked with a bounce in his step. At one time the old master had hoped Iwilla would take Achille for a husband. She had refused, and when he was sent to her anyway, she had thrown some of her witching powder on the fire and frightened him away with a powerful spell. He had been afraid to ever cross her doorway again and had married Beulah, now long dead. Their grandson was Mars, the blacksmith, and he looked remarkably similar to the way Achille had in his youth.

Now Achille was too old to walk without a cane and his head nodded and wavered all the time. Iwilla felt disgust every time she saw him. He had allowed himself to become old. It pained her to think she was the same age as Achille.

The last winter had been hard on her. The cold seemed to have seeped into her bones more than ever before, and she had even been sick. That was still surprising to her. She couldn't recall ever having been sick in her prime. She would have said that she was stronger than any disease.

But she had been sick more than once that past winter, and now her knees and back ached for no reason at all.

But what bothered her the most was the inability to remember spells. Her voodoo was her only hold over the others. True, there were no followers left in the cabins. Her few converts to voodooism had gone back to their former beliefs one by one. But they still held her in awe and fear. She couldn't let them know she was growing old.

Iwilla knew of the voodoo queen in New Orleans, Marie Laveau. Marie had reputedly ruled there since near 1800 and still showed no signs of aging. Iwilla had spent many dark nights wondering how Marie had managed to evade time. Those who had seen her reported that she looked nowhere near the ninety years she must claim. She still danced at the ritual fires and had outlived the other two powerful queens, Sanite Dede and Marie Saloppe. Some said Marie Laveau had made a powerful spell to make Marie Saloppe become insane, and that she stayed that way, broken of her power and muddled in her mind, until the day she died. Iwilla didn't know about that, but she knew Marie Laveau must be incredibly powerful if she could hold back time.

During the night it had come to Iwilla that she had cast the wrong spell on the doll under her floorboards. Because she was determined to do everything exactly right in this, her most powerful spell, she had waited until she found guidance in what to do. If she hadn't begun fasting, she knew she might never have realized her mistake until it was too late. Fasting had always made her mind sharper after the first day. Somewhere between midnight and three in the morning, Iwilla's best time of the night, she had realized her mistake.

If she wanted to keep Emma and Jody away from Whitefriars, she couldn't bury the doll under the floor in Whitefriars' dirt. That might have the opposite effect. However, Iwilla had never before interfered with a spell once it was begun. She was afraid to interrupt this one.

She went back into the cabin and got down the small bag of bones she used for divining purposes. Going back outside, she found a stick and drew a circle in the dirt. She knew everyone in the cabins nearby was watching, and she was careful to move as if her joints didn't hurt. It was good for them to see her at her voodoo work. Iwilla didn't want any of them to see she was weakening.

When the circle was complete, with her in the middle, Iwilla looked up at the sky and held her arms outstretched, palms up. She closed her eyes and began to summon the wind. This was a simple spell, but one that struck fear into those who couldn't do it. Within moments she felt a breeze on her face, and the breeze strengthened quickly. She opened her eyes and looked down at the circle. Using the words she had devised so long ago, she began to shake the leather bag, and the bones inside clicked together, as if eager to answer her questions.

She formed the image of Emma in her mind and that of the doll under the floor. Opening the bag, she tossed the bones onto the dirt. Iwilla crouched, still in the circle, and studied the way they had fallen. Correct interpretation was essential.

A finger bone lay beside a knuckle bone. The smaller bones of a hawk were close to the toe bone. Iwilla nodded as if the bones had spoken to her. She had been wrong to bury the doll. It was trapped there, and Emma was bound to Whitefriars as a result. Iwilla poked at the bones with her long finger. The bone from the hawk's wing rolled aside. She understood. The doll must be disposed of in a way that would take it away from Whitefriars. But how?

She considered putting it in a wagon, but any wagon leaving Whitefriars would eventually return. She was too old to walk to town and too proud to ask for a ride, and even if she found a wagon unattended, there was no guarantee it would be leaving the area. She waited for a sign.

Across the way, a woman tossed a panful of water out the door of her cabin. It splashed onto the dirt and rolled into muddy balls before seeping into the earth. Iwilla's eyes narrowed. Water was the answer.

She gathered up the ancient bones and returned them to her bag. Once again they had guided her correctly. The bones were powerful, and she never used them frivolously. There was a bond of respect between her and them, or so it seemed to Iwilla.

When the bones were again hanging beside the hearth she knelt on the floor and began working the board in her floor loose. When it lay to one side, Iwilla gazed down at the doll. This doll had been in and out of the hole several times since she had first cast the spell. No wonder it had not worked.

She picked it up and dusted all of Whitefriars'

dirt from it. It would not do to send any of Whitefriars with it, or Emma might find a way to come back.

Painfully Iwilla pushed herself up from the floor and muttered some curses as she kicked the board back over the hole. She was angry at herself for wasting so much time. The wedding was set for the next day. There were only a few hours left before dark. She had almost waited too long. As it was, she would have to cast away the doll in the daylight.

She put the doll in her pocket so it couldn't see where she was taking it. She didn't want Emma to have a single clue to return on. It lay there against her thigh like a lump, reminding her at every step how close she had come to failure.

Iwilla held herself as erect as she could with the pain in her joints as she passed down the row of cabins. She looked neither to the right nor to the left, but knew the eyes of those who lived there followed her. Knowing they still feared her renewed her strength. Her mind and body might be getting weaker with age, but no one else knew it.

Soon she entered the woods out back and made her way toward the river. She chuckled mirthlessly at what Micah would say when he discovered his yellow-haired bride had gone away only the day before the wedding. He would be heartbroken. Iwilla's revenge on him would be complete. She had heard that Jody had already moved to Camilla's house and soon would be farther removed from Micah than that. Iwilla was working on a charm that would take her from him forever.

She drew her mind back to Emma. It would not do to work on two spells at once. Both would be diluted by her lack of concentration. Instead, she filled her mind with Emma, how she looked and what her voice sounded like and how she made those little birdlike movements that were so irritating to Iwilla. Birdlike—that was good. She was going to make the bird fly away.

At the river she looked into the muddy water, swollen and quick due to a hard rain to the north. Red mud swirled in the churning water, blocking any possible sighting of fish. That was good. Evil spells worked best when there was no evidence of abounding life.

Iwilla took the doll from her pocket, being careful to keep its face toward the water. She didn't want Emma to look back at all. Iwilla held the doll up in both hands and began to speak the words that were a mixture of her native tongue and broken English. The breeze quickened.

She spoke louder. "Go away," she commanded the doll in the mixed language. "Go away from this place. Leave Whitefriars and never come back no more. I command you, by the power of the moon. I command you by the power of darkness. I command you by the power of unseen devils. I command you by all the beasts with teeth and the birds with claws and the snakes with venom. These have no home and neither do you. These don't live at Whitefriars and neither do you. As surely as these creatures roam, so will you."

Iwilla drew back her arm and threw the doll as far out into the water as she could. The doll arced through the air and dropped with a quiet splash into the river. Quickly bobbing back up, the doll floated away, twirling with the current.

Iwilla watched it go, her lips moving in silent curses. Emma was going to leave this place and go somewhere far away. She was going to take a path she had not intended. Quickly, the doll grew small in the distance and disappeared. Iwilla nodded resolutely. It was done. Emma was taken care of. Now she had only Jody to deal with, and then she, too, would be done.

As she went back to Whitefriars, she refused to let any thought of Emma enter her head. She wouldn't bring her back in any form. Iwilla felt a measure of her old power return.

Emma was in a particularly good mood. Jody had moved to Camilla's and Emma would marry Micah on the following day. Now that Jody was out of the picture, she let herself admit that she had been worried. Since Jody had come to Whitefriars Micah had been less attentive to her, and she had sensed that she was losing him. That couldn't be tolerated. Not when everyone in town knew she was engaged to marry him.

Micah had come to see her the night before. He had been in a terrible mood, and she hadn't enjoyed his visit at all. For a while she had been afraid he was going to say that he was calling off the wedding, but he hadn't. He had only told her that Jody had moved out a few days before and that she was staying at Camilla's. She wondered why it had taken him so long to tell her, but she decided not to worry about it. She rarely understood the things Micah did and this was only another example.

Emma herself had been having doubts about the marriage, although she never voiced them to anyone, not even to Claudia. In another day she would be a married woman, and she wasn't too sure she was eager for the change now that it was upon her. As long as she thought Micah was about to back out, she hadn't allowed herself to consider what married life would actually be like, but now that he was secure, she had reservations.

Once married, women tended to stay pregnant. Emma didn't like the idea of having children, and she detested the thought of losing her figure, even temporarily. Although she was insistent on their having separate bedrooms, she knew she would be expected to accommodate Micah from time to time, and it might be enough to leave her with child.

Also, a married woman didn't attend parties and have men fawn at her feet. If she went to a party, it was more likely to be as a chaperon. Emma wasn't entirely sure she wanted to be shelved just yet. She was still young and pretty, and it seemed a shame not to enjoy herself a bit more.

A married woman had status that an unmarried one didn't. That was an advantage, but it also meant that she would have responsibilities. Emma had been taught how to do all the things necessary to keep a plantation home running smoothly, but she didn't feel capable of putting those lessons into practice. She knew how to tell if a maid had properly aired the linens, but how was one to know when they needed it? She had recipes for jellies and preserves, but when were the fruits to be picked? No, Emma wasn't eager to have control of her own house. If she didn't do it perfectly, she would lose face with her mother, and she hated to do anything she couldn't do perfectly.

The Oaks was in a turmoil of last-minute preparation. At every turn, Emma ran into maids with loads of tablecloths and napkins. The gardeners were busy clipping the lawn and weeding the flower beds for the party to follow the wedding. Father Graham had been out half a dozen times in the past three days to talk to her about her coming vows and how it would mean that she would be flesh of Micah's flesh and bone of his bone. Emma wasn't sure she cared for the simile. As a Catholic, she knew there could never be a divorce, and while that made her position more secure, it opened the worry of what would happen if she changed her mind.

Emma liked to change her mind, and she did it often about small matters. Wasn't it possible she might someday change her mind about how she felt about Micah? What if she came to positively detest him, the way Zelia Ternant seemed to hate Valcour? There was no reprieve for Zelia, and there would be none for herself. How was she to know how she would feel next week, let alone a year from now?

At last the preparations fretted Emma to the point of exasperation, and she decided to do what she always did when she was determined to avoid thinking of a thing. She went shopping.

Everyone in town knew her wedding was set for the next day, and they all seemed determined to speak to her and wish her happiness. Emma smiled and blushed and thanked everyone, but she wished they would all go away. After she married Micah she would be merely Micah's wife, not Emma Parlange of The Oaks. Whitefriars was lovely and she was already connected to the Deveroux family by blood, but after the wedding she would be one of them entirely. She wasn't eager to give herself up so completely.

"Good day, Miss Parlange," a familiar voice said as she neared the glove counter.

"Good day, Mr. Percy." Her thoughts had been so confused she hadn't realized she had walked to the counter.

"Tomorrow is the big day," he said awkwardly.

"Yes. I suppose it is." She felt she could speak more openly with George Percy. After all, they didn't move in the same circles, and he couldn't pass anything along to any of her friends.

"You don't seem entirely happy." George's brow furrowed as he studied her. "I hope nothing is wrong."

Emma looked up at him, for the first time actually seeing him. George was taller than she was, though he was no more than average height. He was passably handsome in a quiet sort of way. Although he would never make a woman's heart beat faster with a smile, he wasn't threatening either. Emma thought of Micah and how thunderous he could look when he was angry, and she found herself preferring George. She hastily looked away. "No. No, nothing is wrong. What could be?"

"I'm sure I don't know, but you seem to be about to cry. Are you feeling well?"

Emma hadn't considered crying up to that point, but at his words, her eyes did fill with tears. She blinked in an effort to contain them.

"Why, you *are* crying." George was around the counter and beside her before she knew what he was doing. "Here. You need to sit down. Come in the back room with me. There's a bench there."

Emma let him lead her to the curtain that concealed the door to the stockroom. She often had been in the dry goods store, but she had never been beyond the salesroom. As he held the curtain aside, she stepped in and looked around with interest. Stacked all about were boxes of shoes, gloves, sewing notions and collars, and all the other items the store stocked.

"Here we are. Sit down here. May I get you a glass of water? I'm afraid we have nothing else to offer you."

Emma sat on the bench and shook her head. "No, thank you. I only need to rest a bit. I guess I was overcome by the excitement."

George sat beside her. "It's no wonder a delicate lady like yourself should be faint."

Emma glanced at him with interest. Micah hadn't noticed how delicate she was in months. If anything, he seemed to be put out at her delicacy, apparently expecting her to be as hardy as Miss Farnell. "Yes. I am rather faint. Perhaps if you have a bit of rose water for my handkerchief?"

George hurried to a stack of boxes and rummaged through them a bit, then returned with a fluted bottle. He unscrewed the top and doused her lace handkerchief with some of the rose water. Emma held the dampened cloth to her nose. "Thank you. I'm feeling better already."

"My sister swears by rose water. She says it's even better than smelling salts unless one is having a bad turn."

"I agree. Smelling salts can be so startling unless it's expected. Roses smell ever so much nicer." She noticed how his hair lay neatly against his head. Micah refused to wear pomade, and his hair always looked soft, as if a breeze might muss it. No breeze could loosen George's hair.

She glanced about. "It seems odd that all this is back here. I never thought the storeroom would look this way. I expected counters rather like you have out front."

"No, ma'am. We save all the prettiness for the customers." He, too, looked around. "I guess I shouldn't have brought you back here, you being a lady and all. But there's no place to sit out there, and you looked as if you needed to compose yourself."

"I never realized you're so observant," she said in a small voice. "You're really quite nice."

George blushed a bright red. "I've noticed everything about you from the first time I saw you."

"You have?"

He nodded. "You were wearing a pink dress with rose lace at the neck and a pink straw hat. I thought you were the prettiest girl I had ever seen." He looked down and kicked at a nail in the floor. "I shouldn't be telling you this. I guess it's because we're back here. In my world, so to speak."

"No, no. That's all right. Tell me more."

"I couldn't, Miss Parlange. Not when you're to be married to someone else tomorrow."

"If you're ever going to say it, today is the day."

She didn't know where she had found the courage to say such a thing, but she waited and held her breath for his response.

George's eyes met hers. "The thought of you married to someone else is almost more than I can bear. I've heard talk that your fiancé might even be interested in Miss Jody Farnell, but I can't believe that. No man would ever look at another woman if he could have you. But all the same, it's being said, and it bothers me that you may be settling for a man who doesn't realize what a diamond you are."

"You think I'm a diamond?"

"Well, more like a pearl, really. You're so soft and sweet and genteel. A diamond is too flashy. You're worth more than a diamond though."

Emma found herself smiling. He wasn't very good at flirting, but his words sounded as if he meant them. "Micah never compares me to jewels."

"He's so handsome, he probably never appreciated you so much. Now take me, for instance. I'm a plain man, and I have ordinary ways. I'm not handsome and I'm not rich. But when I marry— if I ever do—I'm going to treat my wife as if she were royalty."

"You will?"

"I surely will. Out of gratitude, you see. I know I don't have so much going for me, and I'll be eternally grateful."

"I never thought of it like that." Emma studied him. "I feel I can talk to you as I can to no other. Don't you ever tell a soul about this, but I'm having doubts."

"Doubts? As to what, Miss Parlange?"

Elizabeth Crane

"Do we really need to be so formal? I'm having second thoughts about my marriage. There! I've said it! Now you'll think I'm just awful."

"I could never think any such thing about you, Miss Emma. Not ever! Second thoughts, you say? In what regard?"

"I don't know if I want to run a huge place like Whitefriars. You just can't know how intimidating it is! I'll have to know all sorts of things, and I don't want to have to be thinking about linens and jellies all day. I'd rather be painting or sewing something pretty."

"I thought every woman wanted a fine house."

"I do! But I don't want to run it. I'd rather have a smaller place like, well like the Hubbard place. It's large enough to be fine, but there couldn't be much in the way of a staff."

George's mouth dropped open. "Why, I own the Hubbard place!"

Emma put her head to one side. "You do, don't you? I had forgotten that it was sold. You must think I'm awful to say such a thing."

"No, no. Not at all. You could be happy in the Hubbard place? In a house like that, I should say?"

"I could. I really could." Emma touched her handkerchief to her eyes. "No one knows I feel this way. I always try to pretend to be so sure of myself, but I'm really not. I'm fearful of so many things that other ladies seem to take for granted."

George patted her hand awkwardly. "You're like a hothouse flower. You should be pampered every day of your life. Now you take my house, for instance. I have a housekeeper who runs everything. She knows what I need before I know it myself."

"You can afford a housekeeper?" Emma said before she thought.

"I'm paid more here than you might think. I hired a widow who had no children and no place to go. She was glad to get room and board, and I profit by having my house run properly. I don't have to pay her much at all."

"Is that right?" Emma became thoughtful. "What do you do for entertainment?"

"I don't go out much. I'm not accepted into the social life here." He turned his head away. "People don't like me because they think I'm a carpetbagger."

"Aren't you?"

"I used to be, but now I own my own place here, and I've worked at this store for years. I didn't come in, make a quick fortune, and leave. I moved here to stay. It's been lonely, I can tell you."

"I never see you at church, either."

"I'm not Catholic."

Emma's eyes widened. "You're not?"

"I go to Siler City to the Methodist church. It's not much farther from my house than the church here, just in the opposite direction."

"I shouldn't be here talking to you," Emma said abruptly. "What would people think if it became known?" She stood up hastily. "What was I thinking of?"

George jumped to his feet. As if he were doing so before he could change his mind, he took her hands in his. "Miss Emma, you may hate me for what I'm about to say, but I have to speak my mind before it's too late. I've fallen in love with you. I know you can't possibly return my affection, but I had to tell you. I'll never speak of it again."

Emma stared up at him. "You really mean that?"

"Yes, I do. Hate me if you must."

"I couldn't hate you for loving me." She felt flattered and happy. What was happening to her?

"If you hadn't admitted to having second thoughts about your coming marriage, I would never have told you. I know we aren't even of the same religion, and that alone would preclude my having you, even if you weren't promised to another. If you're thinking of calling off your marriage, however, I want you to know someone else loves you."

"I don't know what to say." Her thoughts were whirling.

"You needn't say anything."

"Are you asking me to forsake Micah and have you? Are you proposing to me?"

George looked startled. "Yes, I suppose I am."

Emma tilted her head to one side and touched her temple with her fingertips.

"Miss Emma, are you all right?"

"Yes. I mean no. It's just that I've been feeling a bit odd today. I have to think about this." Emma backed away from him. To her surprise, she was reluctant to go. "I have to think," she repeated, as if to herself.

George put out his hand as if to detain her, but she turned and fled from the back room. By the time he reached the doorway and pushed aside the curtain, she was halfway across the store, clearly on her way out. As other customers had come in while they were in the back, he could hardly call out to Emma from this distance without shouting and had no choice but to let her go, for the time being. George let the curtain fall back into place and silently cursed himself for having said too much. He had never been in love before, and he wasn't adept at its expressions.

Chapter Twenty-two

Micah dropped the book he was pretending to read and leaned his forehead against his fingers. As he rubbed the furrows in his brow, the muscles tensed in his jaw. Tomorrow he was to marry a woman he no longer loved and be forever denied the woman who meant more to him than life itself.

Taking a steadying breath, he let his head fall back against the chair and gazed up at the ceiling. Had it been only six months since Jody had come into his life? In some ways it seemed as if he had known her forever. In others, it was as if everything she said or did was new and delightful to him.

He rose and paced to the wall where the tiny, secret room was hidden. It had all started here: the most unlikely meeting he ever could have conceived. His life would never be the same again. Nor did he want it to be. Before Jody had tumbled into it, he had never known the full heights of happiness or what it meant to be really in love. But he also hadn't known what it meant to have a broken heart.

His eyes fell on a book that had belonged to his grandfather, a man of whom he had only a dim recollection but a definite impression. Lucien Deveroux had been a formidable old man with a white beard and thinning white hair and black eyes that could see right into a person's soul. Micah had been frightened of him more than he had loved him. Lucien had been one to pound his ideas into whomever happened to be standing within earshot. From the cradle, therefore, Micah had learned from him the importance of family devotion, reliability, responsibility, and the necessity of keeping his pledges. Lucien would have died on the spot rather than break his word.

Antoine, Micah's father and Lucien's eldest son, had been less a taskmaster, but he had held the same beliefs. There were things a gentleman did not do and still remain fit for society, not the least of which was to jilt a fiancée at the altar. Some years before, one of Micah's numerous cousins, a young man with an excitable temperament, had argued with his fiancée, then disappeared three days before the wedding. No one gave a thought to any possible explanation for his actions, other than the obvious, and they all castigated him for his willful betrayal. Even after he returned, his family had treated him more or less as a stranger and an outcast. No one ever trusted him again. Now Micah could see the young man might have had a good reason for what he did. Nevertheless, Micah knew that if he jilted Emma on the eve of their wedding, he would be ostracized. More important, so would Jody.

But how could he marry Emma when Jody had all his heart? He had no answer, and the clock on the mantel continued to tick away the minutes.

Jody couldn't stop pacing. A late evening thunderstorm was building, and the house was dark and heavy with the dampness in the air. Earlier in the day she had tried to tell Camilla's children a story, but her mind hadn't cooperated. All she could think of was Micah and that he would be married to someone else in less than twenty-four hours.

She could remember sitting down to supper, but she couldn't recall whether she had eaten anything. Camilla had tried to help her hide her restlessness from the rest of the family, but Jody knew Reid wasn't fooled into thinking her uneasiness was caused by the approaching storm. Jody seldom exchanged confidences with Reid, but this particular evening she had found what she thought was sympathy in his eyes, and she had been touched by it.

When the children were sent up to bed, she kissed them all and received their hugs and kisses in return. Her heart ached to think she would never have children of her own. Without Micah, she didn't care to marry, and she knew this was a decision she would never reverse.

Nighttime had settled in early due to the cover of clouds, and although lightning flickered through the heavy clouds, the storm was still too distant for Jody to hear the thunder. Too restless to join the others in the parlor, Jody went out onto the porch and listened to the trees being whipped by the rising wind.

"It will be a bad one," Reid said from behind her.

Jody jumped. "I didn't hear you come out. Yes, it seems so."

As Reid leaned against a porch support and looked out into the night, he said, "I never interfere in other people's business if I can avoid it. However, under the circumstances, I think I should express my opinion."

Jody waited. Although she had thought she had seen sympathy for her in Reid's eyes earlier, she wasn't sure how Reid stood on any of this. He was unfailingly polite to her, but she wasn't as close to him as she was to Camilla.

"My youngest brother once fell in love with a girl who was entirely wrong for him. She wasn't Catholic or Creole and was the daughter of a man who worked only when he ran out of rum. The family was beside itself and insisted Jacques marry the girl they thought was a much better choice for him, even though he didn't love her. Her family was friends with mine, and she was prettier than the girl he wanted. Everyone thought she would make him a splendid wife."

"What happened?"

"Jacques gave in and married her. Then two months later, he and the girl he loved ran away together. When they were found, they committed suicide rather than be parted again."

Jody put her hand on Reid's arm. "I'm sorry."

"We never talk about Jacques or what happened. It's much too painful."

"Why are you telling me this now?"

He turned to face her. "Because we would rather have had Jacques alive and married to a girl my family found inappropriate than to have Jacques dead."

"I'm not one to commit suicide and neither is Micah."

"I know that. But there are forms of suicide that don't end in death. Vincent Landry is a prime example. Vincent was my friend long before he married Claudia, and as her brother-in-law I shouldn't say anything against her, but he went from being a happy man to one who never smiles. I don't want that for Micah."

"Neither do I, but there seems to be nothing I can do about it. He's determined to do the *proper* thing." Jody couldn't keep the exasperation out of her voice.

"I know. I shouldn't have told you all this, I suppose. I only wanted you to know that I'm on your side."

She gave him a weak smile. "Thank you, Reid. I appreciate that."

He nodded and went back into the house as if he thought he had said too much.

Jody went to the porch rail and looked in the direction of Whitefriars. Was Micah on the veranda? Was he looking toward her? Was he as unhappy tonight as she was? Jody knew he must be.

Iwilla sat beside her fire, chanting and tossing gray-black herbs on the hungry flames. A sour, greenish smoke curled up her chimney. In her lap she was fashioning a new doll, her fingers twisting the straw into arms and legs as she chanted the songs her mother had taught her deep in the jungle, long before she had ever seen a man with white skin. With one of Jody's handkerchiefs, which she had stolen from the clothesline, she began dressing the doll. She had prepared for this spell for weeks.

Outside a storm rumbled, drawing ever closer. Iwilla was using its power to aid her own. She had always felt a kinship with thunder and lightning, and no storm had ever been fierce enough to frighten her. In her younger days she had gained the fearful respect of all those about her by standing outside during the fever pitch of storms with her arms extended overhead as if she would embrace the lightning while she shouted in unison with the thunder. It made her chuckle to recall how everyone had cowered away from her in those days. This charm, when it succeeded, would restore that awe.

From a hidden pocket she drew some fine, dark brown hair. She had gleaned it from Jody's hairbrush a few days before she had left Whitefriars. No one had seen her do it. Iwilla was adept at coming and going undetected. The only one who had seen her where she shouldn't have been was that Bessy girl, and Iwilla had given her a severe bellyache as punishment for daring to upbraid her. Her dark eyes narrowed. Maybe once she had her power back, she would cast a spell to get rid of Bessy, as well. The girl had made a serious mistake by challenging Iwilla.

Using wax from a black candle, Iwilla attached the hair to the doll's head. Her voice rose in the chant.

Elizabeth Crane

*   *   *

Jody was filled with a nervousness that barely could be contained. She paced from the parlor hearth to the harpsichord and back. Camilla and Reid exchanged a glance, but they pretended not to see anything unusual in their houseguest's actions. Jody realized how obvious she was being and sat down. She tried to read, but she couldn't focus on the words. Thoughts of Micah filled her mind to overflowing. She put the book aside and resumed her pacing.

The storm was nearer; she could hear thunder now. Jody had never been particularly afraid of storms, but neither did she like them. "It's the storm," she said to excuse her behavior, although no one had asked. "It's making me uneasy."

"Perhaps if you drink some tea," Camilla suggested. Her gray eyes, so like Micah's, were filled with compassion. "I have to admit the storm is making me nervous as well." She went to the door and asked the butler to get it for them.

Jody tried sitting again, but she couldn't be still. Back on her feet, she went to the harpsichord and picked out a tune, but the music sounded tinny and small coming from the old instrument. Her head jerked up. Camilla's harpsichord was almost new. Not old. A deep fear swept over her, and she frantically looked around the parlor. "No," she whispered. "Not now!"

Reid and Camilla looked up questioningly.

Jody backed away. She was beginning to feel dizzy. As dizzy as she had felt the day she stumbled into this time. "No," she whispered, her eyes growing large.

"Jody, what's wrong?" Camilla was beside her

430

at once, Reid behind her to catch her if she fainted.

"I have to go! I have to get to Whitefriars!" Jody turned to run from the room.

"In this storm?" Reid tried to stop her. "Wait until morning."

"No, no. I can't wait!"

"Then let me get the carriage and I'll drive you."

Jody opened her mouth to speak, but with the dizziness almost overwhelming her, the words wouldn't form. She had to reach Micah, and she couldn't wait for a carriage to be brought around. She shook her head, her eyes imploring them to understand, then ran from the room.

The night closed around her as soon as she left the porch, but she didn't care. She only knew she had to reach Micah. Jody lifted her skirts and began running toward the stables to get a horse. Behind her, she heard Reid and Camilla call out her name, but she dared not pause.

Iwilla's chant built in strength. Her throat ached with the power of the words she was voicing. The doll was almost finished and the storm was nearly upon her. The vile smoke puffed back into the room on a downdraft, but Iwilla ignored it. The spell was almost cast. She couldn't let herself be deterred by anything. She was impressing even herself with the power she was building.

With her knife, she made a small cut in her little finger and used the blood to draw a face on the doll, trying to make it look as much like Jody as she could. Around its neck she tied a string from which dangled a piece of the torment root she had gathered on the moonlit night. She sang her magic and made the doll dance to the chant.

A flash of pink lightning ripped from cloud to cloud directly over her cabin, and thunder roared on its heels. Iwilla threw back her gray head and laughed wildly. She made the doll dance the steps that would bind her to Iwilla's fierce will.

Jody rode as fast as she could toward White-friars. The night was thick around her, and the houses were becoming farther apart as she neared the edge of town. Soon the light from their windows would be of no help in guiding her, and she would have to find her way through the darkness with only the aid of an occasional flash of lightning. A dog barked at her passing, and as she looked in its direction she thought she saw in the window of one of the houses the unmistakable blue flickering of light from a television screen. Almost at once, it was replaced by yellow lamplight. A sob caught in her throat. She couldn't lose Micah!

The realization of what she had been about to throw away spurred her on. Love could never, should never, be wasted. Whatever social convention dictated to the contrary, whatever sacrifice they had to make to be together, it was worth it. She was willing to face anything to have Micah by her side. Without him, she would be sent back to the time from which she had come, bereft and lonely for all time. Surely it had been her decision to give him up that had triggered whatever it was that was trying to pull her back to her modern-day life. She had to get to Micah. As the first raindrops spattered around her, she dug her heels into the horse's flank, urging him to a faster pace.

The road seemed endless. Wind swirled the treetops into a frenzy, and lightning had begun flashing more frequently the closer she got to Whitefriars. Rain poured down from the black skies, hiding the road from her, but Jody didn't let it slow her. Reaching Micah was all that was important.

Suddenly two horses raced into view, and Jody cried out as her horse dodged to one side. The horse nearest her reared, and in the flash of lightning, Jody recognized Emma's face. She was wearing a riding cloak with the hood drawn close about her face, but there was no mistaking her. Their eyes met and Jody stared. Then it was dark again.

"Come on," she heard a man's voice say, his accent touched with a northern twang. "We have to reach Shreveport before your absence is discovered."

Emma kicked her horse and galloped after the man, who had evidently not seen Jody in the darkness. Jody steadied her own mount with a firm rein as she watched them go. Her mind whirled with the dizziness, and she thought for a moment she saw the twin beams of an approaching car's headlights. "No!" she gasped as she whipped her horse back toward Whitefriars and raced away into the face of the raging storm.

Micah had gone upstairs when the storm broke so his people could go to bed. There was no need to keep Gideon and the others up just because he couldn't sleep. Once they were settled for the night, Micah could light himself back down if he chose.

The storm was a fierce one. It wasn't a night for anyone to be out. He opened the veranda doors, and as he watched it for a minute, he wondered if Jody was afraid of storms. This was one to put fear into most people.

Sheltered from the rain by the roof over the deep veranda, he walked to the door of the room Jody had stayed in and opened it. As he peered into the blackness of the room's interior, he almost convinced himself she was there, waiting for him. But then reality came crashing back along with the thunder, and he knew she was gone.

A deep restlessness overcame him. He lifted his head and looked about uneasily. Something was happening. He didn't know what was going on, but something was wrong. He went back to the veranda and, ignoring the rain, he leaned out over the rail to look for signs of trouble. The hair on the back of his neck prickled in warning.

With a frown he stepped back under the roofline. He had felt this same sensation before, but when? Alertness strummed all his nerves, and he found it impossible to stand still. He paced to the corner of the veranda and stared into the blackness. Town lay in that direction, and so did Jody. Was she afraid and was he so keyed to her that he knew her thoughts even from a distance?

"No," he said firmly. Then he shouted at the rainy sky as lightning tore across it, "No! I won't give her up! I can't!"

Thunder shouted back at him as it chased a

streak of lightning into the earth only a few yards from the house. Micah glared at the night. He had an enemy out there that was trying to pull Jody from him. "No!" he bellowed again. "I won't give her up!" A strength he had never felt before filled him, and he shouted back at the storm again. "She belongs with me!" Wind filled with rain lashed at his face, but he didn't care.

Iwilla removed the loose floorboard in her cabin once again, chanting as she worked. The power she had felt this day was greater than it ever had been, but already it had peaked and was ebbing away. She had to finish the spell before the power was gone. She summoned all her strength, even knowing she might never be able to recall it again. Robbing Micah of happiness was more important than any spell she could do in the future.

With her hands beginning to shake, Iwilla removed the objects she had taken from the brew in which they had been soaking for four days. They were imbued with renewed vigor and ready for use in the spell she was concocting.

"Work my will, fence wire," she muttered as she coiled the wire into a circle on the dirt beneath the flooring. "Contain Jody Farnell. Work my will, fishnet. Catch and hold Jody Farnell." She lifted the dog's tooth. "Work my will, tooth. Tear apart any who would break my spell." She put the tooth, taken from a rabid dog the summer before, in the circle of fence wire and net.

She placed the blue-black feathers from a crow in a design all around the dirt circle. "Make her fly away home, feathers. Lose her way so she can never return." She took the rest of the torment root and laid it outside the wire. "If she ever tries to leave where I'm sending her, let your torment work on her."

Into a pot simmering in the ashes, she dipped a ladle and ceremoniously poured droplets of the liquid onto the dust, then watched as it balled into dirty beads. "As sure as rain, as sure as rivers, send Jody Farnell where she belongs. As strong as my spell and as strong as my herbs, keep her there when she arrives." Iwilla's mix of English and her native dialect combined to make a spell stronger than either language could summon alone. She felt a surge of power. Before it could wane, she picked up the doll.

"I send you home, Jody Farnell," she hissed, her eyes black and oily as jet. "I send you back where you belong, never to stray no more." Iwilla got down on her hands and knees and put the doll exactly in the middle of the charmed circle. Her dark hands waved in symbolic movement to bind Jody to the place and to prevent her ever straying again. For good measure, she covered it all with the remaining net.

Holding her breath, Iwilla lifted the ladle to her wrinkled lips and drank. She refused to let it gag her even though it nearly choked her to swallow it.

Less than a second after Jody caught sight of the drive that led to Whitefriars, the thunder attending that illuminating bolt of lightning boomed loudly overhead, causing her horse to rear and plunge. Jody slipped from the animal's wet back and landed in the mud. As she gasped for breath to replace the wind that had been knocked out of her lungs, she saw her frightened horse galloping back toward town and his dry stable. Her side felt as if it were on fire, and she knew she would have bruises by morning, but otherwise she appeared to be unhurt. Rain sluiced down in sheets and as lightning again limned the ground and trees for an instant, she saw Whitefriars in the distance. This time she braced for the boom of thunder as darkness plunged about her. Squinting in the direction of Micah's home, she could see glimpses of light from one window.

Lifting her sodden skirts from the clinging mud, she pressed ahead on foot. The mud seemed to suck at her feet, determined to keep her from her destination. Jody lowered her head and forced herself forward. This was like nightmares she had had in which she was trying to run and couldn't move. Frustrated tears joined the raindrops on her cheeks.

Behind her she heard the unmistakable sound of a car engine and saw its lights slice through the night, then disappear. "No!" she cried out. "I won't leave him. I won't throw all this away for convention's sake!" Whether Micah would have her no longer mattered. She had to reach him and somehow convince him that they must be together.

She remembered seeing Emma and George Percy in the rain and wondered if that had been a hallucination. For Emma to be out in a storm and be with a man she professed to detest seemed too unlikely to be true. Was she going mad? For an instant the thick mud beneath her feet became gravel and she sobbed. After having tried so hard for all these months to return to her own time, why did it have to happen now? With all her will, she forced herself to think of Micah in the house ahead and struggled onward.

Iwilla felt her powers waning as she scrambled to her feet. Puffing from exertion, she went to the pot and dipped the ladle into the brew. "Work my will, fire. Send my message, smoke. Do my bidding, storm." As she drizzled the brew onto the flames, the fire hissed and guttered. The smoke poured thick and green up the blackened chimney. The fire seemed to fight against Iwilla, as she ladled the brew on all the embers.

Finally, her cabin grew darker, lit only by the thick black candles that sputtered as if in consolation with the dying fire. Iwilla knew she would have a hard time relighting the fire to drive away the rainy dampness, but she had to finish the spell properly. That meant ridding the hearth and cabin of all the components of the spell, including the fire.

One by one she went to each candle, thanked it for doing her bidding, then blew it out. When the last candle was extinguished, plunging the cabin into darkness, Iwilla drew a shaky breath. She was exhausted and ached to the bone. Feeling her way through the inky darkness, she found her bed and dropped upon it. Later she would build a fire. Later she might have more strength. Her lips drew back in a grin as she thought of Micah and how she had triumphed over him and all his kin at last. Jody had been sent home and Emma had been driven away.

In the darkness, Iwilla chuckled.

For a minute Whitefriars, in the distance ahead of her, seemed full of light. Not the golden illumination of oil lamps, but the harsher type given off by incandescent light. Jody wavered. Gravel, not dirt, was beneath her feet. During the next flash of lightning, she could see the dim shape of her car parked at the side of the house. "No!" she screamed with all her might. "Micah!" she pleaded.

As she struggled forward, her shoes embedded in mud, the house grew dark again. She pushed on ever harder, calling Micah's name as loudly as she could, even though she knew he couldn't hear her over the storm. She had to reach him before she was trapped in a time other than his.

As if she knew Micah would be there, she lifted her head and looked through the rain at the upper veranda and caught sight of him. He was leaning over the rail, straining toward her as if he couldn't believe his eyes. "Jody?" he called out. "Jody!"

Micah did see her, and as he ran across the porch and down the outside stairs, Jody's feet took wing. They met on Whitefriars' front steps. He wrapped his strong arms securely around her, and she clung to him with a fierceness she had never known before. Her sobs melted into the storm, and she held to him so nothing could separate them.

"Jody! Jody, what are you doing here?" His voice sounded as strained as her nerves.

439

*   *   *

At that same moment, in the darkness of Iwilla's cabin behind Whitefriars, the old voodoo woman was shuffling across the floor toward her bed, feeling weaker by the second. The spell she had just finished was the most potent she had ever cast, and it had taken more of her strength than she had expected.

Turning and groping behind her, she found the edge of her bed, and as she eased herself down, she heard the familiar rustle of the corn shucks in her mattress. She had done it! She had cast a perfect spell, a spell no one could break, one that would last for a lifetime.

She lay there motionless for a moment; then like a tendril of swamp fog, a doubt touched her mind. Iwilla strained against the mattress and managed to get back up to a sitting position. It was almost as if the ashes, cooling in the hearth, were mocking her. Carefully she went back over every detail of her spell. She had cast her magic with all the proper elements; she was sure. Yet something had gone wrong. What was wrong? As her lips moved silently and she mentally repeated the exact words she had used in the spell, her eyes grew wide with realization. "No!" she cried out, but her voice was lost to the roaring of thunder. "Don't bind her here! Bind her to wherever she came from. Not here!"

Iwilla lunged from her bed onto the floor and began clawing at the loose floorboard. "She don't belong here!" Twice more she wailed those words; then the last of her strength failed her and she fell dead onto the floor. In the last flashes of lightning as the storm rapidly dissipated, her wide eyes reflected the horror of her last thoughts and her bared teeth marked her undiminished hatred. But Iwilla herself was gone.

"I had to come to you," Jody shouted above the storm. "I love you, Micah. I love you!" For another terrible moment, she thought she saw him waver before her eyes, and although she had her arms tightly about him, she couldn't feel him. Past his shoulder, she saw the windows brighten with electric light, then thankfully dim again as the feeling returned to her body. "I'll never leave you, Micah. Never!"

"No." He held her close and pressed her head against his chest. "We'll never be apart again. You're home, Jody. You've come home."

She lifted her head to look up at him. "You'll never send me away? You want me enough to stand up to whatever happens?"

He nodded. "Yes. It was wrong of me to let you go. I realized that just before I saw you down here. I love you, Jody, not Emma. If no one understands, that's the way it will have to be. This is your home, and you're going to stay with me forever."

The dizziness suddenly lifted and Jody looked around in surprise. Although the rain continued pouring down and the house remained dark, something was different. She drew in a deep breath. She was home. She would never leave Micah and Whitefriars again. "I'm home," she whispered.

Arm in arm, they went up the porch steps and

out of the storm. At the door they paused, and Micah bent to kiss her gently, his face mirroring the love he saw in her eyes. Together they went inside.

VICTORIA BRUCE

"Victoria Bruce is a rare talent!"
—Rebecca Forster, Bestselling Author Of *Dreams*

A faint scent, a distant memory, and an age-old hurt aren't much to go on, but lovely Maggie Westshire has no other recollections of her missing father. Now she finds herself on a painful quest for answers—a journey that begins in Hot Springs, Arkansas, and leads her back through the years, into the strong arms of Shea Younger. He is from a different era, a time of danger and excitement, and he promises Maggie a passion like none she has ever known. And while she is determined, against all odds, to continue her search for her father, Maggie doesn't know how much longer she can resist Shea's considerable charms, or the sweet ecstasy she finds in his timeless embrace.

_52064-8 $4.99 US/$6.99 CAN

Don't miss these passionate time-travel romances, in which modern-day heroines fulfill their hearts' desires with men from different eras.

Traveler by Elaine Fox. A late-night stroll through a Civil War battlefield park leads Shelby Manning to a most intriguing stranger. Bloody, confused, and dressed in Union blue, Carter Lindsey insists he has just come from the Battle of Fredericksburg—more than one hundred years in the past. Before she knows it, Shelby finds herself swept into a passion like none she's ever known and willing to defy time itself to keep Carter at her side.
_52074-5 $4.99 US/$6.99 CAN

Passion's Timeless Hour by Vivian Knight-Jenkins. Propelled by a freak accident from the killing fields of Vietnam to a Civil War battlefield, army nurse Rebecca Ann Warren discovers long-buried desires in the arms of Confederate leader Alexander Ransom. But when Alex begins to suspect she may be a Yankee spy, Rebecca must convince him of the impossible to prove her innocence...that she is from another time, another place.
_52079-6 $4.99 US/$6.99 CAN

Dorchester Publishing Co., Inc.
P.O. Box 6640
Wayne, PA 19087-8640

Please add $1.75 for shipping and handling for the first book and $.50 for each book thereafter. NY, NYC, and PA residents, please add appropriate sales tax. No cash, stamps, or C.O.D.s. All orders shipped within 6 weeks via postal service book rate. Canadian orders require $2.00 extra postage and must be paid in U.S. dollars through a U.S. banking facility.

Name_____
Address_____
City_____State_____Zip_____
I have enclosed $_____ in payment for the checked book(s).
Payment <u>must</u> accompany all orders. ❏ Please send a free catalog.

THE OUTLAW HEART

VIVIAN KNIGHT-JENKINS

Bestselling Author Of *Love's Timeless Dance*

A professional stuntwoman, Caycee Hammond is used to working in a world of illusions. Pistol blanks firing around her and fake bottles breaking over her head are tricks of the trade. But she cannot believe her eyes when a routine stunt sends her back to an honest-to-goodness Old West bank robbery. And bandit Zackary Butler is far too handsome to be anything but a dream. Before Caycee knows it, she is dodging real bullets, outrunning the law, saving Zackary's life, and longing to share the desperado's bedroll. Torn between her need to return home and her desire for Zackary, Caycee has to choose between a loveless future and the outlaw heart.

_52009-5 $4.99 US/$5.99 CAN